Berkley Sensation titles by Marie Force

ALL YOU NEED IS LOVE
I WANT TO HOLD YOUR HAND
I SAW HER STANDING THERE

I SAW HER
STANDING THERE

Marie Force

BERKLEY SENSATION, NEW YORK

THE BERKLEY PUBLISHING GROUP
Published by the Penguin Group
Penguin Group (USA) LLC
375 Hudson Street, New York, New York 10014

USA • Canada • UK • Ireland • Australia • New Zealand • India • South Africa • China

penguin.com

A Penguin Random House Company

I SAW HER STANDING THERE

A Berkley Sensation Book / published by arrangement with HTJB, Inc.

Berkley Sensation Books are published by The Berkley Publishing Group.
BERKLEY SENSATION® is a registered trademark of Penguin Group (USA) LLC.
The "B" design is a trademark of Penguin Group (USA) LLC.

For information, address: The Berkley Publishing Group,
a division of Penguin Group (USA) LLC,
375 Hudson Street, New York, New York 10014.

ISBN: 978-0-425-27531-3

PUBLISHING HISTORY
Berkley Sensation mass-market edition / November 2014

PRINTED IN THE UNITED STATES OF AMERICA

10 9 8 7 6 5 4 3 2 1

Cover photos by Shutterstock.
Cover design by George Long.
Interior text design by Kelly Lipovich.

CHAPTER 1

Sugarmakers in Vermont feel a bit tender about the weather this winter, what with memories of the heat wave in March last year that choked off the sap runs. In response, we decided to start tapping earlier than ever, on February 6. What's two weeks? It sounds insignificant, but it feels akin to moving Christmas Day up to December 11.

—Colton Abbott's sugaring journal, February 11

Colton Abbott had never considered himself a particularly private person—that is, until he had something big to hide from his loving but overly involved family. His six brothers, three sisters, two parents and one grandfather were *dying* to know how he was spending his weekends lately, and Colton was *loving* that they had no idea. Not the first clue.

A smile split his face as he drove across Northern Vermont, from his home in the Northeast Kingdom town of Butler to Burlington, where his family owned a lake house and where his "secret" girlfriend would be meeting him in a couple of hours. He wanted to get there early and hit the store for supplies so they could relax and enjoy every minute of their time together.

Colton had big plans for this weekend, the sixth one he'd spent completely alone with her. During that time, they'd talked about nearly every subject known to mankind, they'd kissed a lot, fooled around quite a bit and last weekend, they'd even gone so far as to take each other all the way to blissful fulfillment. But they'd yet to have sex.

He intended to fix that this weekend before he lost his mind from wanting more of her. He'd tried to respect her wishes to "take things slow" so they didn't "get in over their heads" when they lived so far from each other and had so little time to spend together. Of course he'd heard people say for years that long-distance relationships sucked, but until he'd experienced the suckage personally, he'd had no idea just how totally the situation sucked.

It got worse with every weekend they spent together when he was left wanting more and having to wait a full week before he could see her again. They'd been lucky so far. Other than the weekend he'd stayed home for the funeral of his sister Hannah's dog Homer, they'd had six weekends with no other commitments to get in the way of their plans, but he knew reality would interfere eventually. They both had busy lives and families and other obligations that would mess with the idyllic routine they'd slipped into over the last month and a half.

They'd met halfway the other times, and this would be the first time that she'd come to Vermont. Since he wasn't quite ready to expose her to the austere life he led on his mountain, he'd asked his dad for the keys to the lake house.

And what an odd conversation that had been the day before . . . With time to think about it during the two-hour ride across the state, Colton had the uncomfortable suspicion that the one person he wasn't fooling with his secret romance was his dear old dad.

Colton had planned his attack stealthily, coming down off the mountain on a rare Thursday to see his dad at the office. Waiting until most of his siblings had left for lunch—except for Hunter, who never seemed to leave the office for any reason except a fire alarm—Colton had sat in his truck and watched his dad step out of the diner and head back across the street to the office above the family-owned Green Mountain Country Store in "downtown" Butler, if you could call Elm Street a downtown.

Colton had emerged from his truck and followed Lincoln up the back stairs that led to the offices where he and five of Colton's siblings ran the store. Colton kept his head down as he walked past Hunter's office and knocked on his dad's door.

"Hey," Lincoln said with obvious pleasure. His father was always happy to see him, which was one of the many things in life Colton could count on. "This is a nice surprise. Come in."

Colton shook his father's outstretched hand and took a seat in one of his visitor chairs.

"To what do I owe the honor of a rare midweek visit from the mountain man?"

"I needed a couple of things in town, so I figured I'd stop by."

"Everything okay up the hill?"

"It's all good. Quiet and relaxing this time of year, as always." Colton thought of early summer as the calm that followed the storm of boiling season, during which he produced more than five thousand gallons of the maple syrup that was sold in the store. After nine years of running the family's sugaring facility, his life had fallen into a predictable pattern governed by twenty-five thousand syrup-producing trees.

"I'm glad you stopped by. I was going to come up to see you today or tomorrow."

"How come?"

Lincoln rooted around on his desk, looking for something in the piles of paper and file folders. "Ah, here it is." He pulled out a light blue page and handed it over to Colton.

As he scanned the announcement of a trade show in New York City, he skimmed the details until he realized what he was reading. "What the hell, Dad? *Pleasure aids and sensual devices?* What's that got to do with me?" He nearly had a heart attack at the thought of his father thinking he needed such things to move the relationship no one was supposed to know about forward.

"I'm considering the line for the store, and I'm looking for someone to send to the show. Since this is your off-season, I thought you might be able to make the trip for us."

While trying to wrap his mind around the idea of "pleasure aids and sensual devices" on sale at their homespun country store, he tried to keep his expression neutral. Though he was slightly appalled at the reason for the mission, the location appealed to him very much.

In the interest of keeping his big secret a secret, he kept his reaction casual and indifferent. "What do the others have to say about that product line?"

"I haven't exactly mentioned it to them yet. I figured I'd let you check it out first and see what you think before I bring it to them."

"Why me?"

"Why not you? Everyone else is up to their eyeballs in work and life stuff, so it seemed to make sense to ask you now that your busy season is over for the time being." Lincoln shrugged. "But if you're not up for going—"

"Never said that." He'd be a fool to pass up a chance to spend a whole week with her. "I'll do it, but with the caveat that I think this product line has no business in our store."

"So noted."

"And I think you're in for yet another battle royal with your kids over it."

"I live for a good row with my kids," Lincoln said with a grin that made his blue eyes twinkle with mirth.

"Don't I know it," Colton muttered. The latest row had involved the website designer Lincoln had hired behind the backs of his children, who'd made it clear they had no interest in taking their store online. Then Cameron Murphy had come to town and won the hearts of the entire Abbott family, especially Colton's older brother Will, who was now madly in love and living with Cam as she designed the website for the store.

Lincoln Abbott had a way of getting what he wanted, and Colton and his siblings had learned to be wary of their father's motivations.

In this case, however, Colton couldn't care less about his father's motivations. Not when he was looking at a full week with his lady.

"Talk to Hunter about getting you registered," Lincoln said, clearly pleased with Colton's capitulation.

"I will." Colton folded the flyer into a square, with the images on the inside, and stashed it in his pocket. "Since you now owe me a favor, I was wondering if I could use the lake house this weekend." When his father gave him an oddly intuitive look, Colton added, "I feel like doing some fishing."

Lincoln didn't move or respond for a long, uncomfortable moment.

Colton had begun to sweat under the steely stare his father directed his way.

"Of course, son," Lincoln finally said, withdrawing a set of keys from his top desk drawer and handing them over. "You remember the code, right?"

Since the code was his parents' wedding anniversary and had been for as long as they'd owned the house, Colton nodded and stood. "Thanks."

"Have a good time."

"I will."

"Are you taking the dogs with you?"

"I thought I would if that's okay."

As Lincoln Abbott was the biggest "dog person" Colton had ever known, he wasn't surprised when his dad said, "Of course it is."

Now as Colton drove to the lake with his dogs, Elmer and Sarah, asleep in the backseat, he pondered the odd look his father had given him when he asked to use the lake house and wondered what it had meant. He thought about the bizarre conversation with his older brother Hunter, who'd questioned what in the hell their father wanted with pleasure aids and sensual devices in the store, before he begrudgingly registered Colton for the trade show that would take place in New York in two weeks.

Colton had merely shrugged and refused to engage in the war of words that would no doubt take place between his father, the CEO, and his brother, the CFO. Let them duke it out. No way was Colton going to get in the middle of their dispute when he'd been handed a free pass to a week in New York.

He couldn't wait to tell her the good news.

An hour later, he pulled up to the lake house that was one of his favorite places in the world. Made of timber and beam and glass and stone, the house sat on the shores of Lake Champlain, right outside Burlington. His parents had gotten a sweet deal on it about ten years ago when it was sold at auction after the previous owner defaulted on the mortgage. The Abbotts had enjoyed many a good time there in the ensuing years.

In fact, his older sister Hannah would marry her fiancé, Nolan, at the lake house in a few weeks.

The house was stuffy and hot from being closed up, so he walked straight through the massive living room to open the sliding door to let in the breeze coming from the lake. He never tired of that view of the lake with the mountains in the distance. Late on this Friday afternoon, a handful of Jet-Skiers and water-skiers were enjoying the warm sunshine and the all-too-short Vermont summer.

Relieved to be out of the truck after the long ride, Elmer and Sarah ran straight down to the private stretch of beach, where they frolicked in the water.

Colton smiled with pleasure and relief at being here, at having pulled off another escape from Butler and the Abbott family clutches, and at knowing he had four full days to spend at his favorite place with the woman who was quickly becoming his favorite person.

Three hours later, Colton had been to the grocery and liquor stores to stock up on necessary supplies, and he was beginning to worry.

While he waited, he made dinner—pasta with grilled vegetables, salad and bread, which was now keeping warm on the stove while he paced from one end of the big house to the other, filled with nervous energy.

When he got tired of pacing, he flopped onto the big sectional sofa that faced the two-story stone fireplace.

Sarah came over to give him a lick, which he rewarded with a pat to her soft blonde head.

"Thanks, girl. I know she'll be here soon, and you and your brother are going to love her." If anyone knew how often he talked to his dogs, he'd be committed. But they were his only companions on the mountain, and he kept up a running dialogue with them during the long days and nights he spent completely alone with them.

For his entire adult life, he'd lived by himself on that mountain, happily content with his no-frills lifestyle. He was the only person he knew who lived without running water, electricity, TV, an Internet connection or any of the modern conveniences most people took for granted.

He'd lived that way since he was seventeen, fresh out of high school and anxious to take over the sugaring facility that had been in their family since his grandparents—the original Sarah and Elmer—had bought the place as newlyweds. His mother had hated the idea of him living up there alone when he was so young, but his dad had encouraged her to let him be, and he'd been there ever since.

Rather than pine for what he didn't have, Colton had preferred to focus on what he did have—a beautiful home in the midst of the majestic Green Mountains, two dogs whose devotion to him was boundless, a job he loved and was good at, a family he adored close enough to see at least once a week and a life that made sense to him.

Until lately.

For the first time in the nine years he'd spent on the mountain, what he *didn't* have had begun to bother him. For one thing, he wished he had a phone so he could talk to her every day. For another, a computer with an Internet connection would come in handy as he navigated a long-distance relationship.

He was twenty-six years old and forced to use his parents' phone to call her because he didn't own one of his own. That was one thing he planned to do something about soon. His mountain was one of the few places around Butler that had reliable cell service thanks to its clear proximity to the cell towers near St. Johnsbury.

But the rest of it, the electricity, the running water, the Internet connection . . . Those were things he needed to think about. He'd yet to bring her to his home on the mountain, mostly because he was afraid of what she might think of it. She was used to the city where she had everything she wanted or needed at her fingertips.

What did he have to offer someone who was accustomed to so much more when he didn't even have electricity or running water? What modern woman would find his lifestyle attractive? And was he willing to change everything about who and what he was for a woman he'd known for only a couple of months?

Unfortunately, he had no good answers to any of these questions, and the more time he spent with her, the more muddled his thinking became on all of them.

And then there was the fact that she was happy in her life, settled in her work and home, living close to her own family and not at all interested in uprooting her existence. He knew this because she'd told him so. But knowing that hadn't kept him from seeing her almost every weekend lately. It hadn't kept him from wanting more of her every time he had to leave her. It hadn't kept him from lying awake at night and wondering what she was doing and if she missed him between visits the way he missed her.

What if she didn't? What if she never gave him a thought from one weekend to the next? He had no way to know if she did or not because he didn't talk to her very often between visits. That had to change, and getting a cell phone would be the first thing he did after this weekend.

Maybe by then he'd have a better idea of how she really

felt about him and what'd been happening between them. He had this niggling fear that for her it was just a fun interlude with someone different from the guys she normally dated, while for him it became something more involved every time he was with her.

He was determined to get some answers this weekend, to figure out what this thing between them was and where it was going. Then the doorbell rang and every thought that wasn't about her finally arriving fled from his brain as he sprinted for the door.

Yeah, he had it bad, and he had a feeling it was about to get a whole lot worse.

CHAPTER 2

———◄❙►———

*Sugar season is an exercise in giving up
control, starting with the weather.
Above all, sugaring is a privilege.*

—Colton Abbott's sugaring journal, February 17

Colton threw open the door and had to hold himself back from grabbing her and dragging her inside so he could kiss her senseless. He forced himself to show some restraint and act like a gentleman when his inner caveman was trying hard to break free.

"You made it."

"Somehow." Lucy Mulvaney's tone was filled with aggravation as she pushed past him into the house, dragging a suitcase behind her.

As she went by, he relieved her of the shoulder bag that was so heavy he assumed it contained her laptop. She'd warned him she would have to do some work while she was there.

"The GPS took me the craziest way. I think I was on forty-seven different roads on the way up here."

"Well, you made it, and that's what matters."

"Yes, it is," she said with a warm smile for him.

As always when they were first reunited, he sensed her

shyness and was grateful for the diversion of the dogs dancing around at their feet, waiting to be noticed by the new arrival. "Lucy, I want you to meet my best friends in the whole world, Sarah and Elmer. Sarah has the pink collar."

She bent to give the dogs her full attention, which earned her tons of points in his dog-loving heart. "Hi, guys. Aren't you beautiful? I've heard so much about you! Your daddy talks about you all the time." She let them smell her and kiss her and Elmer even dropped to his back and gave her his belly to rub. Lucy did as directed, laughing at his shameless appeal for attention. "They're adorable."

"They're spoiled rotten, but I love them."

"This place is incredible." She rose to take a good look at the house while Colton leaned against the counter and indulged in a long look at her until she brought her gaze back to him.

"Took you too long to get here." He smiled and held out a hand to her.

She took his hand and let him draw her into his embrace. "You live too far away."

During the five weekends they'd spent together, he'd learned to go slow at first, to ease her back into their relationship rather than going right to where they'd left off, the way he'd prefer. Haste wasn't what she needed, and since he wanted her to keep coming back, he aimed to give her what she needed.

Colton couldn't deny that the two steps forward, one step back approach to dating Lucy was sort of frustrating. He'd found someone he enjoyed being with, and for the first time in his adult life he was interested in a genuine relationship. But he wasn't sure she wanted the same thing, thus his approach to following her lead when he'd much prefer to take charge and make things happen for them.

"Something smells good," Lucy said after a long moment of silence as he held her.

"I made dinner."

"I was talking about you," she said, looking up at him with big blue eyes.

Without giving much thought to what he was about to do, he bent his head and kissed her. He knew a moment of pure satisfaction—and relief—when her arms came up to curl around his neck and her mouth opened to welcome his tongue. They didn't normally get right to it like this, preferring to ease into the physical stuff after some food and conversation, but Colton wasn't about to complain.

Things had gotten pretty hot and heavy last weekend, and he was glad to know they might be able to pick up where they'd left off rather than taking the usual step backward. He loved how she felt in his arms, the way her soft curves pressed against him and the taste of her on his tongue. Framing her face with his hands, he focused entirely on the kiss, not touching her anywhere except for the tight press of his body against hers.

By the time they finally came up for air, Colton wanted to drag her to the nearest bedroom and see this through to the conclusion they'd been heading toward for weeks now. But again he chose restraint, afraid to scare her away by showing her how badly he wanted her. He kept his arms around her as he kissed her neck and made her shiver.

"What a long-ass week," he whispered, breathing in the scent he'd become addicted to.

"Mmm. A very long week."

"I couldn't wait to see you." He'd never come right out and said that before, even though he'd certainly felt it.

"Me, too."

"Are you hungry?"

"Starving."

Serving dinner gave him something else to focus on besides how it felt to kiss and hold her, how amazing she smelled, the way her shorts hugged her sexy ass and how great her hair looked.

"What happened to your curls?" he asked as he dished up the pasta, vegetables and bread while she opened the chilled bottle of chardonnay he'd gotten for her.

"They met a straightening iron."

"I like it, but I like the curls, too."

"I hate the curls. They make me look like a five-year-old."

"Not to me they don't."

Her cute smile exposed the dimples he'd come to adore. "You're racking up all kinds of points, Mr. Abbott. This pasta is amazing."

"Don't be too impressed. It's about the extent of my culinary expertise."

"I'm very impressed, and it's very good."

"I'm glad you like it."

Over dinner they talked about the week they'd had at work, and Lucy shared some more insight into what it had been like to run her web design company alone since her partner, Cameron, moved to Vermont to live with Colton's brother Will.

"You know when you blow up a balloon and then let it go and it flies all over the place?"

Nodding, Colton refilled their wineglasses.

"That's me since Cam left. I'm all over the freaking place trying to plug all the holes with only ten fingers." She looked up at him, a faint blush occupying her cheeks. "And that's kind of a gross sentence."

Colton laughed. "Have you talked to Cam about it?"

She shook her head. "What would be the point? She's thrilled with her new life with Will. I'd never do anything to take away from her happiness. God knows, she deserves it."

"What about your happiness? Don't you deserve it, too?"

She propped her chin on her upturned fist and smiled at him. "I'm happy enough. Work is crazy, but we're in transition. I suppose that's to be expected."

"And here I am taking up all your weekends when you've got so much going on."

"The weekends are keeping me sane, so keep them coming."

"How would you feel about a whole week?"

She raised a brow in question.

He told her about the trade show and watched her eyes go wide with surprise and then laughter. "Your dad is seriously considering offering that stuff in the store?"

"I'm not really sure what he's up to, and once he said 'a week in New York' I didn't ask a lot of questions. Although now I'm wondering if I should've asked you before I committed. I know how busy you are."

She reached across the counter for his hand. "I'd love to have you in New York for a week. That'd be awesome."

Colton bent his head to kiss the hand she'd wrapped around his. "I'm glad you agree. I thought it sounded pretty damned good, too." He looked over at her and gave her hand a gentle tug, encouraging her to come closer. "You know what else sounds good right now?"

She stepped between his legs and flattened her hands on his chest. "What's that?"

"More of this." He kept his eyes open as he tipped his head and kissed her softly. "And some of this." More kisses to her neck. "And then there's this." He raised his hands from her hips to cup her breasts, running his thumbs over nipples that tightened in response.

Lucy sighed and relaxed against him.

"How does that sound?"

"Really good. Exceptionally good."

"I'm glad you agree." He kissed her again and withdrew from her reluctantly to deal with the dishes as quickly as he could while she finished her wine.

"I can help, you know."

"No need. I got it."

"Good with his hands *and* good in the kitchen."

Amused, he waggled his brows at her. "And you haven't even seen the full extent of my bedroom work yet."

Lucy's face turned bright red, forcing her to turn away from him. She wandered to the windows that overlooked the lake.

Regretting that he'd embarrassed her, Colton wiped his hands on a dish towel and went over to her. When he wrapped his arms around her from behind and kissed her neck, he noticed how tense she seemed. "What's wrong, Luce?"

"Nothing."

"Come on. I made a joke and you went all tense on me. Talk to me." He encouraged her to turn and face him and was shocked to see tears in her eyes. "Lucy . . . What's wrong? I didn't mean to upset you. I was only joking."

"I know you were, and you didn't upset me."

"Then what is it? And don't say it's nothing when I can see it's something."

He could also see that she was trying to summon the courage to tell him, and watching her struggle made Colton ache.

"After last weekend, when things got kind of. . . heated . . ." She cleared her throat and looked away.

Hearing her describe the previous weekend as "heated" made him hard as he remembered the feel of her hand stroking him. Shaking his head, he willed those memories from his mind to focus on what was happening right now. "What about it?"

"I'm not very experienced at all of this, Colton. I know I should be at twenty-nine, but I'm not. I've had a few boy-friends and done some stuff, but I don't really know a lot about, you know . . . Any of it."

His mind raced as he tried to process what she was saying. "By 'some stuff,' does that mean you haven't—"

"I have. A few times with less-than-stellar results." Her face got even redder, if that was possible. She quickly added, "I've been really busy with my work and my family and friends. And I'm shy. Painfully, awkwardly shy. With guys." She looked up at him, slaying him with the open, innocent look she gave him. "I don't want to disappoint you."

"Jesus," he muttered as he pulled her in tight against him, not caring that she would immediately feel what her sweetness did to him. "You could never disappoint me."

"Still . . . You probably know more than I do."

"No one's keeping score here, Luce. Least of all me. I told you before—we don't have to do anything. If you're not ready, you're not ready. I'm not going anywhere, and I'm not looking to pressure you."

"You haven't pressured me. You've been amazing and very patient."

He kissed her forehead and looked out at the lake as he held her. "I hate that you've been stressed out about this. You should've told me."

"It's embarrassing."

"It's endearing."

"It's *embarrassing*."

"Fine," he said, laughing. "Have it your way, but don't be embarrassed around me. I think you're amazing, and I love being with you."

"I love being with you, too, but . . ." She looked up at him. "Before this goes any further, I feel like I should say again that I'm not going to move, and I understand that you can't either. Just because Cameron did—"

"I get it. What worked for them won't necessarily work for us."

"I don't want anyone to get hurt here, Colton."

"Neither do I. Let's just have fun, like we have been, and not let it get too serious. Okay?"

"All right . . ."

"Why do I hear more questions in there?"

"I just wondered . . . If not getting serious means not getting *serious*." Her coy smile was positively adorable, and he couldn't refrain from smiling back at her.

"Doesn't that count as fun?"

"I suppose it could. It's never been particularly fun for me."

"Oh, honey, we need to fix that."

"Right now?" she asked hesitantly.

"Whenever you want."

"I'd love to take a shower."

"Follow me." He took her by the hand, picked up her bag and led her to the spacious master bedroom that was located down a short hallway from the kitchen.

"This house is so beautiful. I can see why you love it here."

"We all do. We've had some really fun times here. You'd be surprised how this big house starts to feel awfully small when all the Abbotts are in residence."

"That must be crazy."

"You can't even imagine."

"Isn't this your parents' room?"

"When they're here, yeah. But they don't care if the rest of us use it." He went ahead of her and flipped on the lights in the bathroom.

"Oh, wow. Is that a hot tub?"

"Sure is. The window above it opens. It's pretty cool. You want to check it out?"

"Only if you do, too."

"You're on." Colton turned on the water and opened the window to let in the soft evening breeze off the lake. "Go ahead and get changed. I'll be right back."

He left her with a kiss and closed the door behind him as he left the room.

CHAPTER 3

───◆◆───

After two days of below-20 temps and a nice
rest for the crew, tapping resumed today. They
tap only when the temp is above 20, to prevent
splitting the tree in the brittle cold, and because
tubing repair goes along so nicely without
stiff hands and tubing. Another day or two
and the sugarbush will be tapped out.

—Colton Abbott's sugaring journal, February 19

After the door clicked shut, Lucy stood in the middle of the huge bathroom and took a moment to calm her frazzled nerves. Sometimes she still wanted to pinch herself because she'd captured the attention of a sweet, funny man who also happened to be so hot he made her blood boil.

When they were together, she tried not to think about the overwhelming issues that hung over their relationship. When they were apart, the issues were all she thought about, especially after last weekend when things had taken a decidedly erotic turn.

All week, those memories had run through her mind when she was trying to concentrate at work, when she was with her friends and family, when she was trying to sleep at night while wishing he was sleeping with her.

From the beginning, she'd told him she had no interest in getting serious with someone who lived in another state. And yet here she was with him for yet another weekend—the sixth she'd spent alone with him. As she looked for the bikini he'd told her to bring for swimming in the lake, she realized her palms were sweaty and her heart was beating fast at the thought of what might transpire between them this weekend.

So much for not getting serious.

"Ugh," she said as she quickly got changed, folded her clothes and stashed them in her bag.

More than anything, Lucy wished she could call her best friend and hash it all out with Cameron, but at the beginning, she and Colton had agreed to keep their "friendship" private for the time being. As the weeks went by, the big "secret" seemed to grow and take on a life of its own until telling Cameron would also mean confessing to having kept something rather huge from her friend for all this time.

She and Cam didn't keep things from each other, especially not potentially life-changing things such as what was beginning to look an awful lot like a legitimate relationship with the brother of her best friend's boyfriend. Lucy sighed, pained by how complicated something supposedly uncomplicated was getting.

"More sighs," Colton said when he came into the bathroom wearing a pair of board shorts that left his incredibly muscular chest, shoulders, arms and belly bare to her hungry gaze. He'd told her before the muscles had resulted from the endless need for split wood to run the sugaring facility. Images of him wielding an axe had fueled many a fantasy since he'd mentioned that.

"You weren't supposed to hear that sigh." She glanced up at his ruggedly handsome face to discover a gaze as hungry as hers taking in the sight of her in a bikini, which naturally made her flush from head to toe. She hated her fair complexion and how it gave away her every thought and emotion.

Thankfully, he chose not to ask about the sigh he'd overheard, preferring to take her hand and lead her into the hot tub.

As she eased into the warm water that circled around her, Lucy sighed for a different reason—pure pleasure. "This feels fantastic."

The steam from the tub made his golden-brown hair curl at the ends. She'd thought he was sexy as hell with the longer hair and furry beard. When she'd expressed an interest in knowing what he looked like without the beard, he'd shaved it off and revealed a stunningly gorgeous face that she never tired of looking at. Looks aside, however, she was even more attracted to his sweetness, irreverent humor and undeniable charm.

"Seriously fantastic," he said of the warm water and pulsating jets. "I've spent all week splitting wood, and I'm sore as hell."

"How can you be sore when you do so much of that?"

"I overdid it the last few days so I could take some time off."

She realized he'd done that so he could spend more time with her. "I don't want you to get hurt on my behalf."

"I didn't get hurt, and it was well worth the extra hours so I could relax this weekend and stay on schedule, too." He glanced at her, the picture of innocence. "But I wouldn't say no to a massage of my aching muscles."

She rolled her eyes. "A little transparent much?"

Now he batted his long eyelashes, which made him even harder to resist. "I'm a hard-working guy looking for some TLC from his lady."

"Actually, you're a schemer trying to get my hands on you."

"And that's different how, exactly?"

"Come over here."

"Oh yay!" He was like a delighted little boy who'd gotten his way, which made him downright irresistible.

She'd found him difficult to resist from the very beginning. He'd walked into the conference room at his family's store the day Cameron was presenting the first cut of the website they'd done for the store, and Lucy had noticed him immediately. She'd never been drawn to the rugged-brawny type until she'd taken one look at Colton Abbott, and all her girl parts stood up to take notice, which had never happened before.

Then his parents invited her to join them for dinner, and he'd tagged along. Her fascination had only grown over dinner at the Abbotts' favorite Italian restaurant, where Colton had eaten enough for two grown men. She'd begun to wonder over dinner what he'd look like under the beard that hid what appeared to be an exceptionally handsome face. She hadn't been wrong about that.

"What're you thinking about?" he asked as he settled between her legs and leaned back against her, sighing with pleasure as she began to knead his shoulder muscles.

"The day we met."

"What about it?"

"I wondered what you'd look like without the beard."

"As I recall, you said as much to me a couple of weeks later, and I ended up shaving it off."

"After you went out to get a pair of hedge clippers."

His laughter echoed through the spacious bathroom. "For your information, they were *not* hedge clippers. And P.S., that was a critical mistake in our attempt to keep our 'friendship' a secret. Everyone was suspicious after I got rid of the beard I've had since high school."

"I'm not sorry. I was right about what was under all that hair."

"Oh do tell. What was under there?"

"An exceptionally handsome face."

"I was quite surprised by that myself. I hadn't seen it in years."

Laughing, Lucy poked him in the ribs. "You're so full of yourself."

"Hey, Luce?"

"Yeah?" she asked, immediately unnerved by the serious way he said her name.

"Tell me again why we thought it was such a great idea to keep this a big secret from everyone."

"You know why."

"Tell me anyway. I keep forgetting."

"Since I don't believe that for a minute, are you asking me because you want to change our status?"

He ran his hand back and forth through the water, sending waves across the wide tub. "Maybe."

Lucy swallowed hard. "We kept it a secret because we didn't want everyone involved in it. And because Cameron and Will had just gotten together, and we didn't want to steal their spotlight."

"Will and Cameron have been together for months now."

"I know."

"So how long are we going to continue to sneak around? I can't even remember anymore why we're doing that."

"Because," Lucy said, feeling more anxious by the second. "We're just having fun. We aren't like them, so we don't need to involve everyone. It's just us, and we like it that way." After a long pause, she said, "Don't we?"

"Sure." He linked their fingers under the water and turned to face her, floating in front of her. "Well, no. I don't think I like it that way. Not anymore."

"Colton—"

"Hear me out, honey."

He made her feel swoony when he called her that.

"I'll admit that I've enjoyed the fact that everyone in my life wants to know what I'm up to and who I'm up to it with, but underneath it all, I'm not much of a mystery man. I'm more of a what-you-see-is-what-you-get sort of guy. And I want to share this, what we have together, with the people I love. I want to bring you to my home on the mountain, to my parents' home for Sunday dinner, to my siblings' homes. I want you to come to my sister's wedding with me. I want us to be a real couple."

Lucy was taken by surprise when she realized how

badly she wanted all the things he wanted. Except none of it was feasible. "We agreed. At the beginning. We set rules."

"Screw the rules, Lucy. That was back when we thought we might hang out for a while and it wouldn't go anywhere. Six weekends later, it's gone somewhere, and I want it to continue to go places. Don't you?"

"Where can it go?" she asked softly.

"I don't know. But don't you want to find out?"

"I don't know. I'm afraid."

"What're you afraid of?"

He looked up at her with clear blue eyes and an open, honest expression that made it easier for her to confess her fears. "Of getting in too deep and not being able to get out. Of getting hurt."

"Aw, Lucy. I'm not asking for a lifetime commitment." He brought her hand to his lips and brushed a kiss over her knuckles. "I'd just like to be able to tell my family about you."

She bit her lip as she thought about that. "If you tell your family, I'd have to tell Cameron."

"And that would be bad?"

"No. Of course it wouldn't. I'm just . . . I don't think I'm ready to go public." She couldn't bear the disappointment she saw on his face. "That doesn't mean I'll never be ready. I'm just not there *yet*. Is that okay?"

"Sure. Whatever you want. Are you starting to get wrinkly?"

"A little."

"Let's get out of here and move on to the next part of tonight's program."

"There's a program?"

"Damn straight there is. Next up is ice cream in bed."

"Oh, I like ice cream in bed."

"Excellent." He helped her out of the tub, kissed her nose and then her lips and wrapped a towel around her. "I'll bring it in."

When he left the room, Lucy let out a deep breath and leaned her hands on the countertop, trying to get her emotions under control. She'd never in her life felt as much for any guy as she did for him. And it had been immediate. She couldn't deny that, as much as she'd tried. That immediate attraction was what had her spending six weekends with him. She didn't do things like that, well . . . ever.

Lucy Mulvaney didn't do serious. It wasn't in her DNA. Or it never had been until Colton Abbott walked into a conference room and put her DNA into a blender and mixed it all up. The result had been someone all new, someone she barely recognized, someone who drove six hours to spend four days with a guy she couldn't stop thinking about between visits. And now he wanted to go public. He wanted to tell people about them. He wanted to change their status.

As long as no one knew, Lucy could delude herself into believing that what was happening between them wasn't serious. It was a weekend fling. If people knew, then it wouldn't be just a fling anymore. It would be a *thing*. And Lucy didn't do *things*. She dated. Here and there. She'd had more first dates than anyone she knew. Her friends teased her about her first-date track record, which Lucy embraced. It kept her from having to deal with things she didn't seem equipped to handle the way other women did.

Sometimes she thought there was something missing in her because she didn't want the same things most people did. She didn't dream of the big white wedding, the house in the burbs, the kids, the dogs. She couldn't picture that life for herself no matter how hard she tried. Work made sense to her, or it had until Cameron left and everything changed.

Now nothing made sense, and she found herself floundering at work like a ship that'd come loose from its anchor, not to mention she was embroiled in a *thing* with Colton Abbott, who lived six hours from her.

How had she let that happen?

"I thought you were going to meet me in bed," Colton said from the doorway, where he stood holding a pint of

Ben & Jerry's and a spoon and wearing a smile that made her want to give him anything he wanted. That smile was one of many reasons she was embroiled in the *thing*.

"What kind is that?"

"Coffee Toffee."

"My favorite."

"I know. You told me." He scooped a spoonful and offered it to her.

Lucy put the towel on the counter and went to him. He'd changed out of the wet bathing suit into basketball shorts that clung to his narrow hips. He sure was beautiful to look at. Placing her hands on his chest, she opened her mouth to let him feed her a bite. As the flavor of the ice cream exploded on her tongue, she couldn't look away from him.

He leaned in to kiss her, his cold lips sending a shiver through her that had more to do with heat than it did with cold. "Why don't you get out of that wet suit and come help me eat the rest of this?"

"Okay."

Kissing her again, he said, "You'd better hurry up. I can eat a pint of Ben & Jerry's in about five minutes by myself."

"You'd better not eat it all!"

"Then you'd better put a move on." He closed the door as he left the bathroom.

After having witnessed how quickly he could consume anything edible, Lucy rushed to change. A fierce debate ran through her mind as she decided whether she should go for sexy or casual, which reminded her once again that she was simply no good at these things. She felt like a bull in the relationship china shop, second-guessing her every move. It was exhausting trying to figure out this increasingly complicated situation, and she was making it worse by dithering over what to freaking wear to bed.

It's not like she hadn't slept with him before. They'd slept next to each other every night they'd spent together since the day they met. But somehow tonight felt different. Tonight felt more important, and if she took this next step with him, she understood that she'd probably be committing to much more than a night of what promised to be amazing sex.

She grabbed the tank and boxers she slept in at home and shoved the sexier, slinkier option to the bottom of the bag. That had been bought in an impulsive moment on her lunch hour the week before, but it would send the wrong message.

No, the message she wanted to send was fun and *temporary*. This was *not* going to get serious. Not on her watch.

CHAPTER 4

*Only 370 taps to go. Lucky for the crew, it was
too cold today, so they took to their skis.*

—Colton Abbott's sugaring journal, February 21

Propped on a pile of pillows, Colton watched her come
out of the bathroom. Everything about her was tentative and hesitant. He was disappointed in her reaction to
his suggestion that they take their relationship public, but
he knew if he pushed her, he'd end up pushing her away.
Since that was the last thing he wanted, he decided to use
his friends Ben and Jerry to smooth things over.

He scooped out another spoonful and held it out her.
"Supplies are getting low. Better get over here and get
yours before it's gone." She didn't need to know he'd
bought three pints of her favorite flavor to get them through
the weekend.

She crawled onto the bed and made a beeline for the ice
cream.

Colton fed her a bite and took another for himself as she
settled into the pillows next to him. He let his gaze take a
leisurely trip from her toenails, which were painted purple,
up smooth legs and a flat belly to breasts that were unencum-
bered under the tank that molded to her body. Remembering

the sweet taste of her nipples had Colton shifting to hide his immediate reaction to her nearness.

Another bad thing about the long-distance relationship, he'd discovered, was too much time in between to think and reconsider and replay what'd happened the last time, which meant they had to start from scratch again every time they reunited.

The stopping and starting could give a guy whiplash if he let it. As much as that frustrated him, he was determined to be patient with her. The last thing he wanted was for her to say she couldn't do this anymore.

He was dying to talk to someone about how he felt about her. Under normal circumstances, he'd seek out one of his older brothers—probably Will. Hunter was more closed off and remote. Will was always more accessible, and he'd have good advice to give, having recently gone through a similar situation with Cameron. But because he'd promised Lucy not to tell anyone, especially Will, that they were seeing each other, he'd kept his mouth shut and respected her wishes.

He would continue to do so for as long as she felt it was necessary, but he hoped it wouldn't be much longer.

"That is so good," she said after most of the ice cream had been consumed. "One of my favorite treats." She turned her head to face him. "Thank you."

Colton placed the empty container and spoon on the bedside table. "My pleasure."

She continued to look at him as if she were making a major decision of some sort. In that moment, he'd give anything to be able to read her mind. After she stared at him for a full minute, he said, "What?"

"I like to look at you."

"I like when you look at me." His suggestive tone made her flush from head to toe, which she'd told him she hated. He quite liked it. "Why are you way over there when I'm way over here?" In truth there was only a foot between them, but that was far too much space for what he had in mind.

She scooted closer to him, and he met her halfway.

"Hey," he said when her lips were only an inch away from his.

"Hey."

"What's up?"

"I don't know," she said with a nervous laugh. "What's up with you?"

"You really want to know?"

"Um, I don't know. Do I?"

"I think you do. I think you really want to know, and you really want to be here with me this way, but you need to give yourself permission to stop worrying about what happens next and just enjoy right now. Can you do that?"

"I can try."

"Then I'll show you what's up." He cupped her shoulder, slid his fingers down her arm and wrapped his hand around hers. Once he had a firm grip on her hand, he placed it over the erection that pulsed between them.

Lucy gasped at his audacity but didn't withdraw her hand. Instead she pressed against him and made his eyes roll back in his head. "Where did that come from?"

"You did that."

"How did I do it?"

"You walked in here looking all sorts of hot and adorable."

She tried to pull her hand back, but he held her in place with his hand on top of hers.

"Don't. Don't pull away from me."

"I'm not hot, Colton. I don't know why you'd say that."

"Are you serious? You've got your hand on the evidence to the contrary, babe." He curled his legs around hers, pulling her even closer to him. "You're extremely hot."

"I'm cute. I'll give you that."

"That, too. But please don't tell me there's something wrong with my eyes or anything equally ridiculous. I think you're hot, and clearly I'm hot for you." He moved his hand from on top of hers and put his arm around her. "Do you know when the last time I spent an entire weekend with a woman was? Before I met you, I mean."

She shook her head.

"Never. I've never done this because I never wanted to spend that much time alone with anyone."

"Colton—"

He had no idea what she planned to say because he never gave her the chance to say it. A week's worth of desire and frustration poured forth in a kiss that only made him want her more than he already did, if that was possible. He didn't want to hear any more about why this was a bad idea or how it had the potential to be a disaster.

No, all he wanted right then was to show her all the reasons it was an excellent idea—possibly the best idea he'd ever had.

She opened her mouth to his tongue and teased him with hers, which only fueled the fire that burned inside him. As he kissed her, he worked a hand under her top and cupped her breast, pinching her nipple between his fingers.

"Colton," she said as she broke the kiss and arched into his embrace.

He pulled her top up and over her head, revealing the plump, full breasts that had starred in all his fantasies over the last week. Kissing his way from her lips to her neck to her nipples, he told himself to go slow, to be patient, to give her time to catch up.

But he'd gone slow. He'd been patient. He'd given her weeks to catch up. He drew her nipple into his mouth and sucked hard, loving the way her body molded to his and her fingers grasped his hair in a tight grip. Colton never would've described himself as a breast man before he caught sight of Lucy Mulvaney's gorgeous breasts last weekend, and now they were all he could think about. He'd always been more of a leg and ass guy, but she'd changed him in more ways than one.

Speaking of her pert ass and smooth legs . . . He cupped a supple cheek and squeezed, making her squirm and moan. "I want you, Lucy. I've wanted you since the first time I saw you standing there next to Cameron in our conference room."

"I'm afraid that we keep getting in deeper." Realizing what she'd said, she squeezed his lips together before he could make a predictable comment. However, even the tight pinch of her fingers couldn't keep the smile from occupying the rest of his face. "You are such a little boy."

He nibbled her fingers until she let go. "That is not true, and I can prove it."

"Yes, it really is true," she said with a sigh.

"I hear what you're saying, Luce, and I get it. Believe me, I do, and I'm worried about a lot of the same things you are. But I absolutely refuse to ruin today by worrying about what might happen tomorrow or the next day." He met her gaze and kissed her softly. "After I lost my twenty-eight-year-old brother-in-law, I promised myself I'd honor his memory by living my life to the absolute fullest extent possible. No regrets, no worries, no fears. That's what I've tried to do ever since."

Colton brushed his lips over her knuckles. "He was two years older than I am now when he died. This was all he got, and he had so much more to give." He closed his eyes when the sadness threatened to derail him. When he'd gotten himself together, he opened them and looked directly at her. "I'm not trying to be dramatic or anything. But that changed me. It changed all of us. It made me realize *this* is all we've got. Right now. Today. And right now, today, I want to make love with you because that's almost all I've thought about since the first time I kissed you."

Her eyes were bright with unshed tears. "The first time you kissed me was the night we met."

He shrugged. "That's how long I've wanted you." Why mince words? At this point, either she was in this thing or she wasn't, but he was no longer interested in hiding how he felt about her. Under his watchful gaze, she processed what he'd said, all the while looking at him with those big blue eyes that gave away her every emotion. Did she think he couldn't see how badly she wanted the same thing he did? Now it was only a matter of whether she would give herself permission to take what she wanted.

"I won't hurt you, Luce. As long as you're mine, I'll take good care of whatever you choose to give me."

A big tear rolled down her cheek, and he brushed it away. She caressed his face, and her touch electrified him the way it always did. "You are extremely irresistible, but of course you already know that."

"No one has ever said that to me before, so I didn't know. Not until you told me." He held his breath, waiting to see what she would do next.

She flattened her hand on his chest and leaned in to kiss him, her lips soft but persuasive. Then the tip of her tongue began to trace the outline of his mouth, and he had to hold himself back from the need to absolutely devour her.

"Lucy," he said in a strangled tone. "Tell me what you want."

"You. I want you, as much as you want me."

"And the rest of it?"

"I suppose we'll figure it out. Eventually."

As his mental traffic light switched from caution to green, he wrapped his arm around her and pulled her in tight against him. He nearly forgot how to breathe when her breasts pressed against his chest. Because he didn't want to miss a thing, he kept his eyes open and focused on her as he lost himself in a deep, sensual kiss full of passion and promise.

He could feel her capitulation, her surrender to the inevitable pull they'd experienced from the first day they met. They'd been drawn to each other before they'd even been properly introduced, and had been heading for this moment ever since. Now that she'd confessed to wanting the same things he did, he was determined to make it unforgettable for her.

With that in mind, he broke the kiss and moved his attention to her neck and throat, nibbling and kissing her soft skin while breathing in the fragrance he'd come to know as hers. It wasn't perfume or soap or anything easily identified. It was *her*, uniquely her.

"Relax, honey." He left a trail of kisses along her collar-bone. "Just relax and let me love you."

Her arms curled over her head as she released a deep breath.

Sensing her complete surrender made him harder than he'd ever been in his life, but he refused to rush. Not after they'd waited so long to get here. He worshiped each breast with his lips and mouth and teeth while she writhed under him, arching against him until he was cross-eyed with lust. But still he didn't rush. Rather, he took his time and didn't move farther down until each nipple was standing at attention and her entire body was trembling in response to him.

Her belly quaked under his lips and her legs shook as he removed her shorts, leaving her covered only in a scrap of see-through lace. He bit his lip to keep from groaning out loud when his own needs threatened to trump hers. But this time was all about her, and he wanted to make sure her faith in him was amply rewarded.

With his palms flat against her knees, he encouraged her to open to him.

Her movements were tentative and almost uncertain.

Colton looked up to find her watching him intently. "Let me in, honey." His voice sounded rough, even to his own ears. He moved his hands from her knees to her inner thighs, hoping he was encouraging her as he went.

She reached for him, but he shook his head. If she touched him now, he'd lose his composure.

"Hands above your head. Grab the slats if you need something to hold on to."

"I want to hold on to you."

"You can. Later."

Lucy did as he asked, wrapping her hands around the wooden slats in the headboard. Her trust overwhelmed him and fired his desire to give her everything.

He ran his hands over her incredibly soft skin as he continued to ease her legs farther apart.

"Colton," she whispered, lifting her hips off the bed.

"Hmm?"

"You're making me nuts, and you know it."

"Now how could I possibly know that?" He smiled as he replaced his hands with his lips, kissing from her right knee, up her thigh and stopping at the place where her leg met her body.

"Colton!"

"Is this what you want?" He pressed his mouth against her core, tonguing her through the lace that covered her.

"Yes! God, *yes*. There. Don't stop."

He kept up the steady pressure of his tongue, while watching the full-body blush that he'd grown to love so much color her soft pale skin. More than anything, he loved that he could do that to her. When he was certain she was past the point of paying attention, he pushed her panties aside and resumed his efforts with nothing between his tongue and her pleasure. They'd never done this before, and the flavor of her on his tongue was like the sweetest honey he'd ever tasted. One taste, and he was already addicted.

She screamed from the new sensations.

He slid two fingers into her and sucked on the heart of her desire, tripping her release, which was about the sexiest thing he'd ever experienced. How in the world could she say she wasn't hot?

While she came down from the release, he removed her panties, leaving her completely naked before him for the first time. The hair that covered her mound was a darker shade of red than the hair on her head. When she saw him taking a greedy look at her, she tried to cover herself.

He took her hands and pinned them to the mattress next to her hips. "Don't hide from me. I love looking at you."

"Colton," she whispered. "I want to touch you."

"In a minute." He bent to kiss her belly. "Do we need protection?"

She shook her head. "I'm on long-term birth control."

"I had a physical a month ago. I'm clean, and I can prove it if you want me to."

"I believe you." She tugged her hands free from his hold and held out her arms to him.

He took a second to remove his shorts before he stretched out on top of her. "God, you feel so good, Luce. Nothing has ever felt this good."

"For me either. I had no idea it could be like this."

"You ain't seen nothing yet," he said with a grin, hoping to get rid of the line of tension that had formed between her brows.

She smiled up at him. "Show me what you've got."

Never one to back away from a challenge, he took himself in hand and pressed into her, slowing when she gasped. "Does it hurt?"

"No. I'm just . . . sensitive. And it's been a while. A long while."

"Mmm," he said, his lips pressed against her neck. "We'll have to take it slow then." Taking it slow would surely kill him, but he'd do it for her.

"Not too slow, I hope." To make her point, she lifted her hips, taking more of him. "God, you're big all over, aren't you?"

That made him laugh, which caused his control to falter, leading to a stronger thrust than he'd intended.

She gasped again and pressed her fingertips into the muscles on his back. Other women had done that, but never before had such an insignificant thing set off an almost electrical current of desire in him. Everything about this—about her—was different and had been from the beginning.

"Luce," he said on a long deep breath. "I can't . . ."

"What?"

"I can't hold back anymore."

"Don't. Don't hold back."

When he heard the desire in her voice, something inside him snapped, shredding what was left of his control. As it was happening, he knew in the back of his mind that he might regret later that he had failed to be gentle, that he'd failed to show restraint or finesse, but in the moment, he could only take and take and take what she gave so willingly.

Her legs curled around his back, her arms encircled his neck and her tongue tangled with his as she took him somewhere he'd never been before. Her shout of pleasure finished him off, and he collapsed into her embrace in a trembling mass of limbs and sweat.

Jesus, he thought. *What the hell just happened?* As the haze of desire lifted, he winced at how rough he'd been with her. He was almost afraid to look at her for fear of seeing shock or horror. Marshaling the courage, he raised his head off her chest and looked down to find her eyes closed and her lips curved into a satisfied little smile. She didn't look the slightest bit shocked or horrified.

"Are you okay?" he asked. His throat was dry, and his lips were sore.

She kept her eyes closed. "Mmm. Hmmm."

"Sorry . . . I was rough. I didn't mean to be."

Her arm encircled his neck, drawing him into a kiss. "You were amazing." She kissed him again. "I get it now."

"What do you get?"

Lucy opened her eyes and looked up at him. "If that's how it is for Cameron with Will, I get now why she ditched her whole life to be with him."

Colton curled up his lip with disgust. "I don't want to talk about how it is for Cameron with *Will*, if you don't mind."

She laughed until she had tears in her eyes, which made her tighten around his hardening cock.

"You know," he said as he rolled her earlobe between his teeth, "we might need to do it again, just to make sure that wasn't a one-off."

"I think we owe it to ourselves to find out."

"I really do like how you think."

CHAPTER 5

Overcast, temps just above freezing. No sap.
Worked on main lines, setting up the vacuum
pump and scouring sap tanks with wet snow.

—Colton Abbott's sugaring journal, February 24

Waking early on Saturday morning, Will Abbott took advantage of the opportunity to watch Cameron sleep. Since she was almost always awake before him, he rarely had the chance to study her in all her gorgeousness without her knowing he was looking.

He focused on the dark circles that had formed under her eyes as she worked long, grueling hours on the website for the store all the while helping Hannah with her plan to turn her home into a bed-and-breakfast for women who'd lost spouses to war. On top of all of that, Hannah had asked Cameron to be a bridesmaid in her wedding to Nolan later this summer.

Unable to resist touching her, Will stroked her fine blonde hair and let the silky strands slide through his fingers. In the weeks that she'd been living with him in his cabin in the woods, she'd also taken to life among the Abbotts like a bee to the sweetest of honey. She'd flitted from one family obligation to another until his parents and siblings were almost as in love with her as he was.

The bruised circles under her eyes told the true story though. She was wearing herself out. He hadn't yet asked what she had planned for the weekend, but inevitably she would work for much of it.

She needed some time away from the computer, and he needed some time completely alone with her. The idea took root as he watched her sleep. He got out of bed slowly so he wouldn't wake her. After letting the dogs out, he filled their bowls with food and then headed for the shower. By the time he was dressed, the dogs were scratching at the door to get in. He wrote Cameron a note to let her know he'd gone to do a quick errand but would be right back and left it on his pillow so she'd see it the minute she woke up.

Will whispered to the dogs to take care of Cameron and he'd be right back. Sensing they weren't invited to join him, Trevor and Tanner went to the bedroom and got in bed with Cam.

He drove his truck into town and across the one-lane covered bridge that led to his parents' home on Hells Peak Road. They still lived in the converted red barn in which they'd raised ten children, who loved to tell outsiders they'd been raised in a barn. His brother Landon liked to add that their upbringing explained their bad behavior. Except none of them were all that badly behaved. Their parents wouldn't have stood for it then, and they certainly wouldn't stand for it now that all ten of their children were adults.

Even Max, the youngest of them, was now officially an adult and had the first Abbott grandchild on the way. Months after hearing that Max and his girlfriend, Chloe, were expecting a baby together, Will was still trying to wrap his mind around the fact that the youngest of them would be the first to become a parent.

They'd all expected Hannah to be the first parent as she'd married Caleb right after college. But they'd yet to have children when Caleb died six years later in Iraq. The rest of them were late bloomers in the marriage and family department. Since he'd met Cameron, Will had begun to think more about the next steps for them. As eager as he was to spend forever with her, they weren't in any rush. Still, it was on his mind.

Will entered the mudroom at his parents' house and was greeted by their yellow labs, George the third and Ringo the third, named for members of his father's favorite band of all time.

His parents were exactly where he expected them to be at that hour—at the kitchen table, drinking coffee and reading the morning paper the way they had every morning for as long as Will could remember.

He bent to kiss his mother and stole a croissant out of a basket on the table.

"To what do we owe this unexpected honor?" Molly Abbott asked as she turned her cheek up to receive his kiss.

"What? A guy can't come by to see his parents without a good reason?"

Lincoln looked over the half glasses that were perched on the end of his nose. "We haven't seen much of you lately."

"I've been busy."

"Busy," Molly said with a chuckle. "Is that what you call it these days?"

"Happy," Will said. "Is that better?"

"That's lovely, and no one deserves it more."

"I don't mean to neglect you guys though."

"You haven't," Molly said. "We're teasing you."

"If you're happy," Lincoln added, "we're happy."

That was the simple truth his parents had always lived by, and it was how he hoped to raise his own kids someday.

Molly got up to refill her mug and poured one for Will, putting the cream and sugar on the table in front of him. "So what brings you by, and where's Cam this morning?"

"Thanks." Will stirred cream into his coffee. "She's

sleeping in, but she's why I'm here. I was thinking about taking her over to the lake for a couple of nights. She's been working nonstop for weeks and could use a break."

"Sounds like a great idea," Lincoln said after a short pause. "I'll get you the key." He jumped up from the table and left the room, the dogs in hot pursuit. Where his father went, the dogs went, too.

Molly twisted her gray braid around her finger as she eyed him. "I've noticed Cam seems sort of worn out lately. I wondered if something else might be afoot."

"Such as?"

Molly shrugged but sent him a devilish grin. "You should ask Max about how tired Chloe has been."

Will felt like he'd been electrocuted as he stared at his mother. "Cameron isn't pregnant, Mom."

"And you're sure of that?"

"Of course I am." Of course he was. Despite his certainty, however, a bolt of panic shot through him.

"Then a few nights away ought to perk her right up."

He downed the last of his coffee, surprised he could get it past the huge lump in his throat. "That's the idea."

Lincoln returned and held out the key to Will. "Have a nice time."

"We will. Thanks." He stood and put his mug in the sink. "I'd better get home and see if I can talk Cameron into a getaway."

"Good luck, son," Molly said.

"Are you taking the boys?" Lincoln asked of Will's dogs.

"I figured I would. They love the lake."

"Yes, they do. Have fun."

"We might be a little late on Monday, but we'll be there."

"You should take Monday off. It's been ages since you had a day off."

"Not that long," Will reminded him. "I had a week off when I helped Cameron move."

"That doesn't count," Lincoln said. "That was work."

Will would hardly consider a week alone with Cameron

work, but he didn't argue the point. "I'll see what she wants to do. She may want to get back sooner rather than later."

"Up to you."

"I'll see you. Have a good weekend."

"You, too, honey," Molly called after him.

Will headed for the door, eager to get back to Cam and make sure she was just tired and not something else. It couldn't be that. Could it?

Lincoln returned to his seat at the table, picked up the paper and settled in to read, his mind racing with scenarios and hoping he'd done the right thing by letting Will go to the lake when Colton was already there.

"That's it?" Molly asked. "You're not going to say a word about what just happened here?"

Lincoln folded the corner of the paper down so he could see his lovely wife, who was, in fact, still very lovely nearly forty years after he met her and had the good sense to marry her. "Excuse me?"

"Don't play dumb with me, Lincoln Abbott. I happen to know you gave the other set of keys to Colton."

He did his best not to squirm under her intense glare. "And how do you know that?"

"I have my sources. So what're you about?"

"It's a big house. They won't even see each other."

Molly raised a brow to let him know she wasn't buying his bullshit. She always could see right through him.

"I don't see what the big deal is. Colton went fishing."

"Is that what he told you?" Molly laughed. "And you believed him?"

What to say? If he admitted he didn't believe him, he'd walk right into her trap. "Why wouldn't I?"

"Oh, Linc, you can fool some of the people some of the time, but not me. What're you up to?"

"Nothing."

"And when Will walks in there to find Colton with a woman, will you still say you weren't up to anything?"

"That's my story, and I'm sticking to it."

She shook her head. "You are too much. I hope your little scheme doesn't blow up in your face."

Her words were a jolt to his system. He hoped so, too.

Cameron was still asleep when Will returned to the cabin. He paced for half an hour, the dogs following him anxiously, sensing something was wrong. When he finally heard her stirring in the bedroom, he went into the room, intending to subtly work his way into the question he needed to ask her.

But seeing her sleep-rumpled and beautiful, subtlety flew out the window. "Are you pregnant?"

Her hazel eyes went wide, and her mouth opened and then closed.

"Cameron, answer me. Are you?"

"Not that I know of. Do you know something I don't?"

"You've been so tired, and the dark circles, and you're hungry all the time, and your breasts, they're well, you know . . ."

"I don't know. Why don't you tell me what my breasts are?"

If he wasn't mistaken, she was enjoying his discomfort. "They're . . . bigger and more sensitive." He cleared his throat. "Lately."

"Who put the idea I might be pregnant in your head?"

"My mom."

"Your *mother*? What did she say?"

"I mentioned you'd been tired lately, and she said she'd noticed that, too. She asked if it was something more than overwork causing it."

"So you totally freaked out and jumped to all kinds of conclusions?"

"Not totally. Only kind of."

"Come here." Smiling indulgently, she held out a hand to him. "You didn't tell your mother about my breasts, did you?"

"Of course I didn't." He was so wound up he could barely function. However, any time Cameron held out her hand to him, he took it. This time was no exception.

She laughed at his discomfort and tugged him down next to her in bed.

"Sorry," he muttered when he was curled up to her. "I let my imagination run wild."

"Did you stop for one second to wonder how I could be pregnant when I'm on birth control?"

"Nothing is foolproof. Just ask Max about that."

"I'm not pregnant, but after seeing you so freaked out, I'm a little concerned about what would happen if I were."

"What does that mean?"

"It doesn't seem like you'd be happy about it."

"Are you serious? I'd love to see you pregnant with our baby. I can't imagine anything that would please me more."

She responded to that with the soft smile he'd come to love so much, especially when it was directed at him. "Then why the freak-out?"

He blew out a deep breath. "I guess it was more the idea that something like that could be going on with you, and I didn't even notice. I was afraid I'd missed something important."

"You haven't missed anything. I promise."

"But you are incredibly tired."

"I won't deny that."

He cupped her breast and ran his thumb over the nipple that hardened under his caress. "And you're more sensitive."

"Probably PMS."

"That I can't do much about, but I've got an idea to deal with the exhaustion."

"What's that?"

He withdrew the key his father had given him from the front pocket of his shorts and held it up for her to see.

"What've you got there?"

"That, my love, is a key to the Abbott family lake house in Burlington."

"Ahh, I've heard about this lake house of which you speak. Something about a wedding happening there later this summer . . ."

"I thought we might run away for a couple of days."

She stared at the key as she contemplated his offer. "Would I be allowed to bring my laptop on this adventure?"

"I suppose I could permit that if you're willing to put a time limit on how much you work. The goal is to rest and relax."

"Three hours a day."

"Two."

"Three."

"*Two*, and that's my final offer."

"Two and a half, and that's *my* final offer."

"Done. How soon can you be ready to go?"

"Twenty minutes if you make the coffee."

One of the things he loved best about Cameron was that she was very much a girl, but she didn't spend hours making herself look like one. She didn't need to. "You're on." He started to get up, but she gave his hand a tug.

"Thanks for being worried about me and for making a plan to get me away from work."

"It's sort of a selfish plan, really."

"How so?"

He kissed her, lingering over the sweet taste of her lips. "Since you've moved here, I've had to share you with my family. I'm ready to have you all to myself for a few days."

She ran her fingers through his hair. "Have I been neglecting you?"

"Not at all. I love how much you love my family and vice versa. But I also love the idea of being completely alone at the lake for a few days."

"I love that idea, too."

"Then let's get to it."

"What about the boys?" she asked of the dogs.

"Coming with us, but don't tell them until we're ready to go, or they'll go nuts."

"Yay, a few days alone with my three favorite guys. What could be better than that?"

Drinking in the bright smile that made her eyes light up with joy, Will couldn't think of a single thing better than that.

CHAPTER 6

—◆—

We are collecting sap. The lower tanks are filling up. Sunshine this morning stirred the trees; the temp finally pushed 40°F. The snow pack on the woodshed roof has begun to curl over the edge, notched at the edge like jigsaw puzzle pieces.

—Colton Abbott's sugaring journal, February 28

Colton came awake slowly but was instantly aware of the soft female curled up to him. Her hand rested on his chest, directly above his heart, which began to beat double time when her scent filled his senses. Dark auburn hair spread out on the pillow next to his, and he was pleased to see that the curls he'd become quite fond of had returned overnight.

He wound one of them around his finger, pulled it straight and then let it spring back into place. She'd told him she hated those curls, but he couldn't imagine why. He loved them. Moving slowly so he wouldn't disturb her, he put his hand on her shoulder and smiled when she burrowed deeper into his embrace.

Then she startled, and her body went rigid.

"Hey," he whispered. "It's just me. Sorry to wake you."

She relaxed in tiny, uncertain increments, as if she weren't entirely sure why she was sleeping naked in his arms.

He vividly remembered the incredible night they'd shared. He'd never forget it. Despite his isolated life on the mountain, he'd been with his share of women, but none of them had ever rocked his world the way Lucy had. Just thinking about how amazingly responsive she'd been had him hard and longing for more of her.

When she shifted to find a more comfortable position, her belly pressed against his erection, making him groan.

"What's wrong?"

Not wanting her to think he let his dick run his life, he pulled his hips back, seeking relief. "Nothing."

"That didn't sound like nothing to me."

"Nothing a cold shower won't fix. Don't worry."

Damn if her hand didn't start to move south, sliding from his chest to his stomach and below. Before his brain could catch up to anticipate her intentions, she had her soft hand wrapped around his extremely hard cock.

"Lucy," he said through gritted teeth. "You don't have to do that."

"Why not?"

The innocently spoken question was in sharp contrast to the way she stroked him, from root to tip, running her thumb over the moisture that gathered at the top.

"Christ."

"Good?"

Was it good? He wanted to laugh at the absurdity of the question. "Mmm. Yeah."

Then she shocked the living shit out of him by pushing him onto his back and kissing her way down the front of him, taking the same path her hand had traveled. He couldn't believe that shy, reserved Lucy was about to—

Holy mother of God and all things holy. The heat of her mouth on him was nearly enough to finish him off—and that was before she brought her tongue to the party.

Colton grasped handfuls of her hair as he tried to ignore the overpowering urge to take control.

"Am I doing it right?" she asked, looking up at him with those crystal blue eyes that were a window to her emotions. In them he now saw concern and hesitation.

"You're perfect in every way."

Her smile lit up her face before she bent to return to the task at hand.

Colton sucked in a sharp deep breath and kept his eyes open to watch as he gave in to the exquisite pleasure. The combination of her hand stroking him, her lips and tongue . . . "Lucy . . ."

She mumbled something that sent a shock wave of vibrations through his cock.

"Lucy."

Stopping what she was doing, she looked up at him with those eyes, her lips gone swollen from her efforts. "Did I do something wrong?"

He sat up, reached for her and pulled her on top of him. "You did everything exactly right."

"I wanted to finish."

He kissed the pout off her lips. "Another time. I want to finish with you."

"Oh." Her entire body flushed with color and heat. He couldn't bear to have her so close and not touch her, especially when her skin turned that appealing shade of pink. With his hands on her back, he encouraged her to lean back so he could reach her breasts as he entered her.

As he took a hardened nipple into his mouth, her slight whimper had him stopping. "What?"

"A little sore from last night."

"Do you want to stop?"

"No," she said, sounding as breathless as he felt.

"Mmm, I'll go easy."

She released a deep breath and combed her fingers through his hair, surrendering to him so completely it was all he could do not to move things along quickly. But he wanted to give her time to catch up before he gave in to the desire that pounded through him relentlessly.

Mindful that she was sore, he remained wedged just

inside her as he sucked gently and licked softly, first one breast and then the other, loving the soft sounds of pleasure that came from her.

"Colton."

"Hmm?"

"I want . . ."

"What do you want, honey?"

"You know!"

"Tell me anyway."

"You. I want you."

"I'm right here."

She groaned with frustration and aggravation as her forehead landed on his shoulder.

He chuckled as he cupped her breasts and ran his thumbs over her damp nipples. "Tell me what you want. Be specific."

"You're trying to embarrass me, aren't you?"

"Not at all. I want to be sure to please you."

"You do please me. You know you do. I gave you ample evidence of just how much you please me several times last night."

The conversation was making her complexion even pinker, if that was possible. He kissed the rosy glow of her cheeks before focusing on her lips, which were pink and puffy and so very tempting. As he captured her mouth in a deep kiss, he cupped her bottom and pulled her in tighter against him.

"You still haven't said the words," he whispered as he went to work on her neck, licking and nibbling his way from her jaw to her throat.

She reached between them, curled her hand around the base of his erection and squeezed, making him see stars. "I want this. All the way inside me. Now. Any questions?"

"Nope. I think I got it." With his hands still full of soft buttocks, he lifted her and brought her back down. Her sharp intake of breath had him slowing things down. "Still sore?"

"A little."

"Want to stop?"

"Don't you dare stop."

"You're in the driver's seat, babe. Go as slow as you want. I'm all yours."

Though it cost him tremendously to turn over control to her, the last thing he wanted was to cause her pain when everything about this felt amazing to him. He propped his hands behind him, reclined slightly to enjoy the show.

Lucy leaned forward to put her hands on his shoulders and began to move in slight increments that had his head falling back and his eyes rolling into his skull as he bit down hard on his lip, hoping the pain would give him something to focus on other than the growing crisis below.

She felt so damned good, and so damned tight and so damned hot. He'd never felt anything even remotely like the pleasure he'd found with her right from the very beginning, before he'd ever even touched her. She was funny and sweet and loyal and talented and sexy as all hell, especially when she wasn't trying to be.

Then he'd touched her and kissed her, which was all it had taken to discover she was different from any other woman he'd ever known. He couldn't begin to articulate what made her so special. There was just something about her, and he'd known that from the first time he saw her.

Last night had demonstrated once again that his connection with her was unique, something to be treasured and nurtured if only she'd let him.

He was almost to the point of no return when she finally took all of him, and suddenly it wasn't enough to only be connected to her there. He needed more. Sitting up straight, he wrapped his arms tight around her and held her close, loving the feel of her breasts pressed against his chest and her racing pulse under his lips on her neck.

The flutter of her internal muscles expanding to accommodate him took him right to the edge of insanity, and they'd barely moved yet. "You are incredible," he whispered. He wished he could tell her everything she made him feel, but he lived in constant fear of going too far too fast and driving her away. "You feel so good."

"So do you."

"Does it hurt at all?"

She shook her head.

He flattened his hands on her back and ran them down to her hips and then to her legs, curling them around him before moving back up to cup her ass. "Hold on to me."

She tightened her arms around his neck but kept her eyes locked on his, watching him carefully as he began to lift her up and down. As a sexy flush overtook her, he watched her lips part and her eyes flutter closed.

Colton picked up the pace, his biceps doing most of the work as they moved together at an increasingly frantic pace. He curled his left arm under her, freeing his right hand to reach between them to coax her. At the same time, he dragged her nipple into his mouth and felt her detonate around him, crying out from the pleasure and sending him into an equally explosive finish.

She sagged against him, pulsating from the aftershocks that continued to ripple through both of them, and held on tight to him.

He buried his face in her hair, breathing in the alluring scent of her as he came down from the incredible high. Still lodged deep inside her, he arranged her so she faced away from him and cuddled into her back, continuing to press into her repeatedly until she trembled in his arms.

The words *amazing*, *incredible* and *life-altering* filtered through his mind in the aftermath. He wanted to tell her that it'd never been like this for him before, not with any-one, ever. But he didn't. He didn't say that or anything. Rather, he reveled in the pleasure of having her in his arms, of the feel of her soft skin under his hands and lips and the internal contractions that massaged him until he was hard again.

"You're out to kill me, aren't you?" she asked with a low groan as she squiggled back against him, taking him deeper.

"Not hardly. I can't help it if you make me want you all the time."

"How do I make that happen?"

He kissed from the end of her shoulder to the sweet curve of her neck. "By being here and being naked and being you. That's about all it takes." Colton smiled when she tipped her head ever so slightly to encourage his kisses. "I had all kinds of plans for today."

"What kind of plans?"

"Beach time. Maybe take the canoe out or the sailboat or the Jet-Skis."

"That all sounds fun. So you don't want to do that?"

"I do, but after what we just did, I can't imagine ever letting you leave this bed again."

"We do need to eat, and a shower would be nice."

"Uh-huh."

She yawned and then jolted when he flattened his hand over her lower belly, his fingers landing just above her mound. "*Colton* . . . I can't take anymore."

"I'm not doing anything. Just holding you."

"You're doing much more than that, and you know it."

"Feels so good. *You* feel so good."

Lucy sighed and reached back to curl her arm around his neck, which he naturally took as encouragement to continue what had started as languid aftermath and turned into round two.

He cupped her breast and tweaked her nipple, drawing a deep moan from her as he continued to slide into her repeatedly.

"Are you trying to show me that Jet-Skis are vastly overrated compared to the considerable charms of Colton Abbott?"

Laughing, he spread his fingers on her lower belly and surged into her. How did she expect him to not fall for her when she insisted on being so damned sexy and funny and cute all the time?

They moved together like seasoned lovers, and once again, Colton found himself fighting to maintain control.

That was also new. With other women, he'd never found it a problem to hang on until they got what they wanted. Now, with Lucy, it took every bit of fortitude he could muster not to give in and let go.

He cupped her breast and teased her nipple, using his other hand to caress between her legs. Again, the combination had the desired effect, making her tremble and moan as she came.

Free to take what he wanted more than anything, he came hard, harder than he had the first time, if that was even possible. Afterward, he held her close and tried to think of something he could say that could properly convey all that he was feeling. But then he felt her relax in his arms, her breathing deepening, and he realized she'd gone back to sleep.

He closed his eyes and released a deep breath of his own, more relaxed than he could remember being, yet still on edge when he thought about where all of this might be leading. Paradise or disaster? He had no freaking clue, and he hated that.

CHAPTER 7

———•❖•———

*The sap is just starting to trickle, and I'm in the
sap shed turning on the vacuum pump. This pump
is ten horsepower large and supplies vacuum to all
of our ten thousand tubing taps. That and the
reverse-osmosis machine are the reason we bring
in generators during the season.*☺

—Colton Abbott's sugaring journal, March 1

Cameron and Will took their time traveling across
Northern Vermont, stopping around noon to buy
sandwiches and drinks that they took to a park in Water-
bury. They fed the dogs from the bag of dog food Will had
brought with them and let them romp around in the open
field while they ate. Tanner and Trevor came over to their
blanket every so often to check in and nose around for
smells. Will rewarded them with a potato chip each time.

"They are so spoiled," Cameron commented after
Trevor had returned a third time for another chip.

"No, they aren't. They're well trained and obedient."

She snorted with laughter. "Is that what you tell yourself when they won't stand still and let you towel them off
when they come inside soaking wet?"

"That's a rare instance of disobedience, and P.S. no one is perfect."

You are, she wanted to say as she took a good long look at him. The blond highlights in his honey-colored hair were particularly golden in the afternoon sunshine, his arms were tanned from shirtless hours outside and his muscles bulged from the way he sat, partially reclined on his outstretched arms. Yes, he was indeed perfect in every way that mattered to her.

"What're you looking at over there?"

"You."

His brows narrowed suspiciously. "What about me?"

"Everything about you."

"That's a pretty broad answer."

"I love everything about you, and I particularly love looking at you. Is that better?"

He stared at her for a long moment before reaching for her hand and bringing it to his lips. "I love everything about you, too. I feel like I'm living in some sort of dream come true since you moved in with me. And then you say something like that, and it gets even better than it already was. How is that possible?"

She leaned forward and kissed him, tipping her head to delve deeper when he hooked an arm around her to keep her from getting away. Somehow she wound up reclined on the blanket as one kiss became two and two became three. Trevor's cold wet nose between them finally interrupted the moment, making them laugh.

"Damn it, Trev." Will scratched the dog's ears while also pushing him back. "You need to leave me alone when I'm kissing my girl."

Trevor whined as he always did on the rare instances when Will actually chastised him.

"It's probably just as well that he saved us from making a spectacle of ourselves in a public park," Cameron said.

Will gathered up their trash and put it in the brown bag their lunch had come in. "It's your fault."

"How is it my fault?"

"You say awesome things to me, and then you kiss me until I forget where I am." He got up and offered her his hand to help her.

Laughing, Cameron took his outstretched hand. "I believe you were a willing participant in the kissing."

He wrapped his arm around her and kissed her again. "You bet your ass I was."

"I don't want to bet my ass. I might lose it, and my boyfriend tells me he loves it."

The low growl that came from Will made both dogs bark.

Cameron lost it laughing and took off running for the truck with the dogs in hot pursuit. A glance over her shoulder told her Will was right behind her, with the blanket tossed over his shoulder and the bag of trash in hand. Nervous giggles escaped from her lips as he caught up to her and hooked an arm around her waist from behind.

She screamed with laughter when he swung her around.

The dogs barked and frolicked at their feet.

Cameron had never felt more "herself" or at home than she did with him, especially in moments like this when they were silly together. For so long she'd affected a tough outer shell that she showed the world, which was how she grappled with the early loss of her mother and the attention deficit disorder that had marked her lonely childhood.

But with Will—and his big, rowdy family—she'd discovered the tough outer shell wasn't necessary. She didn't need to protect herself against him or them. She'd allowed herself to believe that his love was forever.

He put her down and kissed her neck from behind.

Cameron covered his hands with hers and leaned back against him, loving the way he surrounded her and made her feel safe in a way she'd never felt with any man before him.

After weeks of living with him and sleeping with him, she wasn't at all surprised to feel the press of his erection against her back, just as he probably wasn't surprised when she rubbed herself against him shamelessly.

"In the car, woman," he said, with a playful smack to her rear end. "I'm suddenly very anxious to get to the lake."

"Why?" She loved that he held the door to his truck for her—always. "Do you want to go swimming?" Feigning innocence, she looked up at him.

He leaned in and kissed her again, with sweeping thrusts of his tongue that had her immediately ready for anything he had in mind. "No, I don't want to go swimming," he said when he came up for air. "You know damned well what I want, so be ready when we get there."

"Oh, yes, sir. Whatever you want, sir."

"Call me 'sir,' and you'll get a whole *other* side of me that you haven't seen yet."

She found the statement both intriguing and titillating. "All this and there's *more*?"

He winked suggestively. "Much, much more."

Cameron suddenly couldn't wait to get to the lake house.

They passed much of the ride in the easy silence she'd come to appreciate in her relationship with Will. He didn't feel the need to fill every minute with useless chatter. If he said something, it was something worth hearing. Though he was quiet, he still kept a firm grip on her hand as he drove, and that small gesture made her feel loved and treasured.

She'd had no idea this kind of happiness was even possible until she crashed into Fred the moose and found Will Abbott in the dark of Vermont mud season. At first she'd worried he might be a chain saw murderer, a thought that now made her giggle softly.

"What's so funny?"

"I was thinking about the night we met and how I worried you might be a chain saw murderer."

"Your fertile imagination never ceases to entertain me." He brought her hand to his mouth and nibbled on her fingers. "Why would I want to cut you up with a chain saw when I'd much rather tie you to my bed and have my way with you?"

Cameron swallowed hard. "Tie me to your bed?" she asked in a squeaky voice. "Since when did my beta boyfriend become an alpha?"

"Since he found the perfect woman for him and let his imagination run wild."

"Personally speaking, I thought his imagination was already pretty wild."

"Oh, babe, his imagination is almost as fertile as yours."

"I'm a little scared of what goes on at this lake house of yours."

That made him laugh.

Cameron loved to make him laugh and to watch him laugh. He was so damned sexy all the time, but when he laughed . . . She really loved that. And his amazing smile . . . She'd fallen in love with that first. Who was she kidding? She was crazy in love with everything about him, and if he wanted to—gulp—tie her to his bed and have his way with her, who was she to get in the way of his fantasies?

She cleared her throat and swallowed the nervous lump that threatened to choke her. "I'd do it, you know."

"Do what?"

"Anything you wanted."

He took his eyes off the road to glance over at her as his jaw throbbed with tension. "Cameron . . . You can't say stuff like that to me when I'm driving. It's not fair or safe."

"What? We're just having a conversation."

"Right," he said with a laugh. "That's all we're doing. How about we table this *conversation* until we get to where I can do something about it."

At the thought of him "doing something about it" Cameron swallowed again, her heart fluttering with nerves and desire and love. She'd meant what she'd said—there was almost nothing he could ask of her that she wouldn't give him. She wanted to be everything to him and make his every fantasy come true.

"I can hear you thinking about it, and that's also not safe when I'm driving."

"What kind of crazy logic is that? I'm not even allowed to think?"

"Not about that. Not while I'm driving."

As she was about to further state how ridiculous he was being, one of the dogs let out a loud snore from the backseat that made them both laugh. Cameron felt the tightness in her chest ease, which she knew was only temporary. The moment they were alone at the house, she had no doubt they'd pick right up where they'd left off. His kind of tension was the very best she'd ever experienced.

Forty-five minutes later, they drove through the picturesque town of Burlington, home of the University of Vermont.

"I want you to show me where you went to school," Cameron said.

"I will. Tomorrow."

"Did Max live at the lake house when he was in school?" she asked of Will's youngest brother, who had recently graduated from college.

"No, he was in a fraternity, much to my mother's dismay. He lived at the frat house—also known as the pigsty."

"Were you in a frat?" she asked, fairly certain she knew the answer before she asked the question.

"Hell no. Max is the only one of us to go Greek."

He was also going to produce the first Abbott grandchild later this year, an event that had once seemed far off in the future but was getting closer all the time. Max's adorable girlfriend, Chloe, had begun to show rather significantly in the last few weeks.

After a few more turns that took them closer to Lake Champlain, Will pulled onto a long, winding dirt road that led to one of the most extraordinary houses Cameron had ever seen. As the daughter of a wildly successful businessman, she'd seen her share of amazing homes, but this was exceptional. "*This* is the lake house?" she asked, incredulous as she took in the glass and stone and wood that made up the house.

"Yep. What'd you have in mind?"

"Not this, that's for sure."

Will drove past the house to the driveway, bringing the truck to an abrupt stop when they saw Colton's truck. "What's he doing here? And who does he know from Pennsylvania?"

A second smaller car with Pennsylvania plates was parked next to the truck.

"Oh my God," Will said in a scandalized whisper. "He's here with the mystery woman! That sneaky bastard!"

"What should we do? If he's here with someone, maybe we shouldn't bother him."

"The hell with that. My dad gave *me* the keys. He shouldn't even be here."

"You know, most people in the twenty-first century would pick up the phone and call the other person to say, 'Hey, what's up? Why are you at the lake house when Dad said I could use it this weekend?' But in Abbott land, you don't have a phone, and neither does he. Is it too much to hope there might be a landline in there?"

"No landline. My dad didn't want to be reachable at the lake."

"Well, then our choice is to either go in there and interrupt what he's got going on or stay somewhere else."

Will shifted the truck into park. "We're not staying somewhere else, and it's high time one of us got to see this mystery woman he's been running off to meet the last few weekends."

The dogs were up and whimpering to get out after the long ride, and apparently they recognized where they were.

"I'm scared to go in there," Cameron said. "What if they're doing it in the kitchen or something?"

"Eww. He'd better not be doing that."

"But what if he is?"

"I'll kill him before you see anything. I promise."

They got out and met in front of the truck, the dogs

dancing around in circles at their feet. Will reached for her hand and pulled the key out of his pocket with his other hand as they walked to the front porch. "Here goes nothing." He opened the door and yelled inside. "Put your pants on, bro! I'm coming in!"

CHAPTER 8

*The temp rose to 34 or so at the sugarhouse for a
few hours, and the skies finally cleared by late
afternoon. We turned the vacuum pump on
for a while but didn't get much sap.*

—Colton Abbott's sugaring journal, March 5

Colton sat straight up in bed, the covers pooling at his
waist. What the hell had woken him up?

"Colton? Where are you?"

Was that . . . *Will*? If Will was here, Cameron probably
was, too. "Oh my God, what's he doing here?" Colton
bounded out of bed, dragged on a pair of shorts, pulled the
covers up over Lucy, who was still asleep, and was heading
for the bedroom door when his brother appeared in the
hallway. Not sure where to look, Colton glanced over his
shoulder at the bed to make sure Lucy was well hidden and
then returned his attention to Will. "What're you doing
here?" he asked in a low whisper.

"I could ask you the same thing."

"Is he decent?" Cameron asked as she joined them.

"Be quiet, will you?" Colton asked as he tried to get
them to leave the room.

But Will wouldn't budge. He looked around Colton. "Who've you got in there?"

"None of your business. Get out, and leave me alone."

"Oh, wouldn't you love that?" Will crossed his arms and leaned against the door frame, an infuriating smirk on his face that made Colton want to seriously punch his older brother in the mouth.

Colton felt like he was having a heart attack as he tried to figure out what Lucy would want him to say to them. And how was it possible that she was sleeping through this?

Will might've been older than him by seven years, but Colton was stronger thanks to a decade of wielding an axe on the mountain. He put his hand in the middle of his brother's chest and gave him a hard shove.

"Hey!" Will said as he stumbled backward. "Watch out for Cameron."

Will's angry cry finally got Lucy's attention. She sat straight up in bed, auburn curls rumpled around her face, bare breasts visible to anyone who might be looking, and Will and Cameron were definitely looking on with shock on their faces.

"What was that?" Lucy asked as she rubbed the sleep out of her eyes.

Colton moved quickly, lunging for the blanket on the end of the bed, which he all but threw at her.

"*Are you freaking kidding me? My* Lucy is *your* mystery woman?" Cameron's shriek could've woken the dead.

Lucy let out a scream of her own when she apparently realized her best friend was now in the room staring at her, not to mention that her best friend's boyfriend—who also happened to be Lucy's boyfriend's brother—had gotten a good look at her breasts. What a mess. "What're you doing here?" she asked Cameron.

"Oh no, *no*," Cameron said with a pointed finger. "We all know what I'm doing here. The question is what're *you* doing here? Someone has some rather significant explaining to do." Cameron crossed her arms and looked between Colton and Lucy. "Well?"

Colton sent his brother an imploring look, which Will thankfully understood.

"Cam, honey, let's give Lucy a chance to get herself together, and then we'll talk." He took her by the arm as he gave Colton a scorching look. "We'll have a good long talk."

Colton slammed the door shut behind them and turned to face Lucy, fearful of how she would react to what'd just happened. "I'm so sorry. I have no idea what they're doing here."

"He . . . Your brother . . . He saw my . . ." She gestured to her chest.

"You couldn't see much of anything. Don't worry." He told himself the lie didn't really count as a lie because he was trying to protect her.

"Nice try, but I was out and proud, and he saw everything."

"Then he knows I'm a lucky man." He crawled onto the bed and leaned in to kiss her.

She turned her face away.

Colton dropped his head to her shoulder. "Don't."

"What?"

"Don't turn away from me, Lucy. We're in this together. We decided together to keep our friendship private, so let's face the music together, too."

"I don't know what to say to her. Cameron was so shocked. And hurt."

"Tell her the truth."

"The whole truth?"

He tried again and this time she let him kiss her. "And nothing but the truth."

Her hand curled around his neck as she leaned her forehead against his.

"Shower?"

"Yes, please."

He got up and reached out to her.

She wrapped herself in the blanket and took his hand.

"We're not showering together when they're out there waiting for us."

Colton led her into the spacious master bathroom and turned on the water. "It'll be quicker that way. We can talk to them, get rid of them and get back to our weekend already in progress."

"It's not going to be that simple."

"It *is* going to be that simple." He tugged on the tight grip she had on the blanket. "We're both adults—consenting adults. We chose to take some time to ourselves before we told the world we were seeing each other. We've done nothing wrong, so please, don't ruin this for either of us by trying to convince yourself that we owe anyone explanations."

"You don't understand," she said softly.

The shine of tears in her eyes infuriated him. She'd been so happy earlier and now it had all gone to shit. "Make me understand."

"Cameron and I . . . We rely on each other. We talk to each other about things. Important things."

"So you're saying this is an *important* thing?" he asked with a cheeky grin.

As he eased her under the warm water, Lucy rolled her eyes, which was a relief. That was better than tears. Anything was better than that. "She's going to be mad at me for keeping this from her. Especially because of who you are. To Will."

"Will's my brother, not my keeper. We're family, and we're close, but we're not up each other's asses."

Her button nose wrinkled adorably. "That's a hideous visual."

"But you get my point. Despite all our ball busting, my business is my business. I leave him alone, for the most part, and I expect the same from him. From all of them." As he worked shampoo into her hair, he planted strategic kisses on her neck, hoping to remind her of the connection they'd shared before they were so rudely interrupted.

"Thank God they didn't get here a little earlier."

"That's the way. Let's be thankful for small favors."

"That's a very big favor."

He pushed his erection against her back. "Why thank you, darlin'. That's really kind of you to say."

"Colton! Not with my best friend and your brother waiting for us. Knock it off!" She moved away from him to finish her shower. "Stay over there, and get rid of that thing."

Colton laughed at the disdainful gesture she directed at his poor, misunderstood penis. How was he supposed to control him when she was standing naked and soapy and close to him? He was only human, after all. Resigned to the condition remaining until she was no longer naked, he washed up and got out to grab towels for both of them.

Lucy combed her hair and secured it in a ponytail.

They got dressed in silence. Colton wished there was something he could say that would make her laugh the way she had last night. He wanted to let her know everything was going to be okay, but he wasn't sure of that himself. They'd been living in their own little bubble, going from weekend to weekend and holding the outside world at arm's length.

Now their bubble had burst and they were forced to confront realities they weren't quite ready to face. He took her hand and gripped it tightly. "It's all good, okay?"

"Sure," she said with a distinct lack of conviction. "Let's get this over with."

They opened the bedroom door and were hit with an ambush. Cameron stepped between them, edging Colton aside with scary agility. He had no choice but to release Lucy's hand or risk losing his own hand as the door slammed in his face and the lock clicked into place.

What. The. *Fuck?* He turned to find Will leaning against the wall, arms folded and lips tight with displeasure and maybe pride at what his girlfriend had managed to accomplish.

"You've got some serious explaining to do, little brother. And there's no time like the present."

Lucy had never been scared of Cameron before. She'd never had reason to be. Until now. Her best friend was probably furious—and with good reason.

"So," Cameron said.

Lucy sat on the edge of the bed. "So."

"Were you going to tell me?"

"Eventually."

"*When?* And how long has this been going on?"

Lucy wished she could find a way out of this mess of her own making. If only she'd shown some restraint where Colton was concerned none of this would be happening. "Um, since the night I met him."

Cameron's eyes nearly popped out of her head. "The night you went to dinner with him and his parents?"

"That would be the one."

Cameron came and sat next to her. "Tell me everything. Don't leave out a single detail."

Lucy sighed and tried to figure out how to explain something she didn't quite understand herself. "As you know, he'd come down from the mountain to hear the web-site proposal," she began haltingly. A big part of her wanted to tell Cameron to go to hell. It was none of her business. Except . . . She would never say that to Cameron, of all people. They'd been through everything together, and she owed her best friend the truth.

"Right . . . And?"

"We went to a place in St. Johnsbury."

"The locals call it St. J. I just heard that. If you're going to hang with the locals, you should speak the lingo."

"I'm not going to hang with the locals. I'm not you, Cameron. I'm not uprooting myself. I'm simply enjoying some fun. It's nothing like you and Will."

Cameron swept that comment away with her hand.

"Back to the night you met. You went to dinner and then what?"

"We had a lot of fun. He's funny, as you've probably noticed, and his parents are . . . Well, I don't need to tell you."

"No, you certainly don't. They're amazing."

"Yes. There was a lot of laughter at dinner. I can't remember the last time I had that much fun with people who'd been strangers a few hours earlier."

"They have that effect. I've experienced it myself."

"When we got back to Butler, Colton told his parents he'd see me back to the inn, so they dropped us off in town and headed home."

"They just dropped you off. They didn't say anything?"

"No, not really."

Cameron tapped her forefinger against her lip. "That's surprising."

"Why?"

"Never mind. Keep talking. You went back to the inn, and then what?"

"There was a guy playing the piano in the lounge, so we went in and had a drink. Well, a couple of drinks actually . . . Too many for him to drive home, so he came upstairs with me."

"Did you sleep with him?" Cameron asked, scandalized.

"He slept next to me, if that's what you're asking. But mostly we talked. And it was nice. Really nice. He makes me laugh and he makes me feel . . ."

"What? What does he make you feel?"

Lucy shook her head. How could she explain what she didn't understand? "I don't know, but I like him. A lot."

"He must like you, too. He shaved off the beard he's had since high school."

"He did that because I told him I wondered what he looked like under all that fur, so he bought clippers and shaved it off."

"And?"

"Obviously I liked what I saw. I've spent six weekends with him."

Cameron fell back on the bed. "I can't believe this! You've been sleeping with him for *six weeks* and I'm just now finding out about it?"

"I haven't been *sleeping with him* sleeping with him. Until well, yesterday." Lucy had no idea what brought on the flood of tears that suddenly streamed down her cheeks. God, she was such a basket case, and she absolutely hated feeling so out of control.

Cameron sat up. "What? Was it bad?"

Lucy snorted out a laugh and shook her head. "Hardly. What's the exact opposite of *bad*, and don't say *good*, because that's not adequate enough."

"I know," Cam said with a sigh. "I get it."

Lucy nudged her friend with her shoulder. "It's really good to see you. I've missed you so much."

Cameron hugged her tightly. "I've missed you, too."

"So you're not mad at me for keeping such a big secret?"

"I'm furious! All this time I could've been getting the juicy details!" She tucked a strand of escaped hair behind Lucy's ear, letting Lucy know she still loved her despite the deception she'd perpetrated. "Why did you feel the need to keep it a secret?"

"I'm not sure exactly. Maybe because it's not going anywhere. It's just a fling, so why bring everyone else in on it?"

"Just a fling?"

"Of course it is. What else could it be?"

"Call me crazy, but six weekends sounds like more than a fling."

"It's not more. It can't be more."

Cameron studied her in a way that made Lucy feel raw and exposed. Few people knew her better than Cameron did. "Oh, shit, Luce."

"What?"

"You're falling for him, aren't you?"

"No! Have you heard anything I've said? It's a *fling*.

That's all. Stop trying to make it into a big bloody deal. Just because that's what happened for you doesn't mean it's going to happen for me. It can't happen. There's no way I'm moving up here, and he knows that." Lucy wiped the tears from her face. "I'm sorry I kept it from you. One week became two and then two became almost two months and the next thing I knew, it was a big secret. It just sort of . . . happened."

"You have to give me some of the juicy details . . . He's got that whole brawny sexy thing going on."

Lucy giggled at Cameron's description of Colton. "So I've noticed."

"And?"

"What do you want me to say? It was amazing. Best sex I've ever had, but you already know that because you're having the best sex of your life with his brother. What's the deal with the Abbott men and their magic . . . wands?"

Cameron dissolved into a fit of laughter that took Lucy down with her. "Did you really just say that?"

Lucy fell back on the bed next to her friend and joined in the laughter. How could she resist? It was kind of funny. Well, sort of . . . Laughing with Cameron gave her something else to think about besides the mixed-up mess that was her "relationship" or whatever you'd call it with Colton.

"I can't deny that Will does, indeed, have a magic wand."

That set them off all over again, and Lucy laughed until her sides ached. She looked over at Cameron, who was breathing hard and wiping tears from her eyes. "I'm really glad you know. I hated keeping it from you."

"You still haven't told me why you did."

"Everything with you and Will was still so new. I didn't want you to think I was butting in on your scene. And I felt like a cliché sometimes. Taking up with the brother of my best friend's boyfriend. It felt sort of tawdry."

"Mmm, tawdry. I love when things get tawdry."

"Stop. I'm trying to be serious here."

Cameron turned her head so she could see Lucy's face. "You know that one has absolutely nothing to do with the other, don't you? Me and Will. You and Colton. Two totally separate and unrelated things."

"Not entirely unrelated."

"You know what I mean."

"It didn't feel unrelated to me."

"Well, it is. Whatever happens with you guys has nothing to do with us, beyond both of us wanting both of you to be happy."

Cameron's sweet words brought new tears to Lucy's eyes. "I feel like such a shit for keeping this from you. I've felt bad all along. I hope you know that."

"Now that you're out and proud, maybe you can relax and try to enjoy whatever time you get with him without feeling like it needs to be a big secret."

"Yes."

"You don't sound convinced."

"I think I'm going to end it with him."

Cameron sat up abruptly. "What? *Why?* Didn't you just say you're having the best sex of your life with him? And I know for a fact he's a really good guy. Just like his brother."

"I know all that," Lucy said, unprepared for the sharp stab of pain that hit her in the chest when she contemplated ending things with him. The thought of never seeing Colton again was just that painful. "But every time I see him, we get in deeper and deeper, and really, what's the point?"

"The point," Cameron said, "is you've found a connection with him that doesn't come along every day. You can either see what becomes of it or spend the rest of your life wondering what might've been."

"Why do you have to put it like that?"

"Because it's true! You just told me it's nothing more than a fling, and now you're saying the fling has to end because it's becoming more than a fling. Which is it, Luce? A fling or more than that?"

"I don't know! I'm so confused and the more time I spend with him the more confused I seem to get. It's a mess!"

"Do me a favor, okay? Don't make any rash decisions. Let it ride for a while and see what happens."

"If I do that, it's only going to be harder to end it later."

"Maybe you won't have to end it. Maybe you can figure out something that works for both of you."

"Why are you fighting so hard to make this work when I don't even know if I want it to work?"

"I like you two together. It works for me."

"Well, as long as it works for you . . ."

"Shut up," Cameron said with a laugh. "You know what I mean."

"You know what the scariest part is?"

"What's that?"

"You know my thing with guys? The thing that always happens?"

"Yeah . . ."

"It's not happening this time. I'm not getting bored and easily distracted. Most of the days I spend with him are weekend days so I don't take my meds, and I'm never bored or distracted with him. I keep thinking it's because we only get the weekends, so I don't spend enough time with him to let the ADD sidetrack me."

"What about when you're not with him? Do you think about him?"

"Um, yeah . . . A lot."

"Shit, Luce. You've found the ADD antidote."

"Don't make jokes! I'm being serious."

"So am I. It's the same for me with Will. I'm always interested in him. I'm never scatterbrained or forgetful or easily distracted when it comes to him. My focus has never been so laser sharp, and no meds are required to make that happen."

Lucy groaned. "That's not helping!"

Cameron took her hand. "Don't do anything you might regret, Luce. I'd hate to see that happen to you."

Lucy would hate it, too, but more than that, she'd hate to have her heart broken or be responsible for breaking his.

CHAPTER 9

——◆——

Today is the first Tuesday in March, the day
designated as Town Meeting Day across Vermont.
Traditionally, sugarmakers consider this day
their deadline for being tapped out. This year,
for us in our little microclimate, all we know
so far is it isn't an early season for us.

—Colton Abbott's sugaring journal, March 5

"What've you got to say for yourself?" Will asked Colton as he made coffee in the kitchen.

"You're not my father, Will. Stop acting like Lincoln."

"I'm not acting like Lincoln. I'm trying to find out when you started messing around with my girlfriend's best friend and why you felt like you had to keep it a big secret."

Colton raised an eyebrow in the direction of his older brother. "Really? You're actually standing in the middle of my weekend with the woman I don't spend enough time with as it is asking me why I felt the need to keep it a secret? Gee, I wonder. And P.S. I'm not *messing around* with her."

"Don't be a smart-ass. You know this is my business. It affects Cameron, so it affects me."

"It doesn't affect Cameron, and it doesn't affect you. It's got nothing to do with either of you."

"You've lost your mind. That's the only possible explanation for such an asinine statement. Maybe it's all the years you've spent in isolation on the mountain. You've forgotten how the real world works."

"I haven't forgotten a thing. I'm perfectly socialized despite my isolation."

"Then how can you possibly think this has nothing to do with me or Cameron? Who do you think will have to mop up the mess if you break Lucy's heart?"

Holding a mug of steaming coffee and wishing he had a shot of something stronger to add to it, Colton leaned against the counter. "Who's going to mop up the mess if she breaks *my* heart?"

Will huffed with aggravation. "You're not taking me seriously."

"Oh, I am. And for your information, I have no intention of breaking her heart. I quite like her heart and everything else about her. If I have any say in the matter, she and I will be *messing around*, as you put it, for a good long time to come. So no need to get out the mops and buckets, no intervention needed. It's all good. In fact, why don't you get the hell out of here and leave us alone? We were having a perfectly nice time until you showed up."

"I'm not going anywhere. Dad gave me the house for the weekend."

"Funny, he gave it to me, too."

Will stared at him, disbelieving. "He totally set us up."

"Looks that way."

"Unreal," Will said with a laugh. "What's his deal?"

"Clearly he wanted to know who I was hanging out with, so he sent you to find out."

"What a conniving pain in the ass he is. Did you hear he and Gramps messed with Hannah's car on a day when all of us were going to be out of town? She had no choice but to call Nolan." Their sister was now engaged to the mechanic who'd come to her rescue.

"Are you serious? Where did you hear that?"

"Nolan told me. He couldn't figure out why her relatively new battery was suddenly failing. After Dad and Gramps kidnapped him—"

"Wait. They did *what*?"

"The day after Homer died," Will said of Hannah's dog, "Mom and Dad found Nolan asleep with Hannah on the sofa. Apparently he'd stayed with her so she didn't have to be alone after such a sad loss."

"That was nice of him."

"I thought so, too. Anyway, that same day, Dad picked Nolan up at work, took him to Gramps's house and they grilled him about his intentions over pastrami sandwiches. He was laughing about it when he told me, and I think he sort of appreciates the nudge they gave her, but still . . . At the time? Not so funny, especially when Hannah showed up in the middle of their lunch and wanted to know what he was doing there."

Colton shook his head even as amusement warred with annoyance. "I'm sure they played all sorts of dumb and acted like they hadn't done anything wrong."

"Something like that."

"One of us needs to give them a taste of their own medicine. You should go home and tell Dad that my 'girlfriend' is a stripper and I didn't want him to know about it."

"We've got to come up with something better than that."

"Maybe you report back that I was here but really just fishing like I told him."

"That's a possibility, too."

"Either way, you can't tell him the truth."

"Why not?"

"Because . . . I wouldn't want to get his hopes up. He likes Lucy. They both do. Hell, I like her, but she insists it's not going anywhere, so . . ." Colton shrugged. "Not really worth starting an Abbott family furor over it."

"Who you trying to sell that to, bro? Me or yourself?"

"What's that supposed to mean?"

"You're trying awfully hard to convince yourself it's no big deal with Lucy."

"It's not. We're just having fun. That's why we didn't see any need to involve the whole family. It's just . . . Fun."

"Hmm."

"What's that supposed to mean? *Hmm?*"

"You and me, we go way back."

"Oh for Christ's sake—"

"Hear me out. I've never seen you like this before."

"Like what?"

"The beard, for one thing. It was your trademark. Your signature. It's on the syrup bottles, for crying out loud. A couple of weekends with her, and it's gone? Just like that?"

Colton tried hard not to squirm under the glare of his older brother's shrewd gaze. "I'd been thinking about getting rid of it for a while now."

"Really."

"Yes, really. Why do you find that so hard to believe?"

"No reason."

"You don't need to be all smug and sanctimonious. Maybe you don't know me as well as you think you do."

"I know you as well as anyone does, and you've been different lately. I'm not the only one who's seen it. Everyone has noticed."

"So what? I mix up my routine a little and suddenly I'm *different*?"

"It's more than that."

Right then and there, Colton hit his limit. He put down his mug. "Look, Will, this has been a nice visit. Glad we had the chance to catch up. But I've got better things to do with the limited time I get to spend with Lucy than try to defend myself to you, when again, it's none of your business what I'm doing or who I'm doing it with."

Will stood up straighter, prepared to engage.

Colton held up a hand to stop him. "I'm done. You're my brother and most of the time I love being around you. This is not one of those times. Take your lady and hit the road. I was here first, and I've got other plans for this weekend than arguing with you."

"I'm not going anywhere. I've got plans for this weekend that don't involve *you*."

"You'd better find somewhere else to have these plans of yours."

"Why? It's a big house. We can coexist. You won't even know we're here."

"No way. There's no way you can make yourself disappear enough for my liking."

"Unless you were planning to get it on in the kitchen—and you'd better not do that or I'll tell Mom—you can have the downstairs. We'll take the upstairs. You won't even know we're here."

"Will—"

"We're not leaving. Cameron needs this weekend away from it all. She's burned out big time, and she's exhausted. So . . . Live and let live?"

"Will you stay out of my business?"

"To the best of my ability."

"That's not good enough."

"That's all I've got."

"Wait, where're you going?"

"To get our stuff from the car and to let in the dogs."

"You brought your dogs?"

"Hell yes, I brought them."

"Great," Colton muttered under his breath. "Four dogs and two extra people. Just the romantic weekend I had in mind."

"Did you say something?" Will asked on his way out the door.

"Nope." What was the point? Will wasn't going to budge and neither was he. Somehow their romantic weekend for two had just turned into a not-so-romantic weekend for eight. The dogs counted. Of course they did. As if she had read his mind, Sarah nudged at his hand. He ran his fingers through her silky hair. "You feel my pain, don't you, girl?"

He thought she was going to agree with him until Trevor and Tanner came barreling through the front door and all bets were off. With Elmer hot on her paws, she galloped toward her littermates, delighted to see them. "Traitors."

Cameron emerged from the bedroom, looking for Will and hoping to figure out what their next move should be. This whole thing had come as a total shock to her, but with hindsight she couldn't believe she hadn't figured it out sooner. Both Colton and Lucy had been acting strangely, disappearing on the weekends, giving vague answers when asked about their plans and generally being evasive.

The old Cameron, the one who spent most of every day in close proximity to Lucy, would've picked up the scent of gossip weeks ago. The new Cameron, the one who was caught up in her new life with her new love, hadn't been paying close enough attention to her best friend. That realization pained her.

She came upon Colton in the kitchen and stopped short. She had a few things she'd like to say to him, but in the interest of preserving family harmony, she kept quiet.

"What?" he asked when he saw her studying him with all-new interest. "Have you got something you want to say to me, too? Your boyfriend already gave me an earful. Feel free to pile on."

"No desire to pile on. I'll just say she's important to me, and I hope you'll be kind to her."

"Jeez. What do you take me for?"

"I'm sorry. I don't mean to insult you. It's just . . . She hasn't had an easy time of it, and all I want is for her to be happy."

"What does that mean? She hasn't had an easy time of it?"

Cameron shook her head, furious with herself for speaking before she thought it all the way through. "I'm sorry. I said too much. It's her business and up to her who she wants to tell."

"You can't just drop something like that on me and then walk away. Where is she anyway?"

"She wanted a couple of minutes to herself."

"What aren't you telling me, Cameron?"

Thankfully, Will picked that moment to come in with their bags. She took her computer bag from him.

"We're upstairs, babe. Come on, I'll show you our room." With a pointed look for Colton, Will added, "It's on the far opposite side of the house from their room."

With a smile for Colton, Cameron followed Will upstairs and down a long hallway with several closed doors. At the end, he opened the door and stepped into a spacious room that had an amazing view of the vast lake. A king-sized bed occupied one side of the room. "This is beautiful!"

"Isn't it? I love it here."

"I can see why." She sat on the end of the bed, which was covered with a denim duvet.

He sat next to her and linked their hands. "What do you make of all this?"

"I don't quite know what to make of it. Lucy seems very involved yet hesitant and uncertain, too. What did Colton say?"

"Sort of the same thing. Mostly he doesn't see how it's any of our business."

"I guess it's not, unless it goes bad, and then it'll be our business."

"Exactly. That's what I said to him."

"So we're staying, and they're staying?"

"Looks that way."

"I'm really happy to see her." She leaned her head on his shoulder. "I've missed her so much."

Will put his arm around her and kissed her temple. "I haven't forgotten our conversation on the way over here, but that'll keep if you want to spend some time with Lucy."

"You're sure you wouldn't mind?"

"I'm positive. We have the rest of our lives to spend together."

She loved when he said things like that. After all the

changes she'd made in her life to make their relationship possible, he made it worth it every day.

Once he'd dispatched Cameron and Will, Colton returned to the bedroom and began throwing clothes into his bag. Some of the clothes were his, some were hers, but it didn't matter because he was taking her with him.

Lucy emerged from the bathroom, where she'd apparently dried her hair, but thankfully she hadn't straightened it. He loved those curls. "What're you doing?"

"We're leaving."

"Why?"

"Because I want to be alone with you, and I can't be alone with you with them here. I'm doing what I should've done from the beginning and taking you to my mountain, where there's no chance we'll be bothered."

"Colton, wait. I'd like to see your mountain, but there's no reason we can't be here with them and do our own thing while they do theirs."

He shook his head. "I'll know he's here and he's listening and taking notes so he can report back to my family. I can't do it."

She pinched her lips with her fingers and seemed like she was trying not to laugh. "You really think he's going to report back to your family?"

"Yes! And the reason I know that is because it's exactly what I would do if the roles were reversed. It's how we roll, and it's important to you that people don't know about us, so I'm trying to respect that."

She came over to him and wrapped her arms around his neck, making his mind empty of every thought that didn't involve the feel of her pressed against him. "I think the proverbial cat is now out of the bag. While I appreciate that you're trying to respect my wishes, it seems we've lost control of the situation."

"This isn't what you wanted."

"But it's what's happened, so now we have to deal with

it. As much as I'd like nothing more than to be completely alone with you, I've missed Cameron, and now that she's here, I'd kind of like to spend a little time with her, too."

Colton gritted his teeth as aggravation battled with his desire to please her. "Fine. We'll spend tonight with them, but tomorrow we're going to my place and we're staying there until it's time for you to go home."

"Isn't that logistically complicated? Two cars, a couple of hours . . ."

"We'll leave your car here, and I'll bring you back on Tuesday morning."

"That's kind of crazy, Colton. Driving two hours to bring me here so I can drive six hours home."

"I'll take your rental to the airport and turn it in and you can fly back. I'll buy the ticket."

"You're being crazy. You know that, don't you?"

"I'm fully aware of that, and I'm fine with it if it means I get to have two more days alone with you."

She placed her hands on his face, a gesture that calmed and soothed him. That she could do that with only the press of her hands against his skin was just another reason to hold on tight to her. "Okay then, mountain man. We'll do this your way, as crazy as it is."

He leaned his forehead against hers. "If we were doing this my way, we'd still be naked in that bed having the time of our lives." Sure enough, his blunt words made her cheeks turn pink. "Instead it appears we're going to be spending some time with my brother and his girlfriend."

She pressed a lingering kiss to his lips. "I'll make it up to you. I promise."

Hugging her tightly, he said, "I'm so going to hold you to that."

CHAPTER 10

———◆◆◆———

*The wait is over. Out-of-doors it was a storybook
sugaring day. Inside the sugarhouse it was, to
quote a neighbor who stopped by to help stoke the
fire, "like ski racing in the world championships
without any practice. Ready, set, go."*

—Colton Abbott's sugaring journal, March 9

They spent an enjoyable afternoon at the beach in front
of the house with Will and Cameron. Lucy loved the
way the brothers bickered incessantly but with an underly-
ing affection that was reminiscent of her relationship with
her sister, Emma. There was nothing she and Emma
wouldn't say to each other and nothing they wouldn't do
for each other. She sensed the same sort of bond between
Will and Colton, even if they were annoyed by the other's
presence at the house.

"I should tell Dad we caught you with a guy," Will said,
sending the girls into fits of giggles as Colton scowled at him.

"If you do that, I'll tell him you drank all his scotch."

"You wouldn't dare."

"Do it and you'll find out."

Even though Colton was clearly pissed off by the turn

of events, Lucy couldn't help but laugh at his distress. She wondered if he knew how adorable he could be, and seeing him with his brother gave her an all-new perspective on his personality. It was a good perspective that only made her like him more than she already did.

She ran her finger around in the sand, stopping only when she sensed him hovering over her shoulder.

"That's amazing. You just sat there and drew that?"

Lucy snapped out of her musings to take notice of what she'd drawn. The man in the sand looked an awful lot like him. She'd drawn him without even thinking about what she was doing.

"That's awesome, Luce," Cameron said.

"You totally captured him," Will added.

Lucy felt like she'd exposed her private thoughts through the image that had appeared at the end of her index finger. She swept her fingers across the sand, erasing the drawing. "Just scribbling."

"Will you do that again sometime on paper?" Colton asked her.

"Maybe."

"Have you shown her your drawings yet?" Will asked.

"No."

"You can draw, Colton?" Lucy asked.

"His drawings are amazing." Will stood as the sun headed for the horizon on the far side of the lake and the temperature began to cool. "Let's make a fire. Do we have hot dogs?"

"*We* have hot dogs," Colton said.

"That we're happy to share with you guys," Lucy said with a pointed look for him.

"We'll get them," Will said, reaching out to help Cameron up.

"You may as well get the s'mores stuff, too," Colton said begrudgingly.

"Yay," Cameron said as she and Will headed for the house with all four dogs following them.

"It's very nice of you to share with your brother," Lucy said.

"Whatever. He didn't give me much choice."

"You never told me you could draw."

"You never told me you can, too."

She smiled at his reply. "Today was fun. Being here with them . . . I haven't gotten to spend a lot of time with them together. It's nice to see how good he is to her and how much he loves her. It makes me happy to see her happy."

"I like seeing how much she loves him. He deserves that as much as she does."

"Awww, underneath all that bluster, you're a romantic!"

"Ew, I am not. Don't say such awful things about me."

Lucy tossed a small handful of sand at him.

"Oh really? We're throwing sand now?"

"*We're* not throwing sand. *I* am." She sent another pinch of sand in his direction and hit him square in the face.

He stared at her, disbelieving, as he spit a mouthful of sand to the side before lunging at her, making her scream with laughter as he came down on top of her. When he had her pinned to the beach blanket, he looked down at her with a sinister expression on his face. "It's a good thing I'm not a vengeful kind of guy. You forget I was raised with six brothers and three sisters. I know everything there is to know about exacting revenge."

She batted her eyelashes at him. "Please don't hurt me, big strong man of the mountains."

With a low growl, he brought his lips down on hers, drawing her into an incendiary kiss filled with the frustration she'd felt coming from him all afternoon. He'd gone along with what everyone else wanted to do, even if it wasn't what he wanted. *Apparently*, she thought as his tongue tangled with hers, *this is what he'd rather be doing*.

"Oh jeez," Will said when he returned to find them making out on the beach.

Colton groaned against her lips but didn't stop kissing her and didn't make any move to end their embrace.

"Don't look, Cam," Will said. "You'll hurt your eyes."

Colton's scowl made Lucy giggle. Since they were no longer alone, like they should've been, he reluctantly moved off her and willed his raging boner into submission. There were some things a guy shouldn't have to share with an audience. "I'm going for a swim," he announced.

"The lake is freezing," Will said.

"Good. It's just what I need."

Before his brother could make any of the predictable jokes—the same jokes he would've made if the roles had been reversed—Colton jogged to the shoreline and dove into water that was, in fact, frigid. It was so cold he worried about freezing his balls right off. But the cold water had the desired effect on his libido. It shriveled right up with the rest of his important parts.

No matter how warm the summer got, Lake Champlain was always freezing. It was one of the things that could be taken for granted when it came to life in Vermont. As he watched Lucy laugh and tease with Cameron, Colton waited until he was sure he had things under control before he emerged from the ice bath to join them on the blanket.

 . The fire Will had lit went a long way toward restoring feeling in Colton's important parts. Living on the mountain, he was used to being cold and usually wasn't bothered by it. Today though, he was annoyed that the deep freeze had been necessary to ward off an embarrassing situation. If this weekend had played out as planned, he wouldn't have to worry about such things. He could've walked around sporting all the wood he wanted and no one would've known except the subject of his desire.

His thoughts left him in a foul mood as the others talked cheerfully around the fire while they roasted hot dogs over the open flame.

Lucy nudged his shoulder. "What's the matter?"

Did she want the whole list or would it be enough to say he was extremely out of sorts from being forced to share her with anyone—even her best friend and his brother—when they had so little time to spend together? "Nothing."

"Then why are you so quiet?"

"Who can get a word in with you and Cameron sucking up all the air?" He could tell by the way her brows narrowed and her lips puckered that she hadn't appreciated the comment. And she wondered why he was keeping his mouth shut? It was because he was in a foul mood that he had no desire to inflict on others.

"So sorry we are talking too much. We haven't seen each other in a while."

"I don't care if you're talking to her. I didn't mean that."

"Have a hot dog," Will said, handing over fully roasted dogs to Colton and Lucy.

"Thanks." Colton ate his in three big bites while Lucy took far more delicate bites of hers. By the time he finished the first one, Will had a second one ready for him. His big brother knew him well.

"Has he always eaten like that?" Lucy asked Will.

"For as long as I can remember. He'll probably have a big old potbelly by the time he's thirty."

"Screw you. I will not." Colton flexed the muscles he'd acquired through endless hard work.

Cameron and Lucy admired his shameless display while Will groaned with disgust.

"It's okay, Will," Colton said. "I don't blame you for being jealous."

Cameron rested her hand on Will's bare chest. "He has no need to be jealous of anyone. I think he's perfect."

Will's smile lit up his face as he leaned in to kiss his girlfriend.

"Barf," Colton said.

"Stop it," Lucy said.

That she sounded sincerely irritated with him caught him by surprise. Although how could he be surprised when he'd been in a grumpy mood all afternoon? "Sorry." He stood and shook the sand off the towel he'd been using. "I'm going up to grab a shower. Anyone need anything?"

"I'll go with you," Lucy said as she rose. "I'm starting to get cold, so I'm ready to get out of this bathing suit."

"Take your time." Will nuzzled Cameron's neck. "We'll be fine without you."

"Just like we were fine without you?" Colton asked.

Lucy gave him a push to direct him to the stairs that led to the house. "You're in one hell of a mood."

"I know. I'm sorry. I'm all . . ." He waved his hand when he couldn't come up with the words he needed.

"What?"

"Out of sorts."

She followed him up the stairs. "Why?"

He waited until they both reached the landing at the top before he turned to face her. "Because! We have so little time to spend together, and I've been looking forward to having you all to myself. I can't help it that I feel greedy where you're concerned."

The smile that stretched across her face surprised him. "I suppose I can put up with your surliness if you're going to say things like that."

"So you like that I'm greedy where you're concerned?"

"What girl wouldn't like to hear that from the guy she's interested in?"

"I feel like I'm totally out of control with you, being flung all over the place and never sure of where I stand or what's going to happen next. It's making me crazy."

Lucy wrapped her hand around his and gave a gentle tug. "Come on."

"Where are you taking me?"

"You'll see when we get there."

Captivated by the warm glow in her eyes, Colton dutifully followed her to the backyard, where they used the hose to rinse the sand off their feet before going inside.

Lucy led him to the bathroom and turned on the water in the shower. With her hands behind her back, she untied the bikini top that had been distracting him all afternoon. She let it drop to the floor and then tugged at the ties on the bottom half. "Are you just going to stand there or are you going to join me in the shower?"

The question and the challenging tone in which it was issued spurred him to action. He shed his swim trunks in record time and stepped into the steam with her.

Lucy turned to him, linked her arms around his neck and kissed him. "I'm sorry our time alone together got interrupted. I'm sorry you feel out of control—"

"Lucy—"

She put her finger over his lips. "Let me finish." Resting her hands on his chest, she looked up at him. "I feel better now that Cameron knows. I wish I hadn't been so rigid about keeping this a secret for so long. The secret made it all far more dramatic than it needed to be."

Colton couldn't argue with that. He felt the same way.

"I want to go with you tomorrow to your mountain. I want to spend more time with you and get to know your family and the people you love. I want you to do the same with me in New York."

"What're you saying, Luce?" he asked in a voice that barely registered as a whisper.

"I'm saying I want this to be real. I want *us* to be real and not just a weekend fling. I'm saying—"

He'd heard enough. He put his arms around her and lifted her so he could kiss her the way he'd been dying to for hours.

Her arms and legs encircled him and her mouth opened to his tongue. If he thought uncertain Lucy had made him crazy, committed Lucy made him positively insane. She kissed him with the kind of abandon he'd only dreamed of, holding nothing back as she gave as good as she got.

Colton turned them so she was pressed against the shower wall and, grasping her hips, he surged into her, stopping only when she broke the kiss with a gasp. "Hurt?"

"No." She tightened her arms around him and tilted her hips to encourage him to proceed. "Not at all."

He stared into her eyes while he took her fast and hard against the shower wall as the steam rose around them.

She held his gaze without looking away until he reached

between them to coax her. Her eyes closed as they reached the peak together.

Only then did Colton realize how tightly he was grasping her bottom. He eased his grip as he left a trail of kisses from her throat to her jaw and then her lips.

She fisted a handful of his hair and held him there as she kissed him back.

"I've never had sex in the shower before," she whispered.

"What do you think of it?"

"I think I quite like it, especially when I know there's no chance you'd ever drop me." As she spoke, she ran her hands over his shoulders and biceps.

"Never." He couldn't stop kissing her.

"I'm sorry I've been so . . . reluctant about all of this."

"You've had good reason." He drew back slightly so he could see her eyes. "So we're really going to do this?"

Her laughter made her tighten around him. "It appears we're already 'doing this.'"

He pushed against her, letting her know he was ready for more. "So it does. Seriously though . . ."

Lucy smoothed wet hair off his forehead. "We'll take it one day at a time and see what happens."

"While I'm more than thrilled to go along with this new plan of yours, I can't help but wonder what changed."

"I don't know exactly. I guess seeing Cameron and Will together made me realize what might be possible if I stop running scared and give you a chance."

"It's a really good decision."

"He said with complete objectivity."

"So you're saying I need to be thankful to them for showing up?"

"It would be better than being surly."

Colton smiled and kissed her again before reluctantly withdrawing from her.

She glanced down at his erection. "Does he ever take a break?"

"You're naked with me in the shower. It's not his fault."

Lucy reached up to adjust the water, sending an icy blast in his direction. "That ought to take care of it."

Colton grimaced as the cold water immediately cured his problem. "I'll get you for that."

She laughed as she stepped out of the shower. "I'll look forward to it."

CHAPTER 11

—❖—

First boil jitters . . . no matter how many times I do this:
Where is the nozzle I need for filling this drum?
Isn't that plug in the back pan in the wrong pipe?
Is this the right rag for scrubbing syrup off the floor?
Don't we have another squeegee?
Isn't it time to flood the pans before they burn?

—Colton Abbott's sugaring journal, March 11

After breakfast the next morning with Will and Cameron, Colton and Lucy drove away from the lake house in Colton's truck. He'd made arrangements to have her car picked up by the rental company and had booked a flight for her from Burlington into LaGuardia on Tuesday afternoon. All of this had been done on Cameron's cell phone while Lucy was still asleep.

She appreciated that he took care of details that normally fell to her. That was her role with her family and coworkers—she was the one who took care of things. It was nice to be taken care of for a change.

"Thank you for the time with Cameron," she said as they drove through Burlington on the way to the highway that would take them east. "It was great to see her."

"I'm glad you enjoyed it."

"I miss her so much. It's very different without her at work and everywhere else for that matter."

"You guys spent a lot of time together."

"*All* our time—work and play. I'd never tell her this because I wouldn't want her to feel bad about going off to live her own life, but I've felt a little lost without her."

Colton reached across the center console for her hand. "I can only imagine how hard it's been." He glanced over at her. "She said something to me . . . Something I want to ask you about, but I'm not sure how."

Lucy was immediately on guard. "What did she say?"

"That you haven't had an easy time of it, and I need to be careful with you. What did she mean by that?"

While Lucy wanted to kill Cameron for telling him that, she knew her friend had only been looking out for her.

"Luce? Are you going to tell me?"

She looked out the passenger window at the scenic views of tall pines and mountains whizzing by. "My mom died when I was nineteen and Emma was eighteen. My dad sort of went off the deep end after my mother died. He did the best he could, but a lot fell to me."

"What happened to your mom?"

"She had cancer. She fought it for years but ended up dying somewhat suddenly. Emma went a little crazy partying and sleeping around and doing everything she could to run away from the pain. Between her and my dad and balancing college, too, I barely had a minute to breathe."

"I'm so sorry about your mom. I can't even imagine what life would be like without my mom."

"It was a rough couple of years, and we were all doing a little better when Emma got pregnant with my niece, Simone. My dad totally flipped out, which was rather unfair when you consider that he'd been largely absent for about two years by then. No one looks at Simone now and thinks about how or why she came to be, but at the time . . ."

"It was rough."

"Yeah. My dad didn't speak to Emma for a couple of

months. He was so damned mad, but I don't think he was mad at her. He was mad at life, but you couldn't tell Emma that. Took a long time for them to get back on track."

"And you were square in the middle of it."

"Right. I met Cameron around that time, and she really helped me through a lot of it. We had an immediate bond because of the ADD, too."

"ADD? You have ADD?"

"I told you that."

"No, you didn't. That's not something I'd forget, because I have it, too."

"You do? Really?"

"Uh-huh. Fully medicated since seventh grade, thank you very much. How have we not talked about this when we've talked about everything else under the sun, the moon and the stars?"

"It's not something I like to talk about," she said with a sigh. "I wasn't diagnosed until I was in college, and neither was Cam. We both slogged through high school thinking we were stupid, and because I felt stupid, I did stupid things."

"Like what?"

"Drinking, for one thing."

"Did that help?"

Laughing, she said, "Not really. It just caused other problems. And then there's my ADD romantic track record, which consists of more first dates than any girl in the history of the universe."

"Well, clearly you've overcome that because this is easily our thirty-sixth date."

She looked over to find him smiling smugly, which made her belly flutter with something that wasn't nerves, exactly. The feeling was far too pleasant to classify as nerves. "How do you figure that?"

"If each day counts as three dates—morning, afternoon and evening—then we are easily at thirty-six by now. Twelve weekend days times three dates per day . . ."

"All that sexy ruggedness and you can multiply, too."

"Ha ha."

"That certainly sets a record."

"Happy to be of assistance." He glanced at her before returning his attention to the road. "So you've never really done the relationship thing. Is that what you're saying?"

"Yes, I guess it is, so it's no wonder I suck at it, right?"

"You don't suck at it, Luce. It's a tough situation. We've both found something here that interests us. We want to spend more time together, but geography and work and life are conspiring against us. The best thing you can do is what you decided to do yesterday—relax and take it as it happens. That's all either of us can do."

"You make that sound so simple when we both know it isn't."

"It can be. There's nothing wrong with enjoying each other's company and seeing each other as much as we can without worrying about where it might be going. That's not something we have to figure out right now—or any time soon for that matter."

"At the risk of overanalyzing things, I'm not really wired to chill and take it as it comes. I've had to be one step ahead of disaster for most of my adult life, so relaxing and rolling with it doesn't exactly gel with my DNA—or my ADD."

"Stick with me, kid. I'll teach you how to relax and roll with it."

His playful smile sparked the flutters in her belly again. She looked down at her hands in her lap as she thought about what he'd said. Could she become someone who relaxed and rolled with it? Probably . . . Under the right conditions. However, the more time she spent with him, the more mixed up and muddled her emotions became where he was concerned. That was especially true after what'd transpired between them this weekend.

"Tell me what's on your mind. Put it out there and get it off your chest."

He made it so easy to tell him things she wouldn't have dreamed of sharing with any other man she'd ever dated. Of course she hadn't gotten to thirty-six dates with any of them. Since she'd decided to take a chance on Colton, she drew in a deep breath and looked over at him. "I'm wondering what happens when this becomes a more emotionally charged situation."

"It isn't already?"

He floored her with the question, and her brain went totally blank.

Chuckling, he said, "Nothing to say? That's not like you."

Since her brain was still empty of all thoughts, she shook her head.

"I don't think you've been paying attention, Lucy, but I don't fault you for that because I know better than most people how hard it can be to focus when you suffer from attention deficit disorder. So let me lay it out there for you, okay?"

Even though she was somewhat apprehensive as to what he might say, she nodded because she was too curious not to.

"You said you've been on more first dates than anyone in the world. That's sort of been my thing, too. I go out with someone once, it's kind of boring or she's not easy to talk to or I have to try too hard, and I don't go out with her again. I've tried the relationship thing exactly once, and it lasted for two months. I knew I was in trouble when two weeks passed between dates and I had no desire to see her. I used to chalk it up to the ADD, you know?"

"Yes." She knew all too well.

"Now I'm not so sure that was it."

"What do you mean?"

"Thirty-six dates, Lucy. Six full weekends together, and I've never been bored. Not once."

"Neither have I."

"Really?"

"Really."

"So there you have it."

She was almost afraid to ask. "There I have what?"

"Our situation. It's already emotionally charged or we wouldn't both still be here. We would've bailed a long time ago."

"That wasn't supposed to happen."

"Says who?"

"Says me. It was supposed to be a fun diversion."

"Hasn't it been that?"

"Well, yeah, but . . ."

"No *but*s. Just because we didn't intend to get involved doesn't mean things can't change. We *are* involved, Lucy. I thought I showed you repeatedly yesterday and last night how involved I am with you. Apparently I didn't do a good enough job. I'll have to try harder tonight."

"Stop it," she said as a flush set her face on fire.

His ringing laughter filled the cab of the truck and roused the dogs in the backseat. When Elmer poked his head over the seat to investigate, Colton rewarded him with a scratch between the ears. "You have no idea how much I love making you blush like that."

"You're very good at it."

"Thank you very much."

"I didn't mean that as a compliment," she muttered. Here she was the supposedly sophisticated city girl feeling like she was way, way out of her league and seriously outmatched by the mountain man. How'd she let that happen?

"Can we talk about my place on the mountain?"

"Sure." Anything was better than allowing him to talk more about the many ways he planned to show her he was emotionally involved with her.

"I've told you before it's kind of rustic, right?"

"Yes, but I'm not entirely sure I get what you mean by rustic. You've been somewhat vague on that."

"Well, there's no electricity for one thing."

"*No electricity?* Who lives without electricity in the twenty-first century?"

"Um, I do. There's no running water or indoor plumbing either." This was said in a rush of words that set her head to spinning. Before she could formulate a reply, he continued. "I promise you'll be very comfortable despite the lack of modern conveniences."

"How do you take a shower?"

"Oh that's easy. I have solar-heated water that's particularly warm this time of year. It's not so great in the winter, but I survive."

"I wouldn't. No hot shower would be a deal-breaker for me."

"Good to know. So have you ever been camping?"

"Not if I could avoid it."

"That's not an answer."

"My parents took us once when we were like eleven and twelve. We hated it. Bitched the whole time about the bugs, the smell, the cold, the hard ground. Everything we could think of, we bitched about."

"So what you're saying is you're a city girl through and through."

"As if that was in question?"

"All I'm asking is that you give it a chance. No bugs, no bad smells, no cold, no hard ground. You'll be warm and cozy the whole time—and I do offer a hot shower at least once a day and a warm body to sleep with." He glanced over at her. "Okay?"

"I promise to give it a chance, and I'll do my best to refrain from bitching."

"Excellent," he said with a satisfied smile.

"I'm looking forward to seeing where you live and work."

"And I'm looking forward to showing you. In a way, I'm sort of glad we ended up with company at the lake. I've been wanting to bring you to my place for a while now."

"Who takes care of it while you're away?"

"There's not much to take care of this time of year, except the retail store, which stays pretty busy all year long. Max was staying there while I was gone."

"Does his girlfriend stay up there with him?"

"I'm not sure if she came this time. She has before."

"Do you like her?"

"Sure, she seems nice enough. I don't really know her all that well. They hadn't been dating long when she got pregnant."

"Are you looking forward to the baby?"

"Definitely. I can't wait to be an uncle. I just can't believe he's going to be first. He's always last at everything."

"Not this time."

"Nope."

"Is he ready?"

"As ready as anyone can be, I suppose."

"I remember when Emma was expecting Simone and how big and scary it was for her—and for me. I wanted to be there for her and help her in any way I could, but like her, I didn't know the first thing about babies."

"You guys survived, right?"

"It was dicey at first. Babies don't come with instruction manuals, unfortunately. But we figured it out. Simone was a good baby. That helped."

"Is her father in the picture?"

Lucy shook her head. "Never has been."

"That's got to be tough on Emma."

"It was, at first. But she figured it out, and Simone is eight now, so it does get easier."

"I'd like to meet them when I'm in New York. Do you think we could do that?"

"I suppose that could be arranged."

"Good. Since we're emotionally—and physically—charged, I'd like to meet the people who are important to you."

"Do you really have to keep saying that?"

"Yeah," he said, bringing her hand to his lips and setting off a jolt of excitement throughout her body when he kissed her knuckles. "I really do. I need to keep reminding you that you're here with me for all the right reasons, and it's going to be fine."

When he put it that way, it became much easier for Lucy to relax and roll with whatever happened next. They might not be preparing to spend the rest of their lives together the way Will and Cameron were, but there was no reason she couldn't enjoy this—and him—while it lasted.

CHAPTER 12

*Steady rain today, temperature holding at
40 degrees. The snow is either washing down
the brooks or being eaten by the ground fog.
The sap is running steadily, but less intensely,
day and night. The tanks are nearly full.*

—Colton Abbott's sugaring journal, March 12

Nolan had given this a lot of thought. He wanted to do
something special for Hannah at their wedding to
show her how much she meant to him and to tell her family
how well he planned to care for her after they were married. He'd considered a number of different gestures that
would accomplish both goals but kept coming back to the
same thing.

That and one other bit of business had brought him to
Hunter Abbott's front door first thing on a Sunday morning. Hannah thought he'd gone in to work at the garage to
catch up for a few hours. He could've used those hours in
the office, but this was more important.

He rang the bell at the restored colonial that was painted
a dark taupe with black trim. The place was almost as
classy as its owner, Nolan thought as he waited for Hunter

to answer the door. His silver Lincoln Navigator was in the driveway, so Nolan knew Hunter was home.

The door opened to Hunter in a T-shirt and sweats.

"Thank goodness."

"What?" Hunter asked. "What's wrong?"

"Nothing. I'm just glad to see you own sweats like the rest of us."

Hunter's brown eyes narrowed with annoyance. Nolan knew that look. Hannah had the same one.

"Did you want something or are you here to critique my wardrobe?"

"Dude, no one in this town would have the nerve to critique your wardrobe. Can I come in?"

"Sure. You want coffee?"

"Wouldn't say no to that." The coffee would probably help to calm his nerves, too, as he turned what had been only a thought into an actual plan that would involve disclosing something about himself that no one knew—not even Hannah.

Hunter put two mugs on the table along with cream and sugar.

Nolan stirred both into his coffee.

"So what's up?" Hunter asked when he joined him at the table.

"Couple of things, actually."

"Is everything okay with Hannah?"

"Everything is great with Hannah."

"Oh," Hunter said, visibly relieved. "Good."

"I know it hasn't been easy for you . . . the last few years since Caleb died. But I'm taking good care of her, so you don't need to worry."

"Worrying about Hannah is my part-time job," Hunter said with a rueful smile. "I don't know how *not* to worry about her."

"She appreciates everything you've done for her. She's said more than once she never would've gotten through it without you." Nolan stirred the cream around in his coffee.

"But I'm not here to talk about the past. I've got the future on my mind."

"What about it?"

"Hannah tells me I have to get on board with the fact that we're getting married in a couple of weeks."

"I thought all you had to do was show up."

"So did I, but apparently I also need a best man, and I was hoping you might be game."

Hunter's eyes widened with surprise. "Oh, wow. Yeah, I'd be honored."

"Thank you," Nolan said, surprised by how relieved he was that Hannah's twin had agreed to stand up for him. Hunter and Will Abbott had been among Nolan's closest friends for much of his life, but he'd chosen to ask Hunter because of his indelible bond with Hannah.

"Of course. I'm happy to do it. This means there's a bachelor party in our future."

"I'd be perfectly fine with avoiding that entirely."

"I'm sure you would," Hunter said with a laugh, "but that ain't gonna happen."

"I suppose there's no way I can talk you out of it?"

"No way at all."

Nolan sighed and sat back in his chair, resigned to his fate. He'd certainly known what he was getting when he married into the Abbott family, and he wouldn't have it any other way. Well, he could do without a bachelor party, but in Hunter's hands, the event wouldn't be trashy or tawdry. At least he hoped not. "There was one other thing I wanted to ask you."

"What's that?"

"Do you still play the piano?"

"Once in a while. Why?"

Nolan withdrew a folded piece of paper from his back pocket and laid it flat on the table in front of Hunter. "Can you play that?"

Hunter studied the sheet music. "Looks easy enough, but I don't sing."

"I know." Nolan cleared his throat and tried to ignore all the misgivings that had kept him from ever revealing his "hidden" talent. "I do."

"Wait . . . You *sing*?"

"Yeah."

"How come I've never heard you before?"

"'Cuz I've never done it in public. It's always been more of a private thing."

"And you're thinking about taking it public at your wedding?"

As much as the idea of singing in front of other people—even people he'd known all his life—terrified him, he wanted to do this for Hannah. "Something like that."

"Wow. You think you know a guy . . ."

"So will you do it?"

"If it means I get to hear you sing, you bet I will."

"You can't say anything about this. I want it to be a surprise for her."

"My lips are sealed," Hunter said with a smile. "I wouldn't dream of telling anyone." He got up and gestured for Nolan to follow him into the other room. "Come on. This I've got to see."

As they approached the turnoff that led to the mountain, Colton became increasingly more nervous about how Lucy would react to his home. He took the hill slowly, giving her the chance to take in the breathtaking scenery that unfolded before them as they headed up, up, up.

"My ears are popping," she said.

"You get used to it after a while. Look down there." He pointed to the stream that rushed through the woods. "You should see that in the winter when it's totally frozen. It's incredible."

"It's really beautiful."

"I think so, too. I never get tired of it no matter how many times I see it." The road curved and the slope got even steeper. "It'll be a lot colder up here than it was at the lake."

"Is it cold all the time?"

"There's cold and then there's *cold*. It's chilly at night this time of year but warm during the day. In the winter, it's frigid."

"And you have no heat?"

"I've got an awesome woodstove that heats my entire cabin. It's warm and toasty in there."

"Somehow I think your idea of warm and toasty might differ from mine."

"Nah. After a long day of working outside, I'm ready to warm up when I go in for the night."

"Still, your thermostat is probably calibrated differently than most people's after all the time you've spent up here."

"Probably."

"What's this hill like when it's covered in snow?"

"It's really fun. Have you seen the bobsled races at the Olympics?" After she nodded, he continued. "Coming down the hill in the winter is a lot like that. Fortunately, I have four-wheel drive, but sometimes even that is no match for this hill." He pointed to a sharp curve. "Ask Cameron about her first visit up here when Will nearly drove them off the road on the way back down. Happened right about there."

"I heard about that! She said he kissed her for the first time right here, and his foot slipped off the brake." Lucy sat up straighter so she could see what was on the other side of the guard rail. "Holy cow. That's one hell of a drop. She must've been freaking out."

"She was until I showed up and got them back on the road." He flexed his bicep for effect, which made Lucy laugh.

Colton navigated the last three bends in the road that led to his cabin and the sugaring facility right next door. "Oh great," he muttered when he saw his dad's Range Rover parked in the driveway. Was there anywhere he could go to escape his damned family this weekend? "What's he doing here?"

"Who?"

"That's my dad's car, and those are his dogs, George and Ringo."

"I remember. I met them the day we did the demo in the office."

"That's right." He turned off the truck and looked over at her. "Sorry about this."

"About what?"

"More family interruptions. I have no idea what he's doing here. Max was supposed to be covering."

"Let's go find out." She reached for the handle on the door, but Colton stopped her from getting out.

"Are you sure this is okay? He'll know about us."

Lucy laughed again, a sound he never got tired of hearing. "Will and Cameron know about us. Our days were numbered until they got back to town."

"True." Colton got out of the truck and went around to help Lucy. The truck was tall and she was short in comparison, so he gave her a hand down.

He was still holding her hand when Lincoln and Molly emerged from the door to the retail portion of the sugaring facility. *Great*, Colton thought. *Both of them*. At least they'd go public with his parents all at once.

"You're back," Lincoln said with a smile for his son as his gaze shifted to the hand that Colton was holding. "And Lucy! So nice to see you again."

"You, too, Mr. Abbott."

"I thought we were past all that Mr. and Mrs. business," Molly said as she came over to give Lucy a warm hug.

Colton had no choice but to let go of her hand while she hugged both his parents, who didn't seem at all surprised to see her. Very interesting indeed.

"We're Lincoln and Molly," his mother said. "And we're not big on formalities."

"What're you doing here?" Colton asked them. "I thought Max was holding down the fort."

"He was until Chloe got hit with a stomach bug and fever, so he went back to Burlington to take care of her."

"Is she okay?" Colton asked. He didn't know much about having babies, but even he knew any kind of flu could be harmful to a pregnant woman and her baby.

"She is now," Molly said. "They admitted her to the hospital last night and put her on an IV. They were worried about dehydration."

"Damn," Colton said. "I'm sorry to hear that."

"We came up to mind the store for a few hours," Lincoln said. "We weren't expecting you back until Tuesday."

"I wasn't expecting to be back, but as you know, we had some company at the lake, so we decided to come here. So we can be *alone*."

"Colton," Lucy said. "Stop it."

"It's all right, honey," Molly said. "We're used to him. I'm sorry if he embarrassed you."

"You don't seem surprised to see me with him," Lucy said.

The comment took Colton by surprise. He wouldn't have expected her to be so forthcoming with his parents, but they did have that effect on people. They put even perfect strangers at ease.

"You forget that we've seen the two of you together before," Molly said. "At dinner the night you first met."

"But that was before . . ." Lucy gestured with her hand. "Anything happened."

"Was it?" Molly asked shrewdly. "Seemed to us like something happened over dinner that night, and we've been hoping to see you again ever since."

"So you haven't been fooled by our secret friendship?" Lucy asked.

"Not really," Molly said with a warm smile. "You have to understand. When you raise ten kids, you learn quickly to pay attention to the little things or you lose control. In this case, the signs were rather apparent. Our boy here has made some rather significant changes lately, all of them occurring after he met you. Linc and I put two and two together . . ."

"Plus there were a few calls to New York on the phone bill," Lincoln added.

"Desperate times," Colton said with a shrug that made the others laugh. "Is this why you picked me to go to New York for the trade show?"

"Perhaps. Just trying to help you out, son."

"If you were trying to help me out, why'd you send Will to the lake to butt into my weekend with Lucy?"

"I didn't do that. Exactly."

Watching his dad squirm gave Colton some much-needed satisfaction. "Yes, you did."

"You're busted, Linc," Molly said, making Lucy laugh. "Give it up."

"All the secrecy was getting a little much," Lincoln said.

"Says who?" Colton asked. "It's our business, not yours. You forced us out of the closet before we were ready, and that's not really your decision."

"You're absolutely right, son, and I apologize."

The apology caught Colton completely by surprise. He glanced at his mother, who seemed equally shocked. "Did he just apologize for meddling in my life?" Colton asked his mother.

"I think he did. I need a moment. This is unprecedented."

"Oh be quiet, both of you," Lincoln said. "Lucy, come with me. Let me show you around our sugaring facility."

Colton curled his hand around Lucy's arm. "She's not going anywhere with you. It's *my* sugaring facility, and I'll show it to her. You can head back to town and leave us alone."

"I assume you'll be down for dinner later," his mother said with a smile that left no room for negotiation.

"Mom, come on! She's only here until Tuesday!"

"And she needs to eat. Don't you, Lucy?"

"Food would be good."

"I hate everyone right now," Colton said.

"Colton Michael Abbott," Molly said. "You know how I feel about that word." To Lucy, she said, "I had to put a moratorium on the word *hate* with ten children fighting incessantly for years. I'm sure you understand."

Of course Lucy was utterly charmed by his parents. Who wouldn't be? Her lips curled with amusement. "I completely understand. In fact, I'm surprised you're not locked in a padded room somewhere."

Molly patted Lucy's arm. "So am I, honey. So am I." To Colton, she said, "I'll see you both at three?"

When he didn't answer her, Lucy nudged him with her elbow, which connected firmly with his ribs.

"Fine," he muttered.

"Great," Lincoln said. "We'll see you then."

CHAPTER 13

———◄►———

An extravagant run today. The sap gushed,
overwhelming the system this morning. Why?
A genuine freezing night, down to 22 degrees
for several hours. A busy day. We stopped
boiling for today, but the reverse-osmosis
machine will run during the night, and
we'll resume in the morning.

—Colton Abbott's sugaring journal, March 31

Standing next to Lucy, Colton watched his parents leave and tried to figure out how they'd managed to completely manipulate him. So much for being a grown man who ran his own life. "Well, that was mortifying."

"How so?"

"They sort of handed me my ass just then."

Lucy pinched her lips together, but her dancing eyes gave away her amusement.

"Oh go ahead and laugh, if you must."

She did just that.

"I hate you, too." He made sure his tone was light so there was no way she could take him seriously.

"No, you don't."

"Yes, I do."

"I bet I can prove otherwise."

"And how do you plan to do that?"

"I assume that one is your house?" She pointed to the cabin.

"You assume correctly."

Lucy took his hand and led him into his own house, which had been cleaned and straightened in his absence. In that moment, he was extremely grateful for Molly Abbott. But then he remembered the mandatory invite to dinner and his gratitude faded. He hadn't expected to spend so much of this weekend aggravated and irritated by his family. "Where are we going?" he asked as he watched Lucy take in his austere living space. He'd wondered how his rough-hewn home would appear to his city girl.

"This is very cozy."

"Told you."

"I like it."

"I'm glad, but you still haven't told me where you're taking me."

She released his hand and turned to him. In her expression he saw something he hadn't seen before—pure happiness. Gone was the edgy doubt and worry. In its place was a lightness he embraced with everything he had.

"You look happy, Luce. Are you?"

Her fingers found the hem of his T-shirt and pulled it up and over his head. "I like your parents."

"Most people do."

"I can see why. Are you surprised to hear they knew all along what we were up to?"

"Not as surprised as I should be. We never have gotten away with much with the two of them watching over us. Nothing has changed in that regard since we grew up and became adults."

"You're still their kids."

"Exactly."

She flattened her hands on his chest and leaned in to drop a series of kisses on his collarbone. "I'm glad they know."

"Are you?"

"Uh-huh."

"You didn't answer my question, Luce."

"Which one?"

"Are you happy?"

"I'm very happy. What time do we have to leave for dinner?"

He consulted his watch. "Two hours."

"Mmm. Good. That ought to be enough time."

"For what?" he asked, even though he was starting to get a very good idea of where this was leading, but because it was the first time she'd initiated it, he wanted to see how far she'd go. Then she tugged on the button to his shorts, and he sucked in a sharp deep breath.

"Is this okay?"

"What do you think?"

Her smile lit up her face and made her eyes dance with pleasure. He loved that almost as much as he loved the dimples that lined her cheeks.

"You were a good sport with my folks just now."

"I like them."

"They like you, too."

"I'm glad."

Colton put his hands on her hips and brought her in closer to him. "Do you think your dad and Emma will like me?"

"I'm sure they will. What's not to like?"

"See? That's what I say, too, but no one—" He never got to finish that thought because she kissed the words right off his lips.

Colton pulled back from her, even though that was the last thing he wanted to do. "I was going to show you around."

"Can you show me around later?"

"Yes, I suppose I can."

"Good." She went back to kissing him, and her enthusiasm had him hot and bothered in record time. Except . . .

"Hey, Luce?"

"*What*, Colton?"

"I just . . . I don't want you to think . . ."

"What don't you want me to think?"

"That this is all I want from you."

Her hands fell from his chest, and he instantly regretted that he'd stopped her from taking what they both wanted. "I don't think that. You spent five weekends showing me that wasn't all you wanted. I'm sorry if I was too forward—"

"You weren't." He took her hands and put them back where they were before he'd been stupid enough to stop her. "Now where were we?"

"I was just about to ask you to show me to your bed."

"That I can do." Keeping his hands over hers, he walked backward ten steps, which brought him to the bed in the corner of the room. "That about completes the tour of the house."

"I like it." She looked around him. "Are those flannel sheets?"

"You know it. A year-round essential in the mountains."

He cupped her shoulders and ran his hands down until he encountered the hem of her dress, raising it up and over her head. "You're so beautiful, Lucy," said, taking a greedy look at her sexy sheer, nude-colored bra and panties.

"I've never felt beautiful before," she said softly, making his heart ache with what was starting to feel an awful lot like love.

He held her face in his hands and looked directly into her eyes. "You're so, so beautiful. You take my breath away."

"Bed, Colton. Now, please."

Never one to have to be asked three times, he shed his shorts and pulled the down comforter back to reveal blue-and-green plaid flannel sheets. "After you."

She crawled in ahead of him, giving him a spectacular view of her ass.

He was right behind her, reaching for her with urgency he'd never experienced quite so acutely before. The sound of a car horn made him groan almost as loudly as Sarah and Elmer were barking to welcome the visitor. "No way. Not now."

"What?"

"Customer at the store." He kissed her. "Don't move. I'll be right back. And don't change your mind while I'm gone."

"No chance of that, but you should really hurry." She propped herself up on one hand, and all he could see was the plump tops of her breasts spilling out of her bra.

He moaned as he got out of bed, found his shorts and pulled on the T-shirt she'd taken off of him.

"It's inside out," she said with a giggle.

"I don't give a shit. Everything is covered." He could only hope his customer wasn't observant because the T-shirt went only so far in hiding his erection. Colton had never expected to spend so much of this weekend feeling frustrated and aggravated. The universe seemed to be conspiring against him, which wasn't fair at all.

Sliding his feet into a pair of old flip-flops, he clomped outside and groaned again when he saw Mrs. Andersen's car. One of the town's busiest busybodies, she was also a regular visitor to Colton's mountain. And she liked to talk. As his grandfather would say, she could talk a dog off a meat wagon.

Most of the time he didn't mind passing half an hour or so listening to Mrs. Andersen's litany of health issues, including her most recent battle with gout. Today, however, he had much better things to do, and the vision of Lucy nearly naked in his bed nearly had him turning around and blowing off Mrs. Andersen.

But tending to customers was part of his job, so he didn't do that. Rather, he pasted on a fake friendly smile and went to greet her.

"Oh, hi there, Colton. I didn't think you heard my horn."

"I heard it." *They'd probably heard it in Canada.* "I'm tied up today, so I can't linger, I'm afraid. What can I get for you?"

"Tied up with what?"

"Um, some, ah . . . business. Did you need syrup?"

"What kind of business?"

He had to tell himself to stay calm, to not scream, to not give her anything juicy that she could blab all over town faster than the speed of light. Her nosiness—and her presence—had succeeded in totally killing what had been a rather promising boner.

"Is there something I can get for you?" he asked again, determined to get rid of her once and for all.

"I'll take a couple of gallons of Fancy Grade."

"Right this way." He led her into the retail store, got the syrup she wanted and rang up the sale on the old-fashioned cash register that dated back to when his grandparents ran the sugarhouse. Naturally, the drawer picked today to jam and none of the usual tricks would get it to open. Since he had no way to make change, he handed the two twenties back to her. "We can settle up next time."

"Are you sure?"

"I'm absolutely positive."

"Okay, then." Right when he thought she was actually going to leave, she took a long, measuring look at him that made him feel like she could read his mind and knew exactly why he wanted her to go. "Is everything all right? You're acting very strange."

"Everything is fine."

"While I have you . . ."

No! No, no, no!

"I was curious as to what you think about your sister marrying Nolan."

"I'm thrilled with it. We all are. He's a great guy."

"But do you think she's *ready*? I'd hate to see Nolan get hurt. He's such a wonderful guy."

"She's ready, Mrs. Andersen, or she wouldn't have accepted his proposal." Colton hoped if he headed for the door she might follow him. No such luck. "We're all looking forward to the wedding. It's nice to see Hannah so happy. She certainly deserves it, wouldn't you agree?"

"Oh yes, absolutely. The poor dear went through such an awful tragedy losing Caleb so suddenly."

The very last thing in the universe Colton Abbott wanted to do right then was take a trip down that particular memory lane. Thinking about the brother-in-law he'd loved and lost always left him feeling hollow and sad.

"Right. Well . . ."

"I suppose I should move along. I've got lots of errands to get done today."

"It was good of you to come by."

"I'll be back soon to settle up with you."

"Don't worry about it."

"Oh, I will. It's all I'll think about."

He held her car door, waved her off and ran for the house, pulling at his clothes as he went and nearly tripping over his shorts when they tangled around his feet. At the edge of the bed, he stopped short when he saw that Lucy was sleeping. "You've got to be freaking kidding me," he whispered.

Without opening her eyes, she said, "I am kidding you."

"Seriously? Oh my God!" He pounced on her, tickling her until she screamed with laughter and begged for mercy. "That was so mean."

"You should've seen your face when you thought I was asleep," she said, wiping laughter tears from her cheeks. "Totally hilarious." She curled her arms around his neck. "I bet you have lots of ladies from town who come up to buy their syrup right from the hunky mountain man who makes it, don't you?"

"A few." He nibbled on her neck and breathed in her bewitching scent. "God, I love how you smell."

"How do I smell?"

"I don't even know how to describe it. You smell like Lucy, which is the sweetest thing I've ever smelled."

He felt her lips curve into a smile against his cheek.

"Let's talk about these ladies who visit you. Do any of them ever come for more than syrup?"

"I've got the biggest case of blue balls in the history of the condition, and you want to talk about my customers?"

She reached down to cup his balls, making him jolt from the unexpected contact with his most sensitive place. "Are they really blue?"

"*So* blue."

"We can't have that, now can we?"

"It's really not healthy."

She pushed him over onto his back and began kissing his chest as she continued to caress his balls.

"Lucy . . ."

"What?"

"Just wondering what you're up to."

"Oh, this and that." She emphasized her words with a squeeze that had him gasping. "I'm trying to properly diagnose your condition."

He laughed even as he groaned.

Outside a car horn sounded.

"No. Absolutely not."

Lucy dropped her head onto his chest and laughed.

"Don't stop. I'm not going out there."

"You have to go out there. It's your business."

"We're closed today."

"No, you're not. The store is wide open."

"Let them steal the syrup. I don't care."

"Yes, you do."

A knock sounded on the door followed by a female voice calling his name. Colton froze when he recognized that voice. This could not be happening.

"Colton! Are you in there? Your truck is out here, so I know you're home." More knocking followed the comment.

Lucy leaned back and looked at him, her brow raised in inquiry. "Another of your admirers?"

"A friend. That's all."

"Uh-huh. Let me take care of this for you since you're in such a bad way with the blue balls and everything." She got up, retrieved her dress off the floor, turned it right side out and dropped it over her head.

"Lucy, wait."

"Relax. I've got this."

As she crossed the small room to the door, she ran her fingers through her hair and fluffed it up. She'd almost made it to the door when he realized he was lying there bare-ass naked, so he grabbed the comforter and covered his important parts, which had once again gone from raging and ready to shriveled up and dead. The extremes couldn't be good for them, could it?

"Lucy . . ." When she ignored his final plea to ignore the visitor, he flopped back onto the bed, resigned to his fate. This was not going to be pretty.

CHAPTER 14

◆◆◆◆

Pause. SNOW overnight, a bitter wind tearing down the valley all day. No chance of a sap run.

—Colton Abbott's sugaring journal, April 2

I n the time it took to walk across the small room, Lucy summoned her inner she-cat vixen and prepared to do battle. Unlike the visitor she'd heard Colton talking to outside earlier, this one sounded young. She'd bet there was no lack of women interested in spending some time with her mountain man.

Her mountain man. Where in the hell had that thought come from, and when had she begun to think of him as *hers*? Probably about five minutes after she met him, if she were being honest with herself.

Realizing she needed to pull out her biggest guns, she tugged the neckline of her dress down to put her considerable cleavage to good use.

She cracked open the door wide enough to poke her head out, but not wide enough that the strikingly gorgeous blonde on Colton's doorstep could see inside. "May I help you?" Lucy whispered.

Cold brown eyes took a quick assessing look at Lucy and dismissed her as no significant threat. She was used to the instant dismissal as well as the disdainful look. She'd been on the receiving end of it from other women for most of her adult life. "Where's Colton, and who are you?"

"I'm Lucy, and Colton is under the weather."

"What does that mean? Under the weather?"

"He's not well."

Blondie took a step back. "Oh . . . Who are you again?"

"Lucy."

"And you're his . . . his . . . ?"

"Nurse," Lucy said. "I'm his nurse. I was called in to manage his injury."

"Injury? What injury?"

"Oh you didn't hear?" Lucy grimaced dramatically. "The axe caught him. In a bad, *bad* place. Don't tell anyone I told you this, but he might not be able to, *you know*, ever again."

Blondie's eyes got all buggy. *"Ever?"*

"Never," Lucy said gravely. "It's as bad as it gets."

"God, that's an awful tragedy."

"Indeed it is. I'll be happy to tell him you came by, but he's on some serious painkillers. It might be a while before he's lucid again."

"Yeah . . . Um, sure. Tell him Angie was here, and I'm really, *really* sorry to hear about his . . . um, his injury."

"I'll be sure to tell him. It was so good of you to check on him."

"I'd better go. I wouldn't want to disturb him."

"That's very kind of you. I'm sure he'll appreciate your consideration."

Lucy watched Angie run more than walk to her car and smiled with satisfaction when Angie left a cloud of dust in her wake. *That*, Lucy thought, *should take care of that*. Pleased with herself and her quick thinking, she shut the door and turned to find Colton standing right behind her.

She let out a shriek of surprise.

Wearing only basketball shorts, he moved toward her, forcing her to back up until she was pinned against the door by his much bigger body. "You are positively evil, do you know that?"

"*Evil* is such a strong word."

"Do you know it'll take about fifteen minutes for all of Butler to know that I chopped up my boy parts with an axe?"

She batted her eyelashes, going for pure innocence. "Will it take that long?"

"Evil," he said through gritted teeth.

"Look at the bright side."

"Is there a bright side?"

"Of course there is." She smiled brightly. "We won't have any more visitors."

"I'll let you explain my devastating injury to my family at dinner since you're the one who started the axe rumor."

Lucy would never admit that she hadn't given his family a single thought as she conspired to get rid of Angie—and anyone else who might be on the way up to visit—as expeditiously as she could. "Maybe they won't hear about it," she said hopefully.

"Oh they'll hear, and so will we. You can count on that."

She flattened her hands on his chest. "I'm really sorry."

"No, you're not," he said with a bark of laughter. "You're not the slightest bit sorry."

"Well, I'm a teeny tiny bit sorry that your mom might hear the rumor and worry about you." She looked up at him. "But I'm not at all sorry if my story keeps all the single ladies off your mountain for the foreseeable future."

"Is that your way of saying you want to be exclusive?"

She recoiled in horror. "We aren't already?"

Colton shrugged. "I wasn't sure. You've been sort of uncertain about this whole thing from the beginning. You only told me yesterday that you want it to be a *thing* and not just a *fling*."

Lucy couldn't believe what she was hearing. "So you've been like . . . *seeing other people* between our weekends? How many other people? Angie and who else?"

"Wow, you sound kind of pissed."

"Kind of?" Infuriated was more like it. Had he been playing her this whole time? She pushed hard on his chest, trying to dislodge him, but the beast wouldn't budge. "Get off me!" She curled her hands into fists and pounded, which only hurt her hands when they connected with solid muscle. "Are you *laughing*?"

His entire body was shaking with silent laughter.

"This is not funny!"

"It's hilarious from where I'm standing."

She grabbed a handful of his chest hair and tugged. Hard.

"Ow! *Shit!*"

"Not so funny now, huh?"

"Lucy."

"Let me go!

"Lucy."

She pushed, she shoved, she pinched, but rather than take the hint that she wanted him gone, he kissed her.

"Lucy," he said between kisses. "There's been no one but you since the first time I laid eyes on you."

Since she was still struggling to break free of him, it took a second for his words to permeate the cloud of rage. And then she realized what he'd said and all her muscles went slack.

"There." He kissed her again, softly. "No one else, Lucy. Only you."

"You're a beast."

"You impugned my manhood."

"So this was *revenge*?"

"*Revenge* is such a strong word."

She punched him in the belly and howled when her hand connected with a cement wall of muscle.

He took her hand and kissed her poor knuckles. "Don't hurt yourself, honey."

"Don't call me honey. I'm mad at you."

Reaching for her other hand, he began walking backward to the bed.

Lucy resisted to the best of her ability, but he'd already

proven that her strength was no match for his. That was how she found herself on top of him looking down at his adorably amused face, held in place by his incredibly strong arms. "You really are a twelve-year-old, you know that?"

Laughing, he raised a hand to tuck a curl behind her ear. "I thought I was fifteen, and besides, you had it coming. Did you really tell Angie, of all people, that I'd lopped off my junk with an axe?"

"I only said you'd had an accident. A bad accident. I never mentioned the word *junk* or the word *lopped*."

"Yet she left here thinking Colton Abbott has been neutered."

"I can't help what conclusions she jumped to."

"You knew exactly what you were doing, you little devil." He framed her face with his big calloused hands and drew her into a scorching kiss that he ended with a groan. "We have to go to my parents' house. We don't have time to be thorough, and I can't let the boys get their hopes *up* again only to have them dashed. They can only take so much disappointment in one day."

"Poor, tortured Colton. So used to being tended to by all the ladies in town. How do you handle the disappointment when things don't go your way?"

"I don't know. It's never happened before."

"You really are a beast. Now let me go so I can make myself presentable for your family."

"You're already presentable. You're gorgeous."

"Keep sucking up. You need all the points you can get right now after that nasty trick."

"Speaking of sucking up, I haven't forgotten what was happening when we were rudely interrupted."

"Dream on, pal. Or better yet, call your friend *Angie*. I bet she'd be happy to kiss your little boo-boo better."

"There's nothing little about it, and the only one who will be kissing it better is you."

She wriggled out of his embrace and stood by the bed, finger-combing her hair. "So what's the bathroom situation in this rustic palace of yours?"

"Outside and to the left."

"Outside."

"Uh-huh."

"And is there water?"

"Yep. We're attached to a well out there and in here. The water pressure isn't great, but it is what it is."

"All right then."

"Want me to get your stuff out of the truck?"

"I'll get it. Are you going to get ready?"

"I am ready."

"I'm coming back in my next life as a guy."

"That'd be a terrible shame, honey."

Riled and out of sorts after their "fight" but always amused by him nonetheless, Lucy pulled open the door and stepped onto the porch. The air was significantly colder here than it had been at the lake, and she was glad she'd brought a sweater as well as a sweatshirt with her. She stepped off the porch and came face-to-face with a giant animal. Screaming, she took a step back and tripped over a tree root.

Lucy landed hard on her backside as the animal let out a loud "moo."

Lucy's scream launched Colton out of bed. He ran for the door and bounded down the stairs to the yard, where he saw Fred the moose having a standoff with Lucy, and judging by the fact that Lucy was flat on her back, Fred seemed to be winning this round.

"Easy, babe." Colton offered her his hand. "He's a friend."

"A *friend*? He's a monster."

"Fred's a pussycat."

"That's *Fred*? Cameron's Fred?"

"The one and only."

Lucy let Colton help her to her feet, and she plastered herself to him, not that he minded. "Holy cow. No wonder her car was nearly totaled. He's massive!"

"Holy moose, you mean, and he's big, but he's a sweet-heart." He brushed the dirt off her backside.

She jolted.

"Are you hurt?"

"Mostly my pride. I landed kind of hard on my butt." Rubbing her backside, she eyed Fred with trepidation. "I may not be cut out for life in the wild."

"This is hardly the wild, babe."

"What's he doing here?"

"He knows I've always got some twigs and leaves and other goodies for him, so he stops by for a visit from time to time."

Sarah and Elmer came running into the yard, barking gleefully at Fred, who nudged at them playfully the way he always did. The three of them were old friends.

Colton kept an arm around Lucy as he walked her to the truck to get her bag and got her safely to what he referred to as the bathhouse. He thought that sounded better than outhouse. He got her a couple of towels and showed her how to work the water.

"How about a mirror?" she asked.

"Oh, um, that might be a problem."

"You seriously don't own a mirror?"

"I don't really need one. I know what I look like, and until recently I hadn't shaved in years." She scowled at him, apparently not finding him as funny as he found him-self. One thing he would say for Lucy is that she was end-lessly amusing. "Don't you have a mirror app on that fancy phone of yours?"

"A mirror app."

"Why not? Don't they have apps for everything else?"

She rummaged through her bag and withdrew her phone. "I thought the signal was supposedly sketchy in the mountains."

"Cameron says the best service in the area is up here." He pointed to the east. "Clear shot to the cell towers over in St. J."

"Ah, look at that. Several mirror apps to choose from."

"Told ya."

"Buzz off and let me get ready without an audience."

He kept his arms propped above his head in the doorway. "What if I want to watch?"

"You're not watching. Go feed your dogs and your moose."

"All right, I'm going, but next time I want to watch you get ready."

She closed the door in his face and slid the lock into place. That door and lock had been there since his grandparents lived here. He figured it was best not to mention that the lock could be temperamental, which was why he never used it.

After he scattered some goodies around the yard for Fred, he brought Sarah and Elmer inside to feed them so Fred wouldn't get any ideas about sharing in their dinner.

No one was entirely sure how Fred had become so domesticated. Rumor had it that Gertrude "Dude" Danforth, also known in town as Snow White, had worked her animal taming magic on him. As much as Fred was a man about town, the residents were careful not to feed him anything other than what he'd eat in the wild. No one wanted to make it so he couldn't care for or defend himself if need be.

While he waited for Lucy, Colton changed into a pair of khaki shorts and a collared polo shirt, which were the nicest summer clothes he owned. He stopped short in the middle of the room to wonder why he'd gone to the trouble of dressing up for her. He didn't dress up for his own mother, so why did he do it for her and why did he do it without even thinking about it?

After a moment of contemplation, he decided he'd done it because he wanted to look nice for her. He wanted to please her. He wanted her to want him, to want to come back again.

She'd certainly dispatched Angie, who was one of the more tenacious of his "groupies," as his brother Landon liked to call the women who came up to visit him on the mountain.

In the past, he'd encouraged the visits, enjoyed them even. But now, the only woman he was interested in spending time with was Lucy. During the weekends they spent together, he couldn't get enough of her. While they were apart, he counted down the hours until he could see her again. There was no point in trying to deny that his feelings for her ran deeper than they ever had for anyone else.

He had no idea how long he'd been standing there thinking about her when she came back into the cabin looking sweet and beautiful and nervous.

"Do I look okay?"

Colton realized he was staring at her.

"What? Do I have something on my face or something? The mirror app wasn't as helpful as it could've been."

Because the attraction was too powerful to resist, he went to her and raised his hands to her neck, using his thumbs to stroke her face. "You look amazing." He bent his head to kiss her and then took a second taste because the first one was so sweet. "And you have no reason to be nervous."

"I'm not."

"Yes, you are. I can tell by now."

"Don't act like you know me so well."

"I know you, sweetheart, and I also know it's no small thing to go to dinner at my parents' house when we were supposed to be spending a quiet weekend alone at the lake. You've gotten way more than you signed on for, including a visit with Fred."

"That is true. You're going to have to make it up to me when we get back."

"I'll try to think of some way I can do that." He collected her into his arms and held her close. "It's a big group but a welcoming one. You'll be fine. I promise."

"I wish Cam was going to be there."

"I'll be right there with you, and I won't leave your side. I promise I won't let them bite you or anything."

"They *bite*?"

"Lucas and Landon had a little problem with biting for

a while there, but they've outgrown that now. For the most part."

"Lovely."

"I'll keep them away," he said with a chuckle. "Shall we do this?"

She took a deep, calming breath and released it slowly. "Yes, let's go."

CHAPTER 15

—◄►—

Sap Surge! A sugarmaker would never admit
there is such a thing as too strong a sap run,
but days like today test that opinion.

—Colton Abbott's sugaring journal, April 3

As they rode down the steep hill from the mountain to the main road, Lucy told herself—repeatedly—that she had nothing to worry about. Molly and Lincoln Abbott had been warm and welcoming to her from the first time she met them. But that had been because she was Cameron's best friend and business partner, and they loved her.

This time, today, she was coming as Colton's . . . friend or girlfriend or whatever she was to him. He'd been right when he said she was getting way more than she'd expected out of this weekend in Vermont. Not only had Will and Cameron forced them out of the closet, but now she was heading for Sunday dinner at his parents' house, where most of his siblings would be in attendance.

They were nice people. And contrary to what he'd said, she didn't expect any of them to bite. However, she was nervous just the same. Everything had changed this weekend. Their fun interlude had become something much more serious, and it wasn't only because they'd finally made love or because his family had found out about them. No, it was more than that. Things between *them* were more serious, and that had nothing at all to do with anyone but them.

"Talk to me," he said after a long period of silence.

"About what?"

"About what you're thinking right now."

"I want to know how many other Angies are out there."

"*That* is what you're thinking about?"

"Among other things. Are you going to answer the question?"

"There've been a few Angies. Here and there. Nothing significant."

"So they're like fuck buddies or something like that?"

"Lucy! Such language from that sweet mouth of yours."

Though he chastised her, she could see he was also amused. "You still haven't answered the question."

"I guess they'd probably qualify as FBs, if we're getting technical. I never said I've lived like a monk. I like women. I've always liked women, and they seem to like me, too."

That made her snort rather inelegantly through her nose.

"You find that funny?"

"You say that so casually. 'They seem to like me, too.' When you know it's more a matter of them loving you and coming up to the mountain to keep you from getting lonely. I see right through your entire operation, Abbott."

"It's not an operation, per se. It's more of a . . . lifestyle."

She rolled her eyes at him.

"It *was* a lifestyle. Past tense. Now I'm a one-woman kind of guy."

"Because that's what you want or because I started a rumor about your egregious axe injury?"

Laughing, he said, "Because it's what I want, although your rumor might help to get the word out a little quicker than it would've happened otherwise."

"Good."

"You're a spiteful little wench when you want to be, aren't you?"

"You know it."

He reached across the console for her hand and linked their fingers. "I do love sparring with you, Lucy. You keep me on my toes."

"Someone has to. You've had it far too easy in the past. It's high time someone gave you a run for your money."

"I'm really glad it's you giving me a run for my money."

As always, his sweetness was hard to resist, which of course was what made him so popular with women. They turned onto Hells Peak Road a short time later.

"Did I ever mention that I was raised in a barn?"

"I don't think you did." Lucy took her first look at the "barn" the Abbotts called home. Like everything else about their family, the red barn was incredible, filled with different-shaped windows, a weathervane on the roof. The acres of land that surrounded the barn were lush and green, and the mountains in the distance majestic and breathtakingly beautiful. "It's amazing," she said softly, trying to imagine what it had been like to grow up in such a place in the midst of such a family.

He brought the truck to a stop behind several other vehicles, all of them big and rugged and built for the harsh mountain winters. Sarah and Elmer bounded out of the backseat and went off to frolic with George and Ringo. Another smaller dog was also running around with them, and Lucy recognized Colton's sister Hannah keeping a close eye on the little one.

"You ready?" he asked when he came around to the passenger side of the truck to help her out.

"Absolutely." He didn't need to know her heart was beating fast or that her hands were trembling ever so slightly or that she'd never done this with any other guy. She'd never gotten this far with anyone else, so meeting the parents and family had never been an issue.

Hannah came over to greet her brother with a hug and kiss. She took a surreptitious glance down the front of him. "Everything okay?"

"Everything is fine. Why?"

"Heard a little rumor about an injury in a very delicate place."

Colton hooted with laughter. To Lucy, he said, "I told you it'd be all over town in no time at all."

"I'm afraid the rumor is all my fault. We had an unwelcome visitor up on the mountain and I took a little liberty with the truth."

Hannah joined in the laughter. "It's good to see you again, Lucy. I understand you've had one heck of a weekend in Vermont."

"That's putting it mildly. I've also met Fred."

"Even better." Hannah linked her arm with Lucy, who immediately felt at ease with Colton's gorgeous older sister. Her dark hair shone in the afternoon sunshine and her eyes were aglow with happiness. "Come on, Homie. Leave the big kids to play and come with Mama."

The multicolored puppy responded immediately to Hannah and trotted after them into the house.

"He's so good," Lucy said.

"I'm proud of him," Hannah replied. "He's a very good boy."

In the spacious mudroom, Lucy noticed the row of hooks with ten names above them. For some reason she found that ridiculously endearing.

A handsome dark-haired man came into the mudroom. "Oh, there you are, Hannah. I was coming to find you and the little monster."

"Lucy," Hannah said, "this is my fiancé, Nolan, who isn't going to be my fiancé for long if he continues to refer to my baby Homer as a monster."

As Lucy laughed at the comment, she shook hands with Nolan. "It's nice to meet you."

"You, too."

"She's Colton's . . . *friend*," Hannah added for Nolan's benefit.

"Ohhhh. I see."

"You don't see anything, so mind your own business," Colton said.

Nolan cracked up laughing. "Right. The same way all of you minded my business a few months ago?"

"That was different," Colton grumbled.

"Really." The more Colton squirmed, the more amused Nolan seemed to get. "How was it different?"

"It just was. Come on, Lucy. He's not officially in the family yet, so we don't have to put up with him."

They left Hannah and Nolan laughing in the mudroom and continued into the enormous kitchen, where Molly was standing guard over the stove with Colton's other sisters, Ella and Charlotte, assisting her.

"There you are!" Molly said, coming over to hug them both. "I heard you were *injured*. Everything all right?"

"Everything is just fine," Colton replied. "It was all a big misunderstanding."

"Is that right?" Molly's shrewd gaze darted from Colton to Lucy.

"Uh-huh," Colton said. "What's for dinner? I'm starving."

"You're always starving, and we're having pork roast with potatoes, vegetables and applesauce."

"The homemade kind?"

"Is there any other kind?" his mother asked.

"I'm drooling," Colton replied.

"See if you can contain yourself," Ella said to her brother as she came over to greet Lucy. "Nice to see you again."

"You, too."

"So you're the mystery woman, huh?" Charley asked.

Though her sharper-than-expected tone put Lucy's back up, she kept her expression neutral. "I guess you could say that."

"Are you going to move here, too?"

"Charley!" Ella and Molly said in stereo.

"Don't ask her that!" Molly said.

"Really, Charl," Colton said. "Way to help a guy out."

"Why is that an unreasonable question?" Charley asked. "Her best friend and business partner just moved here."

"I'm sorry about her," Molly said, patting Lucy's arm.

"We've been trying to purchase a filter for her for nearly thirty years to no avail."

"She's fine," Lucy said with a nervous laugh. Charley's question had caught her off guard, and now she wondered if all the Abbotts would expect her to move the way Cameron had. But she wasn't Cameron, and she'd said from the beginning that she wouldn't move.

"Stop," Colton whispered in her ear. "I can feel you spinning."

Before Lucy could formulate a reply, two identically gorgeous young men came rushing into the kitchen. They fixated on Colton's crotch. Both wore firefighting gear that only added to their supreme hotness. Lucy had once referred to the Abbott men as a DNA wonderland, and these two were a big reason why.

"Oh, dude," one of them said, his tone full of relief. Lucy thought he might be Lucas, but she couldn't say for sure. "We heard the weirdest thing about you at the firehouse, and we came over here as soon as we heard."

"Let me guess," Colton said with a sideways glance at Lucy. "Something about an axe and my junk?"

Both twins shuddered.

"Yeah, that," Landon said. "What the hell?"

At that moment they both seemed to notice Lucy.

"Oh," Lucas said. "Are you—?"

"The mystery woman?" Lucy replied. "That'd be me. I'm Lucy."

"I remember," Landon said as he shook her hand. "Nice to see you again."

"You, too. I might be responsible for the axe-and-junk story."

"Might be?" Colton asked.

"One of his groupies came up for a visit and I might've told her he'd had an unfortunate run-in with the axe." As she spoke, Lucy felt her face get very warm.

"That is hilarious and brilliant," Ella said. To her brother, she added, "I love her. You have to keep her forever."

Lucy felt like she'd been gut punched by the wallop of

emotion that overtook her at the thought of Colton keeping her forever.

"Who is Colton keeping forever?" another male voice asked as he joined the crowd in the kitchen.

"Shut up, Hunter," Colton said.

Lucy remembered Hunter from the last time she'd met him. He was the oldest Abbott, the one who dressed like he'd just stepped out of the pages of *GQ* magazine.

"Oh hey, it's the eunuch," Hunter said dryly, starting a wave of laughter that took down everyone in the room except Colton. "Don't try filing a workman's comp claim when we all know you never had much to lose in the first place."

"Oh *burn*," Charley said, giving Hunter a high five.

"That's not at all true," Lucy said. The words were out of her mouth before she took a second to think about what she was saying—or who she was saying it to. She couldn't let Colton take all this abuse when she'd been the one to start the rumor. Everyone stared at her for what felt like an hour of face-heating misery until Charley started another wave of laughter.

"She must *really* like you, Colton," Charley said.

"She does *really* like me," Colton said with a pointed look at his sister.

"I can't believe I said that," Lucy muttered, making them all laugh harder.

"I'll love you forever for it," Colton said for her ears only, smiling as he kissed her temple.

Hearing him say he'd love her forever did weird things to Lucy's insides, even if they both knew he was only joking.

"Lucy, honey," Molly said, "I sincerely apologize for the band of hooligans I raised."

"It's okay. I know you did the best you could."

Hannah came through the kitchen carrying Homer and patted Colton on the chest. "She's a keeper."

Colton straightened out of the slouch he'd fallen into. "I heard there was going to be food here. Was that another rumor?"

"Oh hush," his mother said. "Go get Lucy something to drink, and you'll be fed soon enough. The rest of you leave him alone, you got me?"

"Why do we have to?" Charley asked. "He wouldn't leave us alone if we were the one bringing a mystery woman to dinner."

"Do you have a mystery woman, Charl?" Colton asked. "That would explain a lot."

"Shut up."

"You shut up."

"Children," Molly said with obvious exasperation. "All of you shut up and get out of here before I start knocking your heads together."

That seemed to do the trick as the Abbott siblings heeded their mother's orders, and most of them filed out of the kitchen.

Lucy was still stuck on Colton saying he'd love her forever. She hadn't heard much of what'd been said after that.

Colton took Lucy's hand and led her out of the hornet's nest in the kitchen, through the dining room to the huge family room, where his father and grandfather were watching a Red Sox game with Wade.

Lincoln and Elmer jumped up to greet Lucy.

"Well, isn't this a nice surprise?" Elmer said as he hugged her. "It's so nice to see you again."

"You, too, Mr. Stillman."

"Call me Elmer, honey. Everyone does."

"Thank you. I will."

"Hey, Gramps," Colton said as he hugged his grandfather.

Elmer patted his grandson's face. "Still can't get used to you without all the scruff, boy."

"That beard hid a whole lot of ugly, if you ask me," Wade said without taking his eyes off the TV.

"This is a tough crowd today," Colton said. "Wade, take a break from being surly and say hi to Lucy."

Wade looked up at her. "Hi, Lucy. Are you the mystery woman?"

"I suppose I am."

"We're very glad to have you here, honey," Lincoln said.

Colton had never appreciated his father more than he did in that moment.

"Thanks for having me."

Watching Lucy interact with his family and roll with the teasing only made Colton like her more than he already did. And when she'd defended his manhood against Hunter's attack, well . . . He'd sort of meant what he'd said about loving her forever.

Her reaction to that statement hadn't been lost on him. It had thrown her to hear him say those words, even in jest. But he didn't regret saying them. The more time he spent with her the more he could see himself loving her forever. What he couldn't picture was how they'd ever work out the logistical issues that kept them living two very separate lives despite what they'd found with each other.

When Lucy nudged him, he realized he'd missed part of the conversation. "Yeah?"

"I was asking how the woodpile is coming," Elmer said.

"About halfway there."

"And the accident with the axe I heard about from Cletus earlier?"

"A misunderstanding," Colton replied.

"Well, that's a relief."

"You know it."

His mother called them in to dinner, where the good-natured teasing continued during the delicious meal. Colton downed two plates in the time it took most of them to eat one.

"Hurry up and get your seconds, everyone, before Colton goes for thirds," Molly said.

"What can I say? I'm a growing boy."

"So, Lucy," Elmer said, "have you always lived in New York?"

"Born and raised in Queens. My father still lives there."

"Were you lucky enough to be blessed with siblings like we were?" Hannah asked sarcastically.

"Thankfully only one. Emma is a year younger than me, and she has an eight-year-old daughter, Simone."

"How did you meet Cameron?" Ella asked.

"We took some classes together in college and discovered we had a lot in common. We've been friends ever since."

"You must miss her," Hannah said kindly.

"I do."

"We're taking very good care of her," Elmer said, patting Lucy's hand.

"She loves everything about being here."

"It's a good place to be," Charley said. "Don't knock it until you've tried it."

"I'd never dream of knocking it," Lucy said.

Colton had reached his limit in both food consumption and family dynamics. "Sorry to chew and screw, but we've got to get going."

"He's got to go screw, all right," Landon said under his breath, igniting the left side of the table in laughter.

"Landon," Lincoln said sharply. "Have some respect for our guest."

"Sorry, Lucy," Landon said as the others continued to chuckle.

"No worries," Lucy said as she stood, bringing her plate with her.

"Just leave that, honey," Molly said. "We'll get it."

Colton took the plate from her, put it on top of his and put his free hand on her back to guide her around the table. On the way by, he bent to kiss his mother. "Thanks for dinner, Mom."

"Thanks for coming."

"Yes, thank you, Molly," Lucy said. "It was delicious."

"We were happy to have you. Same time every week, so I hope you'll come again."

"I'd love to." She made a friend for life when she bent to give his gramps a kiss. "It was nice to see you again, Elmer."

"The pleasure was all mine, honey. You come back again soon."

Colton rinsed their plates and put them in the dishwasher. Then he led her through the mudroom to the yard, where he whistled for Sarah and Elmer. The dogs came running, followed closely by George and Ringo. "Hey guys," Colton said, rubbing four blond heads at once. "You missed dinner."

He opened the back door for George and Ringo and called after them, "Incoming!"

With his dogs settled in the backseat of the truck, Colton held the passenger door for Lucy and waited until she was buckled in before he closed the door and walked around the front of the truck. He couldn't get a read on her, and that made him anxious.

Had dinner with his family turned her off completely? He was almost afraid to ask. Driving down Hells Peak Road, he took a couple of tentative glances at her. She was staring straight ahead out the window and seemed a million miles away from him.

CHAPTER 16

——◆◆◆——

*Quite the sap run. It kicked in during the
night as a southwest wind kept the temp up.
Then today, a chilly northwest wind with
intermittent sun and snow kept the sap
gushing clear as a glacial lake.*

—Colton Abbott's sugaring journal, April 5

"Sorry if they were a bit much," he finally said when he
couldn't take the silence any longer.

"They were wonderful. I can see why Cameron loves
them all so much."

"Oh. Really?"

"Yes. Did you think I wasn't enjoying myself?"

"I couldn't tell if you were charmed or appalled."

"Definitely charmed. Who wouldn't be, Colton? They're
amazing and funny and beautiful—every one of your siblings is beautiful. You know that, don't you?"

"Ew, gross. They are not. I'll give you Hannah and Ella
maybe, but the rest of them . . . Yuck. My stomach just
turned."

"Don't be ridiculous. By the standards of anyone with a
heartbeat, your brothers are hot and your sisters are gorgeous."

He curled his lip in mock horror. "Lucas and Landon are *not* hot."

Lucy laughed at his reaction. "You've been spending far too much time alone on your mountain. While you weren't looking, your baby brothers turned into gorgeous men who are *firefighters*. Do you understand the significance of that?"

"I guess they've saved a life or two. So what?"

"Now you're just being obtuse."

"That's a big word."

"Dense. Is that better?"

He bit his lip to keep from laughing out loud. She was so damned funny.

"Firefighters are the sexiest men in the *universe*. Not only do they save lives, they run into burning buildings, they get cats down from trees, they pry people out of mangled cars, and they do it all in those suits. What're they called?"

"Turnout suits?"

"Yes! Those."

"You think turnout suits are sexy?"

"Turnout suits are a huge turn-*on*."

"You're not right in the head, Lucy Mulvaney. That's all there is to it."

"You're the one with the vision problems. Not me."

"Well, even though you're not right in the head, you were a good sport back there, and I appreciate it. Especially the boost you gave to my flagging manhood. Up until that point, it hadn't been a very good day for my boys and me. Lots of *ups* and *downs*—and not the good kind. You turned things around rather nicely."

"I still can't believe I said that in front of your mother."

"With the ten of us underfoot, there's nothing she hasn't already heard. Don't sweat it. She was probably impressed that you stood up for me. She's big on loyalty. That goes a long way with her. And with me. You were very, *very* loyal to me. And my boys. We intend to show our appreciation as soon as we get back to the mountain."

Laughing, she shook her head. "You're incorrigible."

"You love me."

A pervasive silence occupied the rest of the ride home, and Colton berated himself the whole way for being flippant about something as important as love. Did he love Lucy? Probably. Was he *in love* with Lucy? He was well on his way to being in love with her, or so he thought. Having never been in love before, he wasn't really sure what it felt like.

All he knew was he wanted to be with her as often as possible. He had no interest in any other woman, which was unusual in and of itself. Under normal circumstances, he preferred variety and had several women who enjoyed hanging out with him on occasion with no strings attached. That had worked for him for a long time. But not anymore. After what he'd shared with Lucy, he couldn't imagine going back to meaningless encounters with women who were nothing more than friends with benefits.

He'd always been up front with them before he got involved. He wasn't looking for serious and he didn't want anyone's feelings to be hurt. If a woman seemed to be getting overly serious about their arrangement, he ended it.

So how was he supposed to know if he was in love with Lucy? When Will got back from the lake, Colton was going to talk to his older brother about this situation. He needed a reality check, and he needed it soon before he did something stupid to mess up the best thing that'd ever happened to him.

Lucy felt like she was floating through a weird dream state as they returned to Colton's cabin. Twice in the last few hours he'd used the word *love* to refer to what was happening between them. In just a few days' time, what had been easy and noncommittal had taken a sharp turn toward serious.

And though she kept reminding herself that none of the obstacles that stood between them and any kind of future together had been addressed, that didn't stop her from wanting more of him.

Even though it was July, the temperature on the mountain had dropped with the sun, so Colton lit the huge cast-iron woodstove in the cabin.

"Do you normally light the stove in the summer?"

"Not very often. When you spend winters up here, this doesn't count as cold. But I know it does for you, so I don't mind heating the place up."

"I want to know everything about how you manage up here without electricity. What do you do for light, for example?" It wasn't totally dark yet, but it was getting there quickly.

"Kerosene lamps." He lit two of them, and they cast a cozy glow over the small space.

"How about refrigeration?"

"I rely on an old-fashioned icebox and get blocks of ice delivered every other day in the summer. I make my own in the winter."

"Where is it?"

"It's over in the sugarhouse. It stays cooler there year-round, so that's the best place for it."

"Will you show me the sugarhouse and tell me how it all works?"

"Sure, I'd be happy to show you tomorrow."

"How about cooking? I'm trying to picture life without a microwave."

"I have my very own microwave right here," he said, gesturing to the iron woodstove. "I can cook both inside and on top, and the heat of the fire gets things done pretty quickly."

"Very impressive."

"It's not fancy, but it gets the job done. I don't want for much up here, except lately."

"What do you want for lately?"

"A phone, for one thing, and an Internet connection. Two things I've lived perfectly fine without until I had someone I wanted to talk to every day."

Smiling, Lucy picked up her bag. "I'm going out to the bathhouse. Will you check to make sure there are no 'visitors' named Fred or anything else out there waiting to scare the crap out of me?"

Chuckling, he said, "I'd be happy to."

Once he'd declared the yard critter free and lit yet another kerosene lamp in the bathhouse for her, he left her to get changed.

As she brushed her teeth and changed into yoga pants and a tank top, Lucy had to admit that she'd been skeptical about what it would be like to live without electricity and all the modern conveniences. But Colton made it look easy—and comfortable. Sure it was different than what she was used to, but different wasn't necessarily bad.

Until she realized she had no way to manage one other nightly task: charging her cell phone. Suddenly different seemed very, very bad.

"Colton," she said when she returned to the cabin. "What do I do about my phone?"

"What about it?"

"I can't charge it here."

"No, you can't. Is that a huge problem?"

She didn't want to overreact, but the thought of her family and employees not being able to reach her made her twitchy. "Not a huge problem . . . It's just . . . I'm not used to being out of touch. What if there's an emergency?"

"I'll tell you what. Tomorrow I'll take you down to town and you can charge up at the office, okay?"

"Yes," she said, relieved. "That'd be great."

"Good." He held up the bedcovers for her. "Jump in so you don't get cold."

She slid between soft flannel sheets and he tucked the comforter in around her.

"Be right back."

Lucy watched him cross the room and leave the cabin, closing the door behind him. She loved looking at him and watching him move. He had a confident way about him, like he was comfortable in his own skin and didn't feel the need to explain himself or his choices to anyone. It was an admirable quality and one she wished she could more fully embrace. At the end of the day, she was a pleaser. She wanted the people who mattered to her to be happy, even if that meant giving up things that might've made her happy.

She'd definitely made sacrifices for her family and had been more like a second mother than an aunt to Simone. As a single mom, Emma relied heavily on her, and Lucy was happy to do whatever she could for both of them. But had that been at the expense of her own life and happiness? These weekends with Colton had shown her what she'd been missing by frantically tending to the needs of others for so many years that she'd forgotten how to tend to her own needs.

Speaking of her own needs . . . He came back inside, bringing the dogs in with him this time and getting them settled on their beds. Then he stripped off his shirt and dropped his shorts, leaving both in a pile on the floor as he headed for the bed with a look on his face that left no doubt about what he had in mind.

Lucy's entire body tingled with interest as he slid into bed next to her. She propped herself up on a bent arm so she could look down at him. "Kind of early for bed, isn't it?"

He played with one of her curls. "This isn't the city that never sleeps. This is the mountain that goes to work—and bed—early."

"What do you do for fun on the rare nights when you have to entertain yourself up here?"

"I'm sensing a bit of sarcasm in that question."

"Just a bit?"

Smiling, he said, "I read a lot, books and sugaring periodicals and other nature stuff. I love to draw." He reached for the bedside table and picked up a book that he handed to her.

"What's this?"

"My living history of the most recent sugar season."

Lucy opened the book and was instantly captivated by his drawings as well as the vivid words he used to describe the season. She wasn't sure what interested her more—the images or the words that went with them. "This is so cool. You're incredibly talented."

"It's just a hobby. I also play with the dogs and fix stuff around here. There's always something to do. I don't get distracted when there's a lot to do, so this life works really well for me."

She put down the book but intended to study it in far more detail when she got a chance. "Don't you feel cut off from your family and friends when you're up here with no way to communicate with them?"

"Not really. I see a lot of my family. They come up. I go down. We keep in touch. People come up to the store, so I hear the latest news from town."

"And of course there's your harem. How does that work? Do you have a scheduler in town who assigns nights to each of the women?"

"Stop it!" he said with a laugh. "There aren't that many of them."

"Still . . . How do they know who is on duty on any given night?"

"I don't know. I've never asked them."

"I bet there's an elaborate system that you have no knowledge of. Maybe Sunday is A Day, thus Angie."

He curled his hand around her neck and tugged her close enough to kiss. "Jealous Lucy is sexy Lucy."

"I'm not jealous of *Angie* or the rest of your harem, and I'm certainly not threatened by them."

"Particularly since you dispatched them by telling Angie I lopped off my package with an axe."

"I never said those words. If she jumped to that conclusion, that's on her. Not me."

He rose up and had her pinned under him before she knew what hit her. "You are an evil minx, and you knew exactly what you were doing when you told her that."

"I have no idea what you're talking about."

"Sure you don't," he said as he kissed her.

"Who's the Monday girl? Mona? Monica? Mary?"

"Shut up, Lucy," he said laughing as he kissed her again.

"Tuesday is Tawny or Tish or Trashy Tina?"

"You know, there are other things you can do with your mouth besides torment me."

"Like what?"

"Seems to me that before you maligned my boy parts, you were thinking about getting to know them better."

"I don't remember that. Maybe you should refresh my memory."

Rather than do that though, he captured her face in those big calloused hands of his and looked down at her.

"What?" she asked, unnerved by the intensity she saw in his gaze.

"I've never had more fun with any woman than I do with you, Lucy Mulvaney."

Far more moved by his words than she probably should've been, she said, "Really?"

"Really."

"Not even Trashy Tina?"

He shook his head. "She can't hold a candle to you."

"She's probably a lot better at the trashy stuff than I am. She's certainly got more experience than I do."

"Are you honestly comparing your skills in bed to that of a fictional woman who you totally made up five minutes ago?"

When he put it like that, she sounded like an insecure nitwit. "Maybe."

"You don't need to worry about comparing yourself to anyone else, Lucy. You're one of a kind. Trust me on that."

She ran her hands up and over his bulging biceps. "Did you mean it when you said you wanted us to be exclusive? No more Angie, Mona or Trashy Tina? And we haven't even gotten to Wednesday yet . . ."

He kissed her. Hard.

When she moaned and opened her mouth to his tongue, he took full advantage of the opportunity to demonstrate the other things she could do with her mouth beside obsess about the other women in his life. He wrapped his arms around her and settled into the kiss as his muscular body pressed against hers.

Lucy curled her arms around his neck and her legs around his hips. She'd never been kissed the way Colton Abbott kissed her, as if kissing her was the only thing keeping him alive. He didn't kiss so much as consume. She felt consumed by him, and it was the sweetest feeling she'd ever known.

As she lay surrounded by his strength and his appealing scent, none of the issues standing between them mattered. She didn't care that he lived six hours from her or that his lifestyle was so different from hers they might be from opposing universes rather than the same country. She didn't care that they'd blown all their plans to not get too serious. She didn't care that she was setting herself up for major heartbreak when this whole thing blew up in her face.

No, all she cared about right now was how magical it felt to be held and kissed and loved by him. Yes, she felt loved, and treasured and strangely safe with him despite all the peril that surrounded this relationship.

He broke the kiss and turned his attention to her neck, licking and nibbling and setting her on fire. "Yes, Lucy," he whispered as his whiskers rubbed against her sensitive skin. "I meant it when I said I want us to be exclusive. The thought of another guy touching you the way I do . . ." He cupped her breast and toyed with her nipple until it tightened. "I'd want to kill anyone who touched you like this."

"So you understand how I felt when Angie came sniffing around earlier."

"You don't need to worry about her or anyone else." He kissed a path to her throat and chest before tugging impatiently at her tank top until her nipple popped free. "I don't want her. I don't want anyone but you."

CHAPTER 17

———◄•►———

*454: that was the tally of gallons at 3 a.m.
when the fire in the arch died down for
the night. Another 50 gallons' worth of sap
sits in the concentrate tank, so "The Gift
Run" did truly yield 500 gallons.*

—Colton Abbott's sugaring journal, April 6

The swirl of his tongue on her nipple made Lucy gasp. She fisted a handful of his hair and held on tight while he licked and sucked and bit down lightly but insistently.

His words and actions made for a powerful combination, and they served to wipe her mind clear of anything other than what was happening right now, right here. He gave her other breast the same treatment before kissing his way down the front of her. Sitting back on his knees, he pulled her yoga pants and panties down and tossed them over his shoulder.

He gazed at her core with barely concealed lust, his intentions apparent.

"Wait. Colton."

Kissing the inside of her knee, he glanced at her. "What's wrong?"

"Nothing. But I was wondering . . . Could I do what I started to do earlier, before we were interrupted?"

"I wouldn't say no to that. Like ever."

She loved that he made her laugh—frequently. "Turn over then."

"I'm thinking about two birds and one stone."

"What does that mean?"

"Come here and I'll show you."

There was something about the way he said the words that immediately set Lucy's nerves on high alert. He turned over onto his back and reached for her, shocking her when he arranged her on top of him so she was facing his feet, among other things. "Colton . . . What're you doing?"

He eased her legs apart and showed her exactly what he had in mind.

"Oh my God."

"Shh. You do your thing, and I'll do mine."

Never one to back down from a direct challenge, Lucy wrapped her hand around his cock and ran her tongue over the wide crown while he tortured her with his tongue and fingers. The whole thing was so wildly erotic and so wildly . . . Well, suffice to say she'd never done this before, and trying to focus on him while he was busy focusing on her was incredibly stimulating and distracting.

"Relax, honey," he whispered against her inner thigh. "Don't think about what we're doing. Just enjoy it."

Just enjoy it. That was becoming a theme between them, and he'd taught her a lot about relaxing and living in the moment rather than obsessing about what was waiting around the next corner. She bent her head again and closed her lips around him, sucking lightly and swirling her tongue through the groove at the top.

He drew in a sharp deep breath and pushed two fingers into her.

The combination of what he was doing to her and knowing she was getting to him was nearly enough to finish her off. She opened her mouth wider and took more of him while stroking with her hand at the same time.

"Ah, Christ, Lucy . . . Don't stop." He curled his fingers inside her and pressed his thumb to her clit.

Lucy moaned, her lips vibrating on his shaft.

His hips lifted off the bed. "So good," he whispered. "Come for me, honey, and take me with you."

At his command, the sensations ripped through her, wave after wave of bliss that she felt in every part of her body. His hand on her bottom held her in place while he came right after her. She swallowed frantically, taking everything he had to give her.

And then he relaxed under her, sagging into the bed for a second before he took control, lifting and turning her as if she weighed nothing. His amazing strength was, as always, an incredible turn-on.

When she was on top of him, looking down at him, he ran his thumb over her bottom lip. "Your lips are red and swollen."

"Gee, I wonder why."

"That was incredible."

"Likewise."

"Have you done that before?"

"No," she said, resting her cheek on his chest. Eye contact was too embarrassing right then. "I've never done either of those things."

"Either of what things?"

"Are you really going to make me say it?"

"You know I am."

She sighed, resigned to her fate. "The position or the ending."

"Ahhh, I see. And? What did you think?"

"Of which part?"

"Both."

"It was very dirty. And very sexy."

"I want to see your face when you say that."

She burrowed deeper into his chest. "No!"

"Lucy . . . Don't be shy with me. You have no need to be."

"Right . . . I'm clearly way, way out of my league with you."

"No, you're not." He ran his hands down her back to cup

her bottom and gave a little tug, moving her up to better align their bodies. And then he sank into her in one deep thrust that made her burn and stretch as she accommodated his girth.

Her forehead dropped onto his chest, and his arms came around her.

"Ahh, Luce, you feel so good. So hot and so tight."

"You have to talk about it, don't you?"

"It feels too good not to talk about it, and wouldn't you rather I talked to you about how good it feels rather than someone else?"

That got her attention. She raised her head and found his eyes dancing with mischief. "You wouldn't dare."

"I wouldn't dare, but you gotta let me talk it out with you."

"If you insist."

"I do." He moved his hands from her back to her breasts. "Sit up, honey."

Lucy flattened her hands on his chest and pushed up, gasping when he slid in deeper. Her head fell back as she absorbed the rippling pleasure.

He pinched her nipples between his fingers and added to the riot of sensation unfolding inside her. "Good?"

"Yeah. Really good."

"Roll your hips. Hold on to me."

She kept her hands on his chest as she began to move tentatively at first and then more eagerly when she found her rhythm.

"God, that's amazing."

Lucy opened her eyes and met his intense gaze. He was so beautiful and strong and sexy. Watching his muscles flex and move under her, his cheek pulse with tension and his lips part nearly undid her. How was it possible that this incredible man had chosen her over all the others who wanted him? How would she ever manage to keep his attention when he had so many choices? And how would she bear to leave him the day after tomorrow after this incredible weekend?

He surprised her when he sat up and wrapped his arms around her. "Whatever you're thinking right now, stop it."

And he was so incredibly tuned in to her. He had been from the very beginning, and that was the first thing she'd found attractive about him. No, honestly, it was the second thing. His rugged sexiness was definitely first.

"Stop it," he said again, more softly this time as he kissed her. "It feels just as good for me as it does for you."

Lucy wound her arms around his neck and held him close as she continued to move on top of him, guided by his hands on her bottom. She once again closed her eyes and gave in to the magic they created together. She turned over the control to him and let him take her away until her world was reduced to him and them and the place where they were joined.

He shifted their position so he was on top of her, pushing into her repeatedly until she could no longer contain the cry that erupted from her lips at the moment they reached the peak together, clinging to each other as they rode the wave of pleasure.

Colton came down on top of her but was careful not to crush her.

Lucy held on tight, running her fingers through hair that was now damp with perspiration. She licked a bead of sweat from his face and absorbed his shudders while aftershocks pulsed through them.

"You'll understand when I say I have no choice but to keep you here with me forever, right?"

"And you'll understand when I say that although that's the loveliest offer I've ever received, it's not possible."

His deep sigh said it all. "I know." He kissed her once more before he withdrew from her and shifted onto his back.

Lying next to him, her body cooling from the heat of passion, Lucy was certain of only one thing. The closer she got to him, the harder it became to picture a life without him in it.

Colton woke early the next morning and watched Lucy sleep for a long time before he decided to get some work done while she slept in. He'd greatly enjoyed the days off with her, but he adhered to such a strict schedule this time of year that he began to stress out if he took too much time off.

Once the woodpile was replenished for the following winter, he could relax. The autumn was usually the quietest of the four seasons on the mountain, and a time he looked forward to every year.

He stepped onto the front porch and nearly tripped over a small cooler that sat right outside the door. "What the heck?" Opening the lid, he found several containers of food and a note sitting on top of the pile.

Dear Colton, I was so sorry to hear about your terrible injury. I am praying for your speedy recovery, and I'm happy to come up and help take care of you. Just let me know. xoxoxo Brandy

"Oh for the love of Christ," he muttered, thankful for the small favor of having woken before Lucy so she wouldn't see Brandy's care package.

With Sarah and Elmer dancing around his feet, he picked up the cooler and crossed the yard to the sugarhouse, where he stashed the food in the icebox. He peeked inside the foil packet to discover a delicious-smelling lasagna that made his mouth water. He'd save that for dinner. Lucy didn't need to know where it had come from.

There was also a container of salad, a loaf of Italian bread and a pan of brownies. He took a couple of them and had them for an early-morning snack. As soon as Lucy got up, he'd make them some eggs and sausage. The thought of it made his always-ready-to-eat stomach rumble.

After he fed the dogs, he settled into an easy routine with the axe, letting his mind wander as it always did during the routine, rote work of splitting wood. Naturally, he thought about the night he'd spent with Lucy, the erotic lovemaking that had left him depleted in every possible way as well as the sweet comfort of sleeping with her tucked in next to him.

He who never let any woman spend the night in his bed

was now addicted to sleeping with one particular woman, and tomorrow he had to let her go again. That truly sucked. For the first time in his life, he had reason to be envious of his brother Will, who had found a way to make things work with Cameron. She seemed thrilled to be living with Will in Vermont. But Lucy had made it clear from the beginning that she wasn't Cameron and she wasn't going to move.

She had a close bond with her dad, sister and niece, not to mention a thriving business that needed her attention. When Cameron left, the business became solely Lucy's responsibility, and he knew she took her obligations to her employees and clients seriously, which was something he admired about her.

He brought the axe down and the log splintered into two pieces. In need of a break, he used his T-shirt to wipe the sweat off his brow and took a long look around at his piece of paradise in the mountains. Would he give this up for her? He might actually be tempted. For the first time since he moved up here at seventeen, something—or *someone*—interested him more than the seasons that governed the sugaring cycles.

But to give up his entire way of life for a woman . . . Not just any woman, of course. The other issue that weighed on him was his lack of marketable skills. He knew how to do one thing and one thing only. He was damned good at that one thing, but running a maple sugaring facility in Vermont didn't exactly translate well to other industries or other locations. His parents had wanted him to go to college, but he'd refused. He'd found his calling early, he told them, and couldn't imagine ever doing anything else.

Maybe if he'd gone to college and gotten a degree, he'd have some options now that life had put an amazing woman in his path and forced him to reconsider every choice he'd ever made.

He was losing his mind. That much was for certain. They'd only made love for the first time two days ago, and here he was contemplating the possibility of tossing his whole life to be with her.

"Hey, mountain man. What's a girl gotta do to get some coffee around here?"

Colton turned and his brain totally froze at the sight of her wearing one of his flannel shirts buttoned once in the middle and nothing else. She was leaning against the post on his porch, arms crossed under her breasts. Her hair was curly and rumpled from bed, and she'd never looked sexier.

He dropped the axe and went to her, so powerfully drawn to her that the emotional wallop took his breath away. Coming to a stop at the bottom of the steps, he reached up to run his hands over her smooth, silky legs, gasping when he encountered naked buttocks under his shirt.

"Fuck, Lucy," he groaned as he pulled her closer and pushed his face into the softness of her belly. "You make me crazy. One minute I'm chopping wood and the next minute I'm sporting it."

Laughing quietly, she put her arms around him and combed her fingers through his hair.

"You've ruined me for every single day that doesn't start just like this," he said.

"Good morning to you, too."

He tightened his grip on her bottom and lifted her into his arms.

She squawked with surprise but recovered quickly, wrapping her legs around his hips and tightening her hold on his neck.

"Kiss me."

"No, I haven't brushed my teeth yet."

"I don't care."

"I do."

"Lucy . . ."

"Colton."

Moaning with frustration, he went to work on her neck, making love to her sweet skin with openmouthed kisses and lots of tongue that had her squirming in his arms. He went up the stairs and into the house, kicking the door closed behind him.

"You'd better be leading me to coffee, mountain man. Ain't nothing else happening around here until I get that."

"Nothing?"

"Not one thing."

He ground his throbbing erection into the V of her legs. "You drive a hard bargain, city girl."

"I'll drive your hard bargain—later. First I want coffee, then a shower, and then I want a full and complete tour of this place. I want to know everything there is to know about making maple syrup, and be prepared. I have a *lot* of questions."

He kept up the kissing and licking and sucking on her neck. "How about we drive the hard bargain now, while it's actually hard, and then we see to all those other things?"

"No deal. I need coffee and a toothbrush and a shower before we do any more driving."

"That's not the way country girls roll."

"So noted. You might've also noted that I'm not a country girl."

No, she wasn't. She was all sorts of refined city girl and was being an exceptionally good sport about roughing it on his mountain. "Does this place sort of horrify you?"

She pulled back to look down at him. "*Horrify* me? Absolutely not. I love it here. It's amazing and beautiful and peaceful. Well, except for the pesky harem, but I think we took care of that problem."

Colton thought it best not to mention the gift he'd awoken to on the porch. What she didn't know wouldn't hurt her, especially since he had no plans to see Brandy or any of the other women who'd once kept him company. Not as long as he was lucky enough to have Lucy in his life.

"I really appreciate you sharing your home with me, Colton. I can't wait to share mine with you." She kissed his forehead. "Now about that coffee?"

He very reluctantly put her down but took another squeeze of soft ass cheeks before he released her and got to work stoking up the fire in the woodstove so he could make her coffee. "You've got a few minutes if you want to grab a shower while it brews."

"That sounds delightful."

"I don't know if it'll qualify as delightful, but at least you'll be clean. Come on. I'll show you how."

"Colton." He stopped on his way to the door and turned to her, raising his brow in question.

"I really do like it here. I'm not just saying that. I like that it's simple and rustic and devoid of all the insanity of modern life. But more than anything, I like that you're here, and I can see how much you love it."

Her words touched him deeply, in a place where no other woman had ever gone before. "Thanks for that. I appreciate that you appreciate it. Means a lot to me." He cleared his throat and gestured for her to go out ahead of him. In the bathhouse, he walked her through the steps of taking a shower.

"When you need water, just tug on this cord and you'll get nice warm water, but when you're soaping up, keep the water off. That way you'll have enough warm water to rinse off."

"Okay. Got it."

"Like I said, not luxurious, but it gets the job done."

"It's fine, Colton. This is an adventure for a spoiled city girl like me." She looked up at the tank that sat above the shower stall. "Where does the water come from?"

"Rain and snow all year round, and it's heated by the sun. There are solar panels on the roof."

"That's very cool."

"It's literally cool in the winter when the sun isn't quite strong enough to heat it."

"I don't think I'd like that."

"You get used to it."

"If you say so. Now if I use all the warm water, what will you do?"

"I can make do with cold. Doesn't bother me."

"Or you could join me and we could share the warm water."

As she said the words her full-body blush traveled from her chest to her cheeks, making him smile. "I know I'm blushing, so deal with it. Do you want to join me or not?"

In answer to her question, he pulled his T-shirt over his head and dropped his shorts, revealing the erection that had never quite subsided after she appeared on his porch wearing only his shirt.

She eyed his poor cock disdainfully as it got even perkier in the fresh air. "Does that thing ever take a break?"

"Not lately, but that's not his fault. It's yours."

"And how is it my fault?"

"You're here and you're breathing and you're you and you're sexy and hot and wearing my shirt oh so well and . . . I'm only human and so is he."

Her lips formed an adorable pucker as she seemed to contemplate what he'd said. "No one has ever found me hot before."

"Maybe you just needed to find me because I think you're very, *very* hot." He kissed her nose, unbuttoned the flannel shirt and pushed it off her shoulders. Then he turned on the water and nudged her into the shower stall that was really only built for one—and how shortsighted had that been? Truth be told, when he'd added the shower to the bathhouse, he'd never expected to share his home on the mountain with anyone.

They stood together under the spray.

"Did I mention the water pressure is somewhat lackluster?"

"It's fine."

"You're a very good sport, Luce."

"I'm not nearly as high maintenance as you'd like to believe."

"I know you aren't." Even still, he was surprised by how well she was rolling with life on the mountain. In some ways that only made it more difficult for him. If she'd come here and hated everything about it, he would've had a much easier time letting her go tomorrow. Instead he was quite certain that after she left, he was going to be extremely lonely for the first time in all the years he'd lived here.

They soaped each other up, which led to the kind of inappropriate touching he loved best with her. If he'd had his way, they would've taken care of business right then and there, but he didn't want her to think that was all he wanted from her. Rather, he rinsed the shampoo out of her hair and then bent his head so she could do the same for him.

When they were clean and dressed, Colton made scrambled eggs, potatoes and toast to go with the coffee, which they enjoyed on his front porch.

"This is really, really good," she said. "You're a great cook."

"I don't know if I'd go that far, but as you well know, I do love to eat."

"I'm impressed, and this coffee is about the best I've ever had."

"It's the fresh mountain air. It makes everything taste and smell better."

"Will you show me your mountain, Colton, and tell me everything there is to know about how you make syrup?"

"You really want to know?"

"I really do."

"Then let's go."

CHAPTER 18

I couldn't get warm all day, though a few weeks ago 32 degrees would have been T-shirt weather. Last night may have been the final freezing night of sugar season. Today began the predicted warm-up on a south wind. The snowpack in the sugarbush is helping to keep the temp in the 40s.

—Colton Abbott's sugaring journal, April 7

"We're going to need to get you some hiking boots," Colton said as he eyed the running shoes she'd worn to climb his mountain. "What size do you wear?"

"Seven and a half."

"I'll get you some at the store for next time."

Next time. Those two little words filled Lucy with excitement and anticipation, both of which were dangerous emotions for a girl who hadn't planned to get overly involved. No sense denying she'd done just that during the course of this weekend, during which everything had changed between them.

His big hand wrapped around hers helped propel her up a well-worn path through the trees that lined the hills above his home. Since she was following him, she had a fantastic view of his muscular ass and legs as he moved easily up the steep incline. While she was huffing and puffing and beginning to perspire, he'd barely broken a sweat. Watching Sarah and Elmer effortlessly bound up ahead of them made Lucy feel like even more of an out-of-shape loser.

After they'd traveled in silence for about twenty minutes, the path leveled off. He stopped and handed her the water bottle he was carrying. "Take a drink."

She did as he directed, grateful for the cool water on her parched throat. "Thanks."

"You doing okay?"

"I'm great."

"Your face is all red."

"Happens a lot in case you haven't noticed."

"Oh, I've noticed." He glanced at the next incline, which was even steeper than the earlier one. "We don't have to go all the way up if you don't want to."

"I do want to. Let's go." She'd pay for this tomorrow, but for right now, it was worth the effort to be able to see everything he wanted to show her. "How many trees do you manage?"

"About twenty-five thousand, give or take a few hundred."

"And you have to tend to all of them every year?"

"In some way or another, yes."

"Tell me how it all works. I want to know everything."

"Everything is a lot," he said with a laugh.

"Start at the beginning, and I'll ask all my questions." If he did the talking, that would give her time to breathe, which was becoming harder the farther up they went.

"Late winter into early spring is our prime season," he began, speaking effortlessly despite the steep climb that was nothing new to him. "The flow of sap begins after the first hard freeze followed by a thaw. The best time for flow is after it freezes at night and the temperature rises to forty to fifty degrees Fahrenheit during the day. So we start around January with drilling new tapholes, checking the lines for blowdowns and critter damage and getting everything ready for that first big freeze. After it thaws, then we need a freezing night to recharge the trees. It's the freeze-thaw 'yo-yo' that we need."

"How long does sugar season last?"

"The taps can be in the trees up to twelve weeks, but the window for making syrup is the end of February through mid-to-late April. The span from the first sap run to the last run can be two weeks or eight weeks, but we only boil—actually make syrup—an average of twenty days. Obviously, if it were a two-week sugar season, we'd boil fewer than twenty days, but that happens some years."

"How many gallons of sap does it take to make a gallon of syrup?"

He smiled down at her. "You weren't kidding when you said you had a lot of questions."

"I've done my homework."

"So I see. It takes anywhere from thirty-five to fifty gallons of sap to make one gallon of syrup, depending on the sweetness of the sap or how much maple sugar it contains. The sweeter the sap, the less sap it takes to produce a gallon of syrup. I could go on and on about reverse osmosis, which makes the sap sweeter before we boil it. There's as much science as there is art behind it."

She fanned her face dramatically. "Reverse osmosis. That's hot."

"Right," he said laughing. "The reverse-osmosis machine makes the sap sweeter before we boil it, but the vacuum pump aids the flow of sap from the trees to the sugarhouse. Two separate functions."

"You're really smart, Colton. It's impressive."

"I'm smart about this one thing, so don't be too impressed."

"How do you power the machine and pumps?"

"We rely on solar energy and generators during the season." He pointed to a copse of trees off in the distance. "We can't run tubes to all the trees, so we still do the bucket method in those cases."

"What kind of trees are these?"

"Most of them are sugar maples. They're the best for

making syrup because they have the greatest concentration of sugar. We use mature trees that are on average about a foot to three feet in diameter that get decent sun exposure. We call the trees a sugarbush. The first step is the tapping, which involves drilling a hole on the side of the tree that faces the sun for most of the day. We drill about three feet from the bottom and an inch or two deep. See right there?" He pointed to a hole the size of a pencil in the lower part of one of the trees. "That's where we tapped last season. Into that hole goes what we call a spike spout that's then attached to the tubing that carries the sap down to the sugarhouse where we boil in what's called an evaporator to get rid of the water and concentrate the sugars. We call this 'boiling down' and that's the most intense part of the process."

"Does the tap hurt the tree?"

"Not as long as we remove the taps at the end of the year to give the tree time to heal in the off season and then choose a different spot to tap the next year."

"When you're installing the taps, how many can you do in a day?"

"Depending on the weather and other factors like icing on the mountain, we can do three or four hundred in a day."

"In a single day?"

"Well, yeah," he said, as if that was no big deal. "We have to move fast if we're going to be ready to run. We have such a small window of opportunity, and we need to capitalize. We tap about ten thousand trees each year. I have to get all of that done before the first good run of sap. It's a pretty delicate balancing act involving weather and timing and a bunch of other factors."

"The boiling is why you need all the wood. I get it now."

"Right. Because we don't have power up here, we still do old-fashioned burn boiling when a lot of outfits are using much more sophisticated equipment these days. It takes a lot of wood to get through a boiling season up here, not to mention heating the house and store."

"Do you ever think about running power up here?"

"We've talked about it, but there's something so ele-mental about running this place almost the same way my grandparents did fifty years ago, with a few nods to mod-ern technology. As long as we meet health codes and pass inspection, we're happy with our output. It suits the needs of the store, and we do a nice little business up here, too."

"What about when the website goes live? Will you be able to satisfy those demands, too?"

"Probably not without bringing sap in from other sources. We've had a couple of meetings about that. I'm in favor of using the site to bring people into the store to buy syrup. Of course my dad wants to be able to sell it online. We're at a standoff on that point. We've been talking to the people who own the spread next door to ours about possi-bly acquiring some more land. If that happens, I'll need someone else up here with me pretty much full time. Max is the most likely candidate, but with the baby coming . . . I'm not sure what he's going to do yet."

"I saw on the website mockup that there're different grades."

"Uh-huh. The early-season syrup tends to be lighter and sweeter, and the maple flavor isn't quite as strong as it gets later in the season when it becomes what we call medium amber or dark amber. The next level is Grade B, which has a much stronger maple flavor, but the color isn't as great. The other thing we have to watch for is that the sweetness tends to be less as the maple flavor intensifies. All syrup, the finished product, is the same sweetness. It's the sap that varies in sweetness."

"I'm trying to picture the boiling season. Do you boil around the clock or just during the day?"

"Sometimes around the clock, but not every day. The whole family pitches in at various times and we make a party out of it. We also hire people from town to help and have a bunch of kids who live on the mountain who come up after school to help feed the fire. Thank God it only lasts about three to four weeks most years. By the end of that I'm so tired I'm like a zombie."

"It sounds like fun, actually." She wanted to offer to come up to help next year but couldn't bring herself to say the words out loud.

"It is fun. It's just very intense."

After a long climb, they reached the top of the hill. On the other side of the peak, the town of Butler was nestled in the hills, the buildings like miniature toys.

With his hands on her shoulders, Colton turned her to face his side of the mountain. "All the trees you see from here down are ours."

"It's amazing, and you were right. I needed to see it from up here to get the full picture." She relaxed against him and smiled when his arms encircled her. "I'm all sweaty."

"I don't care." To prove his point, he nuzzled her neck and kissed her, lingering for a long moment that filled her with utter contentment that was short lived when she remembered that tomorrow she'd be on her way back to her real life. This was a fantasy that couldn't possibly last.

"Why did you just get all rigid on me?"

He was far too insightful for her own good. "No reason. So is going back down easier than the trip up was?"

"Sort of, but you have to go slow. If you get too much momentum, you'll end up on a bumpy ride to the bottom." He took hold of her hand. "But don't worry. I won't let that happen to you."

There it was again. That sense of overwhelming safety and security she felt in his presence. She'd never thought of herself as a "little woman" who couldn't take care of herself. In fact, she'd always been the exact opposite of that. She took care of herself and everyone around her. But Colton was a caretaker, too, and he seemed to like taking care of her. Most intriguing to her, however, was how much she *liked* being cared for by him.

With other guys, she'd refused to let them open doors for her or treat her like a princess. She believed that if women were going to fight for equal treatment in their work lives, they should practice it in their personal lives as well. But now that she'd been cared for and treated like a queen by Colton Abbott, she had reason to question the veracity of those beliefs.

Sure enough, he held her hand all the way down the steep incline, preventing a few tumbles along the way. More than two hours after they'd set out, they landed back in the yard, where Sarah and Elmer were chasing each other around while they waited for Lucy and Colton to catch up.

Lucy sat gratefully on the bench outside the store and took the water bottle Colton handed her. "Those dogs make mountain hiking look as easy as you do."

"They come to work with me every day. These hills are home to them."

"What if you were to have an emergency up here? Like if you really got hurt and you were all alone?"

He sat next to her, stretching his long legs out in front of him. "I'd probably be screwed."

"Seriously."

"I'm really careful because I know a serious injury would be a problem."

"I don't like that answer."

"Sorry," he said with a sheepish grin. "It's the best one I've got."

"What if there's an emergency in your family?"

"That's only happened twice since I've been up here."

When his smile faded, Lucy almost regretted asking. But curiosity got the better of her. "What happened?"

"Landon fell off a roof during a fire once and broke his arm. It was a bad break, and he needed surgery. Hunter came up to get me." He kicked at some pine needles on the ground with the toe of his hiking boot. "The other time was when Caleb died. My dad came. I'd never seen him cry before. I'll never forget it. When I saw he was crying, I thought it was my grandfather, and my stomach dropped. And then when he said it was Caleb . . ."

Colton blew out a deep breath. "That was . . ." He looked off in the distance, lost in painful memories.

"Losing him was the most horrible thing that's ever happened to any of us. Even all these years later, I still can't bear to think about him being gone."

"I'm so sorry. It's obvious you all loved him very much."

"He was an incredible guy. Everyone loved him."

"Hannah seems really happy with Nolan."

"She is, but it took a really long time for her to get there. And for a lot of that time, Nolan waited for her."

Lucy leaned her head against his shoulder. "God, that's so sweet."

"Will you come to their wedding with me, Luce? It would be so great to have you there."

"I'd love to go. Thanks for asking me."

He slid his arm around her and held her close to him. "I know you're spun up about tomorrow and what happens next and what happened this weekend and how everything changed between us. I want you to know I'm spun up, too. I'm in this thing every bit as much as you are, and I have to believe we're going to figure it all out. Eventually. So don't give up, okay?"

"I won't." Sitting here with him in this peaceful place with the warm sunshine beating down upon them and his gorgeous dogs lying at their feet, it was hard to believe they had a single problem or challenge to confront. Everything seemed possible as long as he was sitting right next to her. What would happen once they parted company was the big question that continued to nag at her.

She blinked his front porch into focus and then sat up for a better look. "What's all over your porch?"

"Huh?"

"Look."

"Oh shit," he muttered under his breath. He got up to walk across the yard to the house, and Lucy followed him. Sensing something was going on, Elmer and Sarah came, too.

The porch was littered with coolers. There had to be at least ten of them.

"Are you having a party that you didn't tell me about?" she asked.

"Um, not exactly."

"Then what the heck is all this?"

"Um, well, now don't get all, you know . . . bent out of shape or anything, but I'd venture to guess that the word is out that I'm *injured*, and some of my friends were concerned I might be hungry. My appetite is somewhat legendary around here."

"These are all from *women*, aren't they?"

"Not all of them. I'm sure one or two are from my guy friends."

"Why do I seriously doubt that?" Lucy went up the stairs to investigate further. She flipped open the lid of the closest cooler to find a note on pink paper that was covered with lipstick kisses. "I suppose you're going to tell me *this* is from one of the guys?"

"Maybe not that one, but I bet that one over there is." The cooler he'd pointed to had seen better days.

Lucy opened the lid and found more food along with flowers and a note that had been drenched in perfume. "Definitely one of the guys."

Colton smiled sheepishly and shrugged. "What can I say? I have nice friends."

"You're a man whore, Colton Abbott."

"Now, Lucy, that is so not true."

"Does your mother know you have so many women tending to you up here?"

At the mention of his mother his aw-shucks grin faltered. "You wouldn't dare tell her. You wouldn't want her to stop cooking for me, would you? I'm a growing boy."

"What're you going to do with all this stuff, man whore?"

"Just for the record, I like when you call me *mountain man* better."

"I'm sure you do. So what are you going to do with it?"

"Um, *eat* it? This rumor of yours might be the best thing to ever happen to my always-empty belly."

She elbowed him in said belly.

"Ow!" He rubbed his midsection and pouted like the little boy she suspected he really was. "That wasn't nice."

"Neither is you having a harem to tend to you when I'm not around."

The pouty little boy morphed quickly into stormy, sexy man. *All* man. "No one will be *tending to me* when you're not around. I need you to believe me when I tell you that. Do you?"

Lucy wrapped her arms around herself. "I want to, but all these coolers make me wonder."

He came up to the bottom step, which put him nearly at her eye level. "I *need* you to believe me." He didn't touch her with anything more than his vehement blue-eyed gaze.

Staring at him staring at her, Lucy decided to believe him. She decided to believe *in* him and in them. "I believe you."

"Do you really or are you just saying that?"

"I really do."

"I don't cheat, Lucy. If I tell you you're my girlfriend, and you tell me I'm your boyfriend, then that's that. I don't need anyone else."

"Even if weeks go by between our visits? We've been lucky so far—" She didn't get to finish that statement because he kissed her, effectively shutting down her arguments. Many minutes of erotic persuasion later, he said, "I don't care if it's a week, two weeks, a month or two months between visits. If I tell you I won't betray you or us, then I mean it."

"Okay," she said softly. Maybe one day she'd regret believing in a guy who'd obviously gotten around in the past, but for right now, today, she chose to have faith.

"Now what about you? How am I supposed to know what you're up to in a city full of guys chasing after you?"

Lucy rolled her eyes at his foolishness. "The guys in that city have never chased after me, so no need to worry."

He kissed her again. "That's completely and totally their loss." More kisses, each one more intoxicating than the one before. "I said you're my girlfriend, but I haven't heard the B word back from you?"

"Which B word are you looking for? Brat? Baby? Boy toy? Or maybe boy whore? That's a good one for you."

His eyes twinkled with mirth. "Very funny. You know exactly what I'm looking for, you brat."

"Oh! Do you mean boy*friend*? You want me to call you my boyfriend?"

"I'd very much like that, as you well know."

"We'll take that under advisement and let you know before we leave tomorrow."

"You do that," he grumbled. "In the meantime, help me carry this stuff over to the ice box in the sugarhouse. And if you're really nice, I'll show you how sap becomes syrup."

She shuddered with faux excitement. "It turns me on when you talk about your sap."

"Is that right?"

"Uh-huh."

They each picked up a cooler and headed across the yard. "So when I tell you that after the boiling comes filtering of all the sugar sand and any other crap that's gotten into the sap, and then finally we bottle, that makes you hot?"

"*So* hot."

"Huh. Well, wait till I show you my woodpile. That ought to make you positively incendiary."

"I can't wait."

CHAPTER 19

———— ◆◆◆ ————

*Boiling continues as we slowly slide down the
backside of the season. The nights are not freezing
but neither are the days heating up. In town,
crocuses must be blooming, but up on the hill the
snow persists, and the buds aren't popping yet.
The brook is speaking up though—and the birds.
Always a good sign that spring is near.*

—Colton Abbott's sugaring journal, April 10

Driving across Northern Vermont the next afternoon,
Colton was tied in knots so tight his stomach ached.
He hated that he was taking Lucy to catch a flight so she
could go home to her real life. He hated that he had to go
back to his mountain without her, knowing he'd see her
everywhere he looked there.

They'd had an incredible afternoon and evening, during
which they'd eaten like kings thanks to the generosity of
his "friends." Lucy had blown him away by coming to bed
in a sexy, silky nightgown that he would think about every
night that he spent alone until he could see her again.

And the last time they'd had sex this morning . . .
They'd truly made love. At least he had. He was almost

certain he was in love with her. If the agony he felt at the thought of letting her go was any indication, he was deeply in love and getting in deeper all the time.

She'd been quiet since they left the mountain and set out for the airport in Burlington nearly an hour ago now. With only one more hour to go until he had to say good-bye to her, he was feeling more desperate by the second, needing to make sure she left feeling confident in him and their relationship.

"So I'll be down there Friday for the trade show. Hunter said I can get a hotel room."

"You can stay with me if you want."

"I'd love to stay with you, but I thought the hotel might be kind of fun."

She smiled over at him. "Yes, it probably would be fun. Let's do that."

"I want to meet your dad and Emma and Simone while I'm there. And your friends, too."

"Sure. We'll do all that."

"You sound really sad, Luce. I hate that."

"I'm sad I have to go home. I had a really fun time this weekend."

"I did, too. Except for the awful injury I sustained."

That made her laugh, which he'd hoped it would.

"Only you could end up with enough food to feed an army because of a rumor."

"They don't know it's a rumor."

"True. Just don't go proving it to anyone."

"I told you I wouldn't, and I won't."

"I know."

Long before he was ready, they arrived at the Burlington airport. They'd already agreed he'd drop her at departures, since she'd be going directly to security. Colton parked at the curb and got out to retrieve her things from the backseat.

She was already standing on the curb when he came around carrying her weekend and computer bags.

"You never used this," he said as he looped the computer bag over her shoulder.

"Turns out I had better stuff to do this weekend than work, and I'll pay for that royally this week."

"Sorry to screw you up at work."

"You didn't. It was well worth it."

He put his arms around her and leaned his forehead on hers. "This is hard, Luce. I don't want you to go."

"If it makes you feel any better, I don't want to go."

"It does make me feel better." He held on tight, breathing in the rich, sexy scent of her one last time.

"We've really screwed this up, huh?" she asked after several quiet minutes spent holding each other.

"How do you figure?"

"I never signed on for a boyfriend in Vermont."

"You used the B word."

"So I did."

"You may not have signed on for it, but I'm really, *really* glad to be your boyfriend in Vermont."

She drew back to look up at him and slayed him with the tears he saw in her eyes.

"Aw, Luce, don't cry. Please don't."

"I'm not. I won't."

He hugged her again and then kissed her, lingering for as long as he could before he had no choice but to let her go. "I'll be down Friday night for a whole week, and then we have Hannah's wedding. Lots to look forward to."

She bit her lip as if she was trying hard not to cry and nodded.

"I'll call you tonight."

"You don't have to. I know it's a hassle for you to get to a phone."

He kissed her forehead and then her lips again. "I'll call you tonight. Now go ahead before I give in to the temptation to toss you over my shoulder and drag you back to my mountain."

"You say that like it's a threat."

"I say that like I wish I could. See you Friday."

"See you then. Make sure you change the dressing on your wound yourself."

He matched her cheeky grin with one of his own. "Wouldn't dream of asking for help from anyone but you." Leaning back against his truck, he watched the gentle sway of her ass and the movement of her hair in the breeze until she stepped through the big sliding doors and disappeared into the airport. Her walk was stiffer than usual, but she'd refused to admit that she was sore from the hike up the mountain. He stood there for a minute before he pushed off the truck and walked around to the driver's side.

Buckled into the truck, he sat there for a long moment, unsettled by how truly awful he felt. Christ, what the hell was wrong with him? He'd see her in three days and they had an entire week to spend together then. There was no reason to be feeling like the world had just ended. Except that was exactly how it felt, like the sun had suddenly decided to stop shining or something equally ridiculous.

He pulled away from the curb, not really certain of his destination. He'd made plans to do some shopping while he was in Burlington, but rather than head for downtown, he found himself at the bungalow his youngest brother, Max, had rented for the summer with his girlfriend, Chloe. Max had been running himself ragged commuting between Burlington and Butler, where he worked on the mountain with Colton several days a week.

Parking in front of the house, Colton was surprised to see Max sitting on the top step, head in hands. *Uh-oh*, he thought as he got out and walked through the gate to the tiny yard. "Hey, bro."

Max looked up at him. "Hey. What're you doing over here?"

"I had to bring a friend to the airport in Burlington."

"A *friend*? Would this be the so-called mystery woman everyone is talking about?"

"Move over."

Max slid to the right to make room for Colton, who stretched his legs out in front of him and propped himself on one elbow.

"She's not such a mystery anymore. Our cover was soundly blown this weekend, first by Will and Cameron showing up at the lake house and then by Mom and Dad being at my house when I tried to bring her there to get away from the crowd at the lake."

Max laughed, but it wasn't his usual belly laugh. "Totally busted, huh?"

"Yep. Hard to keep a secret for long in this crowd."

"Well, you kept it for weeks, so props on that. Do I get to know who she is?"

"I'm surprised you haven't already heard."

"I've been a little tied up this weekend."

"I've been seeing Cameron's friend Lucy."

"Oh wow! And Cameron caught you with her at the lake? That must've been interesting."

"You could say that. It's kind of a relief that people know now. I wasn't digging all the secrecy, but it was what she wanted so I went along with it."

"Why did she want it?"

"Mostly because of Will and Cam and giving them a chance to get settled. Or something like that."

"So you like this girl, huh?"

"Yeah, I like her. I hated taking her to the airport just now. We had a really great weekend."

"I'm glad someone did."

"How's Chloe feeling? I heard she was really sick."

"She was. She's better now."

"Then what's wrong?"

"What *isn't* wrong?" Max ran his fingers through hair that was much lighter and longer than Colton's. "This isn't working out at all."

"You and Chloe?"

"Yeah. It's a fucking mess. All we do is fight. Nothing I do is good enough. I say the wrong things. I do the wrong things. I'm getting to the point where I don't even like her anymore, which makes me feel like shit to even say since she's pregnant with my kid."

"Just because she's pregnant with your kid doesn't mean you have to be in a relationship that makes you miserable."

Max blew out a deep breath and shook his head. "I don't know what to do."

"I have an idea that might give you a break from it all. I'm going to New York next week, and it would help me out if you could hold down the fort on the mountain while I'm gone. It would give you an excuse to get out of here for a while and give you both some breathing room."

"Does it make me an asshole if I say that's the best offer I've had in a long time?"

"Nah, it doesn't make you an asshole and trust me, I'd tell you if you were."

Max barked out a laugh that was much more in keeping with the way he usually laughed. "I have no doubt you would."

"Look, just because she's your baby's mama doesn't mean she's it forever, you know? As long as you take good care of her and the baby, you're holding up your end of the deal. Nowhere is it written that you and she have to make a go of it romantically to be good parents to the kid."

"I know, and I've been thinking a lot about that lately. The thing is . . . Before the baby and everything, I thought she might be my forever. It was that good between us. Now . . ." He shook his head. "It's a goddamned mess."

"I don't know much about pregnant women, but from what I've heard it does a number on their hormones and emotions and everything else. You probably ought to let it ride until after the baby comes before you make any big decisions. I'd hate to see you have regrets later."

"That's true." Max glanced over at him. "When did you get so wise anyway?"

"I've always been wise. You've just never noticed before."

"Oh my God, I think I just threw up a little."

"Ha ha."

"So if I wanted to take on more hours on the mountain, you'd be cool with that?"

"I'd love it, but when Lucy's there, you have to stay at Mom's."

"You'd really make me stay at Mom's?"

"If it meant being alone with Lucy, yes, I would. And besides, Mom will cook for you."

"That's true."

"Let me ask you this . . . If a guy happened to be in the market for a cell phone, where would he get one around here?" Unlike most of his siblings, Max had had a phone for years.

Max stared at him as if Colton had just told him he'd seen Bigfoot in Lake Champlain. "Are you freaking kidding me? *You* want a cell phone? Holy shit! You must be in love!"

Colton resisted the sudden urge to squirm as Max tossed the L word around. "Shut the fuck up and just tell me where to get one."

"Better yet, I'll take you. *This* I've got to see."

"I don't think I want you there."

"Too bad. I'm going. Let me just tell Chloe I'm leaving." Max went inside, leaving Colton alone to ponder whether he was in love with Lucy. He still wasn't sure, but if the shitty way he'd felt watching her walk away from him was any indication, he was well on his way.

"Let's go," Max said brusquely as he came back outside.

"You just had *another* fight?" Colton asked.

"Everything is a fight. Every. Fucking. Thing."

Colton followed Max down the sidewalk to the truck. "Dude, that's no way to live."

"You're telling me."

"Go over to the mountain while I'm away. Take some time off from the situation. It might do you both some good."

"I'm going to. Even though I feel like I should be here, clearly she doesn't want me here, so I'm probably doing more harm than good."

"She can call you if she needs you."

"Yeah." Max turned to him. "Thanks for listening and everything."

"No problem. Sorry it's such a shitty situation."

"So am I."

They rode in silence into downtown Burlington, where Max directed Colton to a store that sold cell phones.

"How are you planning to charge this phone on your mountain anyway?"

"Aw shit."

Max howled with laughter. "You're such a dumbass."

"Screw you."

"I can show you where to get a generator, too."

"Fuck," Colton said with a groan. This whole thing was getting way too complicated for his liking.

"Welcome to the twenty-first century, bro. Allow me to be your tour guide."

"I hate you right now."

"Whatever. You'll *love* me when you're talking to your lady later."

"If you say so."

"I say so."

By three thirty that afternoon, Lucy was home at her cozy Soho apartment, and all she wanted to do was sleep. The muscles in her legs were so sore from the hike up the mountain that she wanted to cry from the pain that she'd tried to keep hidden from Colton. She didn't want him to think she was a total out-of-shape mess, even if she was. Curled up on the sofa, she tried not to think about the piles of work she'd let slide during the fantastic weekend in Vermont. She tried not to think about Colton and the many ways he'd turned her world upside down during said weekend.

Try as she might not to think about him, however, he filled her every thought.

Her cell phone rang, and she thought about ignoring it,

but she reached for it on the coffee table and saw it was Cameron, so she took the call.

"Hey," she said.

"How's it going? Are you back in the city?"

"Just now, yeah. What about you? Still at the lake?"

"No, we got home last night. We took yesterday off, but we had to work today."

"Good time?"

"Great time, but I didn't call to talk about me. I want to hear how the rest of your visit went. What did you think of Colton's mountain?"

"I loved it."

"You did? Really? I wasn't expecting you to say that."

"Why not?"

"Come on, Luce. It's me you're talking to. I know how you are about your hot showers and your modern conveniences."

"That doesn't mean I can't do without them for a day or two here and there. It was fun to rough it a little, and it's not like we did without much. There was hot water and hot coffee and a hot man. What else do I need?"

"He is hot. I'll give you that."

"Hands and eyes off. You've got your own hot Abbott brother."

"Yes, I do, and I have no interest in anyone but him. However, I have eyes that work perfectly well, and Colton Abbott is hot."

"So I've noticed. Apparently, every woman in Butler has noticed, too."

"We heard the weirdest thing when we got back to town yesterday."

"Let me guess. Something about an accident with the axe?"

"Yes!"

"That might've been my doing."

"Oh, this I've got to hear!"

By the time Lucy finished relaying the story of the rumor she'd started, Cameron was laughing so hard she wasn't making any noise. "Then the food started arriving from his fan club. I'll bet one of them is there now tending to his festering 'wound.'" The thought of another woman tending to him made Lucy want to scratch the eyes out of the imaginary woman's head, which was certainly a first. Jealousy was an entirely new experience.

"Are you really worried about that? How did you guys leave things?"

"No, I'm not really worried. We're tossing around the BF/GF words."

"Oh my God! That's awesome!"

"I'm glad you're happy about it."

"Aren't you?"

"I am . . ."

"Why do I hear a *but* in there?"

"When I'm with him, everything is great. Everything seems possible. The minute we're apart, I start second-guessing the whole thing and wondering how in the world this could ever really work. Especially after yesterday."

"What happened yesterday?"

"He showed me his mountain and told me how he makes the syrup. I could really see how much he loves what he does. I mean really, really loves it."

"I saw that, too, the first time I was there and he showed me the sugarhouse and everything."

"That's his life, Cameron. His calling. He wouldn't be *him* without it. And I can't leave my dad and Emma and Simone. Not to mention the business . . . I just can't."

"I know," Cam said with a sigh. "I told Will that this weekend. I'm sorry it's all so messy."

"It is what it is."

"Do you love him, Luce?"

"Oh God, don't ask me that after I just told you how hopeless it is."

"That's the most important question. Why wouldn't I ask it?"

"I don't know if I love him. How am I supposed to know that?"

"Want to hear the questions I asked myself when I was trying to figure out how I felt about Will?"

"Sure. Why not?"

"Is he all I think about? Can I not wait to spend more time with him? And is it impossible to keep my hands to myself when he's around?"

To her eternal mortification, Lucy broke down into gut-wrenching sobs.

"Aw, shit, Luce. I wish I was there so I could hug you."

"I wish you were, too."

"It might seem too easy for me to say it's all going to be fine, but it will be. If it's meant to be, you guys will figure it out just like we did."

"I can't see that happening for us." Lucy wiped the dampness from her face. "This is so not me. Crying over a guy. Ugh."

Cameron, that bitch, laughed. "Welcome to the club, my friend."

"What club? What're you talking about?"

"It's *love*, and it's wonderful, maddening, frustrating, amazing . . ."

"I think you've been spending too much time with Will and his magic wand to be objective."

"Perhaps," Cameron said with a chuckle. "His wand is quite magical—and never more so than this weekend. There must be something in the water at that lake house."

New tears fell from Lucy's eyes when memories of Colton's magic wand chose that moment to remind her of the bliss she'd known in his arms. "Stop."

"I've been where you are, Luce," Cameron said softly. "Everything seems hopeless except for what you feel for him. I get it. The best advice I can give you is to let it ride for a while. Nothing has to be decided today or tomorrow or next week or even next month."

"That's true. I just wish I didn't feel so shitty when I'm not with him, which is most of the time."

"Now you know how I felt when I left Will to come back to the city."

"Yeah, and I feel bad because I didn't get it then. But I do now, so I'm sorry if I wasn't sensitive enough to how miserable you were."

"You were fine, and you might not want to hear it, but you sound an awful lot like a woman in love."

"I'm not in love."

"No?"

"No. Definitely not." The phone line beeped with an incoming call. "Hang on. I'm getting a beep. Oh hey, it's Emma. I need to take this. Call you this week?"

"Please do, and hang in there, okay?"

"I will. Love you."

"Love you, too."

CHAPTER 20

—◄►—

How's the sap running? Choose your adverb:
swimmingly, phenomenally, copiously, amply,
abundantly, generously, very well indeed. In
other words, the tanks are close to overflowing;
twice as much sap is coming in per hour as the
reverse osmosis can handle. It will run all night.

—Colton Abbott's sugaring journal, April 13

Lucy took the call from her sister, somewhat relieved to
be spared any further speculation as to whether she
was in love with Colton. "Hi, Em."

"Hey, are you home?"

"Just got in."

"How was the weekend?"

"Fine."

"Still not ready to spill the beans?"

Since his family knew all about them it probably was
time to tell hers. "I might be more ready than I was."

"Good. Come over for pizza with me, Simone and Dad.
Invite Troy if you want."

Lucy had a lot to do after being away for four days, but

the idea of spending hours alone with her own thoughts wasn't very appealing. "What time?"

"Around six."

"I'll be there."

"Simone will be excited. She's been missing her Auntie Lu on the weekends."

A pang of guilt struck in the vicinity of her heart. "Tell her I'll make it up to her."

"I'll do no such thing. She's already a spoiled monster as it is."

"She is not! She's an angel."

"We'll agree to disagree. See you soon!"

"See you." Lucy ended the call with Emma and sent a text to their friend Troy, inviting him to Emma's for dinner.

He replied right away. Would love to. I've been missing my friends lately.

Once again Lucy felt guilty about the people she'd been neglecting while she ran off every weekend to meet Colton. Her friends and family had propped her up after her mother died and had been so supportive since Cameron decided to move. They deserved more from her than weeks of silence and mystery.

She spent the next couple of hours doing laundry and wading through the swamp that was her e-mail inbox. It had exploded in her absence with messages from clients, potential clients, past clients and employees seeking guidance on ongoing projects. All the activity should've made her ecstatic, especially when she thought about how hard she and Cameron had worked to begin the business and how badly they'd struggled during the economic downturn.

Things were flush again. They were busier than ever. And she couldn't have cared less. "This is bad," she whispered to herself and her empty apartment. "Really bad." How could one weekend—albeit an amazingly awesome weekend—totally screw her mojo?

It couldn't. That was all there was to it. Tomorrow she would hit it hard and get back to work with a vengeance.

She'd had two extra days off and had three days to make it count at work before Colton arrived for a week in the city.

She'd see him in three days. There was no way she was spending the next three days moping around like a love-sick puppy. She wasn't lovesick or any other kind of sick.

Three hours later, she was sitting on the floor of her niece's pink bedroom, dressing and undressing the American Girl dolls she'd bought for Simone for Christmas and taking orders from the tiny princess who had her firmly wrapped around her little finger.

The voices of Emma, their dad and Troy filtered in from the living room, chatting away as they watched a Yankee game and waited for the pizza Emma had ordered to arrive.

"Put this one on Rebecca," Simone directed, handing Lucy a red velvet gown.

"I like that with her dark hair."

"That color doesn't look good with our hair, does it?" Simone asked. She'd been either blessed or cursed—depending on who you asked—with the exact same auburn curls as her Aunt Lucy.

"It's not our best shade," Lucy agreed. She'd made it a priority to prepare her niece for life as a redhead to the best of her ability. Whereas Lucy tended to be a somewhat mild-mannered redhead, Simone had gotten the more fiery personality that often accompanied red locks, and Lucy adored every feisty inch of the little girl with the big personality.

The doorbell ringing in the other room had Simone bolting from the bedroom.

"I guess that means playtime is over, Rebecca," Lucy said to the doll as she placed her carefully on Simone's bed. Those "toys" cost an arm, a leg *and* a foot.

After the pizza had been devoured and Simone sent off to take a shower, Lucy felt three sets of eyes homing in on her and sensed the inquisition she'd been putting off for weeks now could no longer be avoided.

Deciding a preemptive strike was in order, she put her

wineglass on the coffee table. "His name is Colton Abbott, and yes, he's Will's brother. I like him. He likes me. We have fun together, and no, I'm not moving. Not now or ever, and he knows that. He'll be here next week on business, and I'd like you all to meet him as long as you promise not to turn a very nice molehill into a mountain of epic proportions."

"Did you just refer to your boyfriend as a molehill?" Emma asked.

"It was a *metaphor.*"

Troy sighed and shook his head. "What's with those Abbott guys anyway?" He'd been less than thrilled when Cameron decided to move to Vermont to live with Will.

The words *magic wand* danced through Lucy's mind, but since her dad was watching her with the wise gray eyes that didn't miss much of anything, Lucy refrained from sharing the thought. "They're nice guys."

"Is he as nice to look at as Will is?" Emma asked. "Will is *dreamy.*"

"Oh barf," Troy said. "Dreamy. What guy wants to be called that?"

Emma stuck her tongue out at him. "You'd probably love to have a woman call you that."

"Right," Troy said. "Pardon me if I pass on that."

"Colton is every bit as nice to look at as Will is," Lucy interjected when she got the chance. "Maybe even more so."

"Oh, damn," Emma said. "This I've got to see."

"He's got four single brothers you need to see, too," Lucy said with a wink for her sister.

"No!" Troy said, startling them with his vehemence. "No more with these Abbott guys! You say you aren't moving, but you probably will. You're just saying what we want to hear."

"That is *not* true, and I resent the implication that I'm placating you. I have no plans to move, and he is well aware of that."

"Seems I've heard that song once before."

"You're being kind of a jerk, Troy," Emma said.

"So what if I am? I'm not supposed to care that my best friends are getting involved with guys who live six hours from me?"

"I'm going to cut you some slack." Lucy rested her hand on Troy's denim-covered leg. "But only because I've been where you are when Cameron was all gaga over Will and trying to pretend otherwise for our sakes. I know how that feels as a friend, and I don't want to make you feel that way. I'm not Cameron. I'm not gaga or any other thing. I'm having fun with a nice guy. That's all it is. All it's ever going to be."

"Sorry," Troy muttered. "I didn't mean to be a jerk."

"Yeah, you did," Lucy said with a grin for him. "But don't worry. We're used to it. We know how you can be."

He scowled at her and then smiled, which set things right between them.

She truly did get how he felt, having just been through losing Cameron from her daily life at work and at play. It wasn't easy, and she didn't blame Troy for being concerned about it happening again.

"You haven't said a word, Dad," Lucy said when she'd pacified Troy. "That's not like you." Ray Mulvaney always had an opinion about what his girls were up to and wasn't shy about sharing those opinions. His wiry hair was all gray now and his face weather-beaten from years of working in construction before he finally retired a few years ago.

"Not much to say. Yet. I'll reserve judgment until I meet this Colton Abbott fellow."

"You are in so much trouble," Emma declared.

"I'm not afraid of him," Lucy said, even though she was a tiny bit afraid of what her dad might think of Colton. He'd pushed both his daughters to go to college and put a lot of value on education. Colton hadn't gone to college, but he was a hardworking guy like her father had been. Surely that would count for something, right?

"You'll bring him home while he's in town? I'll make dinner."

Even though he'd asked a question, they all knew it was a statement and not a question.

"Of course. He wants to meet you. All of you."

She stayed to tuck in Simone, who had no interest in going to bed. "Do you have a boyfriend, Auntie Lu?"

"What makes you ask that?"

"You've been going away a lot on the weekends, and Mommy said it's because you have a boyfriend."

Lucy rubbed noses with Simone, which made her niece giggle. "Mommy has a big mouth, but don't tell her I told you that."

"So you don't have a boyfriend?"

The word *boyfriend* reminded Lucy of how badly Colton had wanted her to refer to him as such. "Yes, I guess I do. His name is Colton, and he's really handsome."

"Do you have a picture of him?"

"I sure do." She scrolled through the photos on her phone until she found a particular favorite from two weekends ago. "That's him."

"He's really cute."

"Yes, he is." The sight of his face on her screen did crazy things to her insides and made her miss him fiercely.

"Are you going to move away like Cameron did?" Simone's bottom lip fluttered and her big blue eyes filled with tears that broke Lucy's heart.

"No, baby. I'm not going anywhere. How could I move away when you're here?"

Simone sat up and wrapped her chubby arms around Lucy's neck. "I don't want you to move away."

"I'm not going anywhere, sweetheart. I promise. I may go to visit Colton in Vermont, where Cam lives now, but I'm not leaving you. Okay?"

"Okay."

Lucy settled her in bed and kissed both cheeks as well as the end of her nose, finishing with a noisy kiss on Simone's lips. "Love you."

"Love you, too, Lulu."

Hearing the nickname Simone had come up with when she couldn't say *Lucy* as a baby set off a tidal wave of memories. Simone hadn't called her that in years.

She closed Simone's door and discovered Emma waiting in the hall for her.

"I hope you're not making promises you can't keep," Emma said.

"I would never do that to her, and you should know better than to imply otherwise."

"I do. I'm sorry. After Cameron moved, she's worried that other people are going to leave, too."

"Well, I'm not." Lucy gathered up her purse and left two twenties on the table for the pizza she knew Emma couldn't afford. "So you can both quit your fretting."

"Luce . . ."

"What?"

"Don't leave mad. As much as we'd both hate to see you go, we'd never get in the way of your happiness."

"I know that." Lucy hugged her sister. "I'll talk to you tomorrow." Wound up after the intense conversations with Emma and Simone, Lucy took her time walking the ten blocks between their place and hers. Unlike most New Yorkers who fled the city in July and August, Lucy loved summer in the city. She loved the sidewalk cafés and the people out and about. She loved the flowers in window boxes and the leafy trees planted between concrete slabs. The frenetic city took on more of a languid pace in the summer. It was too hot to rush anywhere, so people tended to take their time in a way they didn't the rest of the year.

Summer in New York suited her. *Life* in New York suited her. It was where she belonged, and nothing—not even a sweet, sexy mountain man—would ever change that.

As he'd feared, his mountain looked very different to Colton post-Lucy. After spending the afternoon with Max and leaving his younger brother in slightly better spirits than he'd found him, Colton drove home from Burlington with his new toys still in their bags and boxes.

Normally, the sound of silence didn't bother him. He usually relished it after growing up in the madness that was the Abbotts' barn. But now the silence was deafening, and it only got worse when he arrived home to more coolers on his porch and no Lucy to keep him entertained. He saw her everywhere, from the bench outside the retail store to the tiny shower stall in the bathhouse to the bed that was still rumpled from their earlier lovemaking.

He never went back to bed during the day, but today he couldn't resist the need to see if her scent still clung to his pillows. It did, and the memories it invoked hit him like a fist to the gut, making him moan from the misery of having to let her go.

Unnerved by his unusual behavior, Sarah and Elmer joined him on the bed, nuzzling him from either side and trying to draw him out to engage with them.

"I'm okay, guys." Colton scratched their ears. "I miss Lucy."

Sarah's whimper let him know she missed Lucy, too.

In all the years he'd lived alone on the mountain, he'd never been lonely. Sure, he had a lot of visitors, and his family was close enough for company if and when he needed it, but this kind of loneliness was all new to him. The only one who could make it better was six hours away in a city he'd never even been to.

Sarah and Elmer finally persuaded him to get up and get on with storing the food that had arrived in his absence and getting some work done before darkness set in. He made himself wait until close to ten o'clock before he withdrew the new phone from its box and fired it up, trying to remember all the things Max had taught him about how to use it.

Max had programmed Lucy's number into the list of favorites, but Colton did some fumbling before he found that list under the phone icon. His brother had taken great delight in making fun of Colton's ineptitude earlier. Nothing worse than a little brother who knew more about something than you did.

Colton finally figured out how to put through the call and then waited with far more anticipation than he should've been feeling to see if she would answer a call from a number she didn't recognize. Max had warned him about that possibility. Hopefully, the 802 area code would tell her it was him.

By the fourth ring he was starting to worry she wasn't going to take the call. And then she answered, sounding breathless and rushed. "Hello?"

"Hey, it's me."

"Oh, hi. I didn't recognize the number."

"It's a new number. My number."

"*You* got a *phone*?"

"I did."

"What brought this on?"

"You did. I wanted to be able to talk to you any time I wanted to—or any time you wanted to."

"Wow. So how does it feel to join the twenty-first century?"

"Don't start on me. I've already taken a year's worth of abuse from Max today. He was my technology consultant."

"I can't believe you actually got a phone."

"Believe it."

"That's really sweet of you."

"I'm a sweet kind of guy."

The comment made her laugh, and the sound of her laughter, even over the phone hundreds of miles away, made him hard. "How are things in the city?"

"Same as ever. Hot and smelly, but I love it. I got to see my dad, Emma and Simone tonight as well as my friend Troy, so it was a fun night."

"Troy? Who is this guy?"

"A friend of mine and Cameron's. One of our best friends."

"So wait, you're allowed to have *friends* but I'm not?"

"My *friend* is not a friend with benefits and never has been, so there you have the difference between my friend and yours."

His smile stretched across his face. God, he loved to provoke her. What did that say about him? "I miss you. It sucks here without you. Even Sarah and Elmer are down in the dumps."

"I miss you guys, too. It was really fun being on your mountain. I'm glad I got to see it."

"I'm glad you did, too."

"And the lake house was great. That's an amazing spot."

"It was much more amazing before Will and Cameron showed up and ruined everything."

She laughed again, and he discovered he'd do just about anything to make her laugh. "I'm glad they know about us."

"I am, too."

"I told my family tonight. About you."

Colton perked right up at that news. "Is that right? What'd they have to say?"

"My dad said I'm bringing you to Queens for dinner while you're here."

"He said that, did he?"

"Yeah, said versus asked. You get the difference."

"Uh-huh. Is he scary?"

"No!" she said with a laugh. "Not at all. He's just protective of his girls."

"I think I'll like him. Will I get to meet Emma and Simone, too?"

"Absolutely. Simone already told me she wants to meet my boyfriend."

"So you're throwing the B word around, huh?"

"My boyfriend told me I had to call him that."

"Damn straight you do. What about *Troy*? Do I get to meet him, too?"

"Not if you're going to act like a jealous ass around him."

"I'll do my best to behave."

"I've seen your best efforts to behave, so you'll pardon me if I'm skeptical."

"That hurts me, Luce. Deeply."

They chatted for more than an hour about nothing in particular until his phone began to beep with a low battery warning.

"So what's your plan to charge that bad boy on your mountain?" she asked.

"I bought a small generator for just that purpose."

After a brief pause, she said, "You brought electricity to your mountain for *me*?"

"I sure did."

"I'm deeply honored by the effort."

"It's no big deal," he said, even though he was pleased by her reaction.

"It's a very big deal, Colton, and don't think I'm not seeing that."

"This situation is tough enough without having a way to keep in touch between visits. It was a small price to pay to hear your voice at the end of every day."

"Colton," she said with a deep sigh. "You know just what to say to make a girl all fluttery inside."

"Fluttery, huh? That sounds promising."

"Mmm. Indeed."

The extended M sound reminded him of her lips vibrating against his shaft, which got even harder. *"Lucy . . ."*

"Yes?"

"Don't act all innocent with me, like you don't know what you do to me even over the phone."

"I can't help that you have the self-control of a fifteen-year-old boy."

"Damn it, the phone is about to die, but we'll discuss my inner fifteen-year-old tomorrow."

"Looking forward to it."

"Me, too. Talk to you tomorrow. Night, Luce."

"Night, Colton."

He couldn't bring himself to end the call or the connection.

"This is where you hit the End button."

"Don't wanna."

"Your phone is going to die."

"That's okay." He listened to her breathe until the phone went dead in his hand. Lying on his bed, staring up at the ceiling as Sarah and Elmer slept on either side of him, Colton decided the purchase of the phone and generator was the best money he'd spent on anything. Ever.

CHAPTER 21

———◆◆———

*Any leftover thoughts of the best run of the year—
yes, that's what it was—dissipated by nine o'clock
this morning when a torrent of ice like you read
about belched out of the main lines. If anything
indicates the end of the season, it is mucky
pumps, tanks and lines.*

—Colton Abbott's sugaring journal, April 15

T he next morning, Colton made an effort to get back to
his routine on the mountain. He tended to some
record keeping, hiked up the mountain to check on trees
that had shown signs of a possible blight earlier in the summer and added another cord to the growing woodpile.

By noon, however, he was hungry and in bad need of
someone to talk to about all the shit that was in his head.
He gave careful consideration to several possible people,
including both his parents, his sister Hannah and his
brother Hunter, all of whom had opinions Colton normally
trusted implicitly. However, Will had the best perspective
on Colton's situation, having recently been through it
himself.

And since Colton needed perspective, he went looking

for his second-oldest brother. He parked in front of the store and was halfway up the back stairs that led to the offices when he met Charley coming down.

"What brings you into town on a Wednesday?" his sister asked.

"I'm looking for Will, if you must know."

"He's across the street at the diner having lunch."

When Colton heard the words *diner* and *lunch*, his stomach let out a huge grumble. "Okay, I'll look for him over there."

"So, you and Lucy, huh?"

"Yeah, what's it to you?"

"Nothing."

Charley could be such a pain in the ass when she wanted to be. "Great. See ya." He turned to head back down the stairs.

"Are you going to move there?"

Colton stopped in his tracks and turned to look up at her. "No plans to move."

"Then she's coming here?"

"That's not happening either."

"So what're you going to do, then?"

"Who knows? For now, we're having fun and not worrying too much about the future."

"Well, good luck with that."

"What's that supposed to mean?"

"I'd hate to see you get hurt when she gets bored and moves on to someone more convenient, Colton."

Her words sent an arrow of fear straight to all his insecurities where Lucy was concerned, especially since she'd told him herself that losing interest had been a problem for her in the past. "Thanks for that cheery thought. Appreciate it."

"I'm sorry. I don't mean to be a downer. Just be careful, okay?"

"I will and thanks for the concern, but it's all good. Nothing to worry about."

"See you later."

"See ya." He trotted down the stairs, the weight of Charley's worries accompanying him across Elm Street to the diner, where he found Will and Cameron having lunch with his grandfather. For a second he was torn about whether he wanted all three of them in his business, but then his gramps caught sight of him and waved him over.

Elmer slid over to make room for Colton on his side of the booth. "This is a nice surprise."

Colton gave his grandfather a one-armed squeeze. Elmer Stillman was one of his all-time favorite people. "For me, too."

"What brings you off the mountain on a Wednesday?" Will asked.

"Am I so regimented that I can't deviate from the schedule without everyone wondering why?"

After a heartbeat of a pause, Elmer and Will both said, "Yes," making Cameron giggle.

"I take it you're kind of predictable," she said with a kind smile.

"Clearly, I need to shake things up if everyone thinks they know me so well," Colton said.

"What is that in your shirt pocket?" Cameron asked with a shriek that caught the attention of diners all around them.

Colton placed his hand over his chest and realized she meant the phone. He withdrew it from his pocket and placed it on the table.

"Oh. My. God," Will said. "This is worse than I thought."

Cameron picked up the phone and programmed her number into it before Colton had a chance to ask her what she was doing. "There." She slid it across the table to him. "Now you have *two* numbers, interestingly, both of them New York numbers."

Colton scowled at her, which only made her laugh.

Megan appeared at the table, casting a frosty glare at Cameron, who smiled sweetly at the waitress. "Something to drink?" she asked Colton.

"A Coke would be great, thanks, and a turkey club."

Megan turned and walked away.

"Was it something I said?" Colton asked.

"Nope," Cameron replied as she took a drink of her soda. "All her hatred is for me."

"For *you*?" Colton couldn't imagine anyone hating Cameron. She was so damned nice to everyone. "What the hell did you do?"

She used her thumb to point to Will. "I cast a spell on him and got him to fall in love with me."

"Sorry," Colton said, plopping a straw into the Coke the busboy delivered. "Still not getting it."

"Apparently," Will said, clearing his throat and seeming embarrassed by the whole thing, "Megan has had a, um, a crush on me for a, um, a while now."

Cameron spun halfway around in her seat to stare at her boyfriend. "A *while*? More like forever, and it wasn't a *crush*. In her mind, it was full-blown *love*."

"Which I have never encouraged."

Cameron leaned in. "And the kicker of it all is that Hunter has it bad for Megan."

"Hunter as in my brother Hunter?" Colton asked, stupefied by this revelation. *Hunter and Megan?* No way.

"One and the same."

"How does she know all this?" Colton asked Will.

"It's her special gift. Abbott 101."

"Damn, I need to get off my mountain more often. I miss out on all the good stuff up there." He watched Megan hustle around the diner, interacting with customers and staff. "I'm not sure I see her with Hunter."

"A wise man once said that a fool in love makes no sense to anyone but the fool," Elmer said.

"I like that one," Cameron said with a warm smile for Elmer. "Can I write that down?"

"It's all yours, honey."

Colton had so many things he wanted to ask them about his own situation, but the words were frozen on his tongue, stuck on the embarrassment of having to ask how he'd know if he was in love with Lucy. If he had to ask, maybe that was a good sign that he wasn't.

"Colton?"

Cameron nudged him out of the contemplative state he'd slipped into. "Sorry. Did you say something?"

"We asked how the rest of your weekend with Lucy went."

"Good. Great."

"Ohhh," Cameron said, "that's what she said, too."

"Is it? She did?" Ugh! Could he sound any more pathetic?

Cameron laughed at his distress. "Yes, she did. She said she really enjoyed seeing your mountain and learning about how you make syrup. She loved it."

"That's good," Colton said, aware of Will watching him intently from across the table.

"She said you're going there for a week on Friday."

"Yeah."

"Wait till you see New York, bro," Will said. "It's unreal. You won't believe how crazy it is."

"I'm looking forward to it." He was far more looking forward to a week with Lucy, but he didn't share that.

"So are you *in love*?" Cameron asked with a goofy grin.

The unexpected question knocked the wind out of him for a second. But he also recognized the opening Cameron had given him. "I don't know." He looked to her and then Will. "How would I even know that?"

Will laughed, and for a second Colton thought his brother was laughing at him. Then he realized he was laughing at himself and sharing the amusement with Cameron.

"Your brother had the same problem not all that long ago," Cameron said. "He wasn't recognizing the symptoms for what they were."

"Give him your list," Will said to her.

Cameron ticked the items off on her fingers. "She's all you think about. You can't wait to spend more time with her, and you can't seem to keep your hands to yourself when she's around."

Colton's palms felt sweaty and his heart beat fast as he

realized all those things applied to him where Lucy was concerned.

"Oh boy," Elmer said, taking a close look at Colton. "Looks like he's caught the love bug."

Cameron reached across the table to cover Colton's hands with her own. "If it's any consolation, I know Lucy is grappling with many of the same feelings."

It was a huge consolation, but before Colton could say so, Megan appeared at the table carrying two plates laden with food. She stared at Cameron and Colton's joined hands. "So one brother isn't enough for you? Now you're after him, too?"

"Ease up, Megan," Will said somewhat sharply.

Megan's face fell, and her eyes filled.

Cameron pulled her hands back so Megan could put the plates on the table.

The two plates landed with a clatter, and Megan scurried off. The busboy delivered the other two meals.

"You've broken her heart," Cameron said to Will as she stole one of his fries.

"Enough is enough. She needs to leave you alone."

As he devoured his turkey club, Colton was grateful for the diversion Megan's jealousy had created because he was still reeling from hearing Cameron's list and his grandfather's comment about having been bitten by the love bug. Was that true? Did that explain the overwhelming sense of malaise that had overtaken him since she left?

Elmer nudged him. "You okay, buddy?"

"Yeah, just thinking."

"Save a couple of minutes for me after lunch."

Colton wiped a smudge of ketchup off his lip. "Sure."

When they finished their lunch, Will swiped the check off the table and got up to pay. Colton noticed him speaking with Megan, who looked at him worshipfully as she nodded at whatever he was saying. "Looks like he's making up with her," Colton said, nodding toward the register.

Cameron turned in her seat to check it out and then quickly turned back around when Will returned to the table. "What was that about?" she asked him.

"I asked Megan to cut out the hostility toward you. I told her it was annoying me."

Cameron's eyes lit up with pleasure. "You really said that?"

"Yeah, I really said that. She's got no reason to be hostile to you. There was never anything between us, which I just reminded her."

"Whoa," Colton said. "You came right out and said that?"

"Among other things."

"What other things?" Elmer asked.

"I mentioned she might be directing her attention toward the wrong Abbott brother."

"Oh, jeez," Colton said. "Thanks a lot. Now it's open season on the other six of us."

"I meant Hunter, you fool," Will said.

"Did you actually mention his name to her?" Colton asked.

"Um, no, I just said she ought to pay attention to one of my brothers."

"Idiot."

"I was trying to help him out," Will said.

"Your intentions were good, William," Elmer said with a patronizing smile.

"Exactly," Will said with a pointed look for Colton.

"I'm out of here before she thinks you meant me," Colton said. "Gramps, can I walk you to your car?"

"That'd be great. Thank you for lunch, Will."

"Yeah," Colton said. "Thanks, Will." He hadn't gotten the one-on-one time he'd wanted with his brother, but he felt a little less wound up than he'd been when he came down off the mountain. And of course, the food had helped, too. Food always made things better. "Where'd you park?" Colton asked his grandfather.

"Behind the store."

They walked to the crosswalk in front of Nolan's garage and waited for a chance to cross.

"Looks like we've got some company," Elmer said, nodding to Fred the moose, who strolled down the middle of Elm Street without a care in the world. Accustomed to his frequent visits, motorists simply waited for him to pass before continuing on their way.

"He scared the living hell out of Lucy up on the mountain," Colton said, relaying the story of her introduction to Fred.

Elmer laughed so hard he had tears in his eyes. "I suppose the old guy can be somewhat intimidating if you haven't yet made his acquaintance."

"Lucy was totally freaked out, to say the least."

"I like her," Elmer said, hooking his arm through Colton's as they crossed the street.

"I like her, too."

"I couldn't help but notice at dinner the other day that you rarely take your eyes off her when she's in the room."

"Really? I do? I mean I don't?"

"Uh-huh. After you left, your dad and I agreed that you seem positively smitten."

"Smitten. Hmm, is that so?"

"Yep. And she seems equally so. Had her eyes on you much of the time, too."

Hearing that, Colton was filled with unreasonable hope that was quickly dashed when he recalled all the reasons it might never work between them.

"I would've thought you'd be happier to have found someone special."

"I am happy. When I'm with her. When I'm not with her . . . Not so happy."

"Absence makes the heart grow fonder," Elmer reminded him.

"So far all it's done is make me crazy."

"That's because you're in love." When Colton began to protest, Elmer held up his hand to stop him. "You're in love with her, or you wouldn't feel so unsettled when you're not with her."

Colton sagged against his grandfather's small pickup truck. "I didn't mean for that to happen."

Elmer replied with a loud bark of laughter. "Welcome

to the club, my friend." He stood next to Colton, leaning on the truck. "Did I ever tell you that when I met your grandmother, she was dating my cousin?"

"*What?* No!"

"Yep. You want to talk about torture. Here was this absolutely lovely gal who made my heart beat fast and my tongue get tied up in knots every time I tried to talk to her, and she was running around to dances and parties with my cousin. I'd always been close to him, but suddenly I was having murderous thoughts about him."

"So what happened?"

"She told him she fancied me."

"She actually said that to him?"

Elmer's eyes shone with pride and pleasure from the memory of the wife he'd adored. "She actually did."

"How did he take it?"

"He punched me in the mouth. That's how I found out she'd chosen me."

Colton couldn't believe he'd never heard this story before.

"But then I told him I hadn't encouraged her nor had I stolen her from him as he'd implied, and he backed down. I was her choice. There was nothing much he could do about that."

"Did he still speak to you after all of this?"

"Oh yeah. We didn't let it fester. He went on to marry someone he was much more suited to, and they were married for fifty-some years. The four of us were great friends." Elmer seemed a million miles away. "I'll never forget that day. I went to her house with my lip still bleeding to ask her if what he'd told me was true. Had she really chosen me?"

Colton hung on his grandfather's every word, fascinated and riveted.

"She said, 'Yes, I chose you, but I'm not going to keep you if you're going to be working things out with your fists.' I told her I had been on the receiving end of a fist in this case, and the fat lip was the price I'd had to pay to clear the way to her. She liked that. We were together from then on. Got married a couple months later."

"I love that story, Gramps. Thanks for sharing it with me."

"I love it, too. It's proof that true love will always win out no matter what obstacles might stand in the way."

True love will always win out. God, what a comforting thought that was. "I think I do love her." For some reason, saying the words out loud felt incredibly freeing.

"Of course you do. She's a great gal, full of spunk and personality and incredibly beautiful, too. Two of you have some things to work out, no question about that. But I have faith in you—and in her. You'll figure it out."

"You're pretty good at this free advice thing, you know that?"

"I've been in this business a long time, son. I should hope I'm good at it by now." His straight face made his grandson laugh.

"This helped. Thanks."

"It always helps to air it out, and I'm always here to listen."

Colton hugged him. "Love ya, Gramps."

Elmer patted him on the back. "Love you, too, boy. More than you could ever know."

Fortified by the conversation with his grandfather, Colton returned to his mountain with far more optimism than he'd had before. Now he just needed to get through the next few days until he could be with her again. He could do that. Couldn't he?

CHAPTER 22

——◄•►——

*It's not over until it's over. We thought
yesterday was it, then we thought today
might be it, and now there's a chance it'll freeze
tonight . . . Like in the movie* Groundhog Day,
we seem stuck on Boiling Day.

—Colton Abbott's sugaring journal, April 17

As the workweek dragged along, Lucy felt like she was marching through hip-deep snow and getting nowhere fast. Her attention issues hadn't been this acute in years, and even double doses of her daily meds couldn't break through the fog in her brain as she tried to concentrate on a mountain of work while her heart and mind were on a whole other mountain six hours away.

She'd begun to live for the nightly calls from Colton, which went on for hours and hours. Last night she'd finally ended the call with him at two a.m. when her eyes refused to stay open for another second. Thank God it was finally Friday, and she was picking him up at eight at LaGuardia for a whole week together.

She was far too excited about his visit for a girl who hadn't planned to get involved. So much for plans. She had one more meeting to get through before she could put a fork in this useless week and get on with the weekend with him. She'd bought hard-to-get, expensive tickets to the Broadway show *Book of Mormon* for tomorrow night and had reservations for dinner afterward at a new place uptown that she'd heard great things about. Lucy couldn't wait to show him her city and to see his reactions to a place that was as far removed from his reality as it was possible to get and still be in the same country.

Her phone chimed with a text from Colton: On the way to Burlington. Can't wait to see you. A whole week! Mmm.

Lucy's smile nearly broke her face in half. Their use of the word *mmm* had become a regular thing on the phone this week, and it never failed to turn her on. Can't wait to see you too! Seven more hours. Hurry up.

I'm hurrying.

Determined to soldier through the two-hour lunch meeting with one of their best and biggest clients, Lucy gathered her files and headed for the conference room where the rest of her team was already gathered. Melanie Upton owned Mel's Cupcakes in the Village and had hired them to help take her booming business national via a new website.

They were about halfway through the planning process and had miles to go before the site would launch, but they all looked forward to their meetings with Mel because of the box of cupcakes she always brought with her.

"Everything okay, boss lady?" asked Diana, the woman they'd hired to replace Cameron, as if anyone could replace Cam. But Diana, who'd once been a competitor, was doing a decent job of bringing in new business, so Lucy couldn't complain. If she'd made an effort to keep their relationship strictly professional, it was only because she hadn't had time to get to know Diana better.

Or that's what she told herself. Truthfully, Diana was a glaring reminder that Cameron was gone for good, and Lucy resented the other woman's presence in the office. Mature, right? Yeah, she was working on it, but at least she could recognize her own limitations, which was rather evolved of her if she did say so herself. Naturally, Diana had picked up on the hint of chill coming from her boss and had gone out of her way to be extra nice, which only aggravated Lucy more. No one ever said she was perfect.

"Everything's fine," Lucy said in answer to Diana's question. Sometimes she wanted to tell her to just be quiet and leave her alone, but she wasn't *that* immature. "Why?"

"No reason. You've just seemed out of sorts this week. I thought you'd be all rested and relaxed after your time off."

"I am rested. And relaxed."

Diana was tall with raven-black hair that fell in waves around her shoulders, which only made Lucy resent her more. She'd taken Cam's place *and* she had great hair and a kick-ass style that would stir the envy of any fashion-challenged woman. It was too much to be borne. "Great," Diana said with a friendly smile. She never gave up. Lucy had to give her credit for that.

Mel arrived a short time later in a burst of excitement and energy. At just over five feet tall, she made up for her lack of stature with a big personality they all enjoyed. Today she wore her honey-colored hair in a messy bun and had a dab of flour on her cheek from the morning's baking frenzy that began every day at four a.m. She'd brought sushi for lunch and cupcakes for dessert.

"Have we mentioned that you're our all-time most favoritest client?" Lucy asked as she devoured a couple of California rolls. She'd been so distracted this week that she'd missed quite a few meals and was famished.

"You only say that because of the cupcakes," Mel said with the engaging grin that had made her a friend as well as a client.

"That is so not true," Lucy replied.

"Oh, whatever!"

Two hours into the meeting, Lucy's stomach began to hurt. What started as an ache quickly morphed into sharp pains and severe nausea. Around the conference table, she noticed the other members of her team were unusually pale and sweaty looking.

"Does anyone else feel like shit?" Diana asked.

"Oh my God," Mel said. "My stomach is killing me." The words were no sooner out of her mouth than she was running from the room with her hand over her mouth.

"*Fuck*," Diana said with a moan, speaking for all of them.

"Everyone go home," Lucy said as a wave of nausea hit her. "Lock up and go."

The staff cleared out, and Mel returned to the conference room looking green around the edges. "I'm so sorry, Lucy. I get sushi from that place all the time, and I've never had a problem before."

"Not your fault. Go on home before it gets worse."

"I'm so sorry again. I'll call you next week."

"Sounds good." Feeling worse by the second, Lucy ran for her office to grab her purse and phone and was hailing a cab at the curb when lunch came roaring back up, leaving her heaving into a sidewalk trash can while people on the street made a wide berth around her. She'd never been so violently ill in her life, even after a few unfortunate drinking episodes during her misspent youth. When the vomit finally stopped coming, she stood upright, the sidewalk swimming before her eyes and the heat making her feel even sicker.

She held up her arm weakly. "Taxi. Please. Taxi." As one of one of New York's famous yellow cabs came to a stop in front of her, she crawled into the backseat and gave the driver her address. "Hurry."

"Are you high or something?" the driver asked in broken English. "Don't want no drugs in my car."

"Not drugs," Lucy assured him. "Food poisoning."

"Don't want that neither."

"Believe me, I don't either. Drive fast and end the misery for both of us."

He drove like the car was on fire and got her home in record time.

Lucy handed him a twenty and didn't wait for her change. She didn't have the time. The two flights of stairs that led to her third-floor apartment seemed like a mountain, and she was sweating profusely by the time she made it to the third-floor landing. She pushed open the door, dropped her purse on the floor inside the door and ran for the bathroom.

The plane landed ten minutes late, which was maddening to Colton after days of counting the hours until eight o'clock Friday night. Then it took forever for people to gather all the crap they'd brought on the plane and get the hell off. By the time he reached the terminal, it was nearly twenty after eight, and he hated that he'd made her wait.

He jogged through the crowds, dodging vehicles and luggage and strollers and general Friday night mayhem in the busiest airport he'd ever been in. Will had warned him about what to expect in the city, but even with preparation, the crowds were overwhelming.

Lucy planned to meet him at baggage claim, since he'd had to check a bag to bring the clothes he needed for a week. Colton took the escalator downstairs but didn't see her bright auburn hair anywhere in the sea of humanity that surrounded him. He collected his bag off the carousel and moved out of the fray to call her. The phone rang and rang before her voicemail picked up.

"Hey, Luce. I'm here. Wondering where you are. Give me a call or text to let me know."

He waited expectantly for the next fifteen minutes, scanning the crowd all the while and looking for the distinctive hair he'd know anywhere. After half an hour had passed, he began to get worried and called her again. No answer.

This wasn't at all what he'd expected, and he had no idea what to do. He didn't even know exactly where she lived. When the clock struck nine and she was officially an hour late, he called Cameron.

Her "hello" was hesitant.

"Hey, it's me, Colton."

"Oh hi. I didn't recognize the number. What's up? I thought you were going to New York today?"

"I'm in New York, at LaGuardia, actually, but Lucy's a no-show, and her phone is going right to voicemail."

"That's weird. She could be stuck in Friday night traffic with a dead cell phone."

The possibility brought relief. "I'm not sure what to do."

"Give her another hour and then grab a cab to her place."

"I'm afraid I have no idea where she lives."

"I'll text you the address."

"Thanks, Cam."

"Try not to worry. Anything is possible in New York."

"You don't think . . ."

"What?"

He looked down at the floor, unsure of how to say the words that had been circulating in his mind since he realized she wasn't there. "That she's changed her mind about me?"

"Not that I'm aware of, and even if she had, she wouldn't do it this way. I probably don't have to tell you that Lucy's a straight shooter. She doesn't play games. If she didn't want to see you, she would've told you so."

"Yes, you're right. I'm sorry. I'm just being paranoid."

"Long-distance relationships will do that to you. But remember, this is Lucy we're talking about. What you see is what you get. I promise she's been delayed and is probably freaking out because she knows you're waiting for her. She'll come running in there any second."

"Thanks, Cam. Appreciate the pep talk."

"Let me know when you connect with her, okay? I'll be worried until I hear."

"I will."

"Have a great time this week."

"Thanks again."

Colton took Cameron's advice and gave it another hour. He tried to reach Lucy several more times with no luck, so at ten he hailed a cab and gave the address Cameron had texted him. On the way he thought about Cameron and how quickly she'd become a good friend to his entire family. Will was lucky to have such a great woman in his life. There was nothing about her not to love. Well, unless you were Megan, that is.

Thinking about something other than where Lucy might be kept Colton from going insane on the long ride from Queens into Manhattan, through traffic unlike anything he'd ever seen before. Forty-five minutes after he left the airport, the cab pulled up to Lucy's place in Soho, information Cameron had included in her text.

He paid the fifty-dollar fare and got his bag from the trunk before the cab pulled away. It was now three hours after Lucy was supposed to meet him, and he'd begun to feel seriously anxious about her safety more than an hour ago. While he'd tried not to go to worst-case scenario, what other reason could there be for her to fail to show up at the airport when she'd been so excited to see him earlier in the day?

Someone was coming out of Lucy's building as he went up the stairs, and the guy held the door for Colton. He suspected that wasn't cool, but he wasn't about to mention it when Cameron had warned him it might not be easy to get into her building if she wasn't home. He trudged up two flights of stairs and saw her door hanging open, keys still in the lock and her purse spilled on the floor.

A sense of unease traveled up his spine, settling into a pang of fear that sent a shiver racing through him. What the hell? He stepped inside her apartment, put down his bags down and called for her. No reply.

Should he proceed or call the police? Knowing she was home and possibly in some sort of trouble had him overruling his sense of caution and moving into the apartment to look for her. He found her out cold on the bathroom floor. A stale odor in the room indicated she'd been sick.

He dropped to his knees beside her, shocked by how ghostly pale she was. The first thing he did was check for a pulse and was relieved to find a steady beat in her neck. "Lucy. Honey. Can you wake up for me?" He got up to wet a washcloth with cool water and ran it over her face. "Luce?"

Her eyes fluttered open for a brief second and then quickly closed again. "You should go to your hotel," she said so faintly he almost couldn't hear her. "Don't want you to see me like this."

"Don't be silly. I'm not going anywhere. What happened?"

"Bad sushi."

"Oh no, honey. How long have you been here?"

"What time is it?"

"Almost eleven."

"Since three or so." Her eyes opened again. "The airport. Was supposed to get you."

"Don't worry about it. I found you. That's all that matters."

Tears spilled down her cheeks. "Don't want you here for this. So gross."

"I'm afraid you're stuck with me."

Her moan was quickly followed by a frantic scramble for the toilet that she could barely manage on her own.

Colton pulled her hair back from her face and held her while she heaved. Her entire body was racked by the effort, which yielded nothing much of anything. "How many times have you been sick, honey?" he asked as he wiped her face again.

"Don't know. Lost count." She began to cry in earnest. "I stink so bad and this is so far beyond disgusting."

He put his arms around her and kissed her forehead. "You don't stink that bad, and I've certainly seen worse than this. There's no way I'm leaving you when you're this sick, so deal with it."

"How did you even find me?"

"Cameron." Colton propped her up against the wall and turned the water on in the big claw-foot tub.

"What're you doing?"

"Getting you cleaned up."

"I can't . . ."

"You don't have to do a thing."

"Colton . . . You should just go to your hotel. I'll call you when I feel better."

"Not happening, so you can quit trying to get rid of me." When the tub was filled with warm water, he shut off the tap and grabbed a towel that was hanging on the back of the door. Then he turned his focus on helping her out of her dress, which had apparently taken a direct hit at some point during the siege.

"You're never going to want to have sex with me again after this."

The unexpected comment made him laugh. "You don't think so? I hate to tell you that's absolutely untrue. As soon as you're feeling better, look out."

"Thanks for the warning."

He lifted her easily and deposited her gently into the warm water.

She let out a moan of ecstasy. "That feels really good."

"I had a feeling it might." Colton used a washcloth to wet her hair, which he washed with products that were sitting on a corner shelf above the tub. "This stuff smells good."

"It's my favorite." She looked up at him. "I haven't had my hair washed by anyone other than a hairdresser since I was a baby."

He winked at her. "I'm at your service."

She reached up to curl her fingers around his wrist. "Thanks."

"It's my pleasure."

"Sure it is," she said with a laugh. "This is exactly the kind of pleasure you had in mind for tonight."

"Any time I get to spend with you is a pleasure."

"Even when I'm barfing and too weak to move?"

"Even then."

"You're crazy."

"About you." The words came so easily that they were out of his mouth before he took a second to consider what he was saying. But he didn't regret saying it, especially because he made her smile.

"The feeling is quite mutual."

"Good."

CHAPTER 23

70 degrees today. By far the warmest day of the year. BUT, a hard freeze is predicted for Saturday night, so we'll hold out to see if the sap runs on Sunday.

—Colton Abbott's sugaring journal, April 19

"Were you mad when I didn't show up at the airport?"

"Not mad so much as worried you might've changed your mind about me."

"I never would've left you stranded like that, even if I had changed my mind, which I haven't."

"That's what Cameron said, too. She said if you were through with me, you would've said so."

"She's right."

"Will you tell me? If you get to a place where this doesn't work for you anymore, will you just tell me?"

"Yes. Will you?"

He nodded. "I'm not expecting to get there any time soon. Just so you know."

"Me either. Just so you know. I'm sorry you had to fend for yourself in the big city. What do you think of it so far?"

"I hardly noticed a thing because I was so anxious to get to you."

"Colton?"

"Hmm?"

"I think I'm going to be sick again."

He moved quickly to grab the small trash can that sat next to the sink and got it to her with no time to spare. When she was done, he helped her out of the tub and into the towel he wrapped around her. He held her up at the sink so she could brush her teeth. "Bedroom?"

"That way," she said, pointing. Like every other part of her, the vomiting had weakened her voice. She directed him to where he could find sweats and a T-shirt that he helped her into. Then he tucked her into bed.

"I know you're going to object, but I'm wondering if you need a doctor."

"No."

"The longer this goes on, the more dehydrated you're going to get, and that can go bad really quickly."

"I don't need a doctor."

"Then you have to drink something. I'll get you anything you want, but you have to stay hydrated."

"Water."

"Cold water?"

"That sounds good." She looked up at him with blue eyes that were bigger than usual in her pale face. "You don't know where anything is."

He leaned over to kiss her. "I'm a resourceful kind of guy. I'll figure it out." It took him less than five minutes to locate glasses and fill one of them with water from a pitcher in the fridge that contained some sort of funky filter system.

When he returned with the water, he found her asleep and debated whether he should wake her to get her to drink something. He decided to let her sleep while she had a break from the vomiting and took advantage of the lull to clean the bathroom and gather her dirty clothes.

Then he sent Cameron a text to let her know what was going on.

She responded almost immediately, as if she'd been waiting to hear from him. Oh no! I hope she's okay!

She's miserable but seems okay. Full of beans as always.

That's a relief. Thank goodness u r there with her.

I'll be with her until she feels better.

Keep me posted.

Will do. Thanks for the help earlier.

Happy to support the Colton and Lucy cause.

We're a cause now?

☺

I'm scared of you.

LOL. TTYL. That means: Laugh out loud and talk to you later.

Smart ass. I knew that.

I wasn't sure you spoke text yet.

Colton laughed at her snappy comeback. She was funny. He'd give her that. The sound of a phone ringing in the apartment took him back to where her purse had spilled inside the door. He picked up Lucy's phone and saw her dad was calling for the third time. Hoping he was doing the right thing, he took the call.

"Hi, Mr. Mulvaney. This is Lucy's friend, Colton Abbott."

"Where's my daughter?"

"I'm with her at her apartment, but she's sick."

"Sick? With what?"

"Food poisoning, apparently. She had some bad sushi."

"Oh no. Well, that explains why she hasn't been answering her phone."

"Is everything all right?"

"Everything is fine, but when your daughter doesn't answer her phone you keep trying until she does, no matter how old she is."

Colton smiled at the feisty reply. He could see now where Lucy's sauciness came from. "You sound a lot like my own father, who would do the same thing if one of his daughters didn't answer her phone."

"Do I need to come there to be with her?"

"No, sir. I'm taking care of her, but I'm sure she'd like to see you when she feels a little better."

"I'll bring her some soup tomorrow."

"I bet she'll be ready for that by then."

"I'll get some for you, too."

"Oh. Thanks. I'll look forward to meeting you."

"What kind do you like?"

"Mr. Mulvaney, one thing you'll soon learn about me is there's absolutely nothing I won't eat."

That drew a grunt of what might've been laughter from the other man. "I'll see you tomorrow." He paused before he added, "You'll call me if she gets worse, won't you?"

"You have my word."

"Very good then. Behave yourself with my daughter."

Colton held back the need to laugh because that really wouldn't have been wise. "Yes, sir."

"Good night then."

"Good night."

Amused by the exchange with Lucy's dad, he placed her phone on the counter that divided her kitchen and living room. With her asleep, he finally had a chance to take a look at her charming living space. He could see her everywhere—in the wide variety of colors that all seemed to work perfectly together to the furniture that had been purchased with comfort in mind to the modern artwork on the walls. Like Lucy, her place was practical yet artistic and modern as well as whimsical.

On the mantel over a gas fireplace, he found a collection of figurines that looked old and priceless. He wondered how she'd come to have them and looked forward to asking her about them. As he was perusing a bookshelf full of romances, mysteries and thrillers, his stomach let out a loud growl that reminded him he hadn't eaten since lunch.

He went into the kitchen and opened the fridge to see what Lucy had on hand. Other than several containers of yogurt, some wilted grapes and the filtered water, there wasn't much of anything to keep a guy alive. Luckily, several takeout menus were affixed to the fridge with magnets. The choices were awe-inspiring for someone who lived alone on a mountain: pizza, Chinese, Japanese, Thai, Indian, Italian, Mexican and everything else anyone could ever want.

The variety of choices had his mouth watering. He wanted all of them, although knowing sushi had made Lucy so sick had him putting aside the Japanese menu. While his first inclination was to order a large meat-lover's pizza and call it a day, he decided it wouldn't hurt him to broaden his horizons and chose chicken pad Thai. He would've killed for a couple of beers, too, but he wasn't leaving Lucy for any reason, especially one as frivolous as beer.

Tomorrow he'd get them stocked up with food, beer and anything else they needed to hunker down for a few days. He peeked in on her curled up in a ball in bed before he went out to see if he could find the Red Sox game on TV since he hardly ever got to watch them play. Mostly he caught the games on the radio and had no idea what many of the players even looked like.

While he had no trouble at all finding the New York Yankees television station, there were no Red Sox to be found on any of the staggering number of channels she had available. Since he had no interest in watching the Yankees, he skipped around until he found an action movie that looked somewhat interesting.

He'd settled into watch the movie when he heard a noise from the bedroom that had him up and running. Colton grabbed the trash can he'd placed by the bed and got it to her just in time to save the bed from a direct hit. This time was much worse than the time before and seemed to go on for ages, when it was probably only ten minutes. But every one of those minutes cost her strength she didn't have to spare.

"I'm getting nervous here, Luce. I really think we need to take you to the ER."

"No," she said when she finally fell back on her pillow. "I'm okay."

Colton chose not to argue with her. He took the trash can to the bathroom to wash it out and came back with a fresh washcloth that he used to wipe her face and mouth. "Your dad called. He was worried when he couldn't reach you. I talked to him. Hope that's okay."

"You talked to my dad?"

"I did. He'd called three times so I figured he was anxious to speak to you. I told him what was going on and he said he's going to bring you soup tomorrow."

"Oh good. Okay." She looked up at him warily. "Was it strange to talk to him for the first time that way?"

"Nah, it was fine. We had a nice chat."

"He wasn't like, you know, weird that you were here?"

"He told me to behave with his daughter, and I assured him I would."

She groaned. "Ugh. I hope that's one promise you don't plan to keep."

"Tonight I plan to keep the promise. But once you're feeling better, look out."

"Good," she said with a sigh. "Sorry about all of this. Not the night we had planned, that's for sure."

"Stop apologizing. It's not your fault. Do you think you could drink some water?"

"I can try."

He held the cup for her while she took two sips. The small bit of effort seemed to further exhaust her.

"I'm so sorry I'm such a mess," she said with tears in her eyes.

Stretching out next to her, he linked his fingers with hers and looked down at her. "Please don't be sorry, and you're not a mess. I'm just glad I was here when you needed me."

"None of the guys I've dated in the past ever would've done something like this for me."

"Then you've been dating the wrong guys."

"Clearly."

"What now?" he asked when her eyes filled.

"Are you ever going to be able to look at me again and not see and smell puke?"

Colton laughed. "Honey, I grew up with nine siblings. Someone was always puking. Dogs were pooping and peeing everywhere but in the yard. We had goats at one point, and they were forever wandering into the house and making deposits. We had chickens and even a cow with an attitude. And then there were the horses Hannah and Ella had. They blackmailed their little brothers into mucking out their nasty stalls. Trust me when I tell you I'm not easily intimidated by a little puke."

"A *little* puke?" she asked, seeming to appreciate his effort to downplay her illness.

"Okay a lot of puke. But you're still incredibly cute even when you're puking."

She wrinkled up her nose and still managed to look adorable. "Something's seriously wrong with you."

"You're not the first person to tell me that. How about a little more water?"

"There're straws in the cabinet over the stove. Could you grab me one?"

He kissed the back of her hand before he released it. "Coming right up." As he walked out of the bedroom, a loud buzzing noise echoed through the apartment. "What is that?"

"Someone's at the door."

"Oh, I ordered food. Hope that's okay."

"Of course it's okay. You must be starving." She talked him through the steps of answering the intercom and buzzing the delivery guy into the building.

After exchanging cash for food at the door, Colton stashed his dinner in the kitchen, brought her a straw and helped her take a few more sips of water. "How about I go get you a sports drink to help restore the electrolytes?"

"What do you know about electrolytes?"

"Search-and-rescue training. There was a whole section on dehydration."

"You've had search-and-rescue training."

"Yep. Me and all my brothers. It's a hobby of ours in the winter."

"Only you would be entertained by going out into blizzards to search for people."

"It's really fun, especially when we find them alive."

"I'll have to take your word for it as you won't catch me alive—or dead—in a snowstorm."

Chuckling, he said, "So, sports drink? Yes?"

"Sure. There's a bodega on the corner where you can get stuff like that, and there's money in my purse."

He leaned over her to kiss her forehead and then her lips. "I gotcha covered, babe. Do they sell beer at this so-called bodega?"

"Yes, they do, but we're right around the corner from one of the best beer stores in the city."

"You have *beer stores* here?"

"We have everything stores here."

"Tomorrow, or the next day when you're feeling better, I want to see the beer store. Tonight, I'll be happy with a six-pack of something cold and American. You sure you'll be okay if I leave for a few minutes?"

"I'll be fine. I'm super sleepy. Go ahead and eat and then get your beer. I'm okay."

"If you're sure. I'll be quick." He put the bucket on a towel on the bed next to her. "Just in case, and I'm going to shut the door while I'm eating so the smell doesn't get in here."

Her wince said it all. "Thanks for that."

"Get some rest. I'll be back soon."

"You'll need keys. Bring them here, and I'll explain them to you. I think they're out there somewhere."

"They were still in the door when I got here, so I know exactly where they are."

"Wow. I have very little memory of that. This whole day is a blur. My dad would have a total cow if he ever knew I left my keys in the door. You can't tell him."

"I won't, but only if you promise you'll never do it again."

"Let's hope I never have another day like this one."

After she'd schooled him on how to use the two keys he needed to get back in, he left her to sleep, went to eat his dinner and then left to do his errand. At the bodega, he bought the sports drink, chicken soup and ginger ale for her as well as eggs, fruit, cereal, rolls, cold cuts, milk and beer to sustain him until she felt better. Even at close to midnight, the streets were busy with cars and pedestrians bustling about like it was midday.

By the time he got back to the stairs that led to her building, his bags were beginning to get heavy, which had him wondering how a city person grocery shopped. He needed to ask Lucy about that. From what he'd seen of it, he decided he liked the energy of the city and that he could go out at midnight, walk around the corner and get what they needed. How cool was that?

So far, the city had a lot to recommend it, and he could see himself spending time here. Although his opinion might change after a few days of nonstop hustle and bustle. One thing he could already see for certain was that her world and his were as different as they could possibly be, and yet here they were with genuine feelings for one another.

Could he see himself living here? Probably not. He would have trouble making a living here since his one marketable skill relied on sugar maple trees in Vermont to be useful.

So much for not getting ahead of yourself. No one was talking about moving, so why was he thinking about such things? There was no need for those thoughts right now. It was too soon, for one thing. And for another . . . He blew out a deep breath. For another, it was becoming increasingly more difficult to imagine a life that didn't include Lucy. Which was why his thoughts were straying into places they shouldn't be going. Yet.

The keys took some juggling with the bags in his arms, but he finally got into the first-floor door and up the two flights of stairs. Inside the apartment, he put the bags in the kitchen and went right to check on Lucy, who was sleeping peacefully. Thank goodness. He'd been worried about her getting sick again when she was home alone.

Assured that she was okay, he stashed the groceries and popped open a beer. Walking over to the big windows that overlooked the street below, he watched the goings-on outside for a while and tried to imagine what it would be like to live amid so much activity all the time. He tried to picture Sarah and Elmer here. They probably wouldn't know what to make of it.

He certainly hadn't seen this evening unfolding the way it had, and it probably ought to scare the piss out of him that he'd rather be with Lucy when she was sick than with any other woman he'd ever met. However, it didn't scare him so much as cement his resolve to figure out a way to make this work. The alternative was no longer an option.

CHAPTER 24

———◆———

Boiling status: When we boil tomorrow,
we'll break the old record for the latest boil.
It feels odd to be still writing about
freezing nights and sap runs. My eyes wander
to the rhubarb and daylily shoots.

—Colton Abbott's sugaring journal, April 22

Lucy was sick twice during the night. After the last time, at four a.m., she finally started to feel a tiny bit better. "I think it might be over," she said to Colton after he returned from rinsing out the bowl he'd placed between them on the bed at some point. He wore only a pair of form-fitting black boxer briefs, and she watched his every move from the bed.

"How can you tell?"

"For the first time since this started, my stomach isn't killing me, and I'm enjoying watching you walk around in your underwear. That has to be a good sign, right?"

His sexy smile lit up his eyes. "It's a great sign."

She tossed back the covers and swung her legs off the bed, blinking furiously when she saw stars.

"What're you doing?"

"I need to pee and brush my teeth."

He bounded around the bed, which was also fun to watch. Nobody bounded quite like Colton Abbott did. And those muscles . . . *Damn*, the man was hot. She saw more stars that couldn't entirely be blamed on being sick. The sight of him mostly naked would make any red-blooded woman swoon. "Give me a second to get here to help you, would ya?"

"I can do it." She started to push off the bed, felt the whole room begin to rotate and sat back down. "Maybe not."

"Take it easy, honey, and let me help you." With his arms around her, she stood and teetered against him until she got her bearings.

"Wow, this is nuts, huh?"

"It's because you're dehydrated. More sports drink after the bathroom."

He stayed with her while she walked slowly to the bathroom. "I feel like I'm a hundred years old."

"I'm sure you'll be much better by this time tomorrow."

"I hope so. I didn't intend to spoil our entire weekend."

"You haven't. Not at all. I was thinking earlier that I'd rather be with you when you're sick than any other perfectly healthy woman I know."

"I think there might be a compliment in there somewhere," she said, teasing even though she was deeply touched to hear him say something so sweet after the night he'd put in with her.

Laughing, he kissed the top of her head. "There's definitely a compliment in there."

"I can take it from here," she said when they were in the bathroom.

"Are you sure? You don't want to fall. That wouldn't be good."

"I'm sure. I'll hold on."

"Okay, call if you need me. I'll be right outside."

"Thanks."

She tended to business and took extra minutes to brush her teeth, loving the taste of the toothpaste after the misery

of the last few hours. Then she made the mistake of looking in the mirror and let out a scream that had Colton
storming into the room.

"Jesus," he said when he saw her standing upright. "You
scared the hell out of me."

"I scared the hell out of myself." She pointed to the mirror. "Look!" Her hair was a tangled mass of unruly curls
after being slept on while wet, her eyes were big and
bloodshot with dark purple circles under them and her face
was so pasty white she looked half dead. "I'm like a creature from a horror movie."

"You are not," he said, shaking his head with amusement at her assessment.

"I look like the walking dead. Don't try to sugarcoat it."

He reached around her and picked up her brush from
the counter. "Come on."

"Where are we going?"

"Back to bed before you fall over." He stayed right next
to her as she shuffled to the bedroom and sat down gratefully on the bed. "Stay there for a second." Standing in
front of her, he brushed her hair gently, which made Lucy
sigh with pleasure.

She tipped her head forward until it rested against his
stomach. "Feels great. You're good at this caretaker stuff."

"Only when you're the patient."

Because he was amazing and because she was falling
more in love with him with every minute she spent with
him, she wrapped her arms around his waist and held on to
him while he continued to brush her hair.

"Um, Luce?" he said after several minutes in which the
only sound was that of the brush sliding through her hair.

"Yeah?"

"Don't be alarmed or anything, but the close proximity
and all . . ."

She drew back from him and saw he was fully erect,
which made her giggle.

"Glad you find it funny," he said through gritted teeth.

"Sorry," she said, making an effort to control her laughter.

The playful scowl he directed her way only made her laugh harder.

"Yeah, you're feeling better if you're up for laughing at me."

She let her hands slide down his back to cup his muscular ass and pulled him in closer to her.

"Lucy . . ."

When he was close enough, she kissed him through the tight cotton that was stretched over his erection, letting the heat of her mouth seep through the cloth.

He sucked in a sharp breath. "Fuck, Lucy . . ."

"I don't mean to be a tease. I'll finish what I started tomorrow."

A shudder went rippling through him, making her feel powerful and feminine despite the fact that she felt like death and looked even worse.

"You don't have to. That's not the only reason I'm here."

"I know," she said with a sigh. "You also came to mop up puke."

"Get your cute butt into bed."

She swung her legs onto the bed, and he pulled the covers up and over her. Then he sat on the edge of the mattress and held the bottle of sports drink for her while she took a couple of greedy sips. Her stomach gurgled noisily, which made him laugh and her cringe.

"I'm so gross."

He leaned in to kiss her. "You are so cute, and I love you."

Lucy stared at his gorgeous, sincere face, looking for indications he regretted saying those words, but saw no sign of regret. Rather, she saw indications of hope and pleasure and the possibility of incredible joy, if only she could find the courage to take what he offered so willingly. "You . . ."

"Love you. Yes. You heard me right."

Lucy had never been more stunned or overwhelmed in her entire life. No one, other than her family and closest friends, had ever said those words to her.

Colton kissed her again, lingering for a minute, and

then pulled away to get into the other side of the bed. He turned off the bedside lamp and reached out to her. "Come here."

"That might not be wise. I think the puking is over, but I can't be sure."

He removed the bowl from between them and reached for her. "I'll take my chances."

Lucy curled up to him, resting her head on his chest. "Keep that close, just in case."

He put his arms around her, making her feel safe and loved and wonderful, despite the awful night she'd had. "It's right here on the table."

"Colton?"

"What, honey?"

"I want you to know . . . I think I love you, too, but this whole thing is really scary to me. No, that's not true."

"It's not scary?"

"No, it is. But I don't *think* I love you. I know I do. If I hadn't already loved you, I surely would after tonight."

"It makes me really happy to hear you say you love me, and I want you to be happy about it, too."

"I am. I'm so happy whenever I'm with you. It's just when I'm not with you . . . That's hard. Really hard and getting worse all the time."

"I know what you mean. But I want you to have faith that somehow, some way, we'll figure this out. Right now, in this very minute, I get to sleep with you in my arms, and that's all I need."

She ran her hand over the rippled muscles of his abdomen. "This is pretty damned amazing."

"Isn't it?"

"Yeah."

"So let's just enjoy the moment and try not to worry about what happens down the road. Can we do that?"

"I can certainly try." She pressed a kiss to his chest and nuzzled the soft hair that tickled her nose. "You were incredible tonight. I'll never forget it."

"It's nothing you wouldn't do for me."

"Well ... um, I probably ought to mention at some point that I'm what's commonly known as a sympathetic puker."

"What in the name of hell does that mean?"

"You puke. I puke."

"What?"

"You heard me right. The sound of puke, the smell of puke ... That's all it takes to make me puke. Just ask Emma about the time I had Simone when she was a baby and she came home to both of us puking, but only one of us was actually sick."

"You are too funny, Lucy Mulvaney. I'll remember that if or when I ever feel the need to puke, although I don't think I've actually puked since I was fifteen and got drunk for the first time."

"I'm great with the plain old flu. If you catch that, I'm your girl."

"You're my girl no matter what." He kissed the top of her head and gave her a squeeze. "Now go to sleep so you can feel better tomorrow."

"It's already tomorrow."

"Sleep, Lucy."

She fell asleep with a huge smile on her face. He loved her. Colton Abbott actually loved her.

A loud noise outside woke Colton the next morning. He glanced at his watch and saw it was after ten. He couldn't recall the last time he'd slept past seven. Yawning, he ran his fingers through his hair and glanced down at Lucy, who was still out cold, her head on his chest and her hand flat against his stomach.

He'd told her he loved her. Just blurted it out like it wasn't the most important thing he'd ever said to anyone. Recalling the shocked look on her face made him smile. How could she be surprised that he was in love with her? After the blurt, he'd wondered if he'd regret saying it, but in the bright light of day, he hadn't a single regret.

He was glad she knew how he felt about her and was relieved to know she felt the same way. Where they would go from here was anyone's guess, but as he'd said to her during the night, nothing had to be decided immediately.

Moving carefully so he wouldn't disturb her, Colton slid out of bed and pulled the covers over her, hoping she would sleep for a while yet.

In the bathroom, he took a quick shower, brushed his teeth and pulled on a worn pair of jeans that he left unbuttoned. After a quick check to ensure Lucy was still asleep, he went into the kitchen to make coffee. As he never had access to TV, he flipped it on to check what was going on in the world while he scrambled all twelve of the eggs he'd bought the night before and made toast with bread he found in Lucy's cabinet.

Hopefully she'd feel up to eating something soft like eggs and toast.

The food was almost ready when the buzzer sounded, indicating someone was at the door downstairs. Recalling his lesson last night, Colton buzzed back, admitting the visitor. He hoped that was the right thing to do and was about to go grab a shirt when a knock on the door had him heading that way instead. Oh God, what if it was her father and he was answering the door half naked?

He peeked through the peephole and saw a blonde woman, so he disengaged the locks and opened the door to the woman and a tiny version of Lucy.

The woman looked him up and down, her gaze settling on his chest.

"Let me guess," Colton said, leaning against the door and trying not to feel violated by the staring. "Simone and Emma." He pointed as he spoke and deliberately mixed up their names, which made the little girl laugh.

"*I'm* Simone and *she's* Emma, and we want to see Auntie Lu 'cuz she's sick."

He stepped aside to admit them. "Come on in."

Emma carried a brown bag that she deposited on the kitchen counter as she took a look at what he was cooking and then went back to staring at him. She was smaller than Lucy, but they had clear blue eyes in common.

"Are you Auntie Lu's secret boyfriend who's not a secret anymore?" Simone asked.

He smiled down at her. How could he not? She was adorable—and precocious. "That'd be me. I'm Colton Abbott."

Simone shook his hand. "Nice to meet you."

"Where's Lucy?" Emma asked.

"Still sleeping. She had a rough night."

Emma's brows furrowed with concern for her sister. "Is she okay? Should we take her to a doctor?"

"She's much better than she was and insists she doesn't need a doctor."

"Typical Lucy," Emma said. "I'd like to see her."

Colton gestured for her to go ahead. Who was he to say it might be better to let her sleep? When Emma disappeared into the bedroom, Colton went to the kitchen to move the eggs around in the pan and refill his coffee mug. Then he moved to the sofa to join Simone, who had changed the channel to something animated.

She sent him a side-eyed glance. "You have a lot of muscles."

"I work really hard at my job."

"What's your job?"

"I make maple syrup on a mountain in Vermont."

She thought about that for a second. "Like the kind Mommy buys at the grocery store?"

"Probably not," he said with a disdainful snort. "I make the good stuff, and if you give me your address, I'll send you some. You'll never want that grocery store crap again."

"I do like presents." She got up to find a piece of paper and a pen and labored over the writing of her name and address. When she was finished, she handed it to him.

"You got it, kiddo. I'll send it to you when I get home next week."

"Thanks."

"So what's your job?"

She gave him that disdainful look that all females did so naturally when men were stupid, which was often. "Duh, I don't have a *job*. I'm eight."

"Since when is that too young to have a job?"

"You're silly. I go to school."

"Oh right. I forgot about school. What grade are you going into? I'm guessing ninth or tenth."

"Third!"

"Wow, I was way off."

She looked at him as if she couldn't decide if he was teasing or just dumb, which amused him greatly.

Emma returned with Lucy, who was wrapped up in a robe and moving slowly.

Colton jumped up when he saw her coming and went over to her, leaning in to kiss her cheek. "How're you feeling, hon?"

"Weak as a kitten, but better than I was."

"Auntie Lu, your boyfriend is silly."

Lucy smiled at Simone. Although she was still frighteningly pale, she looked a lot better today, and he was relieved to see a spark of animation in her glorious eyes. "Believe me, honey," she said. "I know he is."

"Hey, don't talk about me like I'm not here," Colton said, earning another giggle from Simone. "I'm going to find a shirt." To Simone, he said, "Don't talk about me when I'm gone."

"I'm going to."

"You'd better not."

Her laughter was deep and adorable, and he was completely taken in by the little girl who looked so much like the woman he loved. He couldn't help but wonder what Lucy's children might look like and decided right then and there that he very much wanted to find out.

Wow, he thought as he went into Lucy's room in search of a shirt. *What happened to not getting ahead of yourself?*

CHAPTER 25

——◆——

*The Crop Is In: Come September when I
mention to a visitor that we made this year's
crop of syrup in twenty-three days it will
sound, even to me, like nothing. "But," I'll
add after a jerk of memory, "we were sure
glad it didn't go a day longer." Woods
cleanup begins tomorrow at 8:00 a.m.*

—Colton Abbott's sugaring journal, April 23

"Holy shit, Luce," Emma whispered. "You didn't tell me he's totally freaking hot."

"I didn't?"

"You know you didn't! He's even hotter than Will, and that's saying something."

Lucy smiled at her sister, pleased with her reaction to Colton. "He was amazing last night. I was sicker than I've ever been in my whole life. I didn't show up to get him at the airport, and Cam told him where to find me. He came in and took over. I'm not sure I would've gotten through it without him."

"That is amazing. What guy wants to deal with that?"

"He was totally unfazed by it. Shhh. He's coming back."

"Were they talking about me when I was gone?" Colton asked Simone.

She dissolved into giggles. "Uh-huh."

"Come and help me in the kitchen. I want to hear everything they said about me."

Simone got up and ran across the room to join him.

"Looks like you're not the only one who's in love," Emma said, watching her daughter interact with Colton.

Lucy couldn't miss the hint of longing she saw in her sister's gaze. Her last relationship had been with Simone's father, and that had ended before her daughter was born.

"Tell me there are more of these amazing Abbott brothers," Emma said with another not-so-subtle glance at Colton.

"Four more single brothers at last count."

"Hmmm, I might be due for a weekend in Vermont one of these days."

"Any time you want. I'd love for you and Simone to meet them all. They're the most awesome family."

"Are you going to move, Luce?" Emma asked softly. "After meeting him and hearing how great he was when you were sick, I wouldn't blame you if you did, despite what I said the other night."

"No, I'm not moving. I could never leave you or Simone or Dad. Not to mention I have a business to run. No, I'm staying put, and he knows it."

"So he's going to move?"

"I don't think so. His whole life is in Vermont."

"Not anymore it isn't."

As Lucy thought about what her sister had said, Colton came over to her carrying a steaming mug.

"Tea," he said. "I found it in the cabinet and thought it might taste good to you."

She took the mug from him with a grateful smile. "Thanks."

"Do you think you could eat something? I made eggs and toast."

"That actually sounds pretty good."

"Emma? Coffee? Tea? Eggs?"

"Coffee sounds good, but I can get it myself."

"I'll do it. How do you like it?"

"Just some cream would be good."

"Coming right up."

When he walked away, Emma made goggle eyes and fanned her face with her hand, nearly making Lucy choke on her tea. Her first sip of the lemon-flavored liquid settled in her tortured stomach and seemed destined to stay there, so she took another.

Colton brought Emma's coffee and a plate with eggs and buttered toast for Lucy.

Her mouth watered at the tempting aroma. "That smells great. Thanks."

"Sure thing. Now don't talk about me while I'm right over there. Simone and I are watching you two."

Simone's giggle made Lucy and Emma smile.

"Hey, Simone," Lucy said. "Will you take Colton with you and go get my mail? The keys are on the table."

"Come on, Colton. Let's go get Auntie Lu's mail."

He dutifully followed Simone to the door. "I know why you're trying to get rid of me."

Lucy gave him the biggest brightest smile she could muster. "I just want my mail, and Simone can't go alone."

"Right . . ." To Emma, he added, "Whatever she says about me, it's all true."

"I have no doubt," Emma replied dryly. As soon as the door closed behind them, Emma pounced. "Spill it."

"He told me he loves me after I'd been puking for hours and looked like death."

"Oh, Luce," Emma said with a sigh. "I'm so happy for you. No one deserves to be loved by a great guy more than you do."

"I'm happy for me, too."

"What did you say when he said it?"

"I told him I love him, too, because I do. I think I have for a while now. I'm trying not to think about all the issues we still have to work out, but whenever I'm with him, it's easy to forget there's anything standing in our way."

"I'm sure you'll figure something out."

"I hope so." Lucy took a small bite of the eggs and toast, which seemed to satisfy her aching belly rather than aggravate it as she'd feared. "So I have *Book of Mormon* tickets and reservations for tonight that I won't be able to use. You should take them and ask someone to go with you."

"You can't just give away tickets like that! You have to try to go."

"I know I won't feel like schlepping uptown and dealing with the crowds. Not tonight."

"Are you sure?"

"Positive. They're all yours. You can bring Simone over here if you can't find a sitter on short notice."

"You don't want her underfoot when you get so little time with him."

"She won't be underfoot, and we'd love to have her."

"If you're sure . . . I suppose I could see if Troy wants to go."

"Send him a text, make some plans, get dressed up, have a night out. Simone can even sleep over if you want. Go have fun. With the way I feel, there's no chance of her seeing anything that'll scar her for life."

"Well, that's comforting." She sent the text to Troy, who wrote right back to say he'd love to go. "I guess I have a date with Troy."

"Simone is thriving, Em. It wouldn't kill you to take some time for yourself once in a while."

Before Emma could reply, the door flew open, and Simone came in carrying the mail and a bundle of yellow flowers.

"Were those in my mailbox?" Lucy asked as Simone presented the flowers to her.

"No, silly, we got them at the corner. Colton said I should bring you flowers 'cuz you're not feeling good."

"Colton said that, did he?"

"Uh-huh."

"Well, thank you, honey. They're lovely. Will you put them in a vase for me? There's one under the sink."

"Yep." Simone took the flowers and dashed into the kitchen to find the vase.

"Thank you for the flowers," Lucy said to Colton.

"They're from Simone. It was all her."

"Somehow I doubt that." Lucy flipped through the mail and found a pink envelope with Cameron's handwriting and new return address in Vermont. "Oh, something from Cam!" She tore open the envelope to find an invitation to Hannah's bridal shower the following weekend and a note from Cameron that said, *Hannah told me to make sure you're invited. Hope you'll come. Let me know if I can pick you up at the airport, train station, etc. You have to come! We all want you here!*

"What is it?" Emma asked.

Lucy glanced at Colton. "An invite to Colton's sister Hannah's bridal shower. She's getting remarried in two weeks. Her first husband died in Iraq seven years ago."

"Oh, good for her." Emma looked up at Colton. "Do you like the guy she's marrying?"

Colton nodded. "Very much so. We've known him since we were kids, and he was a close friend of Hannah's husband Caleb's, too. She and Nolan are great together."

"That's awesome," Emma said with that same hint of wistfulness Lucy had noticed earlier. She made up her mind to continue encouraging Emma to get out more now that Simone was older and becoming more independent all the time.

"Will you come for the shower, Luce?" Colton asked casually, but she didn't miss the look of longing he sent her way. "You could fly back with me, and I'll drive you from Burlington."

"Let's talk about that later," she said with a warm smile so he'd know she wasn't dismissing him or the idea outright. The invitation had filled her with yearning to be part of Hannah's special day and to see Cameron and the rest of the Abbotts again.

"We should get out of your hair," Emma said as she stood to leave. "I brought you some muffins and ginger ale. If you change your mind about tonight, text me."

"Not going to."

"You should at least ask him if he minds."

"If I mind what?" Colton asked from where he sat on a bar stool at the counter that divided the kitchen and living room. He was reading the paper and drinking coffee. She couldn't deny he seemed to belong there in the midst of her home and her stuff and her people. Nor could she deny that she loved that he'd made himself at home in her place.

"Watching Simone while Emma uses the tickets I'd gotten for a show I'm not going to feel up to."

"Someone has to watch Simone? I figured she probably babysat other people's kids by now."

"*I told you*," Simone said indignantly. "I'm *eight*! I can't stay alone yet. Don't you know anything about kids?"

"Apparently not much, but if we *have* to watch you, I suppose it's okay." He made a show of acting put out, but they all knew he was kidding.

"When I come back I'll bring Rebecca and my pretty princess game. It'll be so much fun! Mommy, can I bring my Dora sleeping bag and sleep over with Auntie Lu?"

"Absolutely," Lucy answered before Emma could object. "And I can't wait to see Colton dressed up as a princess. He will be *so* pretty."

"Yes, he will," Emma muttered under her breath, making Lucy snort with laughter.

"What kind of snacks do I need to have on hand for this sleepover?" Colton asked Simone.

She recited a long list of treats that he dutifully recorded. "Got it."

"If you give her all that, you'll be cleaning up more puke," Emma said.

"I'll be selective," Colton said with a wink for Simone.

"Come on, Mommy." Simone dragged Emma to the door. "I've got to go home and start packing."

Emma rolled her eyes at them and allowed her daughter to tug her through the door.

Colton closed it behind them and came to join Lucy on the sofa. "You look better."

"I feel a little better, but still weak."

"Sorry you had to give up the tickets."

"Me, too, but I know I won't feel like it, and I'd hate to see them go to waste." She reached for his hand. "I was looking forward to taking you to the theater."

"We'll do it another time."

Lucy leaned her head back against the sofa and looked over at him, drinking him in.

"What?"

"Nothing. I just like to look at you."

"I like to look at you, too."

"Especially when I look so fantastic." Smiling, she said, "Thanks for being so great with Simone. She's crazy about you."

"She's adorable, and oh my God, she looks just like you!"

"I know. Em says she huffed and puffed and gave birth to her sister."

Laughing at her description, he said, "You ever think about having kids of your own?"

Damn that creep of heat that overtook her face. Why did she have to light up like a stinking firecracker every time he flustered her, which was *all* the time? "Not really. It's not something I see happening for me, with the business and everything. That's somewhat all consuming. Plus I have Simone, and she's like my kid, too." She glanced at him. "What about you?"

"Not something I've given much thought to. Maybe in the far-off future. After meeting Simone though, I can't help but wonder what a little Lucy would look like." This was said with that charmingly adorable smile that made her insides flutter every time he directed it at her.

Lucy was suddenly overwhelmed with yearning for things that might never be possible for them. She tugged her hand free. "Why are we even talking about this?"

He tightened his grip on her hand, refusing to let her escape. "Because it's what people talk about when they're building something together."

As quickly as the yearning came, it drained away when

the realities of the situation reminded her she had no business pining for anything permanent where he was concerned.

"Why are you frowning?"

"Am I?"

"Uh-huh."

"The usual reasons." She forced a smile, determined not to spoil the time they had together with worries about a future neither of them could predict. "It's so nice to have you here."

"It's nice to be here."

"I'm sorry for what happened yesterday. I feel terrible about leaving you stranded at the airport."

"It worked out fine. I'm just glad you're all right and feeling better."

She diverted her gaze to the invitation on the coffee table.

"I have an idea," he said.

"About?"

"About how you can come to Vermont for Hannah's shower and stay there until the wedding."

"This I've got to hear."

"What if you spent this next week doing all your meetings and getting everything together you needed to work in a quiet, peaceful setting with only a horny mountain man to disturb you every couple of hours. Imagine all the work you could get done in this peaceful, bucolic setting I've described for you."

In addition to his many attractive qualities, he was also endlessly entertaining. "You seem to have given this some considerable thought."

"Only since you got the invitation from Cam, which I knew nothing about in case you wondered." He rubbed at the whiskers on his jaw. "When I got my cell phone, the guy at the store tried to talk me into one of those mobile wireless thingies. What do you call them?"

"Broadband?"

"Yeah that. Do you have one of those?"

"I do."

"Excellent. I have a generator that you can use to charge your computer and phone and broadband thingie. The connectivity on the mountain is some of the best in the area because of the unrestricted access to the towers in St. J. You could get a ton of work done. And you could be with me for two whole weeks in a row." He bent his head to leave a line of kisses on the back of her hand before turning it to deliver one very persuasive kiss to her palm. "Two whole weeks together, Luce. Wouldn't that be awesome?"

She caressed his cheek. "It would be very awesome."

"So you'll do it? You'll come home with me next Saturday and stay through Hannah's wedding?"

"Will you hate me if I ask for a little time to think about it and to figure out if I can make it happen with work?"

"No, Lucy, I won't hate you. How could I hate you when you know I love you?"

She closed her eyes and took a deep breath that she released slowly. "So I didn't dream that you said that in the middle of the night?"

"Look at me."

Forcing her eyes open, she met his intense gaze. "I love you. I want to be with you as much as I can. I'll take whatever I can get. A day, a weekend, a week, two weeks, a month. I'll take it."

"But at what point will that stop being enough for you? For both of us?"

Colton curled his hand around her neck and drew her in for a soft, tender kiss that brought tears to her eyes. He made her feel safe and cherished and protected from everything other than the heartache she knew had to be coming right around the next corner.

CHAPTER 26

And now for some stats . . . First boil:
March 9. Last boil: April 23. This date
broke the record by three days.

—Colton Abbott's sugaring journal, after the boil

"Kiss me back," he whispered as he stretched out next to her on the sofa, their legs intertwined, arms wrapped around each other.

Lucy pushed aside all her worries and fears to give into the sweetness of his kisses. Nothing had ever been better than the way she felt when she was surrounded by him, consumed by a kind of pleasure she'd never experienced before. At times like this, when she felt closer to him than she'd ever been to anyone, it seemed hard to believe anything could keep them from having it all.

But then reality intruded, as she thought of her company and the people who relied on her, the clients she'd worked so hard to cultivate, the family that counted on her, and it all seemed quite impossible to reconcile with her growing love for a man who lived and worked six hours from her.

She turned her face away from the kiss.

Breathing hard, Colton held her close and burrowed

into the curve of her neck, leaving a trail of fiery kisses on her sensitive skin that made her shiver in response to him.

"God, Lucy, what you do to me. I promised myself I wouldn't touch you today when you've been so sick, and the minute we're alone I'm kissing you like I'm drowning and you're my only source of air."

He sounded so angry with himself and maybe frustrated, too. She regretted being the cause of either emotion when he'd done so much for her while she was sick. "There's no reason you can't touch me, Colton. I'm much better, and I love when you touch me."

"I shouldn't touch you. Not now." Though his words sounded pained, he made no move to release her.

"Why not?"

"Because one touch is never enough with you. I always want more, and you need to rest and relax and recover, not be pawed by your boyfriend."

"I love being pawed by my boyfriend."

"Lucy." His low growl made her laugh.

She took his hand and guided it down the front of her until it was pressed against the heat between her legs. "Does that feel sick to you?"

"God, no. It feels hotter than hell."

"Touch me, Colton. Make love to me. I promise I won't break."

"You need to rest, Lucy."

"I will. After . . ."

He moved quickly off the sofa and slid his arms under her, lifting her into his embrace effortlessly.

Lucy put her arms around his neck and peppered his face with kisses as he walked them into the bedroom, where he deposited her gently on the bed.

Leaning over her, he gazed at her reverently as he moved slowly and carefully to untie and open her robe. Underneath she wore only a T-shirt and a tiny pair of panties she'd bought with him in mind. At some point during the night, she'd kicked off the sweats that had made her feel overheated.

His hands trembled ever so slightly as he moved them over her body, setting her on fire with his gentle strokes, and he hadn't even touched her skin yet. "Sit up." He helped her up, pushed the robe off her shoulders and reached for the hem of her shirt, lifting it up and over her head before helping her to lie down again. Standing by the side of the bed, he gazed down at her as he pulled off his shirt and unzipped his pants. Then he was propped above her on one elbow, looking down at her with love in his eyes. "You are so beautiful. So incredibly beautiful."

Her first inclination was to object. She wasn't beautiful. At best she was attractive. But he made her feel beautiful with the way he looked at her, the way he touched and kissed her.

She curved her hands over his shoulders and down his back, which rippled from the effort to hold himself above her. "It's okay," she said. "I want to feel you next to me."

"I don't want to hurt you."

"You couldn't."

Rather than put his weight on her though, he turned them over so she was on top of him. "Is this okay?" he asked, running his hands up her arms to her shoulders and then down to cup her breasts.

"It's more than okay."

"I wish you could see what I see when I look at you."

"Back atcha. You've got my sister and my niece dazzled."

"As long as you're dazzled, that's all I care about."

"I am well and truly dazzled by you, Colton Abbott."

"Excellent," he said with a smugly adorable smile.

She was looking down at him when the room seemed to spin around her. She flattened her hands on his chest and closed her eyes before the spinning could make her nauseated.

"What?"

"Just a little dizzy."

"We shouldn't be doing this." He turned her again so she was on her back and pulled the covers up and over them. After kissing her softly and sweetly, he said, "We have all week for this kind of fun. We need to get you better."

"I know you're worried about me, and I do love you for that, but you've got me all hot and bothered over here. If you leave me in this condition, I'm just going to feel worse—and I'm going to be cranky, too." As she spoke, she cupped her breasts and ran her thumbs over her nipples, watching his eyes go hot with lust. It was the most overtly sexual thing she'd ever done in the presence of a man, and his reaction made her feel powerful and desired.

"Christ have mercy, Lucy. You know how to drive a guy wild."

"I only know how to drive *you* wild."

"That's all that matters." He leaned over her and drew one of the nipples she had teased to life into his mouth, sucking and tugging lightly but firmly enough to make her squirm.

She held his head to her chest and arched into him, needing to get closer.

He moved above her, giving her other breast the same treatment as he caressed her body with his work-roughened hands.

Lucy raised her arms over her head, surrendering to him completely.

"Yes, honey, *yes*. Let me love you." His words, whispered against her belly, were nearly her undoing. He touched her profoundly with the way he spoke to her as he showed her how much he loved her. By the time he leaned back and pulled her panties off, Lucy was more than ready for him. But he tested her readiness just the same. It took only one touch of his fingers to her core to make her come.

"Colton," she said, gasping as she reached for him. "Need you."

"I'm here. I'm right here."

At some point, he'd gotten rid of his jeans and boxers and was now poised over her, guiding himself with a hand wrapped around the base of his cock. On his knees, he pushed forward, stretching her as he went.

"Mmm," he said against her ear, making her shiver and tremble. "So tight. God, it's all I can do not to come right now. You make me crazy, Lucy. I've never wanted anyone the way I want you."

Swept away by his words and the tender way he moved above her, she wrapped her arms and legs around him, wanting him as close as she could get him. His powerful muscles flexed under her hands as he devastated her with his gentleness. He held her tight, but not too tight while he gave himself to her completely, holding nothing back. All the while, he kept a close watch for any sign of distress from her. But all she felt was bliss—pure, amazing bliss.

"Come for me again, Lucy. I want to feel you." He reached down to where they were joined to coax her, teasing and touching her until she exploded, clinging to him as he joined her. "Wow," he said after a protracted period of silence during which the only thing she could hear was the roar of her own heart and his breathing. He raised his head to look down at her. "I used to think it was kind of funny when people talked about making love, as if sex isn't sex, no matter how you do it. But now I get it. It's different when you're in love."

Lucy reached up to push the sweaty hair off his forehead. "It certainly is. Nothing has ever felt that good. Ever."

"For me either," he said with a soft kiss before he withdrew from her and turned onto his back, reaching for her.

Lucy curled up to him, putting her arm and leg around him.

He cupped her bottom and pulled her in even tighter against him.

She wanted to stay right here, in this moment with him, forever. This kind of contentment had eluded her in the past. Sure, she had a great job and family and friends who loved her. But this . . . This was something else altogether, and now that she'd had it, now that she'd been loved by him, everything was different—*she* was different, and there was no going back to who she'd been before.

"What're you thinking about?" he asked her.

"That I want to stay right here for as long as I possibly can."

"Me, too." He stroked her hair and kissed her forehead. "Close your eyes and rest for a while. We've got nowhere to be and nothing to do but be together."

Hearing that, Lucy was able to relax and enjoy the rare luxury of nowhere to be and a full day to spend cuddled up to her favorite person.

Colton had never been one to laze a day away in bed, but he was happy to make an exception to that rule today because it meant he got to spend hours cuddled up to naked Lucy. That was the closest thing to paradise he'd ever experienced, and he never wanted to let her go.

While she slept on her belly, he ran his hand up and down her back, reveling in the soft smoothness of her pale skin.

"Mmm," she said. "That feels good."

"You feel good."

She yawned and stretched. "What time is it?"

"About two thirty."

"In the *afternoon*?"

"Uh-huh."

"Oh my God. I never do this."

"Neither do I, but if you ask me, we've been missing out. Lying around in bed naked all day might be my new favorite way to spend a Saturday."

"I'm trying to picture you on your mountain, lolling about naked in bed."

Laughing, he kissed her shoulder. "The only way that's happening is if you're there with me."

"I want to come home with you next weekend. I hope you know how much I want to do it. I just need to be sure I can pull it off at work."

"I understand completely. We both have obligations that have to be seen to. You'll never get any flak from me about seeing to yours. I promise."

"I'm trying to figure out . . ."

"What, honey?"

"How our casual weekends turned into wanting to spend every minute of every day together."

"It was never casual for me, Luce. I've felt something different for you since that first minute in the conference room. You looked at me, and *pow*. Different."

"I felt it, too."

He reached over to tuck her hair behind her ear and cup her cheek with his big hand. "We're lucky, you know? Most people never experience that. Sure, there're all sorts of challenges standing in the way, but they don't seem insurmountable because I get to be with you this way even some of the time."

"You make me believe it's all going to be okay."

"It will be. One way or another, we'll figure it out." His stomach let out a loud rumble that made her laugh. "Time for lunch. Do you think you could eat something?"

"I'm actually hungry, too."

"That's a good sign."

"I need a shower first though."

He got out of bed. "Funny, so do I. Shall we?"

"You're very obvious, you know?"

"How so?"

"You want me naked and soapy in the shower so you can have your way with me again."

"That is so not true."

Lucy glanced down to watch his cock harden before her eyes. "Uh-huh. Right."

"You're the one who said the words *naked and soapy*. How is that his fault?"

"It's true," she said gravely. "He can't help that he's attached to a fifteen-year-old boy."

"I'm insulted on his behalf." He hooked an arm around her waist and hugged her from behind, pressing his insulted erection against her bottom. "And only a couple of hours ago you were all like '*Oh*, Colton, *yes, yes, yes, harder, Colton*,' and now you're being totally rude to him. He's not going to forget this."

She elbowed him. "I never said any of that."

"I heard it."

Wrenching free of him, she went ahead of him into the bathroom and turned on the water. "You're making things up."

"I'll remind you of this later when you're all about him."

"If you keep this up, there'll be nothing happening later."

Approaching her from behind again, he slid his hands up the front of her to cup her breasts, and sure enough her legs went weak. "Yes, there will. You can't resist me."

Since she could hardly argue that point and had no interest in resisting him, she decided to cede the point to him.

CHAPTER 27

———◄●►———

*Length of season: 46 days. The range in our
records since 1980 is 15 to 49 days. Technology
is pushing the boundaries of sugar season,
since modern tubing systems prevent the tap
holes from drying out as quickly.*

—Colton Abbott's sugaring journal, after the boil

With her wedding coming up soon, Hannah couldn't
seem to keep up with all the details swirling around
her. In the midst of a hot and sultry summer day in Vermont, all she wanted to do was sleep, which was extremely
unusual for her. No matter how much she slept at night
lately, it wasn't enough. She told herself that once they got
past the wedding and settled into normal life that she'd feel
better.

"God, I hope so," she said out loud as she headed downstairs.

"You say something, hon?" Nolan called from the
kitchen where he was making a late lunch after working
all morning. He was putting in extra time at the garage so
he could take a week off after the wedding. It would be the
longest he'd ever been away from the garage. His faithful

but unreliable sidekick, Skeeter, had assured him he'd keep the place running in Nolan's absence. They were hoping for the best.

"I was talking to myself," she said when she joined Nolan in the kitchen where he was eating a sandwich standing up. "Leftover habit from years of living alone." He'd left the deli turkey on the counter and the sight of it turned her stomach.

Hannah hoped she wasn't coming down with something so close to the big day. That would truly suck.

"You okay?" he asked, taking a closer look at her. "You're kind of pale."

"I'm just tired."

"You're sleeping a lot lately. How can you be tired?"

"I was just wondering that same thing. Too much on my mind, I suppose."

"Are you going somewhere?"

"To meet Cameron to talk about the inn. We've got a lot to do before the grand opening over Labor Day. With the wedding and our week at the lake coming up, we're getting short on time."

Nolan finished the sandwich, wiped his mouth with a paper towel and came over to her, resting his hands on her shoulders. "May I make what might be an unpopular suggestion?"

"What's that?"

"How about you push back your grand opening a little to give yourself a break from this pace you're keeping? It's enough to wear anyone out. I want you to enjoy our wedding, Hannah. Not have it be a box you check on your endless to-do list."

Hannah gaped at him. "Did you honestly just say that?" She pulled back from him, appalled that he could think such a thing, let alone say it.

"Maybe I said that wrong."

"Maybe?" She picked up her purse and keys and headed for the garage.

"Don't leave mad, Hannah."

"I'm not mad." In truth, she was trying very hard not to cry, which was infuriating. Her emotions were all over the place lately—highs, lows and everything in between. She'd chalked that up to the naturally emotional process of getting remarried seven years after being widowed. But still, her reactions to everything seemed overly extreme, even to her.

Nolan followed her to the garage with their puppy, Homer Junior, scurrying along behind him. "Babe, wait. I'm sorry." He reached for her arm to stop her. "Oh, damn. Are you crying?"

"No, I'm not crying."

"Well, um . . ." He used his thumbs to clear the moisture from her cheeks. "You're leaking, then."

The comment made her laugh even as more tears spilled from her eyes.

Nolan gathered her into his embrace. "I'm sorry. That was a shitty thing to say."

Hannah rested her head against his chest and put her arms around him. "It's okay. I can see why you said it with the way I've been lately, running around like the proverbial chicken without a head."

"Still . . . You didn't deserve that, and I'm sorry I said it."

She looked up to offer him a smile. "Did we just have our first fight?"

"I think it was more a matter of me being an insensitive clod. I'm still new at this relationship business. You've got a lot of work to do to whip me into shape."

"And I'm looking forward to every minute of it." She went up on tiptoes to kiss him. "What're you going to do while I'm gone?"

He scooped up the puppy, who'd been circling their feet. "Homie and I are going to cut your grass."

"You don't have to do that."

"Yes, we do." Nolan kissed her nose and then her lips. "Go ahead and hurry back. You're taking the rest of the day off when you get home to snuggle with me."

"Snuggle, huh? With clothes or without?"

"The good kind. No clothes."

"I'll look forward to that."

He kissed her again, lingering this time. "I love you, Hannah. I can't wait to be married to you."

"I can't wait either. Fourteen days."

"That many?" He held the car door for her and waved to her as she drove off. By the time she returned, he'd have the grass cut for her even though he had his own grass to cut. They were planning to move to his place once the inn opened to the public but weren't rushing that with everything else they had going on. For now, he was all but living with her at the house she'd shared with Caleb.

It was time for a change, in more ways than one. The years she'd spent alone in the huge Victorian after Caleb died had healed her to the point where she was ready to move forward with Nolan. But she'd never forget the happiness she'd known in that house with Caleb and his dog, Homer Senior, who was now buried in the backyard.

The plan to use the house as a retreat for women who'd lost their husbands to war was coming together nicely, and the first weeks after the grand opening were already booked thanks to Cameron's marketing forte. In record time, she'd launched a website, a Facebook page and a mailing list, things that would've taken Hannah months to accomplish on her own. And Cameron had done all that while moving to Vermont to live with Will and while building a complex website for the Abbott family store.

To say Hannah admired her new friend greatly was putting it mildly. She'd quickly become one of Hannah's favorite people, and she looked forward to the day when Cameron would officially become an Abbott.

Hannah got to the diner about fifteen minutes before Cameron was due to arrive and since the place was all but empty, Hannah had her choice of tables. She slid into a booth facing the door so she could watch for Cam. Knowing Cameron's issues with Megan, Hannah had suggested they meet at the coffee shop instead. But Cameron had said she refused to hide from anyone, least of all Megan.

"Hi, Hannah," Megan said. "What can I get you?"

"Coffee would be great and an ice water, please." Hannah studied the woman who'd captured the attention of her brother Hunter and tried to look beyond the crankiness to see what might've attracted him to her.

Megan had long blonde hair, delicate features and high cheekbones. While her personality could be formidable at times, now that Hannah looked closer, she decided there was something distinctly fragile about her. She wondered if Hunter had noticed that, too.

Hannah was almost ashamed to realize that she'd seen Megan several times per week for years but didn't know much more about her other than she was the sister of Nina, who owned the diner with her husband, Brett. She also knew that Megan and Nina had lost their parents in a car accident quite some time ago.

Megan returned to the table with a mug of coffee, a glass of ice water and a small pitcher of cream.

"Can you sit for a second?" Hannah asked her, surprising herself almost as much as she seemed to surprise Megan. She told herself she was doing this for Hunter.

"Oh, um, I'm working."

"Can you take a break? Just for a minute."

"Ah." She looked over her shoulder to her sister, who was busy doing paperwork at the counter. "I guess. Sure."

Hannah stirred cream into her coffee and added a dash of sugar. She'd pay for the late-day caffeine later when she was staring at the ceiling wide awake in the middle of the night. "I was thinking we don't know each other all that well, despite living in the same town for so many years."

"Oh. I thought you were going to chew me out for being a jerk to your friend like your brother did."

"So you admit you've been a jerk?"

"Sort of." Megan flipped a pen back and forth between her fingers. "Yeah, I have. I know it's not her fault that he chose her."

"Maybe you ought to tell her that, huh?"

Megan nodded. "Maybe. I heard you're getting married. Congratulations. Nolan is a really nice guy."

"Yes, he is, and thank you."

"I was, um, sorry about your husband. He was a nice guy, too."

"Yes, he was. I appreciate your kind thoughts of him."

"I ought to get back to work. Let me know if you need anything else."

"I will. Thanks."

As she got up, Cameron came rushing through the door and stopped short at the sight of Megan talking with Hannah.

Megan hesitated. "I'm sorry," she said to Cameron. "For being a jerk. It's not your fault. And it's not his. It's mine."

"Apology accepted. Thank you."

"Can I get you something?"

"I'd love a tuna on wheat toast and a Diet Coke, please."

"Coming right up."

Wearing a gobsmacked expression, Cameron slid into the booth across from Hannah. "What just happened?"

"I heard Will chewed her out the other day."

"Yeah. He said enough was enough, and apparently told her so. She cried a little."

"She was just really sweet congratulating me about the wedding and saying what a nice guy Nolan is and Caleb was."

"There may be hope for her yet."

"I've known her for such a long time, but I barely know her at all, really. I thought I should make an effort for Hunter's sake."

"You think anything will come of that?" Cameron asked.

"Hard to say. He has to know he faces an uphill battle in light of her affection for Will, but you never know what'll happen."

"Anyway . . . How are you?"

"All right. I think Nolan and I just had our first fight."

"Really? What happened?"

Hannah relayed the story, including his heartfelt apology.

"I suppose no man is ever perfect, even one who's perfect for me."

"That's true. So listen to this . . . Colton is in New York nursing Lucy through a vicious bout of food poisoning."

"Oh my gosh! Poor Lucy!"

"I know, right? From what I heard, bad sushi took down the whole office and one of our best clients. I got out of there in the nick of time."

The words *bad sushi* made Hannah's stomach turn.

Megan returned with Cameron's drink and sandwich.

"Thank you," Cameron said.

While she ate, they talked about the changes Hannah wanted to make to the inn's website while Cameron took notes and asked questions that led to more changes.

The scent of the tuna coupled with the overly warm temperature in the diner made Hannah feel nauseated, which was odd because she loved tuna and ordered it all the time. "Is it hot in here, or is it me?"

"I'm not hot, but you're kind of pasty around the gills, girl."

"I think it's you and your tuna."

"Oh sorry! I thought you loved tuna."

"I do. Just not today."

"I'll get it to go."

"No! Finish it. I'm fine. I'm just hot. And tired all of a sudden. Really, really tired."

"Are you sick? Because you aren't allowed to get sick for the next three weeks."

"I'm not sick. I just feel weird today. I think it's the heat."

"I know this counts as hot to you guys up here in Vermont, but to a city girl like me, unless you can fry an egg on the sidewalk, it's not really hot."

"The thought of eggs fried on a New York sidewalk doesn't do much for my stomach."

"Sorry."

"So did Lucy say anything about how it's going with Colton?"

"She thinks she in love."

"Really? That's amazing! Is she going to move here, too?"

"I don't think so. She's really tight with her dad, sister and niece. And then there's the business . . . I walked away. It's not like she can, too. I feel kind of guilty about that."

"You shouldn't feel guilty. I doubt she'd want that."

"Still . . . What do you think they'll do?"

"I don't know. I can't imagine him anywhere but on his mountain."

"Having just lived through it myself, I don't envy them the decisions they'll have to make at some point."

"Why does it have to be so hard for two people who obviously love each other and totally deserve to be happy?"

"Because if it wasn't hard it wouldn't be worth the payoff."

"That's very well stated and certainly true."

"Are you okay, Hannah?"

Damn her unpredictable emotions these days. Her throat tightened around a lump that had her waving a hand to buy a minute to collect herself. "It's all very bitter-sweet," she finally managed to say, so softly it was nearly a whisper.

"Oh, honey, I can only imagine."

"I love Nolan so much. I never thought I'd feel this way again."

"But you're thinking a lot about Caleb, too. Right?"

Hannah pressed her lips together tightly and nodded. "He's very present in all of this."

Cameron dabbed at her eyes. "Of course he is. You both loved him."

"Sometimes I worry I'm not being fair to Nolan by thinking so much about Caleb."

"From all I've heard, Nolan is better able to understand what you've endured than any other man ever could."

"You're right. He's amazing and understanding and everything I could've hoped for."

Cameron reached across the table for Hannah's hand.

"Be kind to yourself, Hannah. Any thoughts or feelings you have right now are yours, and you're entitled to each and every of them. No one is judging you, least of all Nolan. He's crazy in love with you."

"Yes," Hannah said, smiling through the tears that continued to come despite how much she wished she could talk about this without them. "He is."

"You should go home and let him give you some TLC."

"That actually sounds rather divine. I think I'll do just that."

Cameron grabbed the check. "I've got this one."

"Thank you for that and everything else." Hannah hugged her. "You've been the most incredible friend."

"Same to you. You've made me feel so welcome in my new home, and I'll always love you for that."

"Stop." Hannah wiped away new tears. "I'm already a hot mess."

They laughed and hugged like two longtime girlfriends.

"I'm here if you need me in the next two weeks," Cameron said. "Anything you need. Any time you need it."

"Thanks, Cam. I'm so glad my brother decided to keep you."

"So am I. I get him and all of the rest of you, too. What a lovely thing that is."

They walked out of the diner arm in arm, laughing and talking, and parted with another hug.

Hannah drove home feeling relieved that she'd unburdened herself to Cameron, who was such a kind and understanding friend. But while she felt better to have gotten a few things off her chest, she was still feeling queasy, overheated and tired. The exhaustion was pervasive, so pervasive in fact that she wondered whether she might need to see a doctor. Maybe she was anemic, and wouldn't that be magical with everything she had coming up in the next few weeks.

She arrived home to a freshly cut lawn but no sign of Nolan's truck in the driveway. He'd probably left to run an errand or to pick up something from his own house where he spent very little time these days.

With some time to herself, Hannah scooped up Homer and went directly to the sofa in her cozy sitting room to lie down, grateful for the house that was hard to keep warm in the winter but cool and comfortable in the unforgiving heat of summer. That was her last conscious thought until Nolan kissed her awake to a room that had grown considerably darker.

"Hey there." He held the puppy in his arms as he gazed down at her. "You were out cold."

Her eyes felt too heavy to keep open. "Mmm, what time is it?"

"Almost six."

She'd been asleep for close to three hours? How was that possible?

"Is everything okay?"

She reached for the puppy, who struggled to break free of Nolan so he could get to her. "Uh-huh."

"Hannah?"

"Hmm?"

"I'm worried about you. I kept thinking you'd wake up, but you've been asleep for hours. It's not like you to sleep like that in the middle of the day. Would you tell me if something was wrong?"

She nodded. "I would, but I don't know what's wrong. I feel sick and tired, and Cam's tuna sandwich nearly made me barf, and I cry over *everything*." She was crying again now and swept angrily at the tears. "It's ridiculous! I'm getting married, not staring down a firing squad."

Laughing softly, he reached for her and helped her sit up. Somehow he managed to smoothly arrange things so she was on his lap, cuddled up to him with Homer cuddled up to her. Nolan smelled of freshly cut grass and cologne that made her want to nuzzle closer. "I suspect there might be something else entirely going on here, my love."

"And that is?"

"Is it possible you might be pregnant?"

"*What?* No. I'm not pregnant."

"You're sure?"

"Of course I'm sure. If I were pregnant, I'd know it. Wouldn't I?"

"Having never been pregnant myself, I couldn't say for certain. It just seems that you're sort of all over the place and tired and hungry—that is, when you aren't nauseated. I'm certainly no expert on such things, but the thought occurred to me, and . . . Oh God, Hannah, why are you crying again?"

"Because! That's it! That's what's wrong with me, and I didn't even know it. And what kind of mother will I be if I didn't even *know* I was pregnant?"

His body shook under her, and for a moment she thought he was crying, too. Then she realized he was laughing.

"You're *laughing* at me? Seriously?"

"Hannah, I love you so much. So goddamned much." His eyes were bright and full of emotion and tears that probably weren't entirely due to the laughter. "You have no idea how adorable you are right now. And if you *are* pregnant, which we'll confirm one way or the other first thing in the morning, the child we made together will be the luckiest kid in the universe to have you and your great big generous heart as his or her mother."

"This wasn't supposed to happen so fast. We just stopped being careful a couple of weeks ago."

"I can't help that I'm a stud, babe. You're just going to have to learn to live with it."

She poked him in the belly, which made him gasp before he laughed. "Is all of this really happening? Tell me I'm not dreaming."

"It's a dream come true," he said, kissing her. "In every possible way." He kissed away her tears and then captured her lips in another passionate kiss that cleared her mind of every thought that didn't involve him and the sublime way he made her feel. "I was promised some naked snuggling," he reminded her, his lips soft against her ear. The combination of his words and the heat of his mouth sent goose bumps down her arm.

"I always keep my promises."

He tightened his arms around her and stood, carrying her upstairs. Not wanting to be left out of anything, Homer Junior followed right behind them.

"Nolan?"

"Hmm?"

"Thank you."

"For what, honey?"

"Everything. You've given me everything."

He laid her on their bed and came down over her, careful not to put too much weight on her. "If I've given you everything, why do I feel like the luckiest guy who ever lived?"

"I guess we're both lucky."

"Fourteen days until you're my wife, Hannah. I can't wait."

"Neither can I."

CHAPTER 28

——◆◇◆——

*Number of boiling days: 22 (not 23 as
reported earlier). March vs. April: April
won with 55 percent of the crop.*

—Colton Abbott's sugaring journal, after the boil

"You're totally cheating! *Snood* is not a word!"

"Then go ahead and challenge me." Lying face-down on the floor wearing nothing more than well-faded jeans, Colton was the picture of sexy insolence. His hair was tousled from their earlier nap. Late-day whiskers covered his jaw, and his blue eyes danced with mischief. The stinker was effortlessly gorgeous, and he knew it.

Lucy had already made the mistake of challenging him twice before and came out on the losing end both times. He was kicking her ass rather significantly, and she was beginning to regret suggesting a game of Scrabble. "I had no idea you were such a cheater."

"I am *not* a cheater," he said emphatically. "Just because I have a more intellectually developed vocabulary than you do doesn't make me a cheater."

Lucy tossed the Q tile she'd been unable to use at him and hit him square in the forehead.

"That's a declaration of war." He moved so quickly she had no time to defend herself before he was upon her.

She let out a feeble squeak of protest but didn't try too hard to keep him from overtaking her—and disrupting the board. Tiles went flying all around them, which was fine with her. "You ruined our game."

"You threw a Q at me."

"Get your snood off me."

"Ah-ha! So you admit it's a word!"

"Too bad you messed up the game and can't collect your forty-six points or whatever it would've been this time."

"Fifty-five, and did you intentionally provoke me to get out of finishing the game?"

"Would I do that?" she asked, batting her eyelashes at him.

"Yes, I believe you would."

"Sadly, you pounced before we finished, which means your ninety-point lead never happened."

"And you say *I* cheat . . ."

"Getting trounced in Scrabble always makes me cranky," she said. "You wouldn't want me to be cranky, would you?"

"Don't you mean *crankier*?"

She scowled at him. "Speaking of declarations of war . . ."

"There're so many better things we can do besides fight over who's a cheater at Scrabble. Like this, for one thing." He kissed her lips. "And this." More kisses to her neck. "And this is a personal favorite," he said of the kisses to the upper slope of her breast.

"Colton?"

"Mmm?"

"My sick day with you was the best day I've ever spent with anyone."

"Your sick day has been one of my favorite days ever, too. I'd say you should get sick more often, but I never again want to see you suffer the way you did last night."

"I never again want to suffer like that either—or have you see it."

"You're still not over that, huh?"

"I may never get over the horror of puking in front of my boyfriend."

"I love when you call me your boyfriend, even if we're talking about puke."

"Again I say there's something wrong with you."

He was smiling and coming in for more kisses when the buzzer sounded. "Ugh. Don't they know I'm busy here?"

"Put it on hold, Romeo. That's probably my dad."

"Oh. Shit." Colton got up comically fast and held out a hand to help her up from the floor.

She patted his bare chest. "A shirt would be good. Just while he's here though. Then I want it off again."

"Right. Going to get a shirt now."

While Colton headed for the bedroom, Lucy went to deal with the intercom.

"Hello?"

"It's your dad."

"Come on up." She buzzed him in and went to pick up the game pieces that were scattered all about on the area rug in her living room. *Snood* . . . That was *not* a word.

Colton returned wearing a red T-shirt that was wrinkled but presentable. He'd combed his hair, too. He seemed nervous about meeting her dad, which was adorable.

She was about to tell him he looked good when he handed her his phone to show her something on the screen.

Snood: a decorative hair net or ribbon worn by unmarried Scottish women.

Damn him! "How do you know about unmarried Scottish women? Do you have one of *them* in your harem, too?"

He pinched her butt. "That'll learn you not to challenge the master, babe."

"You're an arrogant ass, and I'm never playing Scrabble with you again."

"You forgot the part about how you love me." He gave her a gentle nudge. "Now get the door for your dad."

Colton stood back and watched as Lucy opened the door to her dad, who came in carrying two brown paper bags. He took a quick look at Colton before continuing to the kitchen with his bundles. "I got chicken noodle for you and beef stew for him."

At the words *beef stew* Colton's stomach let out a loud growl that made Lucy laugh.

"I'd say he approves of your choice." Lucy took hold of her father's hand and led him into the living room. "Colton, this is my dad, Ray Mulvaney. Dad, my boyfriend, Colton Abbott."

Never had the word *boyfriend* carried more significance than it did at this moment. Colton shook hands with Ray. "Nice to meet you, sir."

"Call me Ray."

"I will. Thank you."

Since he hadn't been much for relationships in the past, he hadn't met many parents and wasn't all that experienced at this. But something about the way Ray Mulvaney sized him up had Colton's hands feeling clammy and the rest of him sweaty. "You're a big guy. Spend a lot of time in the gym, do you?"

"Um, no. Never been in a gym in my life."

"He works on a mountain, Dad, making maple syrup. It's very physical work."

"Is that right?"

"Yes, sir. I mean Ray. I'd be happy to send you some of our syrup. There's nothing quite like it in the world."

"So I've heard. I wouldn't say no to trying some."

"I'll get your address from Lucy."

Ray sat on one of the bar stools and crossed his arms, settling in. "I understand you come from a big family."

"There're ten of us kids."

"Ten kids." Ray shook his head. "How many girls?"

"Three."

"Well, at least your poor parents only had to deal with three teenage girls." His gray eyes twinkled with glee at his own joke.

"Thanks a lot, Dad."

"My parents would probably tell you their boys were far more of a handful than their girls."

Ray raised a brow. "Is that right? You were a hellion, were you?"

"If enjoying all forms of extreme skiing, snowboarding, snowmobiling, mountain climbing and other such exploits make me a hellion, then I guess I was. Our form of trouble was more in the way of broken bones and stitches than anything illegal."

"Hmpf," Ray said. "You don't plan to take my daughter on any of these extreme adventures, do you?"

"No, sir. The kinds of things we consider fun in the mountains are far too dangerous for a nice city girl like Lucy."

"That's a good answer."

"However, I do think she might enjoy cold-weather camping, and I hope we get to do that sometime."

"Oh boy," she said dryly. "Can't wait for that."

Both men laughed at her obvious distress at the thought of camping in the cold.

"You're feeling better, honey?" Ray asked his daughter.

"Much better. Colton was a saint. Thank goodness he was here last night. It got kind of ugly."

"She was a trooper," Colton added.

"When I wasn't puking my guts up."

"I heard you guys have Simone tonight. I can take her if you want."

"We're happy to do it," Colton said. "She's adorable."

"Yes, she is," Ray said, once again studying Colton with those shrewd eyes that seemed to see right through him.

The guy had a good penetrating stare. Colton would give him that. He did his best not to wilt until Ray looked away, his focus once again on his daughter. "Is there anything else I can get for you?"

"No, Dad. We're good."

"You'll come home for dinner tomorrow night." He glanced at Colton. "Both of you."

"We'd love to," Lucy said. "Thanks for the invite and for the soup, too."

Ray got up and kissed Lucy's cheek. "Glad you're feeling

better, honey. You gave me a scare when you didn't answer your phone all night."

"I guess I scared a few people by dropping off the radar."

"Yes, you did," Colton said as he shook hands with Ray. "Nice to meet you, Ray."

"You, too. See you tomorrow."

"We'll be there."

"Lock the doors behind me."

"I will, Dad. Be careful going home."

Ray waved as he headed down the stairs.

As instructed, Lucy closed and locked the door and set the deadbolt. She turned to him. "He liked you."

"Really? I didn't think he did."

"No, he did. I can tell when he doesn't like someone, and he liked you."

"He seemed . . . I don't know . . . Suspicious or something."

Lucy took the containers of soup out of the bag, which also contained two crusty loaves of freshly baked bread. "He's worried I'm going to move like Cameron did."

"I take it you told him that's not going to happen."

"I did, but I'm not sure he believes me."

Colton crossed the room to her, unable to stand being so close to her but not able to touch her. He slid his arms around her and enjoyed the way her satin robe clung to all her curves. "I have no desire to take you away from the people you love, Luce. You'd never be happy living that way, and I want you to be happy."

"And you'd never be happy living away from your mountain or your family."

"I don't know if that's true."

She drew back from him, looking up at him tentatively. "What're you saying?"

"That I'm not ruling anything out. My mind is wide open to the possibilities as long as those possibilities include you."

"Are you thinking you might want to move? At some

point, I mean. I'm not looking to put pressure on you to decide something I don't even want to talk about."

"Not ruling anything out at the moment." He held her face in his hands, compelling her to look at him. "But I heard you when you said you can't move, and after seeing you here with your family, I get it. I truly do, and I'm not going to suddenly expect you to change your mind. I promise."

"That's good to know, but you forget that I've seen you with your family and in your element on the mountain. I can't imagine you happy anywhere else."

"I've been really happy right here with you this weekend."

"And I was puking for much of that time."

"You just proved my point, Luce." He kissed her. "I'm happiest when you're in the room with me. It doesn't matter what we're doing. Although some things are a lot more fun than others."

He made her laugh. He made her smile. He made her think. He made her mad and glad all in the same ten-minute period. He made her *want* like she'd never wanted anyone or anything before. More than anything, he made her happy.

"I'm happiest when I'm with you, too. I don't care where we are."

"I want you to remember that and stay focused on it. This isn't going to be easy. It's going to be challenging beyond belief at times. But if we both remember when we're happiest, I think we can make it work."

"You're starting to make me a little hopeful."

"It's safe to be hopeful. I've been giving our situation a lot of thought, and I'm not quite ready to talk about it yet, but will you trust me for a little while longer?"

"I trust you, Colton. I've thought a lot about our situation, too. I feel like it's all I think about lately when you're not scrambling my brains with kisses and other such things." She flattened her hands on his chest. "I've also thought about what you said about losing your brother-in-law and how you've tried to live in the moment ever since, to enjoy right now and not ruin that by obsessing about what might or might not happen. I'm trying to do that, too."

"Right now is really, really good."

"Yes." She let her head fall to his chest. "It is."

He wrapped his arms around her. "Right now is as close to perfect as perfect gets."

"I want to hold on very tight to right now."

"Hold on to me, Lucy. I won't let you down. I promise."

Because she wanted so badly to believe him, she held on as tight as she could.

On Monday morning, Colton took a cab uptown to the hotel where the trade show was being held. As he rode through rush-hour traffic, he thought about the weekend he'd spent with Lucy. Saturday night, they'd played pretty princess, watched movies and eaten popcorn with Simone until she fell asleep leaning against him. After settling her on the sofa, he and Lucy had gone to bed.

The next morning, he'd awakened to a little face looking down at him. He'd held his breath, waiting to hear what she had to say about finding him in bed with her aunt.

"What's for breakfast?" she'd asked.

Colton had breathed a sigh of relief and got busy making pancakes for Simone and Lucy, who'd finally felt a lot better. After Emma came to pick up her daughter, he and Lucy had gone out for a long walk around her neighborhood. She'd taken him to the beer store, where she said he acted like a kid in a candy store. They'd had lunch at a sidewalk café and then returned to her place to spend the rest of the afternoon in bed before they left for dinner in Queens.

Colton had loved seeing the home where Lucy had grown up, and he'd enjoyed spending more time with Ray, who was gruff on the outside but warm and welcoming to Colton, which was a relief. Lucy had told him later that

Ray had liked Colton a lot better after hearing Lucy say yet again that she wasn't going to move to Vermont.

Leaving her to go their separate ways for a few hours this morning had made him sad, which was ridiculous. He knew that. Still, he was bummed to have to spend any time away from her when they were in the same place at the same time. "You'd better get used to it," he said softly to himself. They were looking at a possible future of more time apart than together, a thought that depressed him profoundly.

He was determined to figure out a way to make this work, however. And he had this week in the city to ponder their options while hoping she'd be able to come home with him to spend next week in Vermont before Hannah's wedding. The thought of her back on his mountain made him smile.

"Here you go," the cabbie said as he pulled up to a mid-town hotel.

Colton realized he'd been so absorbed in his thoughts that he'd barely paid attention during the ride. Here he was in a new place full of things to see and experience, and all he was thinking about was how he could spend more time with Lucy. "Live in the moment, man," he reminded himself on the way into the hotel, where signs directed him to a ballroom on the third floor.

He'd had good intentions about doing some preliminary work to prepare for the event, such as finding out where he might find the exhibitors his father wanted him to talk to. But with Lucy sick for most of the weekend and too many other things he'd rather do, he was walking in cold.

The first indication of what was to come was the security guard checking IDs to ensure attendees were over eighteen. Inside the bag he was given at registration were samples of things he'd enjoy looking at later with Lucy.

He proceeded into a massive exhibition hall that was packed to the gills with people. Other than the time he'd gone to a Rolling Stones concert in Boston, he'd never been in a room with so many people. Or penises. The penis seemed to be everywhere he looked, in a dazzling array of colors and textures and materials. And they were all big. Really, really big.

Choking back the need to laugh, he wished he had the nerve to whip out his phone and take some pictures. He and his brothers would have a field day with those photos. But the people around him were engaged in serious conversations—and demonstrations—so he reined in his inner fifteen-year-old and proceeded into the hall, determined to do what he'd been sent here to do and then get the hell out of here as quickly as he could.

A woman wearing a bustier with thigh-high stockings and spike heels approached him with a tray of cookies. Only these cookies were little penises wearing cock rings and breasts with clamps affixed to the nipples. Hiding his amusement from the server, he took one of each, wrapped them in a napkin, and stashed them carefully in his bag to share with Lucy later.

"Thank you."

"You're welcome."

He continued down the aisle and happened upon an ongoing demonstration about the different types of lube. Fascinating. He'd had no idea there were types—or flavors for that matter. He hoped they'd included some of that strawberry stuff in his goodie bag.

Don't think about what you might do with that. Not here and not now. Although in this room, another hard penis would be right at home. Lucy was correct. He was a fifteen-year-old boy pretending to be twenty-six. In fact, he was probably the worst possible person his father could've sent on this mission. No, Landon and Lucas would've been worse. And Max. They would've been totally ridiculous here—especially together.

Colton was the picture of maturity compared to the three of them. And then he tried to imagine Hunter here and nearly lost his shit laughing. He sent a text to Lucy. I'm traumatized.

She wrote right back. Is it crazy?

Pretending to text, he took a photo of a woman in an adjacent booth demonstrating the proper application of nipple clamps—on her own nipples—and sent it to Lucy.

OUCH! Bring me something—not that though.

I've got a whole goodie bag to share with you.

I like goodies. Don't look at strange boobies. You'll go blind.

For the first time in my life, I actually wish I were blind right now.

Hahahahaha. Wish I'd gone with you. Sounds like more fun than writing html.

Going to do what I came here for, and then I am out of here.

Stay strong, little scout. See you when you're done.

I'm going to need you to hold me.

Any time. Xoxo

CHAPTER 29

———◆◆◆———

*Sugar content of sap: The range was
2.3 percent to 1.3 percent. Others reported
a sweeter season than ours.*

—Colton Abbott's sugaring journal, after the boil

Smiling after the exchange with Lucy, Colton stashed the phone in his pocket and continued through the exhibit hall until he found the area he'd come to see. A woman wearing a tag with the name *Joyce* was overseeing the booth. She had blonde hair and wore a sharp red suit. When Colton arrived, she was talking to a couple about her product line and how it brought sizzle back into the love lives of postmenopausal women and their partners.

An image of his mother popped into his head, and he quickly suppressed it. Under no circumstances would he think about her right now. Or his aunts. Or any other over-fifty women he'd ever known in his life. While he waited his turn to talk to Joyce, Gertrude "Dude" Danforth's face appeared in his mind, along with her "boyfriend," Skeeter, who helped Nolan out at the garage. *Make it stop*, he said silently to his overactive imagination as he perused the line of vibrating devices, lubricants and personal "massagers." Um, okay.

As his eyes wandered to the Kegel and prostate "exercising" devices, he reached his limit and stopped looking.

"Hi there. I'm Joyce. May I help you?"

"Colton Abbott from the Green Mountain Country Store in Butler, Vermont."

"You're a long way from home."

"You have no idea . . ."

Joyce laughed at his response and the grimace that went along with it. "So what brings you to the show?"

"My dad and his big ideas about how products like yours would be a good fit for our store."

"I take it you have a lot of customers who are over fifty?"

"We do."

"In that case, I bet my products would fly off your shelves. Let me tell you all about them. All of our products are also adaptable to people with special needs," she began.

Colton wanted to beg for mercy. But rather, he let Joyce lead him around the booth, filling his head with words and images that all the booze in Manhattan couldn't erase.

He emerged from the hotel several hours later a changed man and in possession of *things* he'd never given a thought to before today. His brain was muddled and filled with thoughts that had his blood racing through his veins, all of it accumulating predictably in one place. He pulled on the collar of the shirt he'd ironed at Lucy's apartment last night. It was some kind of hot in this city.

Colton pulled out his phone and called Lucy.

"Did you survive?"

"Just barely. How soon can you meet me at your place?"

"About an hour or so."

"I should be able to make it until then."

"What does that mean?"

"You'll find out when you get home."

"You're sort of scaring me right now," she said with a laugh.

"I've been scared all day."

"How are you getting home?"

"I thought I might walk."

"Don't be crazy. It's too hot to walk. Grab a cab. You've got the keys, right?"

"Yep. Hey, Luce?"

"Yeah?"

"Did you know the sex toy and novelty industry brings in fifteen billion dollars a year in this country?"

"Is that billion with a B?"

"Sure is. If you're ever in the market for penis-themed bachelorette party products, I can hook you up."

"That's very good to know. You never know when you might need a good rubber penis."

Her quick retort made him groan, among other reactions. "Don't talk about penises. It makes mine want you more than it already does."

"You brought it up."

"Don't use the word *up* around him right now. He's very fragile after the day we've had."

She laughed so hard she went silent for a full minute. "Fragile my ass."

"Great. Now I'm thinking about your ass. Get home, will you."

"I'm coming."

"Lucy!"

Her laughter made him smile as he continued to walk along busy, congested sidewalks. He wondered if his goofy grin would have people thinking he was strange, but no one paid any attention to him. They were all frantically moving toward their next destination, many of them wearing earbuds or walking with their noses to their phones.

He bought a hot dog and an icy-cold Coke from a sidewalk vendor with a thick New Yawk accent. It was the best hot dog Colton had ever had. He'd planned to get a cab but was still walking twenty blocks later when he came to a stop outside a gourmet shop. After checking his reflection in the window to make sure there was no leftover ketchup on his face, he stepped into the cool store.

It was the kind of place that carried a hundred different types of olive oil and another hundred kinds of vinegar. There were bins of coffee beans waiting to be ground to order, pasta and grains, homemade sauces, jams and breads of all kinds.

"Help you with something?" a male voice asked.

"Just looking," Colton replied.

"Let me know if you see something that interests you."

"I do have one question."

"Sure."

"Do you carry any kind of maple syrup?"

"I'm afraid we don't."

"Would you have any interest in stocking syrup made in Vermont? Perhaps under your own label?" The idea took hold as he said the words.

"How do you mean?"

"We make it, you carry it, and we put it in packaging that meshes with your corporate brand." Colton hoped the guy couldn't tell he was making this up as he went along.

"I'm intrigued. How would it work?"

Colton spent an hour talking to Stefano, who turned out to be the owner of the store, and when he emerged into the heat of the day, he'd landed a client in New York.

Lucy had a million and one things to do, especially since she was moving heaven and earth to be able to go home with Colton on Saturday. However, hearing he was on his way back to her apartment—and apparently revved up after his day at the trade show—had her making all kinds of excuses at the office.

"I might leave early, too," Diana said. "Still not a hundred percent after the weekend from hell." Her face was ghastly pale, but Lucy didn't look much better.

"Has anyone heard from Mel? Did she survive?"

"She called this morning to make sure we were okay. Her husband made her go to the ER on Friday night, and they kept her overnight. That's what I should've done. I still feel like hell, and she's a lot better. All apologies again, of course."

"Wasn't her fault. You should go home."

"I think I will."

"Before you go, could I talk to you for one second about something?"

Diana eyed her warily, which Lucy deserved. "Sure."

Lucy closed the door and took a seat in one of Diana's visitor chairs.

"This is worrisome. You closed the door."

"Nothing like that. Sorry."

"Oh good. I'm never quite certain where you're concerned."

"And that's entirely my fault. You replaced my best friend. I miss her. That has absolutely nothing at all to do with you, and I'm sorry if I've been an ass to you."

"You haven't been an ass, and I knew you and Cameron were tight. It has to be hard to see things change."

"It's been really hard, but I'm thrilled for her. Will is an awesome guy, and they're so happy together." Lucy bit her lip and forced herself to press on. "Which brings me to my own awesome guy. His brother. Colton."

"Oh," Diana said. And then her eyes got very big. "*Oh*. Are you moving, too?"

"No, nothing quite so dramatic. However, I do find myself wanting to spend more time in a place that's six hours from here on a good day with no traffic."

Diana tapped her pen against her chin. "That is a dilemma."

"His sister is getting married the weekend after next. I'm invited to the shower this weekend and the wedding the following weekend. I was thinking if I jammed a bunch of meetings into this week, I could go up there next week and do the creative portion. Would you have a problem with that?"

"Me? No, not at all."

"I might need you to handle a few things here that aren't technically in your job description."

"Which is also fine."

"Why are you being so nice to me when I've been a total ass to you?"

Diana laughed. "Because I've been where you are. I don't do change very well myself, and I knew you were working it out and you'd come around eventually. Or I'd find another job." Diana shrugged. "It's just work. It's not my whole life."

"I don't want you to find another job. You're doing fantastic work for us, and we're all very pleased. And that you're willing to cover for me while I'm out of town is extremely helpful."

"Happy to do it. I bet you'll get a lot done up there in the mountains without all the distractions of the office."

"That's the plan. Although there will be distractions of another kind."

"The best kind," Diana said with a knowing smile.

"Indeed."

"What's he like, this guy of yours?"

"He's . . . He's amazing. He showed up in the midst of Friday night's disaster and totally took over."

"Oh wow. I can't imagine a guy around for that."

"Neither could I, but he was incredible through the whole thing. Never batted an eye—and he still wanted to have sex with me afterward."

Diana howled with laughter. "He sounds like a prince."

"He is."

"You're in love."

"Very much so."

"And he lives in Vermont."

"Yes, he does."

"So what's the plan?"

"We don't have one. This week he's here. Next week I'm there. The week after that? Who knows? But he says we'll figure it out, so that's what we're doing. We're figuring it out one week at a time."

"Good for you, Lucy. You deserve to be happy."

"That's nice of you to say, and I'm sorry if I was less than welcoming."

"You were fine, and I'm glad I waited you out. I have a feeling you're a good friend to have once you come around."

"I will be. And thanks for being willing to help me spend time in Vermont."

"It's no problem. This is the best job I've had in a long time. I'm happy to do whatever you need me to do."

Though she didn't have the time, Lucy chatted with Diana for another fifteen minutes, time well spent in getting to know her new colleague a little better. She returned to her own office and was startled to find her dad waiting for her. He hadn't been there in years, since right after he helped her and Cam move into the office space a year after they started their business.

She gave him a kiss on his cheek. "What're you doing here? Is everything okay?"

"I'm sorry to bother you at work. They told me you were in a meeting, and they said I could wait for you in here. Hope that's okay."

"Of course it is. Do you want coffee or tea? I think we have Coke, too."

"No, I don't want anything."

"Why do you look all spun up? What's wrong?"

"I am. I'm wrong. What I said to you last night about not moving away from me. I was awake all night thinking about it, and it was wrong of me to say that to you."

"Dad—"

"Wait. Hear me out." He took a moment, seeming to be searching for the words. "Ever since your mother died—and for a long time before that, if I'm being entirely honest—you've been the glue that's held our family together. We all rely on good old Lucy, and she's always there for us no matter what."

"I love you guys, Dad. You've never been a burden to me."

"I know that, Lucy, but there comes a time when you have to live your own life and do what you need to do to be happy. If that means moving to Vermont to live with a man who's clearly in love with you—and vice versa—then that's what you should do. As much as I'd miss you, I want you to be happy."

Lucy went to him and wrapped her arms around him, fighting back tears as he did the same. "I'm not moving, Dad. I meant it when I said that."

"You shouldn't rule it out. Not yet anyway."

"I ruled it out weeks ago when I started to realize this thing with him was turning out to be much more than a weekend fling."

"Why, Lucy? If Cameron can be happy there, why can't you?"

"Because she doesn't have what I have here. She doesn't have a dad like you and a sister like Emma, a niece like Simone. Not to mention she walked away from the business, which was totally her prerogative, but it leaves me with fewer options, you know?"

"Businesses can be sold or disbanded or even relocated."

She eyed him skeptically. "Why are you pushing so hard to get rid of me?"

"That's not what I'm doing. Believe it or not, I know what it's like to be young and crazy in love. I didn't get nearly enough time with your mom," he said softly, his eyes filling. He never talked about his late wife. Ever. Lucy had wondered if he was angry at her for dying, but now she could see he was heartbroken, even after all these years. "Time is a very precious commodity, honey. Don't squander it. Spend it with the people you love the most."

"That's what I'm doing, Dad. And besides, I promised Simone I wouldn't leave her."

"Simone doesn't have the right to ask that of you. None of us do."

"And none of you have. I'm doing what *I* want to do. Being here with you is what I want."

"What about marriage and children and a family of your own? How does that happen if he doesn't move or you don't?"

"We haven't even begun to discuss things like that," she said, though the question caused a wave of yearning deep inside her. To be married to Colton, to have his children, to laugh with him and wake to his gorgeous face on the pillow next to hers every day . . .

"Lucy, honey, I'm sorry. I didn't mean to make you cry."

She shook her head, furious with herself for letting her emotions take over. "You didn't. It's a tough situation, and I knew going into it that it wouldn't be easy, but he's always been worth it. You should've seen him when I was sick."

"I've met him twice, and I can already tell he's made of good stuff. He's got the right kind of hands, for one thing."

"The right kind of *hands*?" Lucy asked, baffled. "Not that I don't agree that his hands are pretty fabulous, but something tells me we aren't talking about the same thing."

Ray grimaced. "Remember who you're talking to, young lady."

Lucy giggled at his stern tone. "Don't blame me. You're the one who said it. I was just agreeing with you."

"What I meant was that you can tell by a man's hands whether he's a hard worker."

"That's not really true anymore, Dad. You've heard of the digital revolution . . ."

"In my world, it'll always be true. Your Colton has working man's hands. You can tell by looking at them that he's a hard worker."

"Yes, he is," Lucy said, ridiculously touched by her dad's assessment—and approval—of the man she loved. "You should come up and see his mountain someday. The process involved with making syrup would fascinate you."

"I might just do that."

"All right then. We'll make some plans."

"Do what you need to do to be happy, Lucy Lu. The rest of us will be just fine no matter what you decide."

Lucy hugged him again. "Thanks for coming all the way down here to tell me that. I'm sorry you lost sleep over it."

"I'm retired. I can take a nap."

She smiled at him as her phone dinged with a text from Colton. Almost home. Are you there yet?

Ray kissed her forehead. "Go ahead, honey. I don't want to hold you up."

"I'm really glad you came to see me," she said as he headed for the door.

"So am I. Talk to you tomorrow."

Watching him go, Lucy's heart broke at the thought of him lying awake worrying that he'd said the wrong thing to her, that he'd discouraged her from following her heart. Speaking of her heart . . . She shut down her computer and grabbed her purse. On the way out of the office, she replied to Colton's text.

Ten minutes away.

Hurry up. I'm lonely for you.

You know how to make a girl all swoony.

I've got a few other ways to make that happen. What are your thoughts on nipple gloss?

For a second, Lucy thought she'd read that wrong, but then she laughed as she remembered where he'd been earlier. Umm, am I supposed to have thoughts on nipple gloss? I don't even know what it is.

You will soon enough. I'm sure you'll have some thoughts about it later.

She was so engrossed in her text conversation with Colton that she nearly slammed into someone on the street. "Sorry," she muttered.

"Watch where you're going," he said with a growl.

Normally, the comment would've pissed her off, but today she didn't care. She had far better things to do than engage in a verbal smackdown with a stranger on the street. Only the fear of smelling sweaty and gross kept her from jogging home—that and the fact that she still felt less than perfect after the weekend's ordeal.

But knowing he was waiting for her had her walking fast. Very, very fast.

CHAPTER 30

---◄►---

Syrup yield per tap: .492 gallons, or nearly a half-gallon of syrup per tap. This calculation is the only meaningful way to compare sugar seasons, since the number of taps varies from year to year. This year ranks a close third behind 2011: .55 gals per tap and 1992: .52 gallons per tap.

—Colton Abbott's sugaring journal, after the boil

The six-block walk had never seemed so long, but Lucy had never been so eager to get home before. She'd never gone home from work knowing Colton was waiting at her place, and that one detail made everything so much more significant. Walking onto her street at last, she saw him sitting on the stairs that led to her apartment. He was looking down at his phone, messing around with it while he waited for her. His long legs were stretched out in front of him, and he looked totally at home in her world, even if it was so far removed from his.

The sense of rightness, of belonging, of homecoming had nothing at all to do with the place where she lived and everything to do with the man sitting outside waiting for her. As those feelings washed over her, she no longer cared about smelling sweaty. She broke into a jog so she could get to him faster.

He looked up, saw her coming and got up to meet her, catching her in his strong arms and lifting her into a kiss that should've embarrassed the hell out of her, taking place as it did in broad daylight on the street where she'd lived for years. But she didn't care in the least if anyone saw her kiss him.

"That was the longest ten minutes ever," he said, letting her slide down the front of him until she was standing on solid ground again.

"I tried to hurry."

"I'm kidding, babe." He kissed her again and escorted her up the stairs, keeping his arm around her until they were in her apartment.

Lucy caught a glimpse of her coffee table covered with stuff. "What's all that?"

He held out his hand to her. "Come see."

She took his hand and went to sit next to him on the sofa to take a closer look at the items on the table.

"This right here would be a cock ring—the vibrating kind. Intriguing if I do say so myself. Over here we have a bullet vibrator and the already-mentioned nipple gloss. Personally, I'm looking forward to seeing your glossy nipples."

Listening to him, Lucy felt her face heat up, but for once she didn't care. By now he'd certainly come to expect that reaction when he was being outrageous, which was pretty much all the time.

"I'm not really sure what this thing is." He held up a tapered object that was thin at the top and wide at the bottom and examined it from all angles.

"Um, I think that's a, um . . ."

He glanced at her, his gaze fixed on her flaming cheeks. "What?"

"Butt plug."

"Huh?"

"You um use it to, you know . . ."

"Oh please. For the love of God and all that's holy, please finish that sentence."

She shoved his shoulder until he fell over on the sofa, laughing his ass off. "You know exactly what that is. You just wanted to make me say it."

"You have no idea how much I enjoyed that."

"I hate you a little bit right now."

"No, you don't. You think I'm adorable and funny and sexy and irresistible, and you may as well admit it."

"I'll do nothing of the sort."

He held up the plug, examining it from every angle and then glancing at her suggestively. "Want to play with my new toys?"

"We don't need toys to have fun."

"True, but I've spent all morning thinking about all the ways I could make you crazy, and I have to admit, my imagination has never been more vivid."

"I'll try the nipple gloss if you try the cock ring."

"Oh baby, you're on." He was up and off the sofa so quickly she barely had time to register the movement before he was sweeping her along on the way to her room.

Clothes went flying in a flurry of color and movement. He was a man on a mission. When she was bared to him, she resisted the urge to cover herself the way she would have only a couple of weeks ago. Now she stood perfectly still and let him take a long perusing look at her. Naturally, the flush she couldn't control overtook her, but he loved that.

She tugged at the button to the khakis he'd worn to the trade show and had trouble getting the zipper down over his bulging erection.

He drew in a deep breath and rested his hands on her hips, drawing her closer to him, but she resisted his attempt to kiss her.

Dropping to her knees, she pushed his pants and boxers down over his hips, encircled his cock with her hand and teased the head with her tongue. "You'll never get the ring on when you're in this condition, so we need to start all over."

"Lucy . . ."

She wrapped her lips around the wide crown and sucked him in.

"Fuck." He grasped the back of her head roughly, which only added to the thrill for her. "This is going to be quick."

Opening her mouth wider, she slid him in, letting her tongue swirl around him as she stroked him with her hand.

His head fell back in total surrender to her and his legs trembled, which filled her with satisfaction. He was so strong and capable, but knowing she had this kind of power over him was the sweetest kind of pleasure.

She stepped up her efforts, letting her free hand wander around to the back of him to squeeze his ass, drawing another sharp gasp from him.

"Lucy . . ."

The note of warning wasn't lost on her. He was giving her the chance to withdraw, but that was the last thing she wanted to do. Rather, she relaxed her muscles and took as much of him as she could accommodate, all the while stroking with one hand and squeezing with the other.

He came hard, flooding the back of her throat with his release, which she swallowed greedily.

She stayed with him until she felt his muscles relax. The instant she released him, he fell back on the bed, wrecked. His arms covered his face and his chest heaved from the deep breaths he drew in and out. Lucy took advantage of his preoccupation and his newly flaccid state to apply the cock ring.

He sat up abruptly to see what she was doing.

"There," she said, patting his thigh. "All fixed."

He reached for her and pulled her down on top of him. "You're a vixen, you know that?"

"Never been one before, so it's all your fault."

"I'm so glad you saved it for me. That was fucking incredible. You are fucking incredible, and I love you more every day. Not just because of things like that either. It's everything. All of you." He reached up to run his fingers through her hair, tucking it behind her ears. "The way you looked at me when you saw me waiting for you on the street. No one has ever looked at me like that before."

"Somehow I find that hard to believe," she said dryly, even though her heart beat madly.

"I'm serious, Luce. Women have looked at me before, but never the way you do."

"How do I look at you?"

"Like you love me. Like you want more from me than a good time in bed. Like you want *me*."

"I do want you and love you. And I want more from you than a good time in bed, although the good time in bed is a lovely benefit."

"I do what I can," he said with that impish smile she loved so much. "Now where's that gloss?"

She found the wand on the bed and handed it to him.

He smoothly rolled them over so he was on top of her and knelt between her legs.

"What flavor is it?"

"I'm almost afraid to say."

"Oh come on! Where's your sense of adventure?"

"Um, it's wrapped rather tightly around my cock at the moment."

Lucy dissolved into giggles. He was so damned funny—all the time. "Spill it."

"Funny you should put it that way. It's 'Cream My Jeans.'"

"That's kind of gross."

"Luckily, you won't be the one tasting it."

"I already took one for the team. This one's all yours."

"Here goes." He withdrew the wand from the barrel and took great pains to carefully paint every inch of her suddenly super-sensitive nipples with the smooth gloss. "Mmm, that's hot. Look how shiny they are."

As he worked, his erection blossomed and stretched nearly to his belly button.

"You young boys recover quickly," she said, caressing his muscular arms as he hovered above her, tongue trapped between his teeth as he created his masterpiece.

"That's what you get for robbing the cradle."

She gave a gentle tug to a tuft of chest hair. "You're only three years younger than me."

"But what a difference those three years make."

"Indeed. I'm hoping you'll reach the maturity of a seventeen-year-old one of these days."

"Don't hold your breath on—" He startled and his face twisted with what might've been pleasure—or pain.

"What?"

"It just started vibrating. Scared the shit out of me."

Lucy cracked up laughing and couldn't stop. She laughed until tears streamed from her eyes and her chest heaved with hiccups. Her laughter died, however, when he bent over her and began to clean up the gloss with his tongue on her sensitive nipples.

"Mmm," he said, ensuring the vibration of his lips had her full attention. "I thought that might quiet you down."

"How's the buzzing down below?"

"Why don't you tell me?" He moved so the bottom portion of the vibrating ring was pressed tight against her most sensitive area.

Lucy cried out from the triple threat caused by the heated gloss, his lips on her nipple and the vibration between her legs. She wrapped her arms around him, trying to get closer.

"You like that?"

"Yeah," she said breathlessly. "What does Cream Your Jeans taste like anyway?"

"It's sweet, but I like the way you taste better." He moved from her nipple to her lips, the flavor on his tongue giving her a hint of what the gloss tasted like.

"If you liked that," he said, "you're gonna love this." He pressed against her slippery flesh, gaining entry one slow inch at a time, giving her time to adjust and accommodate. Then he was fully seated, and the vibrating ring was pressed tight against her clit. The combination of his lips tugging on her nipple, the tight squeeze of his cock inside her and the vibration set off the most explosive orgasm of her life, and he hadn't even moved yet.

"Lucy," he whispered against her ear, holding her tightly as she came back down to earth. "God, that was amazing."

"Why does my throat hurt?" she asked between deep breaths.

"Maybe because you screamed your head off."

"I did? Really?" That had certainly never happened before.

"Uh-huh."

"Thank goodness my neighbors aren't home at this hour. They might've called the cops."

He laughed and pressed deeper into her, which was when she realized the screaming orgasm had been hers alone.

"You didn't . . ."

"Nope. You took the edge off. I'm good to go for an hour now."

"An *hour*?"

"Uh-huh. Hold on tight babe. Here we go."

Lucy was completely ruined for all other men. True to his word, he'd made love to her for a solid hour, until she finally begged for mercy and used a couple of dirty tricks to finish him off. She'd been in every possible position and a few she never would've thought of before him. His imagination was as robust as his stamina. Now she was face-down on the bed as he kissed a series of circles on her back while his hands kneaded her bottom.

"You're out to kill me, aren't you?" she asked when his efforts resulted in yet another throb between her legs. She was surprised she still had feeling there after what they'd just done.

"Not hardly. It's your own fault for taking the edge off earlier."

"I'll have to remember the consequences of that in the future."

"I want to play with that plug," he whispered, his lips brushing over her backside and leaving her tingling with goose bumps.

"Not now. I'm wrecked. You've completely destroyed me."

"You wouldn't have to do anything."

"Colton!"

He flopped on the bed next to her. "Fine. Be that way." Lying on his back, he looked over at her. "That wasn't a *no* though, was it?"

"No, it wasn't."

His eyes went dark with lust, which she found remarkable. How could he have anything left after that marathon? "So you'd be game for doing that sometime?"

"You like to embarrass me, don't you?"

"Not at all. I like to keep it real with you." He turned on his side and continued to run his hand up and down her back, as if he couldn't stand to be that close to her and not touch her. She loved that. "I like that I can be myself with you and say whatever I'm thinking, even if it might embarrass you."

"I like that you're yourself with me. I don't think I've ever been more myself with anyone than I am with you."

"That pleases me more than you could ever know." He leaned over to kiss her shoulder, punctuating the kiss with a little nibble. "So the plug? Sometime? Yes?" The eager-little-boy side of him was almost impossible to resist.

"Only if you do it, too."

The face he made was positively priceless. "What? No way."

"Why not?"

"Because, babe," he said with grave seriousness. "That's a one-way street. Exit only."

"That is a double standard of the highest order."

"Call it what you will. Rules are rules."

"Then I guess we're at a standoff on this topic."

His hand slid down her back to cup her bottom. "I could make it really good for you . . ."

"I could make it really good for *you*."

"Not happening."

"Okay, then. Your loss."

His head dropped onto her back. "This isn't fair. You got my hopes up."

Lucy smiled. "You get that you're being totally ridiculous and narrow minded and sexist and—"

He shifted on the bed and kissed her before she could finish the thought, and because she loved kissing him so much she turned onto her side to give him better access to her lips. For the longest time, they did nothing more than lie there wrapped up in each other, kissing and touching and snuggling.

As hard as she tried, Lucy couldn't imagine anything better than whiling away a summer afternoon in bed with Colton Abbott.

CHAPTER 31

———◦‹›◦———

Syrup grade: 66 percent Fancy Grade, a reflection of good sugaring weather. Only 1 percent Grade B this year. Syrup made in one day: On April 12 we beat the record-breaking Gift Run by 10 gallons, for a total of 464 gallons.

—Colton Abbott's sugaring journal, after the boil

On Saturday morning, Lucy flew to Vermont with Colton, armed with her laptop, broadband device and a week's worth of work to do for clients—not to mention a stack of paperwork she'd let slide the last couple of weeks. Diana was holding down the fort at the office with orders to call Lucy whenever she needed her.

She'd decided not to feel guilty about doing what she wanted for a change. She and Colton had spent extra time with Simone, picking her up from school on Friday afternoon and taking her to the park and for ice cream. Lucy had promised to call her niece while she was gone and to take lots of pictures at the wedding, which seemed to satisfy the girl.

In between spending time with Colton, showing him her city and seeing her family, Lucy had worked like a demon to set herself up to be out of the office all next week. Tucked into her suitcase was the silver frame from Tiffany's that she'd paid extra to have engraved before she left the city. She'd give that to Hannah and Nolan as a wedding gift, and she had ordered crystal goblets from Hannah's registry to be delivered to Colton's parents' house in time for the shower.

"What if the shower gift doesn't get there in time?" she asked when they were on final approach to Burlington. He'd held her hand the entire way, even as he dozed off.

"It'll get there," he said without opening his eyes.

"How can you sleep on a plane?"

He opened his left eye to look at her. "How can you not sleep on a plane? What else is there to do?"

"Fret and worry about every bump and dip and sound. How can you do that if you're asleep?"

He opened both eyes, smiled at her warmly and brought their joined hands to his lips. "Have I told you yet today how much I love you and how thrilled I am that you're coming home with me for this special week with my family?"

"You might've mentioned those things a time or two."

"Is it okay if I mention them again?"

She nodded and fixated on the seat across the aisle as all sorts of thoughts spiraled through her overactive mind.

"What're you thinking about?"

He was always so attuned to her, which was something she was slowly becoming accustomed to. "Nothing much."

"Don't lie to me. I know that look. You're overthinking something. All the signs are there."

"Quit knowing me so well. It's unnerving."

"Get used to it, babe. You're stuck with me."

His words filled her with longing so sharp and so powerful it nearly took her breath away. She wanted to be stuck with him forever. Lately, that want, that desire overrode everything else that had ever been important to her. From the very beginning, she'd been firm in her conviction that moving wasn't an option for her. She hadn't changed her mind, but with every day she spent with him it was becoming harder to imagine a day without him.

Another week together wasn't going to make anything easier. If anything, it was getting more complicated and confusing all the time. The one thing that remained blissfully uncomplicated was the way she loved him. It was the purest, simplest, most natural thing she'd ever felt for anyone.

After the plane landed, he stood behind her in the aisle waiting for the people ahead of them to disembark. He slid his hand around her, laying it flat against her belly and keeping her close to him. "I brought the plug with me," he whispered in her ear, making her shudder from his words as much as the heat against her ear.

She turned her head to return his whisper. "Let me know when you're ready to try it."

His low growl made her laugh out loud, causing the crowd of people around them to look at them curiously.

Thirty minutes later, they'd collected their bags from baggage claim and ridden the shuttle to the long-term parking lot. Loaded into his truck, they set out for Butler.

"I can't wait to see Sarah and Elmer," he said. "This is the longest I've ever been away from them."

"I'm sure Max took good care of them while you were gone."

"He better have or I'll kick his ass."

"So what's the plan for this bachelor party that's going on tonight?"

"The guys are all coming up to camp on the mountain for the night. Beer and poker and Jäger and maybe more beer." He glanced over at her. "You're sure you don't mind spending the night with Cameron at their place?"

"As long as there aren't strippers coming to the mountain, I don't mind."

Colton's bark of laughter made her smile even though she was dead serious about the strippers. His laugh was that contagious. "Have you met my brother Hunter?"

"Yes, a couple of times now."

"Then you ought to know that as Nolan's best man, he's the last guy on the *planet* who'd arrange for strippers at a bachelor party. With him in charge, we're far more likely to end up with tenderloin and pâté than we are tits and pus—"

She slammed her hand over his mouth. "If you finish that thought, I'll kill you."

"What?" he asked, his voice muffled by her hand. He nibbled at her until she removed it. "You got a problem with pussycats or something?"

Lucy rolled her eyes at him. "Like that's what you were going to say."

"Now you'll never know, will you?"

Lucy watched the scenery go by, captivated once again by the pure, majestic beauty of Vermont. Even the highways were scenic. "Colton?"

"Yeah?"

"I just want you to know that I have more fun with you than anyone I've ever known in my whole life."

He looked at her for a moment before returning his attention to the road. His hand came over the center console in search of hers.

Lucy happily joined their hands.

"That's the nicest compliment I've ever gotten from anyone. And P.S., same to you. If I'm not dying laughing with you, I'm dying from wanting you. It's a pretty amazing thing we've got here, and I hope you know I'm never going to let you go."

"I'm sort of counting on it." Under normal circumstances, a statement like that would've made her feel wildly vulnerable and exposed. But saying it to Colton was different. She knew she was safe with him and could say what she really meant without fear or regret.

He squeezed her hand. "Good."

The invasion of the Abbott men began around four o'clock. Cameron had driven Will and would be taking Lucy with her, but now that the hour was upon them, Colton resented the intrusion. They hadn't spent a night apart in more than a week, and the thought of even one night without her was unbearable.

He knew he was being ridiculous, but every minute with her was precious, and he didn't want her to go.

Lucas and Landon were fighting over how to put up a tent, and Max was right in the middle of it, refereeing. Wade was telling them all to shut the hell up while Elmer and Lincoln worked on building the bonfire in the yard. In summers past it would've been too dry to have a fire, but this year there'd been plenty of rain and thus there were no burn warnings keeping them from enjoying the fire.

George, Ringo, Trevor, Tanner, Elmer and Sarah ran around in circles, adding to the chaos with their enthusiastic game of dog tag.

Colton clung to Lucy from behind as she took in the scene unfolding around them. "Please take me with you." Just an hour ago they'd had the mountain to themselves with only Sarah and Elmer for company, and now it had descended into chaos.

"You need a night with the boys, and I need a night with Cameron. You'll survive."

"Who's bringing Nolan?" Lucas asked as he hammered a stake into the ground. He had his shirt off and was sweating profusely from the effort.

"He's coming with Skeeter and the racing team," Hunter said.

"Put a shirt on, will you?" Colton said to Lucas. "There're women present."

"It's fine," Lucy said, patting Colton's hand. "You don't have to put a shirt on for me, Lucas."

"Me either," Cameron said with a goofy grin.

Will threw Lucas's T-shirt at his head. "Put the shirt on."

"They're just jealous," Landon said to his twin. "Probably starting to sag around the middle. Happens to old dudes like them."

"He hasn't started to sag—yet," Lucy said, "but that doesn't mean I don't enjoy a good man chest when I see it."

Lucas flexed his muscles dramatically, making the others groan.

"Maybe it's best if you get out of Dodge." Colton kissed Lucy's temple. "I can't be responsible for what happens here." He held her close to him for another minute. "I'm going to miss you tonight."

"Me, too. Have fun with the boys."

"Can I come with you guys?" Hunter asked Cameron and Lucy. His attempt to dress down for camping consisted of a T-shirt that looked like he'd ironed it, khaki shorts and fancy hiking boots.

"This is your party, pal," Colton said. "You aren't going anywhere."

"So what's the verdict?" Cameron asked Will. "Are the boys coming home with me or staying with you?"

Will whistled for Trevor and Tanner, who came rushing over to him. "You guys want to stay with me or go with Cam?"

Both dogs jumped up on Cam, practically knocking her over.

"I guess they answered the question," Wade said with a laugh.

"Good," Will said. "They'll take care of you while I'm not there." He bent to give both dogs some love before he sent them to Cameron's SUV. "I'll see you in the morning, hon." He kissed and hugged Cameron while Colton did the same with Lucy.

Lucy patted his chest. "Don't get into any trouble."

"I'll try to behave." He kissed her again. "Love you."

"*Awwwwwww,*" Lucas and Landon said together, holding and hugging each other while pretending to sob. Next to them, Max laughed his ass off.

"Dad," Will said. "Do something about them."

"Boys, leave your brothers alone."

"I don't want to," Lucas said.

"Neither do I," Landon added.

"Me neither," Max said.

"They don't want to, Will," Lincoln said. "Sorry."

Elmer's guffaw echoed through the yard.

Will and Colton were saved by the arrival of Nolan and Skeeter in one truck and three other trucks behind them, presumably containing Nolan's racing team.

"Don't block in the black SUV," Will called to them. "They're leaving."

"Let's get out of here while we still can, Lucy." Cameron stole one more kiss from Will and headed for the truck.

"I'll come get you in the morning," Colton said before he released Lucy. "Early."

"If you end up having too much fun, you can get me later. Hannah's shower isn't until two."

"It'll be early." He kissed her soundly right there in front of his father, grandfather, brothers, future brother-in-law and a bunch of other guys he didn't know. Even Lucas and Landon's catcalls didn't deter Colton from the kiss. "There," he said when he was done. "Now I should be able to make it until tomorrow."

As expected, Lucy's face was bright red, but she didn't seem mad at him for kissing her in front of everyone. "Have fun."

"You, too. Text me later."

"You'll be too busy partying to text."

"Text anyway." He leaned in close to her. "Love you."

She smiled at him. "Me, too."

"Say it."

"Here?"

He raised his brows, issuing a dare. "Right here."

"Love you, too."

Lucas and Landon started up again, kissing and hugging and weeping dramatically—and loudly.

"Dad!" Colton said.

"Boys, knock it off."

"We don't want to," Landon said.

"They don't want to," Lincoln said.

Aggravated, Colton ignored the whole lot of them and

walked Lucy to Cameron's car and held the door for her. "I can't wait until this happens to them. Payback is a big hairy bitch named Colton."

Lucy laughed and kissed him one more time. "Have fun, you big hairy bitch."

He let out a low growl. "That sounds so hot coming from you."

She pushed him back and got into Cameron's car.

Colton waited until she was belted in and then closed her door.

With Will's help, he directed Cameron to drive forward and then turn around so she was facing downhill.

"Be careful going down," Will said.

"Believe me," Cameron replied. "I remember what can happen on that hill." She winked at him, and his face lit up in a big smile.

Colton recalled when Will had nearly driven off the icy road the first time he brought Cameron up the mountain. Colton had suspected at the time that his brother had been distracted. Watching them now, he was sure of it.

Colton stood with Will to watch them go.

"How'd this happen to us?" Colton asked. "How'd we become the guys who'd rather be going with them than spending the night boozing with these douchebags?"

"I have no idea, but at times like this, I blame Fred."

"I can blame him, too, right? If he hadn't snagged Cameron for you, then I wouldn't have met Lucy, and I wouldn't be standing here feeling like I just got run over by a steamroller because I don't get to sleep with her tonight."

"You can blame Fred, too."

"Good. Thanks. That helps."

"Let's go do this so we can get to tomorrow faster."

With his hand on Will's arm, Colton stopped his brother from walking away. "Nothing says we have to stay here all night."

"What do you mean?"

"After everyone crashes, we could head down the hill and go find our girls."

"Not planning to drink?"

"Not really in the mood. You?"

"Not so much."

"So it's a plan?"

Will smiled at him. "If they ever find out, they'll call us pussy-whipped assholes for the rest of our lives."

"I'm willing to risk it."

Will fist-bumped his brother. "Me, too."

CHAPTER 32

———◆———

*Cords of wood burned: 32. Without the reverse-
osmosis machine, we would have needed five
times as much wood. Granted, the reverse-
osmosis machine uses a lot of fuel, but the overall
fuel and cost savings are high. Bags of oranges
eaten while boiling: 26.*

—Colton Abbott's sugaring journal, after the boil

Surrounded by most of his favorite men, Nolan settled in
to enjoy his last hurrah as a single guy. While he
couldn't wait to be married to Hannah in one short week, a
night away from it all with the guys was no hardship. He'd
thought everyone who was coming had already arrived
when two huge SUVs came into the yard and almost all of
the Sultans came pouring out of the two trucks.

"What's this we heard about a bachelor party?" Turk
asked in the loud bellow that was his trademark. He had an
unlit cigar hanging out of his mouth as he came toward
them, followed by Jack, who had his guitar strung over his
shoulder, then Austin, Ethan, Liam, Josh, Mark and
Dylan—all of them Caleb Guthrie's best friends. Over the
years, Caleb's friends from his years as an Army brat, college hockey star and later as an Army officer had merged
with his childhood friends in Butler, including Nolan,

Hunter and Will. No one had been more adept at blending all his friends into one big group he called the Sultans than Caleb.

"Oh my God," Nolan said to himself more than anyone else. The guys had come from all over the country. He hadn't expected to see them here. As close friends of both his and Hannah's, they'd been invited to the wedding, but to have them here now, too, was almost more than Nolan could process.

He stood to receive their handshakes and man hugs. "What're you guys doing here?"

"We came for the week," Turk said. "Our brother Nolan is getting married to our patron saint Hannah. Where else would we be?"

Nolan shook his head in amazement. "I'm so glad you're here."

"We wouldn't be anywhere else," Austin said with a squeeze for Nolan's shoulder. "Now where's the beer? We were promised beer!"

"We brought the Jäger," Liam said, proudly producing a bottle from behind his back.

"Of course you did," Nolan said, laughing. As the son of a drunk and a drug addict, he'd realized early on in life that it wasn't in his best interest to drink the way a lot of his friends did. He enjoyed a beer or two. Sometimes, on nights like this, he might even have three. But you wouldn't catch him anywhere near a bottle of Jägermeister.

"Good surprise?" Hunter asked when he joined Nolan.

"Amazing surprise. It's very . . . humbling . . . to have Caleb's crew here. I was wondering though . . . Is Gavin coming?" Nolan asked of Caleb's brother, another of Nolan's close friends from childhood.

"He's supposed to be bringing his dad. I hope they get here soon. It's almost time to eat."

Hunter and the other Abbott brothers had been manning the grill for an hour now, cooking steaks and baked potatoes, the smell of which was apparently enough to bring Fred strolling through their makeshift camp for a look-see.

"Holy shit," Turk said, the cigar falling from his mouth as he backpedaled out of the way of the moose, knocking over his chair as he went. "Why're you guys just sitting there? Do something."

"That's just Fred," Landon said, taking a swig of his beer.

"He's harmless," Wade added as he threw another log on the fire.

"That thing is fucking huge," Austin said, the other Sultans nodding in agreement while they kept a close watch on Fred.

When he'd satisfied his curiosity, Fred continued on his way.

"Jesus," Turk said when he returned to his seat by the fire. "Took five freaking years off my life."

Laughing at the Sultans' reaction to Fred, Nolan said, "This is a pretty fancy bachelor party, Hunter." He gestured to the steak on the grill. "Thanks for going all out."

Hunter laughed. "Only you would think camping on the mountain was fancy."

"I can't think of anything I'd rather do or any guys I'd rather do it with." He held his bottle up to Hunter. "Thank you."

Hunter touched his bottle to Nolan's. "My pleasure. Enjoy yourself. It's your big night."

His big night. As Nolan looked around at the men who'd come from near and far to celebrate his upcoming wedding, he felt blessed beyond measure. After growing up without much family to speak of, the family he'd chosen for himself and the one he was marrying into had more than filled the void left by his absent parents. Still, he couldn't help but wish the people who'd brought him into this world would care enough to see him marry the love of his life.

But that wasn't going to happen, so he'd found contentment with what he had and didn't spend much time wishing for things that would never be. His glass was way more than half full, especially now that he had a family of his own to look forward to with Hannah. On Monday they'd had an appointment to confirm what multiple pregnancy tests had already indicated—she was pregnant, and they were thrilled beyond measure.

Only because he was keeping half an eye on the hill did he see the sweep of headlights that preceded the arrival of Gavin Guthrie and his father, Bob. Honored that Gavin and his father had come, Nolan held back, giving them a chance to see the others first. Each of the Sultans greeted the Guthries with warm hugs and lots of laughter.

Nolan was deeply, profoundly thankful for the future he had planned with Hannah. But in that moment, he would've given up his own happiness and everything else he had to see Caleb Guthrie standing in the middle of this gathering he would've enjoyed so much.

Bob came over to Nolan and greeted him with a hug. "Congratulations to the groom-to-be."

"Thank you, Bob. And thanks for being here."

"Glad to be here. Gav had a last-minute crisis at work or we would've been here earlier."

"You're right in time for steak," Hunter said, pressing a beer into Bob's hand. The two of them headed toward the grill.

Gavin wandered over a few minutes later and shook hands with Nolan. He'd initially objected to Nolan's relationship with Hannah but had since come around. Even knowing that Gavin's objection came from a place of relentless grief over the loss of his brother, it had been hard for Nolan and Hannah to handle. The three of them were good now, but Nolan knew the idea of Hannah getting married again had to be tearing Gavin up inside. "Nice turnout you got here, pal," Gavin said.

"It's incredible. I had no idea the Sultans were coming."

"You're one of them. Where else would they be?"

"That's what they said, too."

"I haven't been up here in years." Gavin took a long look around at the familiar buildings that made up the Abbott family's sugarhouse and Colton's cabin. "Brings back a lot of memories. Remember all the nights we spent up here when we were kids?"

"Those were some good times. The best of times."

"Yes, they were. I'm really happy for you, Nolan. For both of you. I hope you know that."

"Thank you. That means a lot to me, and I know it will to Hannah, too."

"I'm ready for a beer. Can I get you one?"

"Sure, I'm due for another. Hey, Gav?"

"Yeah?"

"I'm really glad you're here."

Gavin's smile didn't light up his face the way it used to, but it was sincere nonetheless. "Wouldn't have missed it."

"The first time I came here, this road was full of potholes," Cameron said as she drove down the long dirt lane that led to her and Will's place. "Mud season."

"Ah yes," Lucy said. "Mud has a season in Vermont."

"It's one of Vermont's many charms."

"A year ago, if you'd told me you'd be living way out in the boonies espousing the charms of something called mud season, I would've laughed my ass off."

"I would've been laughing right along with you."

"Look at us now. In deep and getting deeper all the time with two brothers from Vermont."

"You forgot sexy. Two *sexy* brothers from Vermont."

"Sorry for the oversight. They are indeed sexy."

"So you're in deep, huh?"

"Yeah."

"You don't sound too happy about it."

"I am happy. When we're together." Lucy blew out a deep breath. "It's just, the rest of it . . ."

"I know, honey." Cameron parked, turned off the car and reached over to squeeze Lucy's arm. "Come in, see my new home, have a glass of wine, get comfy and we'll talk it out."

"Sounds good." Lucy got out of the SUV and took a

good look around at the gorgeous spot where Will had built the home he now shared with Cameron. "This is beautiful, Cam."

"Isn't it? I felt at home the first time Will brought me here, before we were even officially dating."

Cameron released the dogs from the backseat and they took off toward the trees.

"Will they be okay?" Lucy asked as they disappeared from view.

"They'll be back in a few minutes. It's part of the routine."

"You already have a routine here."

"I do. It's home."

Carrying the backpack she'd brought to spend the night with Cam, Lucy walked into the cozy cabin. "This is fantastic."

"Not much to it." Cameron spread her arms. "Living room, kitchen, bedroom, bathroom, loft up there where you'll be staying. Everything we need, but no frills."

"Is the bathroom inside the house?"

"Yes. Why?"

"Then compared to Colton's place, this is the Ritz. Though both places have plenty to recommend them. It's so quiet. Does that ever drive you crazy?" She dropped her backpack on a chair inside the door.

"Not at all. I thought I'd miss the action of the city, but I don't. I'm so busy and engaged here that I don't have time to miss New York. I miss you and my dad and everyone there, but the city itself? Not so much."

"I like it here. I honestly do. But I don't think I could ever really leave the city."

Cameron opened a bottle of red and poured them both a glass. "It's in your blood."

"It wasn't in yours?"

"Not the way Will is." She leaned forward, elbows on the counter. "Talk to me, Luce. What're you thinking?"

"The truth?"

"And nothing but."

"I need to end this with Colton before I get in any deeper. There's no way this can work long term with the two of us living so far apart, and the more time I spend with him, the harder it gets to think about leaving him."

"If you end it with him, you'll spend the rest of your life wondering if you let the love of your life get away."

"So which awful scenario is better—that or ending up a few months from now crushed and heartbroken when the whole thing blows up in our faces?"

"What if it doesn't blow up? What if it works out perfectly? Here, there and anywhere the two of you are together?"

"How can it work perfectly when we don't live in the same place?"

"You love him. He loves you. Why not have faith that it's all going to be fine?"

"Because I'm far more convinced that it's not going to be fine."

"Will said Colton has never been this way with any girl. Ever."

That news sent a happy jolt to Lucy's heart. "What way?"

"Smitten, gaga, demonstrative. Obviously in love. I told him I've never seen you this way either."

Lucy fiddled with the stem of her wineglass. "I want to be happy and enjoy it and say to hell with all the worries. I want to be that person, the one who can go along like it's no big deal that we have this huge obstacle standing between us. But I'm not that person. I haven't been her in a very long time."

"Since your mom died and you had to grow up overnight and take care of everyone and everything."

Lucy dropped her head to her folded arms.

Cameron came around the counter to rest her hand on Lucy's back.

"I can't let this crush me, Cam. I just can't."

"I understand. I don't like it, but I get it. When will you tell him?"

"After the wedding."

"That's a week from now."

"I know. I thought about telling him before we came here, but I'd already agreed to go to the wedding with him. And I wanted to see everyone again. One more time. At least until your wedding when I'll have to see him again. I guess I'll have to deal with that when it happens."

"That and when Will and I have kids and other events and things I'll want you here for. You'll see a lot of him. Are you prepared to see him with someone else? Maybe even married to someone else?"

Tears rolled freely down Lucy's face. "No, I'm not prepared for that. But hopefully I will be by the time it happens. It's what he deserves. He should have someone who can be with him freely."

"I want you to do something for me."

Embarrassed by her emotional meltdown, Lucy wiped her face and tried to find her composure. "What?"

"I want you to take this week to really think this through. I'd hate to see you do something you might regret."

"Of course I'm going to regret it. I already regret it, and it hasn't even happened yet. But it's the right thing for me, even if it hurts like hell. It'll hurt a hell of a lot worse a few months from now when we realize there's no way we can make this work."

"I worry you're underestimating him, Luce. Obviously I don't know him as well as you do, but I know him pretty well, and he doesn't seem likely to go quietly."

"He'll respect my wishes." As she said the words, Lucy hoped that was true, but suspected Cameron was right.

"I hope it's okay I told Hannah, Ella, Charley and Molly to come by for some wine and snacks tonight. I thought it would be fun to give Hannah something to do during Nolan's bachelor party, but if you don't feel up to it—"

"I'm fine, and that does sound like fun." She welcomed anything that provided a distraction so she didn't have to think about what it would be like to say the words to Colton, to crush him after he'd been so amazing to her.

Telling herself it was in his best interest—and hers—didn't make it any better.

While Lucy helped Cameron put together some appetizers, they talked about everything other than the topic that had upset Lucy earlier and continued to weigh on her more than an hour later. It stayed with her all evening, during a fun get-together with Colton's sisters and mother, who made her feel like a part of the extended Abbott family. They acted like she was one of them rather than a temporary visitor.

She felt like she'd led them on the same way she'd led Colton on.

"So I have something to tell you guys," Hannah said, glancing at her mother.

Molly smiled and reached for Hannah's hand.

"Do you want to tell them, Mom?"

"Oh no. It's your news, honey."

"Someone had better tell us," Charley said.

"I'm pregnant."

The women erupted in screams and tears and hugs that Lucy watched with an odd sense of detachment. She wouldn't be a part of this. She wouldn't get to see Hannah round with pregnancy or visit her in the hospital after she had the baby. Colton would want to be there with his sister and the rest of their family, but she wouldn't be with him.

"Congratulations, Hannah," Lucy said, hugging her. "I'm so happy for you and Nolan."

"Thank you. We're so excited."

"And you're feeling all right?" Ella asked.

"I'm so tired and nauseated pretty much all the time. But other than that, I feel great."

"I propose a toast," Cameron said, "to the new mom, the new grandma and the aunts. This will be one very lucky baby."

"Hear, hear," Lucy said, forcing a cheerful tone. She ached from the desire to be part of it all, to be there at the moment when Colton found out whether he had a niece or a nephew, to see him holding the fragile little body in his big hands. Her chest ached from the pain of the desire to see that.

"Lucy?" Molly studied her intently. "Are you all right, honey?"

She was going to cry. There was no way to stop the flood that was coming. "I, um, excuse me."

CHAPTER 33

❧❧❧

Default Sugarhouse Cleanup Music:
Paul Simon's Graceland. *Default Music to*
Boil By: O Brother, Where Art Thou*; any of*
William Elliott Whitmore's CDs.

—Colton Abbott's sugaring journal, after the boil

Fighting to control her emotions, Lucy got up and went into Cam and Will's bedroom. With her hand on her chest, she sat on their bed and fought to get oxygen to her air-starved lungs.

She sensed a presence in the dark room. "I'm okay, Cam. Really. Go have fun with your family. I'm good."

"You don't look too good."

Shocked to hear Molly's voice, Lucy tried to pull herself together. "Sorry. I'm fine. Just PMS and stuff."

Molly came into the room and sat on the bed next to her. "I used to suffer terribly from that. I know how awful it can be."

Lucy nodded in agreement.

"I also know how awful it can be to find yourself in love with a man who wants to be somewhere other than where you are."

"Wow. You saw right through that PMS thing, huh?"

Molly flipped on the bedside light and winced at the carnage that must've been evident on Lucy's face. "Ten kids. I'm good at this."

Lucy hadn't expected to laugh, although she shouldn't have been surprised. Colton was one of the funniest people she'd ever met, and there'd been nothing but laughter during the time she'd spent with his family.

"Linc was on his way to Oxford when I met him. All he talked about was going to England. He was so excited. It was his dream. To spend time in England, to live and study there."

Lucy listened, although she couldn't figure out where Molly was going with this.

"I loved him, you know? Nothing in my life had ever been more instantaneous than the way I felt about him. It was like lightning striking, and he was going to England for two years. God, that sucked. It was all I could think about. It colored every minute that I spent with him. I kept asking myself, 'What's the point?' But oh, Linc . . . He was persistent. I'll give him that."

Her smile was infectious, and Lucy couldn't help but return it. "His son gets that from him, then."

"I'd imagine Colton can be quite persistent when he has his heart set on something." Molly reached out to push Lucy's hair back.

The gesture stirred poignant memories of what it felt like to be mothered.

"He has his heart set on you, Lucy. You know that, don't you?"

"Yes. Yes, I know."

"And your connection to him was every bit as instantaneous as mine was with Linc. His father and I saw that the night we went to dinner with you two. I told him on the way home that I'd felt like I was intruding by being there, and he agreed."

"We were that obvious, huh?"

"Oh yes. Am I being presumptuous to think you might have your heart set on him, too?"

Lucy shook her head. "You're not being presumptuous."

"It's a difficult situation. I'm not making light of that. Cameron was coming after you, but I asked if I could. I wanted you to know I've been where you are, and I know how hard it is."

She didn't want to cry all over Colton's mother, but Molly was so kind, so caring and so understanding. Lucy covered her mouth to muffle the sob that escaped from her tightly clenched jaw.

Molly put an arm around her. "It's okay, honey. Let it out. You're among friends here."

"I'm sorry. I'm a hot mess tonight. And hearing that Hannah's pregnant . . . I wondered if I'd get to meet the baby or see Colton hold it. He'll be a really great uncle. You should've seen him with my niece. She's more in love with him than I am."

"You know what I think?"

Lucy shook her head and wiped at her tears.

"I think if it's important enough to both of you, you'll find a way. You'll figure it out. Like we did." As she spoke, Molly continued to stroke Lucy's hair, and Lucy wanted to purr from the pleasure of being tended to by a professional mother. "Linc didn't go to England. At first, I didn't agree with that decision. I thought he'd regret it and grow to hate me because I kept him from following his dreams. But you know what he said when I told him that?"

"What?"

"He said dreams change. He said he had a new dream now, and that dream was me."

"For what it's worth, I would've married him, too."

Molly laughed. "I know, right? Who says no to that?"

"Did his dream also include ten kids?"

"Oh hell no! That just sort of happened. By the time we figured out what was causing it, we had ten kids!"

Once again, a gurgle of laughter took Lucy by surprise.

"I've never once, in thirty-seven years married to him, caught even the slightest hint of regret coming from him. Not once."

"You guys are really lucky."

"We are lucky. We'd never deny that. But we were also willing to do whatever it took to be together. He doesn't know this, but if he'd gone to England, I was going with him."

"You would've done that?"

"In a New York minute," she said, winking at the play on words. "But he made his decision first and seemed to be at peace with it, so it never came to that." She paused before she added, "I don't want to be dramatic or overplay my hand, because we're talking about my beloved son here, and I'm biased where he's concerned. But things like this, what you have with Colton, they don't come along every day. Although the obstacles might seem insurmountable, I assure you they are not."

"I want so badly to believe that, to hold on to it with everything I've got."

"But?"

"But I can see this ending badly down the road when the distance gets to be too much, and if it hurts this badly now, what will it be like then?"

"None of us can predict the future—and thank goodness for that. I've got all I can do to live in the here and now. I can't help but wonder if you've considered the other possibility. That it could all be fine and work out swimmingly."

"You're quite convincing, and you make me want to believe that anything is possible."

"Anything is possible—if you want it badly enough." She gave Lucy a kiss on her forehead and patted her shoulder. "I'm here if I can help."

"Mrs. Abbott?"

"Please, call me Molly."

"Molly . . . I just want to say thank you. I miss my mom a lot, especially lately, and . . . Well, thank you."

"My pleasure, honey."

After Molly left the room, Lucy took a few minutes to pull herself together. When she rejoined the others, she was incredibly thankful that no one said a word about the obvious evidence that she'd been crying.

Hours later, after Hannah, Ella, Charley and Molly had left and Cameron had gone to bed, Lucy lay awake staring at the ceiling in the loft thinking about everything Molly had said. She wanted so badly to believe that Molly was right, that anything was possible and no obstacle was too great to overcome when you were facing the challenges with the right person by your side.

But she kept circling back to the same thing over and over again—a vision of herself months in the future, wrecked by the breakup she'd seen coming all along. Tears leaked from the corner of her eyes as she allowed her mind to wallow in the pain of that far-off inevitable moment.

Her brain spun around in circles until she finally dozed off only to wake sometime later to realize she wasn't alone.

"It's me." Colton kissed her face and lips as he drew her in close to his naked and fully aroused body. The scent of fresh air and smoke from the fire came with him into bed.

"Colton."

"Were you expecting someone else?"

"Of course not, but I wasn't expecting you either."

"Will, Nolan and I snuck out and came back to town. I couldn't stand to know you were a few miles away and sleeping alone." He kissed her cheeks and eyes. "Why do you taste salty?"

"Do I?"

"Uh-huh. Have you been crying, Luce?"

"Maybe a little."

"How come?"

What could she say? She couldn't very well tell him she'd been crying because she'd been thinking about how best to end this thing with him while she still could.

"Lucy?"

"I've been thinking."

"About?"

"This. Us. All of it."

"Why do I get the awful feeling I'm not going to like what you've been thinking about?" His hand slipped beneath the long T-shirt she'd worn to bed. As always, his touch set her on fire.

She heard Molly's voice in her head, reminding her that things like this didn't come along every day.

"You're not going to tell me?"

"You know I love you, right?"

"Yes, Lucy. I know. And I love you more every day."

"That's just it. I love you more every day, too, and I keep thinking about what happens a few months from now when it all goes bad. When living between two places gets to be too complicated. When we decide we can't do this anymore. I'm afraid of that day, Colton. It's all I can think about as I seem to get deeper into this all the time."

"I want you to know that I understand what you're saying, and I get why you're afraid. We'd both be a little bit crazy not to be afraid of what's going on here. But I'm asking you to trust me, to have faith in me and in us for a little while longer. Will you do that for me?"

"I want to have faith. You have no idea how badly I want that."

"I know, honey." He kissed her then, pouring all the love he felt for her into a kiss that made her body hum with the kind of desire that only he could arouse in her.

She needed to get closer to him, to hang on to the one thing that made sense in all of this. The T-shirt disappeared over her head into the darkness, followed soon after by her panties. His lips and hands were everywhere as he made her forget everything other than the powerful connection they'd shared from the very beginning.

He grasped her hands and held them over her head as he entered her in one smooth thrust that had her biting her lip to keep from crying out.

"Shh," he whispered, his mouth curving into a smile against her lips. He pressed deeper into her, and Lucy arched her back. "Lucy . . . God. I love you so much. You have no idea." He barely moved, but he touched her everywhere.

"Love you, too." Lucy tugged her hands free and wrapped her arms around him. She held on tight, her fingers sifting through the hair he'd cut for her as his muscles flexed and his chest hair abraded her nipples. He overpowered all her worries with sweetness and tenderness that brought new tears to her eyes when she imagined how empty her life would be without him.

"Stay with me, honey. Give me this week. I promise you won't regret it."

"Okay."

Her acquiescence seemed to spark a flame in him. Without making a sound, he took her somewhere she'd never been before, somewhere she already knew she'd never go with anyone but him.

The week passed in a flurry of activity that led up to their departure for Burlington on Friday. Every night, there'd been some sort of gathering with the friends who'd come to town for the wedding. Though Hannah had intended to keep her pregnancy a secret until after the wedding, it didn't take long for the whole family to hear about the baby who would arrive in the spring.

While they spent a lot of time with Colton's family and friends, they also spent much of their time alone on the mountain. Lucy powered through a ton of work during the day while he took care of his own work outside. He came in at lunchtime for what he called "conjugal visits."

By the end of the week, Lucy had succeeded in pushing aside most of her worries about the future, mostly because she hadn't had the time to dwell on them. With everyone around her in high spirits as the big day approached, she had no desire to be a downer in their midst. The Abbotts had waited a long time to see Hannah happy again, and though the weekend promised to be emotionally fraught for them, Lucy was determined to enjoy the celebration of two people who deserved as much happiness as life could bring them.

"Are you ready to go?" Colton asked her when he came in from securing the retail store for the weekend.

"Just about."

"Elmer and Sarah are waiting by the truck."

"I can't believe everyone is bringing their dogs."

"The Abbotts go nowhere without their dogs. You should know that by now."

"But still, Colton. A wedding?"

"Wouldn't be a family occasion without everyone there."

"You're nuts. You're all nuts. I bet that huge house is going to get awfully small with everyone there."

"That's why we're not staying there."

"We aren't?"

"Nope." He came over to her and slipped his arms around her. "I want you all to myself this weekend with no prying eyes or ears anywhere near us."

"We need to talk about all of this at some point, Colton. We've been in this dream state all week, pretending we don't have anything to worry about when we both know that isn't true."

"You're trusting me, remember?"

"Yes, but—"

He kissed her. "No buts about it. I promised you it would be okay, and it will be."

"You shouldn't make promises you can't keep."

"I never do. Let's get going. The rehearsal dinner is at

five. We don't want to be late." He picked up her bags and headed for the door.

Lucy followed him, but a sense of foreboding came with her. As Hannah and Nolan prepared to begin their life together, why did she feel like hers was about to come unraveled?

CHAPTER 34

——◆◆◆◆——

*What I learned this year about boiling: If the
trough bubbles like fish eyes it's not ready; if
it bubbles like sheep eyes it's syrup.*

—Colton Abbott's sugaring journal, after the boil

The unease stayed with Lucy all the way to Burlington
and throughout the festive party at the lake house that
evening. Gathered around a bonfire on the beach, the
Abbott family and their friends were in high spirits and
looking forward to the wedding the next day.

Sitting on Nolan's lap next to the fire, Hannah looked
serene and happy. The peaceful aura that surrounded her
was contagious, and for a short time, Lucy nearly forgot to
be worried about her own situation. But then she would
think about the flight back to New York that was booked
for Sunday, and she'd remember that she had just two more
nights with Colton before they'd return to their separate
lives.

"Are you ready to go?" Colton asked her.

"Any time you are."

"I'm ready." He stood and held out a hand to help her up
from her seat on a blanket that had been spread out on the
beach.

"Can I hitch a ride with you guys?" Nolan asked.

"Me, too," Hannah said.

"Where are you going?" Molly asked her daughter.

Hannah used her thumb to point to Nolan. "With him."

"But it's bad luck to see the groom before the wedding."

"I've used up my lifetime share of bad luck," Hannah told her mother. "I'm taking my chances."

"Nolan," Molly said. "Do something!"

"Sorry, Molly," Nolan said as he put his arm around his fiancée, "but I'm with Hannah on this one."

"Of course you are."

Hannah bent down to kiss her parents good night. "I'll be back in the morning, and you can fuss over me to your heart's content."

Molly tugged on Hannah's long hair. "I'll look forward to that."

"Nolan," Lincoln said, "take good care of my daughter and get her back here on time tomorrow."

"You have my word."

After they'd said their good nights to the rest of the group, the four of them headed up the stairs to the house, where they collected their belongings. Hannah let out a squeal and jumped onto Nolan's back.

He grabbed her legs to keep her there. "Christ, woman. Don't break me before the honeymoon."

"I expected my mom to put up a much bigger fight about me leaving."

"Let's get these kids back to the inn so they can have a good night's sleep before their big day," Colton said to Lucy.

Hannah nibbled on Nolan's ear. "Sleep is highly over-rated."

Colton put his arm around Lucy. "I couldn't agree more."

"You two are so cute together," Hannah said. "I predict you'll be the next to tie the knot."

The statement hit Lucy like a punch to the gut, making her gasp. "*What?* We aren't getting married."

Hannah shrugged off Lucy's protest. "Call it a hunch."

"You're wrong." She looked to Colton, hoping he would back her up, but his expression was unreadable.

Lucy and Colton traveled the short distance to the inn in silence as Nolan and Hannah whispered and giggled in the backseat. Lucy envied them. All their questions had been answered, and their future stretched out before them bright with promise and all the joy they both deserved.

The more Lucy thought about the many unanswered questions in her life, the more exhausted she became.

They parted company with Hannah and Nolan on the second-floor landing. Hannah hugged them both. "We'll see you tomorrow."

Colton gave his sister a second hug and a kiss. "Happy for you, Hannah Banana."

"I'm happy for you, too."

Colton smiled but his eyes were sad. "Get some sleep."

"Uh-huh," Hannah said.

With his hand on her lower back, Colton guided Lucy up one more flight of stairs. Inside the room, they took turns in the bathroom. Lucy put on the new silk gown before she brushed her hair and teeth. When she emerged from the bathroom, Colton was already in bed. The covers hugged his waist, leaving his muscular chest bare to her hungry gaze. Would she ever look at him and not want him? Probably not.

Lucy got into bed and turned on her side to face him. She expected him to turn to her, but he stared up at the ceiling for a long time. "What's wrong?"

"I could ask you the same thing."

He sounded truly upset. "What do you mean?"

"We aren't getting *married*. As if it's the most preposterous thing you've ever heard."

"You're mad about *that*? We've never even talked about getting married and your sister is predicting we'll be next. What was I supposed to say to that?"

"I don't know, but your emphatic denial makes me wonder what the hell we're doing here."

His words filled her with fear. "You want to talk about getting married when we can't even figure out a way to be in the same place at the same time for more than a few days."

"We've just put together two full weeks."

"And now what? Now I go home the day after tomorrow and see you again when?"

"The following weekend?"

"And then what?"

"I don't know! I don't have the answers you want. All I know for sure is if we give up now we'll never know what could've been. You're giving up. I've felt you pulling away from me for days now, and then you say something like that to my sister, and . . ." He blew out a deep breath. "It's got me questioning everything."

"I'm sorry. I didn't mean to hurt you. She caught me by surprise when she said that."

"It sounded to me like you'd given the matter some considerable thought and already made up your mind that it's never going to happen."

"That's not true."

"Isn't it?"

Her throat tightened and closed, making it impossible to speak over the lump that settled there.

"Thought so." He turned on his side, facing away from her, and turned off the light.

Lucy lay awake for a long time, staring into the darkness, wishing she could find the courage to stay the course and hope for the best, but she just wasn't built that way. Tears slid down her cheeks and dampened her hair. She tried to be quiet in her misery, but a sob escaped anyway.

Colton turned over and put his arm around her. "I'm sorry, Luce." He kissed her shoulder and arm. "Please don't cry."

"I wish I was different."

"What? Why would you say that?"

"Because I'm not courageous the way Hannah is. I'm not strong or resilient like Cam. I hurt easily, and I wish I didn't. I'm afraid if I don't stop this now, it'll ruin me later." The darkness that surrounded them made it possible for Lucy to speak her truth, to say the words that had been in her heart all week.

He slid one arm under her and put the other around her middle, pulling her in tight against him. "I happen to love you exactly the way you are, tender heart and all."

Surrounded by him, warmed by him, her body shook with sobs. "I'm sorry, Colton. I'm so sorry. I kept telling myself just one more weekend, just one more . . . I never should've let this happen."

"Please don't say that. Don't have regrets. The time we spent together has been the best time of my life."

"I'll understand if you don't want me to come to the wedding. It's such a special day for your family. I wouldn't want to do anything to take away from it for you. Or them."

"I'd really like you to come with me."

"Okay." After a long silence, she said, "I really am sorry, Colton."

"So am I, honey. So am I."

In the pearly predawn, Hannah slept in Nolan's arms, floating in that narrow space between wakefulness and dreams. Her one conscious thought was that she would marry Nolan today and begin her new life with him. Warm and cozy, she drifted, letting the dreams carry her for a while longer.

He came to her then, in that in-between place, brushing the hair back from her face and kissing her forehead. He lingered for a long moment, his lips pressed to her skin, his fingers stroking her hair.

She held her breath, waiting to see what else he might do, but as quickly as he'd come he was gone again.

Hannah opened eyes that were filled with tears. Had she been dreaming? She reached up to touch the place on her forehead that still tingled from the touch of his lips. In all the years since she'd lost Caleb, it was the most vivid dream she'd ever had about him. She hadn't seen his face or touched his skin, but she'd felt his presence as powerfully as she ever had when he was alive.

Why today of all days would she feel him so potently?

Nolan's hand shifted from her hip to her belly, pulling her in closer to him as his lips touched her shoulder.

Hannah covered his hand with hers, holding on tight to him.

"What's wrong, babe?"

"Nothing."

"I can feel how tense you are. Are you having cold feet?"

"No. Of course not."

"Would you tell me if you were?"

"I'm not, Nolan. I promise."

"Then what is it?"

After a long pause, she said, "I had a dream. At least I think it was a dream. Caleb was here. He . . . He pushed the hair back from my face, and he kissed my forehead. It was only a few seconds, but he was here. I've never felt him like that before."

"He was wishing you well, love. He was letting you know he's with you always, even today. Especially today."

"It was just a dream."

"I'd like to believe it was more than that. I'd like to think he was actually here and that he knows you're all right. I'd like to believe he knows I'm taking care of you for him."

Needing to see his face, Hannah turned over.

He wiped away her tears with the gentle stroke of his finger on her face.

"I love you," she whispered. "Thank you for letting me share that with you."

"I'd never want you to feel you couldn't share something like that with me. Believe it or not, it brings me some comfort to know he was here, that he knows about us, that maybe he approves."

"Of course he would approve. He loved us both."

Nolan gathered her in close to him, tucking her head under his chin.

She breathed in the fragrance of soap and clean skin that had become so familiar to her in the last few months. It was the new scent of home. "I'm glad I was with you when that happened. It might've messed me up if you hadn't been here to tell me it was okay."

"I'm glad I was here. I'll always be right here, Hannah. There's nowhere else I'd rather be in this entire world than right here with you."

"In that case, what do you say we make it official?"

He grunted out a laugh. "I say you're on."

Hannah looked stunningly gorgeous as she came down the stairs to the beach, accompanied by her parents. Her dark hair was piled on top of her head in what some might call a messy bun, but on her it was nothing short of glamorous. She wore a simple off-white silk dress, carried a bouquet of wildflowers and was chased down the stairs by her overly excited puppy, Homer.

Molly and Lincoln were teary-eyed as they delivered their eldest daughter to her groom, who had been riveted by the sight of his love coming toward him as their friend Jack played his guitar. He only took his eyes off Hannah long enough to bend and scoop up Homer Junior, who sported a black bow tie collar for the occasion.

Nolan wore a white dress shirt with a blue tie and khakis. Hunter stood beside him, while Ella, Charley and Cameron were Hannah's attendants.

Both the bride and the groom were barefoot, a touch that Lucy found particularly perfect. Standing in front of Colton to watch as his grandfather officiated the ceremony, it was difficult to wallow in her own misery while watching two such deserving people get their happy ending.

It was excruciating to know that she and Colton wouldn't have a day like this. They wouldn't have any more days after today, and it was all because she was too afraid of what might happen tomorrow to enjoy today. Knowing what Hannah had endured to get to this moment in her life made Lucy feel ashamed of her own inadequacies.

As she listened to Elmer talk about the incredible journey Hannah and Nolan had traveled to reach this day and heard them pledge their eternal love to each other, Lucy yearned to someday say those same words to Colton and to hear them from him. She yearned for the forever they weren't destined to have. Maybe he was feeling the same way because his hand found hers and held on tight. It was the first time he'd touched her all day, and she clung to the welcome feel of his hand in hers.

After Elmer declared Hannah and Nolan husband and wife, a cheer went up from the friends and family who surrounded them, including the Guthries, Caleb's beloved Sultans and Nolan's racing team. The group tossed rose petals at the bride and groom as they went up the stairs to the house where the reception would take place.

"So beautiful," Cameron said as she wiped tears off her face.

Will put his arm around her and drew her into his embrace.

"Incredible," Colton agreed. He continued to hold Lucy's hand as they made their way up the stairs and only let go to hug the bride. "So happy for you, Han."

"Thank you." Hannah glowed with happiness as she stood next to Nolan on the deck, accepting hugs and kisses from everyone. She hugged Lucy as if they'd been friends for years rather than months. "So glad you were here with us today."

"Me, too," Lucy said sincerely. It was comforting to know that sometimes things worked out the way they were meant to. She followed the crowd inside where Molly was supervising the caterers. Despite her depressed state, Lucy was swept up in the party atmosphere as everyone ate and drank and celebrated the happy couple.

The effort to hide her own pain in the midst of such incredible joy was exhausting, but Lucy kept a smile on her face, determined to get through this day and night so she could go home and lick her wounds in private.

Outside on the deck, a trio provided music that only added to the festive atmosphere. She was standing with Colton, Will, Cameron, Ella and Charley when Hunter took the microphone from the singer and waited for the group to quiet down. Then he turned his attention to Hannah and Nolan.

CHAPTER 35

‹•›

*Interesting: A visitor from Kuwait remarked that
oil and maple syrup producers have this in
common: You drill, you collect, you boil, you
filter, you grade. You end up with something
amazing at the end of all that.*

—Colton Abbott's sugaring journal, after the boil

Nolan stood behind Hannah, his arm hooked around her waist as they waited to hear what her brother had to say. So far their wedding day had exceeded Hannah's wildest hopes. They had wanted simple, elegant and intimate, and had managed to achieve all three in this beautiful spot by the lake.

"Every time I saw Nolan the last few years," Hunter said, "he'd ask how Hannah was. He asked me, he asked my parents, he asked my grandfather, he asked my brothers and he asked my sisters. He never missed a chance to ask about Hannah. And being the concerned, *involved* family we are, we never missed a chance to pass along his thoughts to Hannah. We thought it was the least we could do to deliver his messages."

Hannah snorted with laughter and rolled her eyes at her brother.

"So I speak for all of us when I tell you, Nolan, how grateful we are that you can now ask her your damned self—every day for the rest of your lives."

When the roar of laughter died down, Hunter continued. "It's my very great honor to welcome Nolan to the Abbott family, although I think we actually did that a long time ago. Again, I speak for my parents and my siblings when I tell Nolan he was an Abbott long before Hannah made it official. I feel extremely fortunate that my twin sister, who is my very best friend, married another of my best friends, and I can't help but think that Caleb is looking down on this happy gathering today with love and approval of the man his beloved Hannah chose to accompany her on the next part of her journey."

Touched by the way Hunter had managed to include Caleb, Hannah wiped away tears. As Nolan pressed his face against hers, she felt the dampness on his skin and knew he was as equally moved by Hunter's words.

"I know he loved you both as much as the rest of us do, and we couldn't be happier to celebrate this amazing day with you." He raised his glass of champagne. "To Hannah and Nolan, may you know many, *many* years of happiness together."

After everyone had toasted them, Hunter gestured to Nolan. "Ready?"

"As I'll ever be."

"What's going on?" Hannah asked.

Nolan turned her to face him and looked down at her, his eyes warm with humor and love. "This is gonna go one of two ways, babe, so bear with me." He took her into his arms, nodded to Hunter, who accompanied him as he began to sing to her in a deep, melodic voice that astounded her. *Where* had he been hiding such a talent?

She recognized the song, "I Won't Let Go," a favorite of hers by Rascal Flatts, but she wouldn't have guessed that he knew it, let alone could sing it so beautifully. Once she got past the shock of him singing to her when she'd had no idea he could, she began to focus on what he was saying and everything else fell away as the emotion of the moment hit her square in the heart.

By the time Hunter played the final notes to the song, everyone around them was sniffling, but Hannah paid no mind to anyone other than the amazing man she'd married and his incredible gift to her.

While their guests applauded and wiped away tears, Nolan leaned down to speak only to her. "I told you I could teach you to enjoy surprises."

Hannah laughed and hugged him tighter. "That was the best surprise ever."

"Glad you liked it."

She looked up at him, filled with the kind of joy she'd never expected to experience again. "I loved it, and I love you."

"Love you, too, Hannah. Forever."

She hadn't meant to watch him all day like a crazed stalker, but Ella Abbott couldn't help that her gaze was naturally drawn to him. It had been for as long as she could remember, and today was certainly no exception. So when he slipped away during Nolan's touching song, Ella went after him.

Everyone was so caught up in the moment between Hannah and Nolan that no one saw her follow Gavin Guthrie down the stairs to the beach, where she found him skimming stones into the lake.

He wore a dress shirt rolled up to his elbows and khaki pants that molded to his muscular legs and ass. His dark, curly hair was on the longish side, the way Caleb's had been before he joined the army. Gavin was, without a doubt, the most incredibly gorgeous man she'd ever laid eyes on, and she'd been in love with him for almost as long as her sister had been in love with his brother. Not that she'd ever told anyone that . . .

"Hey," she said when she joined him on the beach.

"What're you doing down here? Don't you have brides-maid duties or some such thing?"

"Nope. Hannah didn't want any of that."

"Keeping it simple, huh?"

"That was the plan."

"You look beautiful."

"Thank you." Hoping to hide her unreasonable pleasure at the unexpected compliment, Ella bent to pick up a flat, shiny stone and sent it flying over the surface of the water, counting at least twenty skips.

"Wow. That was awesome. Where'd you learn to skip like that?"

"I have seven brothers. You'd be surprised at all the stuff I know how to do." The moment the words left her mouth, Ella realized there were a number of ways he could interpret them.

Thankfully, other than one rakishly raised brow, he didn't comment.

"Are you okay?" She hadn't spoken directly to him since the day of Homer Senior's funeral, when he'd con-fessed to how acutely he still felt the pain of his brother's death.

He looked over at her and then back at the lake as he let another stone go flying. "Truth?"

"Please."

"I've had better days."

"I'm sure it has to be very difficult for you—and your parents. I know how much it means to Hannah that you're here."

"Of course we're here. We love them and wouldn't have missed sharing this day with them. But still . . ."

"It hurts."

"All the goddamned time. Sometimes more than others."

Ella knew it wasn't wise, but that didn't stop her from moving closer to him. It didn't stop her from putting her arms around him, and it didn't stop her from wishing she could do something to ease his pain.

For a second, he seemed too startled to react, but then his arms came around her, too.

She looked up at him as he looked down at her. And then he was kissing her, roughly, without finesse or any of the things she would've expected from him. But finesse didn't matter. She was kissing Gavin Guthrie, and her entire world was reduced to the feel of his lips on hers, the press of his tongue in her mouth and the tight clasp of his arms around her.

She curled her hand around the nape of his neck, wanting to keep him anchored to her.

Then he pulled away abruptly, leaving her bereft. "Christ, Ella. I'm sorry. I don't know what I'm doing. I'm so fucked up today. I'm sorry. I shouldn't have done that."

She wanted to tell him not to be sorry, that she'd loved kissing him and wanted to do it again. But all she managed to say was "Wait."

He turned to her, looking tormented and regretful.

"Don't be sorry. I'm not."

"You're beautiful, Ella." He stole her breath when he caressed her face. "Inside and out. If I were going to let something like this happen with anyone, you'd be the first one I'd call. But I've got nothing to give you, and it wouldn't be fair. It just wouldn't be fair."

Before she could begin to formulate a response, he walked away, heading down the beach. She watched him go, noting the curve of his shoulders, an obvious indication of the pain he carried with him everywhere he went.

He said he had nothing to give her, but he'd just given her the one thing she'd never had where he was concerned— hope.

Colton was dying inside. All around him, people smiled and laughed and celebrated the beautiful bride and her handsome groom. He was so happy for his sister and her new husband, but inside, he ached.

Lucy was leaving him for good tomorrow, and he had to

pretend like everything was fine when he felt like complete and absolute shit. He could tell by watching her as she talked to Charley and Cameron that she felt the same. Her smile was forced and her eyes were puffier than usual after she'd cried herself to sleep the night before.

He'd run out of ways to assure her that everything would be fine. He'd failed to persuade her to give him a chance to show her they could make this work if only she had faith. The effort to pretend that everything was fine when it wasn't was wearing him out.

Looking to escape the prying eyes of his family, he went into the kitchen to grab a beer.

"Make it two," his grandfather said.

Colton turned. "Where'd you come from?"

"I followed you."

"Oh. Okay then." Colton opened a second bottle of beer and handed it to Elmer. "Fantastic day, huh?"

"One of the best I can ever remember."

Colton nodded in agreement. "Great job on the ceremony."

"Glad you liked it." Elmer took a sip of his beer. "What's on your mind today, son? You're not yourself."

The last thing he wanted to do was introduce his problems into a day that should be trouble free for everyone. "Nothing much."

"You may as well tell me. You know you want to tell someone."

Colton laughed at his audaciousness, but he knew it came from a place of pure love. "Lucy and I have decided to break up. I'm bummed out, to say the least."

"Huh." Elmer leaned against the counter and thought about what Colton had said. "So that's it? Over and done with?"

"I guess so. We're both firmly rooted in our lives in two separate places."

"Seems to me you've been working around that rather well for quite some time now."

"I thought so, too, but she's worried about what happens when it stops working."

"So she's going with a preemptive strike."

"Something like that."

"And how do you feel about it?"

"How do you think I feel? I've never felt worse about anything, but what choice do I have if this is what she wants?"

"I don't believe for one second that this is what she wants. I believe it's what she's convinced herself needs to happen."

"What's the difference?"

"There's a huge difference, Colton. Think about it. She wants the same things you do, but she's convinced it can never happen. So you have to show her it *can* happen. Do what you do best and draw her a picture. Make a case. Prove to her you're in it for keeps. You know what you have to do."

"How do I do that when she's telling me it's over?"

"First, you give her a week or two to miss you, and then you go in for the kill."

"You make it sound so dramatic."

"You're fighting for the life you want with the woman you love. If that's not dramatic, I don't know what is. You can't leave anything on the table, my boy."

Colton's mind raced as he contemplated what his grandfather had said. "So I let her go tomorrow, and I let her think it's what I want, too, even though it isn't?"

"For starters."

"And then I don't call her or talk to her in any way for a week, maybe two . . ."

"That's right. And you use that time very, very productively."

"What if I do all this, and she still says it's not what she wants?"

Elmer placed his hand on Colton's shoulder and looked him square in the eye. "Then at least you'll know you did everything you could and you'll respect her wishes. But if I had to guess, I don't think that's going to happen."

"You really think that will work?"

Elmer touched his beer bottle to Colton's. "I really do."

"I sure hope you're right." The alternative was unimaginable.

Saying good-bye to Colton the next morning at the airport was the most excruciatingly painful thing Lucy had ever done. In deference to the wedding and the happiness of the day, they hadn't said a word to anyone yesterday about their decision to end their relationship. Lucy hadn't even told Cameron.

After two nights of awkward silence between her and Colton, it was almost a relief to finally leave. He hadn't begged or pleaded with her to change her mind. Rather, he seemed to have accepted her decision, albeit reluctantly. That was for the best, she'd told herself during that second night as she lay awake next to him. Though he'd been right there with her, he'd been a million miles from her.

Gone was the teasing, the laughing, the loving, the talking, the playful bickering, replaced by a pervasive silence that shattered her already broken heart all over again.

When they arrived at the airport, Elmer and Sarah stuck their heads out the back window of the truck, and Lucy reached up to pet and kiss them both.

Almost as if she knew this was really good-bye, Sarah whimpered.

Lucy clung to her composure like a life raft in a stormy sea, determined to get through this without making a scene.

Colton deposited her suitcase and computer bag on the curb. "If you forgot anything, I'll send it to you."

"Thanks." There was so much she wanted to say, but none of it mattered now. She placed a hand on his shoulder and went up on tiptoes to kiss him. "I'm sorry, Colton. I truly am."

He hugged her—tightly—but he didn't say anything. And then he let her go, because it was what she'd told him she wanted.

Lucy looped the strap of her computer bag over her shoulder and reached for the handle on her suitcase. She forced a smile for him and then walked away, all the while resisting the urge to look back. She'd made her decision. There was no point in looking back.

Once again feeling like she was wading through hip-deep snow, she went through the motions at security and moved like a zombie through the airport in search of her gate. She held it together on the short flight and in the cab ride home from LaGuardia.

Only when she reached the comfort of her own bed did she finally give in to the tears that had threatened to consume her for two days. She cried until her eyes and chest ached, until there was nothing left but the loneliness she'd inflicted upon herself.

Other than to tend to essential needs, she never moved from her bed for the rest of the night. Hours later she realized she'd been waiting for him to call her. But he didn't call. He wouldn't call again. She'd seen to that. It had been the right thing to do, even if it hurt like hell right now. It would only be worse a month or six months or a year from now.

It was for the best. If she just kept telling herself that, soon enough she might actually believe it.

During the next two weeks, she threw herself into work with an almost religious fervor. She worked twelve, fourteen and even sixteen hours a day, stopping only for an occasional meal with her sister and Simone or her dad, all of whom repeatedly expressed concern. But Lucy didn't want to talk about it—not with her family and not with Cameron, who called several times hoping to talk it out.

Lucy had put her off each time, telling her best friend

she wasn't ready to talk about it. She didn't tell Cameron she might never be ready to talk about it.

The goal of every day was utter exhaustion so she would fall into bed and drop off the cliff without taking even a minute to dwell on the agonizing pain that made its presence known every minute of every day, no matter how hard she tried to run from it.

Still trying to convince herself it was for the best, she worked late into the night on the second Friday without a weekend with Colton to look forward to. When her eyes gave out on her just after nine, she packed up a bag to bring home to get her through the long weekend that stretched before her.

She locked up the office and set out on foot for home, stopping to pick up takeout. Everything reminded her of him, even the takeout box that stirred memories of a picnic they'd had at Battery Park. In the short time he'd spent with her here, he'd managed to touch almost every aspect of her life. She saw him in her apartment, in her office and at many of her favorite local haunts. She heard his voice and his laughter in her dreams, and a thousand times each day she thought of something she wanted to tell him.

As that second week came to a slow, quiet, painful end, she finally began to question whether living like this was better than living with him any way they could.

That question was weighing heavily on her as she walked the final block home. She was so deeply mired in her own head and unhappy thoughts that she nearly tripped over the large foot on the bottom stair that led to her front door. The near fall finally jarred her out of the contemplation, and she looked up to bitch out the owner of the offending foot.

The words died on her lips when she saw Colton sitting there, beer in hand, smile on his face, as if he had not a care in the world. "Working late, huh?"

For a second, she was too stunned to speak. "What . . . What're you doing here?"

"I had some business to take care of in the city, so I

figured I'd stop by to see how you're doing." He took a closer look at her, no doubt seeing the deep, dark purple circles under her eyes, the pale pasty skin, the dull, lifeless hair that had required more energy than she could bother to muster. "How're you doing, Luce?"

"Great. I'm great. You?"

"Fantastic. Never been better."

"That's good."

"No, wait," he said after a long awkward pause. "That's not exactly true. I'm actually terrible. I'm a goddamned mess, and it's all your fault."

She couldn't hear this. She couldn't go backward. Not when it had taken everything she had to move forward for the last few weeks. "Colton, please don't—"

"You've had your say, Lucy. Now I'm going to have mine." He got up and headed for the door to her building, using the key she'd given him and apparently forgotten to get back. "Are you coming?"

The part of her that still favored self-preservation wanted to run for its life. But the other part of her, the part that loved this man with her whole heart and soul, had realized the moment she laid eyes on him that there was nowhere she could go to fully escape the power of what she felt for him.

So she went up the stairs and through the door he held for her. She trudged up the two flights of stairs knowing he was behind her, coming with her to say whatever it was he had to say. She stepped into her apartment and sucked in a sharp breath when she saw it was filled with flowers of every imaginable kind.

She turned to him, overwhelmed with questions, but the words escaped her.

He relieved her of the bag she'd carried from the office, took her hand and led her to the sofa. A wrapped box with a bow on top sat on her coffee table. He pointed to it. "Open it."

Lucy's hands trembled as she tugged at the satin bow and unwrapped the book that looked like one of the journals he kept on the mountain. "What is this?"

"Look at it."

She looked first at him and then directed her attention to the book, which was filled with drawings of the two of them—in her apartment in the city, on his mountain, with the dogs, with his family, with her family, at her office, in his bed in the cabin. The drawings were heartfelt and amazingly true to the time they'd already spent together. "This is . . . it's incredible, Colton. You're so talented."

"Keep going."

She turned the pages until she came to one that was marked *Chapter 2*. The first page carried a heading that said *Life in New York* that showed them eating dinner on her sofa while watching TV. On the next page they were in her bed. The story unfolded from there on the streets of New York, at her father's home, with Simone and Emma at their apartment, on a sidewalk café and at her office.

The heading on the next page said *Life in Vermont*, and it showed her working at the desk space he'd made available to her in the retail store while he chopped wood outside. He'd included a picture of Sunday dinner at his parents' home and a scene at the beach at Lake Champlain.

Touched and filled with longing for all the things depicted on the pages, she stopped for a moment to deal with the flood of tears that cascaded down her cheeks.

He took the book from her. "This is my favorite part." The heading said *Chapter 3: Colton and Lucy, Life Together.* The first picture was one of Colton with her dad. "That was my first order of business in New York. Speaking to your dad."

Startled to hear that he'd been to her father's house, Lucy said, "Why?"

"Keep reading."

The next page included a picture of a wedding and pregnant Lucy and another of Colton grinning widely as he held a baby who had red hair. "Colton . . ."

"We could have all of this, Lucy, every single thing on these pages and so many other things we can't yet imagine. All you have to do is agree to be with me in any way we see fit. We're both self-employed and can make up the rules of our own lives. One week here, one week there, one week in the Caribbean on a beach together, two weeks in Vermont, three weeks in New York. Together every day."

She wanted what he offered so badly she could almost taste it. "You can't be away from the mountain for that long."

"Yes, I can. Max is coming on board full time, and my family has decided to buy the place next door that's been on the market for some time now. We're going to add to our acreage and hire some more help. I'll have Max with me to help manage everything. The only time I absolutely have to be there is from January to April. I figure you can come and go as you need to then."

"What about when you're here? What would you do?"

He pointed to a picture he'd drawn of a store with two men talking. "The last time I was here, I spoke with the owner of a gourmet shop who's interested in stocking our syrup in his store. I suspect there are many others who might be convinced to carry our product once they hear about it. That's what I'll do while I'm here—sell syrup."

She ran her hand over the leather-bound book full of drawings. "You've thought of everything," Lucy said, truly wowed by the obvious time and effort he'd put into showing her how their unconventional life together could work.

"Except for one thing—protecting that tender heart of yours." He knelt before her, took the book from her and placed it on the table. "I've loved you from the first time I ever laid eyes on you. I'll always love you. I've missed you more than you could ever know these last two weeks, and I never want to be away from you again. I want you to have the commitment you need to believe that we can really make this work, so I'm asking you, Lucy Mulvaney, to marry me and to live with me in our two places, to make a life with me that works for both of us." He produced a ring that he held up to her, almost daring her to take everything he offered. "Will you marry me, Lucy?"

She stared at the ring and then at him, trying to process

everything he'd said. "Yes." The single word seemed somehow insignificant in light of all he'd said to her, but judging by the joyful light in his eyes, it was the only word he needed to hear.

Blinking back tears, he slid the ring onto her finger and took her into his arms.

She returned his embrace, holding on for dear life to him and his assurances that they really could make this work as long as they had love and commitment to depend on.

He drew back from her and framed her face with his big, rough hands and kissed the tears off her cheeks before focusing on her lips. As he kissed her and held her, all of Lucy's worries drained away, gone in a sea of desire and love and need for the one thing she couldn't live without—him.

"You have no idea how happy you've made me—or how relieved I am that you said yes," he said.

"You have no idea how happy I was to see you sitting on my stairs. To say I missed you doesn't do justice to how awful I've felt the last two weeks."

"My grandfather told me two weeks would be long enough to make you feel bad enough to say yes."

Lucy gasped and then laughed. "So he coached you through this?"

"He told me what I needed to do, and he was right. But two weeks was way too long to be without you."

"What about Sarah and Elmer? I'm not allowed to have pets here."

"They're with Cameron and Will this weekend, enjoying some time with their cousins, and the good thing about my gigantic family is that there's always someone who'd be willing to help us out with them when we're here."

"So Cameron knew you were coming?"

"Yes, but she didn't know why. No one does, except for my gramps. He helped me pick out the ring."

Lucy took a good long look at the gorgeous diamond set in a platinum band. "It's beautiful. You guys did good."

"I went with simple over fancy because I thought you'd like that better."

"I love it, and I love you. Thank you for this, for showing me how foolish I was to think I could live without you after everything we'd shared."

"I was prepared to let you go if that's what you really wanted, but Gramps told me it wasn't what you really wanted. It was what you felt you *needed*. Want and need were two very different things in this case."

"He's very wise."

"Thank goodness he helped me to see the difference."

"Thank goodness is right."

He reclined on the sofa and brought her with him, arranging her so she faced him, their legs intertwined. The way he looked at her made her melt from the inside out. "So we're really going to do this?"

Lucy nodded. "We really are."

"Could we start doing it now? Because, you know, it's been a really long two weeks."

Laughing as she caressed his adorable face, she said, "Yes, Colton, we can start right now."

EPILOGUE

———◆———

"We have a problem," Elmer said as he slid into the other side of the booth.

"What kind of problem?" Lincoln asked.

"I heard a rumor that Nina and Brett are selling the diner. He got a position overseas to teach next year, and they're looking to unload the place quickly."

"How is that our problem? And is this why you made me drive all the way over here to meet you for lunch?" *All the way over here* in this case meant a sandwich shop in St. Johnsbury.

"I didn't want anyone to overhear us. There's going to be a lot of interest in that little gold mine of a diner. We have to keep this top secret."

"Keep *what* top secret?"

Elmer looked at his son-in-law with exasperation. "Are you paying attention? We can't let anyone know we're interested in the diner."

"Interested in the diner? Have you lost your mind? I'm not interested in the diner."

"Yes, you are."

"Please, enlighten me. Why am I interested in the diner exactly?"

"And here I thought you were such a smart guy. *You're* not interested in the diner. *Hunter* is."

"He's never said so to me. How do you know that?"

"Lincoln, have you been drinking?"

"No, I have not been drinking in the middle of the day, as you well know. How about you stop talking in circles and give it to me straight?"

Elmer leaned in, speaking quietly. "Hunter wants Megan, Nina's sister. If Nina sells the diner, where does that leave Megan? And where does that leave Hunter?"

"Ahhh, okay. I'm starting to get the picture."

"Thanks goodness. I was beginning to worry about you for a second there."

As Linc scowled at him, Elmer ordered a grilled cheese sandwich with a cup of tomato soup.

"That sounds good," Linc said to the waitress. "I'll have the same."

"So what're we going to do about this situation?" Elmer asked when they were alone.

"I don't know what we can do. We just committed to buying the acreage on the mountain. That on top of the website . . . I don't want to get us overcommitted. Hunter would never allow that to happen."

"Hmm," Elmer said as he stirred cream into his coffee. "That is a problem."

"How'd you hear about all this anyway?"

"Cletus's son works at that fancy school where Brett teaches. He heard rumblings that Brett applied for an overseas position and got it. After he did a little extra digging, he found out they're planning to sell the diner before they go."

"What about Megan? What will she do?"

"That's the big question. I'll be honest with you . . . I don't get what our boy sees in that girl. Don't get me wrong . . . She's very pretty. That's undeniable. But she can be . . . What's the word? Cranky. Extremely cranky.

But from what I've heard, Hunter sees past that. If he wants her, we can't let her get away."

"All this time, she's been right across the street from where he works all day every day, and he hasn't done a thing about it."

"That's because she's been carrying a torch for Will for years. Apparently, she's only just recently given up on him, which opens the door to other possibilities."

"So you're actually suggesting we buy the diner to keep Megan in town in the hope that Hunter might actually— finally—do something about these so-called feelings he has for the pretty but cranky waitress who's worked across the street from where he works for years?"

Elmer squirmed in his seat. "When you put it like that, it sounds kinda farfetched."

Lincoln's laughter had other patrons looking at them with curiosity. "How do you propose I go around my CFO to buy this diner you want me to acquire for my CFO?"

"I'm not proposing you go around him, per se. I'm proposing you make him think it was his idea."

"And where's the money coming from? He'll never go for it after we just agreed to buy the property to expand the sugaring facility."

"If you can get him to agree to the purchase, I'll come up with the money."

"We've had a good run, you and me," Lincoln said, eyeing his father-in-law skeptically. "We're three for three, on a roll and running the risk of getting a little full of ourselves and our successes. But this one . . . I don't know if she's the right choice for him."

"That part ain't up to us. We're just here to give a little *encouragement* where we can. The important stuff . . . That's up to *them*." Elmer sat back in his seat, gazing at Lincoln shrewdly. "So . . . Are we getting into the restaurant business, or what?"

Lincoln let out a deep sigh, knowing defeat when he saw it. "I guess we're getting into the restaurant business."

Elmer smiled. "Excellent. If it goes the way I think it

will, this one counts in my column. That'll make us tied at two, even though Colton should count as mine since I saved the day there."

"I already told you—Lucy came to us through Cameron, and she was my doing."

"I'll give you that, even if I know the truth about how Colton managed to pull off an engagement."

"You're a worthy adversary, Elmer Stillman."

"And don't you forget it." He held up his coffee mug in a toast. "Number four, here we go."

Lincoln touched his mug to Elmer's. "Here we go."

ACKNOWLEDGMENTS

Thank you, Audrey Coty, proprietor of the Nebraska Knoll Sugar Farm in Stowe, Vermont, for allowing me to borrow liberally from her blog (nebraskaknoll.com/vtmaple2013) detailing her facility's 2013 sugaring season for Colton's journal entries at the start of each chapter. She also helped to ensure the accuracy of Colton's descriptions of how he makes syrup. My visit to Nebraska Knoll was one of my favorite moments in researching the Green Mountain Series, and I'm grateful to Audrey for her generosity. Thank you to "Jack's" team—Julie, Lisa, Holly, Isabel, Cheryl and Nikki—for all you do for me so I can write, write, write. To my agent, Kevan Lyon, my editor, Kate Seaver, and everyone at Berkley Publishing, thank you for your support of the Green Mountain series. A very special thanks to the Orton family, proprietors of the Vermont Country Store, as well as the awesome staff in the Weston and Rockingham stores, for their incredible generosity toward me and the books that were inspired by the store and the Orton family. The series launch parties we held at the stores were the most fun I've ever had as an author, and I hope we can do it again sometime.

Thanks to my family—Dan, Emily and Jake—for supporting my writing career, and to my dad for enjoying this wild ride with me.

I usually thank my readers last, not because you are the least important, but because I like to save the best for last. I couldn't do what I love to do without all of you. Your love for my books overwhelms and honors me every day. Thank you, thank you, *thank you*! I hope you loved Colton and Lucy's story. If you did, be sure to leave a review on the retail site of your choice and/or Goodreads to help other readers discover the Green Mountain series.

When you're finished reading, join the *I Saw Her Standing There* Reader Group on Facebook at facebook.com/groups/ISawHerStandingThere to discuss the story with other readers and fans with spoilers allowed and encouraged. Much more to come from the Green Mountains! Keep up with all the series developments and qualify for occasional giveaways as a member of the Green Mountain Reader Group at facebook.com/groups/GreenMountainSeries. The best way to stay up-to-date with all my news is by joining my mailing list at marieforce.com.

Watch for Hunter and Megan's story in *And I Love Her*, coming in March 2015. Keep reading after the Colton and Lucy short story, "Lucy in the Sky With Diamonds," for a sneak peek at Hunter and Megan's story. Thanks for reading!

xoxo
Marie

Turn the page for a bonus short story
featuring Colton and Lucy,

LUCY IN THE SKY
WITH DIAMONDS

A Green Mountain Series Short Story

CHAPTER 1

————◆◆————

"You want to do *what*?" Lucy asked, certain—absolutely *certain*—she'd heard him wrong.

"Come on, Luce," Colton said in that charming, cajoling tone that usually worked wonders on her, especially when he was trying to separate her from her clothes. "It'll be a blast. And you'll get two whole days with Cameron, your second favorite person in Vermont. Come on . . . *Pretty please?*"

"Don't do that."

"What am I doing?"

"That whole I'm-too-cute-for-words thing you do whenever you're trying to talk me into something you know *I* don't want to do."

"I'm too cute for words? Awww, thanks, honey. You say the sweetest things. I'm so glad I was smart enough to ask you to marry me."

"There! You're doing it again! Stop trying to distract me, and the answer is still no. An emphatic no-way-in-hell-are-you-talking-me-into-going-camping *no*. Any questions?"

"Just one."

"And that is . . ."

"Do you love me, Luce?"

"Oh don't do that either! What kind of question is that? You know I love you. I tell you I love you every day—at least ten times a day."

He came to her then, his eyes warm and amused as he looked at her, and put his arms around her. "Then let me share something I love with you. Trust me enough to ensure you'll have a great time and be perfectly comfortable. Please?"

"My idea of camping is an all-inclusive resort with a spa and room service."

"We'll do that sometime, too. Any time you want."

"And Cameron actually agreed to this plan of yours and Will's?"

"She's in."

"I won't believe that until I hear it from her."

"You aren't calling me a liar now, are you?"

"*Liar* is a strong word. *Occasionally truth challenged* might be a better way to put it."

He threw his head back and laughed. "You do crack me up, Lucy Mulvaney." Sliding his arms around her, he drew her in close to him and kissed her neck until her knees went weak.

"Don't do that either," she said with far less conviction than she'd shown a few minutes ago.

"What?" he whispered, setting off goose bumps down her arm. "What am I doing?"

"Seducing me into going along with this harebrained plan of yours."

He pulled back to look down at her, his brow raised rakishly. "Harebrained? Really?"

"Yes! Do you have any idea what a pain in the ass I'll be on a camping trip? Do you have the first clue how much bitching, moaning, pissing and groaning there'll be?"

"I have a fairly good idea."

"And you still want to take me?"

"Very badly."

She shook her head with dismay. "You're a glutton for punishment."

"Your kind of punishment is my favorite kind."

"Colton! I'm being serious. I'll hate every minute of it, and you'll hate me for ruining something you love."

"I could never, ever, *ever* hate you, Lucy. Ever."

"Even if I complain for two straight days without taking a breath?"

"Even then."

Lucy wished she were still eight like her niece, Simone, and could get away with a full-blown temper tantrum followed by a good old-fashioned pout. But that wasn't going to happen, and it was beginning to look like the camping trip was. So she had two options—flat-out refuse to go and run the risk of disappointing him or suck it up and compromise. This relationship thing was not for the faint of heart.

While she had her own internal argument with herself, he waited patiently, his gaze never straying from her face as she weighed her extremely unappealing options.

"Fine," she said sullenly. "I'll do it. But, you're taking me to a fabulous spa in the next month."

"Deal." He kissed her then, sucking the oxygen from her lungs and all thoughts from her head that didn't involve the exquisite pleasure of being kissed—devoured, in fact—by Colton Abbott, love of her life. "Wait till you see how hot tent sex is."

Damn if he didn't always make her laugh, especially when she was on the verge of starting a great big fight with him. "It better be the hottest sex of my life, or this will be the last time you ever get me into a sleeping bag, you got me?"

"Oh, baby . . . I got you, and I do love when you throw down the gauntlet."

The look he gave her was full of sexy determination. Maybe this wouldn't be so bad after all.

It sucked. It absolutely, positively *sucked*. *Suck, suck, suck* was the only word bouncing around Lucy's mind as she pretended to participate in the paddling of a canoe against a strong current in a river located smack in the middle of nowhere. She was hot, sweaty, smelly and apparently the daily special on the mosquito buffet despite multiple doses of bug spray.

Even though she'd lathered on sunscreen and reapplied frequently, she could feel her fair skin burning as the sun beamed down on them. And her arms ached from the effort required to help propel the canoe forward.

She glanced over at Cameron, sitting in the front of Will's canoe, laughing and splashing with her boyfriend and appearing to have a jolly good time. Lucy wished she'd brought a slingshot and some acorns she could shoot at Cameron, who was ruining everything. How was she supposed to bitch and moan when perky Cameron had embraced this fiasco as a great big adventure?

Naturally, Colton had failed to mention the canoe part of the program when he talked her into this ridiculous outing. She kept telling herself—two days and one night and then they'd be back to his place on the mountain, which was positively plush compared to this. It was funny to think that she'd once found his cabin to be rustic. *This* was rustic—trees and water and birds and a cloudless blue sky above them.

On most days, Lucy appreciated a cloudless blue sky. Today she'd kill for a cloud or two between her and the hot sunshine. If there was one perk to this nightmare, it was the opportunity to occasionally glance back at Colton in all his shirtless glory as he paddled and steered the canoe from the back.

The play of his finely honed muscles was a sight she usually enjoyed. When they were in Vermont, one of her favorite pastimes was sitting on the porch of his cabin and watching him swing the axe as he split the wood he'd need for the next sugaring season.

Today, however, even the sight of his sexy body failed to cheer her the way it usually did.

"How're you doing up there?" he asked after a long period of silence.

"Great. Never been better."

"Do you think I can't hear the sarcasm in your voice after all this time together?"

"I'm getting eaten alive. Are you sure that was actual bug spray you gave me and not something that actually appeals to them?"

He stopped paddling and stood, coming toward her and making the canoe tip precariously.

Lucy dropped her paddle into the boat and grasped the sides, preparing to be dumped into the freezing water at any second. No matter how warm the summer sun got, Colton had told her, the river never really warmed up. "What're you doing?" she asked over her shoulder as he came toward her.

"Turn around," he said.

Lucy moved carefully to accommodate his request without pitching them both into the river.

"Time to reapply." He pulled the can of bug spray from one of the pockets of his cargo shorts and squatted before her, spraying her legs and arms. "Do your neck."

Lucy took the can from him and did as directed.

From the pocket on his other leg, Colton retrieved the sunscreen. "How can you still be getting burned under that big hat when I put eighty-five on you earlier?"

"Irish skin. You knew this about me."

"Still . . ." His brows furrowed with concern. "I don't want you getting burned."

"Might be too late for that."

Working with intense concentration, Colton reapplied the sunscreen to her arms, her legs and the tops of her feet. Though she wished she could click her heels together and be anywhere but floating on a freezing river in the mountains of Vermont, she had to admit the slide of his hands over her skin had her thinking about the amazing tent sex she'd been promised.

Then he handed her the sunscreen stick she preferred to use on her face.

"Don't forget your lips," he said. "I've got big plans for them later. We can't have them sore or burned."

"Everything okay over there?" Will called as he and Cameron circled back to check on them.

"Yep," Colton said. "Just reapplying bug spray and sunscreen."

"Are you getting bitten, Luce?" Cameron asked.

"Like crazy."

"You must be sweeter than me. They don't like me."

"Good thing I do," Will said suggestively, making Cameron laugh.

Everyone was in such a great mood, excited for the getaway and the chance for the guys to share one of their passions with the city girls they'd fallen in love with. Lucy felt a little guilty for being so grumpy. Perhaps if she tried to embrace it as an adventure and time away from the rat race of life with the man she loved, she might actually enjoy it.

She snorted inelegantly. As if. *Okay, so you might not be enjoying it, but maybe you can let him think you are*, she reasoned with herself. If she did that though, he might want to do this again, and that was not happening. Several hours in, Lucy already knew this was going to be a one-time thing.

She's miserable and trying to hide it, Colton thought as he propelled the canoe forward along the lazy river that wound through the Green Mountains. He'd been coming here all his life and had wanted to share it with Lucy, but that might've been a mistake. He could *feel* her agitation despite the three feet that separated her seat from his. He could *see* it in the unusual slump of her shoulders.

Since her happiness and comfort were always foremost on his mind, he decided to try to cajole her out of her bad mood by showing her how much fun the outdoors could be when you were with the one you loved.

"We're going to take a little detour," Colton called to Will as they reached a fork in the river. "Meet you at the campsite?"

"Sounds good."

Cameron waved as they took the left side and Colton directed their canoe to the right.

"Where are we going?" Lucy asked.

"Just down here a little ways. I've got something I want to show you." He paddled along for another half mile or so before he steered the canoe around a bend and into a small cove that had been carved out of the earth by water rushing by over thousands of years.

"This is pretty," Lucy said as Colton beached the canoe, jumped out and dragged it up onto the small stretch of sand.

"It's one of my favorite spots along this river." He held out a hand to help her out of the canoe, which again tipped when she moved. Luckily she pitched right into his arms, and he lifted her onto the beach.

"I suck at this," she said glumly.

"No, you don't. It's just new to you. That's all."

"You don't have to pretend to be glad you brought me here."

"I'm never pretending to be glad when I'm with you, Lucy. I don't care what we're doing or where we are. If you're there, I'm happy."

"I don't deserve you."

"*Why* would you say that?"

"Because I've been thinking really mean thoughts about you all morning."

Colton tossed his head back and laughed hard.

"You think it's funny that your fiancée is thinking mean things about you?"

"What kind of mean things?" he asked when he'd stopped laughing.

"Mostly all the reasons I hate you for making me go camping—bugs, sun and bathrooms were tops on the list."

"Bathrooms? I hate to tell you . . ."

"You don't have to tell me there's no indoor plumbing out here, Colton. I have eyes. So what's a girl supposed to do when she needs to pee? Urgently?"

"She tells her big studly fiancé that she has to pee—urgently—and he sets her up."

"Sets her up how?" she asked, eyeing him skeptically.

"Leave it to me." He went back to the canoe, rooted around in the huge pile of stuff that he'd tied into the back of the boat and returned with a roll of toilet paper and a plastic bag. "Let's go."

"You're not coming with me to pee."

"Hmm, well, I thought you'd want me to check for bears and bobcats and snakes, but if you've got this . . ." He held out the toilet paper and bag.

"You can come with me."

"Thought you might say that."

"Are there really bobcats in these woods?" she asked as she followed him into the trees, looking everywhere for glowing eyes ready to pounce.

"I've never seen one, but they're native to this area. I'd hate to have one find you when you've got your cute little butt out on display. That would be a tragedy."

"It would be just my luck," Lucy said.

Colton led her into an area so dense with trees, the sun's rays only faintly penetrated, sending weak beams to the ground. He took a deep breath of fresh air and pine. "Smell that?"

Lucy breathed deeply. "Uh-huh."

"One of my favorite scents. Second only to the scent of Lucy, which is my all-time favorite."

She rolled her eyes at him, but a smile tugged at her lips. He considered that a small victory.

"This one will do," he said, sizing up a huge pine tree that was bare on the bottom with branches beginning about ten feet above them.

Lucy looked at it with apprehension. "How will it do?"

"My sisters swear by the tree trunk strategy of outdoor peeing. You drop your shorts, lean your back against the tree, keeping your feet and clothes in front of you and out of harm's way, and let her rip."

"Seriously?"

"Your other choice is to squat, but I'd recommend against actually sitting anywhere. You never know what's on the ground, and that cute butt wouldn't be so cute with poison ivy or sumac all over it." He scratched his own rear to make the point.

She took the paper and bag from him and turned her hand in a circle, telling him to look away.

"I'll be right over here taking care of my own business if you happen to see any bobcats or bears."

"It's not fair that you can just whip that thing out and go, and I have to lean against a freaking tree. I'm coming back in my next life as a man."

Laughing at her way with words, he said, "Don't do that. You'd ruin my next life if you come back as a man." He kissed her cute, sunburned nose and left her to do her business while he did his, all the while listening closely for any signs of trouble.

CHAPTER 2

———◆———

"How ya doing?" he called to her when he was finished. "Fine." She came out from behind the tree a minute later, carrying the roll of paper and the bag. "Now what do I do with this?"

"I've got a garbage bag in the canoe."

"This whole thing is kinda gross."

"The first time or two, but after a while you get used to it and it's just routine. We can't leave the paper out here. That would be littering."

"God forbid."

"Indeed."

Back at the beach, Colton produced the garbage bag and then opened the cooler. "Hungry?"

"Starving."

"How does turkey on rye with lettuce, tomato, cheese, mayo and pickles sound?"

"You made my favorite turkey sandwich from the deli in the city?"

"Yep."

"Oh my God, I think I might love you again."

"So wait," he said, withholding the sandwich, "you actually didn't love me?"

"It was only for a minute. Maybe two. Right around the time the mosquito stung me on the butt. There was a little bit of nonlove at that moment. But it passed and now I'm all the way back in love again."

"You wound me, Luce." He rested his free hand on his heart. "Right where I live."

She went to him and kissed him, wincing when her lips connected with the stubble he'd let go without shaving.

"What?"

"My lips are sunburned, too."

"I'll shave later so you can kiss me without pain."

She kissed him again. "It doesn't hurt that bad, and your kisses are worth the sacrifice."

He hooked his arm around her waist and drew her in close to him. "I know this isn't your thing, but I love having you out here with me. All I ask is that you roll with it and let me show you how fun it can be, okay?"

"I'm sorry if I've been a poor sport. I'm trying."

"You're not a poor sport. You're adorable, and I love you."

"I love you, too, but I'll love you even more when you hand over that sandwich."

Smiling, Colton kissed her again and then gave her the sandwich along with a canister of lemon-scented wet wipes. He pulled a blanket from the canoe, spread it out on the sand and then went back for his own sandwich and a couple of sodas for them.

Lucy shook her head when he offered the drink to her. "I'll just have to pee again."

"I'll find you another tree. You have to stay hydrated out here."

"Fine." She took the soda, popped it open and took a delicate sip. "Are you happy?"

"Never been happier."

Surrounded as they were by majestic trees, birds of all kinds, wildflowers of every imaginable color, blue sky and bluer water, there was plenty to look at. But Colton's gaze was drawn again and again to her as she ate her sandwich and took in her surroundings. He'd give just about anything to know what she was thinking.

"It sure is pretty here," she finally said.

Her appreciation of the scenery went a long way toward relieving some of the stress he felt about dragging her along on a trip he knew she didn't want to take.

"Wait until you see it at night. The stars are unlike anything you've ever seen."

"I'm kind of scared to be out here at night."

"Why would you be scared, honey? Do you think I'd ever, ever, *ever* let anything happen to you?"

"No, but still . . . I've never slept outside before."

"You won't be outside. You'll be in a tent with me. I promise you'll be perfectly safe and very comfortable." He leaned over to kiss her, resting his forehead against hers. "Have a little faith in me?"

"I have all the faith in the world in you. Why do you think I'm here?"

Lucy curled her hand around his neck to keep him close enough to kiss again. He was so adorable and sweet and wanted so badly to show her a good time that Lucy decided to let go of all her worries and fears as well as her irrational need for all the creature comforts of home. She was alone with Colton, one of her favorite places to be. What did it matter where they were?

While she was perfectly content to kiss him, apparently he had other needs that became apparent to her when he lifted her T-shirt to gain access to her belly. "What're you doing?"

"This," he said, placing kisses on her belly that made her squirm under him. Pushing her shirt up as he went, he kissed the slopes of her breast and then tongued her nipples through her bra. "And this."

"Um, Colton?"

"Hmm?"

"Not here."

"Yes, here. Right here." He released the front clasp on her bra and was devouring her right nipple before she caught up and realized his intentions.

Lucy began to squirm more intently, determined to end this before it got any further out of control. However, since she was no match for his formidable strength, she decided to fight like a girl and pulled his hair.

"Ow," he said while continuing to stroke her nipple with his tongue.

"We need to stop! I can't do this here."

"Yes, you can."

"No, I can't!"

He looked up at her, slaying her with those eyes that never looked at her with anything other than love. "Yes," he said softly, "you can. We're completely alone here. No one around for miles."

"Will and Cam are around."

"They went the other way, and he knows I wanted to be alone with you. They won't be back."

"How can you know that for sure?"

"Because I know my brother, and he knows me. Relax, Luce. Let me love you."

"We can do this later. When it's dark."

"We'll do it then, too." He drew her nipple into his mouth, sucking hard enough to ensure there wasn't room for any other thoughts in her head than the divine pleasure she always found in his arms. Then he was tugging at the button to her shorts, unzipping them and pushing them down her legs. His hand slid inside her panties where he discovered at least one part of her was fully on board with his plan for outdoor, middle-of-the-day, broad-daylight sex on a riverbank.

"Ahh, God," he whispered as he kissed his way down the front of her. "That's so hot."

"Come back up here." Her heart beat frantically at the thought of what he obviously planned to do.

"In a minute."

"Colton . . ."

"I love the sound of my name coming from you."

"Please come up here."

"I will as soon as I make you come. So the faster you come, the faster I'll be back to protect you from the prying eyes of the wildlife." This was said between kisses to her belly and nibbles to her hip bones that made her squirm with interest rather than retreat.

Her panties slid down her legs and were discarded over his shoulder.

"Don't lose them!"

"I'll find them for you. Don't worry."

"Don't worry. Right."

"Relax, honey," he said as he kissed his way from her knee up her inner thigh and then back down the other side, skipping over all the places that mattered most. Clearly, he was in no particular hurry as he propped her legs on his broad shoulders.

She really ought to seriously call a halt to this. That was her last cognizant thought before he used his thumbs to open her to his tongue. Staring up at the bright blue, cloudless sky, Lucy gave in to the overwhelming desire he aroused in her so easily. All he had to do was look at her in that certain way, and she was a goner. But when he did this, when he made love to her with his mouth and fingers, she became a blathering idiot, incapable of anything other than holding on to his thick hair for dear life as he took her on the wildest of rides.

Outside, in the bright light of day, the effect seemed to be intensified by the fear of getting caught. Her skin felt like it was on fire, and not from the sun. Her legs trembled violently and her sex clenched around his tongue, but the orgasm she needed to move things along was elusive and out of reach.

Moaning, she buried her fingers in his hair.

He sucked hard on her clitoris, making her see stars as he sent his fingers plunging into her. With his free hand, he squeezed her ass, which tripped her over the edge, screaming from the incredible pleasure that ripped through her body.

Moving quickly, he managed to push his shorts down over his hips and align his cock with her still-clenching channel, surging into her and triggering another release.

"God," he whispered in her ear, his hot breath giving her goose bumps. "You are so hot, Luce. You make me crazy with wanting you."

"Obviously, you make me crazy, too, if I'm actually having sex outside in the middle of the day."

"Isn't it fun?"

"It's scary, so hurry up." She raised her hips, trying to move things along so they could get their clothes back on as soon as possible. Of course, her desire for haste only had him slowing down, his pace languid and unhurried as he moved above her.

"I could do this all day," he said before he captured her lips in a deep, erotic kiss.

Lucy turned away from the kiss. "We can't do this all day. We have to hurry up."

"Do you want me to stop?"

"You ask me that when you're overpowering me in every possible way," she said with a nervous laugh.

Poised on top of her, he smoothed her hair back from her face and compelled her to meet his gaze while he continued to throb inside her. "I love you," he said, kissing her softly.

"I love you, too."

"Then trust me to take care of you and to keep you safe."

"I do trust you."

"Let go of your worries and just feel the pleasure." He grasped her hands and raised them over her head as he picked up the pace again. "Close your eyes and don't think. Just feel."

Since there wasn't much else she could do while completely overtaken by him, she did as he directed and closed her eyes, relaxing into the now-familiar rhythm they always found together.

"That's it," he said, bending over her to suck on her nipple. "Ahhh, I love that full-body blush."

Lucy hated that her skin gave away her every emotion, but she'd learned not to tell him that every time he said how much he loved it.

He released her hands so he could slide his under her. Gripping her ass, he went for broke. "Touch yourself, Luce," he said in a harsh whisper that told her he was close.

Before him, she would've been mortified by such a demand from one of the few lovers she'd had in the past. Now she slid her hand down to where they were joined without hesitation, anticipating the sublime pleasure they found together.

"*Yes*," he said in the same gravelly tone. "Just like that. So hot. So incredible."

His words were every bit as powerful as the deep thrusts of his cock.

"*Lucy . . .*"

She opened her eyes to find his closed, his jaw throbbing from the effort to hold back and wait for her.

He surged into her, and the combination of that and the press of her fingers against her clit had her forgetting everything that didn't involve him and the way he made her feel every time they made love. With a protracted groan, he came with her and then rested on top of her, his head nestled between her neck and shoulder.

Lucy ran her hand over his back, which was damp with sweat. "There's definitely something to be said for outside, middle-of-the-day sex."

"Told ya." His lips curved against her neck as he kissed his way to her lips. "There's something to be said for sex with you no matter where we have it."

"This isn't going to be a regular thing."

"You said yourself it was amazing, and—" He stopped himself midsentence and cocked his head, listening to something.

"What?"

"Is that . . . singing?"

"Did I make you hear music?"

Grunting out a laugh, he pushed himself up on his arms to peer above the row of low-cut bushes that hid them from the river. "Oh, shit." Colton moved quickly, grabbing the blanket and rolling them without withdrawing from her.

"What the hell?"

"Shhh."

"What is it?"

"If I'm not mistaken, it's a Boy Scout troop."

"*Are you freaking kidding me?*" she whispered in an angry hiss.

"Shhh, be quiet. Maybe they won't notice us."

She was going to punch him the second she could do it without fear of being caught—*naked and having sex*—by a bunch of kids! And was he . . . *getting hard* again? Lucy began to struggle against his tight hold. "Don't even think about it," she said through gritted teeth.

He shook with silent laughter that only made her madder.

"I'm going to kill you for this."

Nuzzling her ear, he bit down gently on her earlobe. "No, you won't."

"Yes, I will!"

"Shhh. Maybe they won't see us."

"What are they doing, Mr. Carson?" a young voice asked.

"Ummm, camping," the adult replied in a terse, annoyed tone.

"They forgot their tent."

"Apparently so. Let's continue on down the river and find another place to stop for lunch."

"Why is there underwear hanging from that bush?"

"Paddle, boys. Right now."

"Why would someone hang their underwear from a bush? A bear might take it."

"You're paddling. Not talking."

By now, Colton was laughing so hard he had tears rolling down his face that fell against her neck and shoulder.

"You're a dead man," she said as the young voices faded in the distance.

"What a great story to tell our kids someday."

"We can't tell them that! You're crazy!"

With his head resting on her shoulder he laughed and laughed and laughed.

Lucy couldn't keep a small smile from occupying her lips as she listened to him. He had such a great, lusty laugh. Speaking of lusty . . . As he laughed, he continued to throb inside her. "Get that thing out of me and find my hanging underwear."

"As long as he's back for round two, it'd be such a shame to waste him."

"Only you could get a hard-on over being caught having sex by a bunch of kids."

"They didn't see a thing, and it was all you, babe."

"None of this is my fault." She pushed on his shoulders and managed to finally dislodge him.

He sat back in a squat, his hard cock standing at attention between them. Colton glanced down, clucking with disapproval. "You're really going to leave him in this condition for hours and hours? Is that what kind of wife you're going to be?"

Lucy sat up, holding the blanket snug against her chest. "Find. My. Clothes. Now."

"Fine. Be that way."

He gathered her shorts, T-shirt and bra and handed them to her. "Oh look at that," he said of her panties, which were, in fact, hanging from a bush. "I bet I couldn't do that again if I tried."

"You won't get another chance."

With his own clothes in hand, he sat next to her on the blanket, leaned in close to her and nibbled playfully on her shoulder. "Come on, Luce. You have to admit that was funny."

"It was mortifying!"

"But funny. *Come on* . . . Admit it . . ."

"If I say it was even kind of funny that'll encourage

you, and I can't do that. You're already totally out of control." She gestured to his still-erect penis. "And so is he."

"On behalf of both of us, I'm hurt."

"Go take a dunk in the freezing river. That'll take care of him."

"Great idea." He stood up, still bare-ass naked, and walked toward the water.

"Colton! Put a bathing suit on or something!"

"Why? There's no one around."

"Where have I heard that before?" She pulled on her clothes while he took a dip in the freezing water.

"Holy shit, that's cold!"

"Maybe it'll chill you out for a few hours."

"Won't last that long."

"Then I'll dip you again."

Even though she was truly mortified that a group of Boy Scouts had nearly caught them having sex, she couldn't help but think about what she'd be doing on a summer Saturday in New York if she'd never met him. Probably hanging out at her apartment, doing laundry, perhaps seeing her sister and niece at some point. That life had been satisfying and filled with people who loved her. But this life . . . Her life with him was one adventure after another, and she loved every minute she got to spend with him—even when he was embarrassing the hell out of her.

Like now as he walked out of the water in all his glory, hands on his hips as he strolled toward her like a sexy panther on the prowl. And he was still hard!

Lucy scrambled to her feet, pulling her shirt over her head as she backpedaled away from him.

He rushed toward her and hooked an arm around her waist, stopping her from going any farther. "Don't move. There's poison ivy right behind you." Lifting her like she was a feather rather than a fully grown woman, he deposited her gently on the blanket.

She looked over her shoulder at the shiny green leaves on the bush behind her and shuddered when she realized how close she'd come to stepping right into it. "Thanks," she said with a kiss for her rescuer. "My hero."

"So I'm forgiven for the Boy Scouts?" he asked as he pulled on his clothes.

"Not hardly."

"Crap. I thought I had just gotten myself a get-out-of-jail-free card with the poison ivy rescue."

"No such luck."

"You'll forgive me before the day is out. I'll make it my mission in life."

"Have at it."

She helped him gather up their trash and fold the blanket that she would never look at the same way again. Thank God there'd been a blanket.

He took it from her and headed back to the canoe. "Hang on for one sec." Returning to where she stood on the beach, he withdrew a tube of sunscreen from his cargo shorts. "Time to reapply. We can't have that beautiful skin burning."

She held out a hand for the tube. "I can do it."

"Oh please. Allow me."

"You're shameless, Abbott."

"Call me what you will, but my hands on your skin is one of my favorite things in the whole wide world."

"Is it better than outdoor, middle-of-the-day sex?"

"It's a very close second to that." He set about applying the sunscreen with intense concentration and attention to detail.

"How is it that you can make the application of sunscreen into a sensual massage?"

"Is that what I'm doing?"

She elbowed his ribs playfully. "Like you don't know."

"I'm completely innocent."

Snorting with laughter, she tugged on his hair. "You weren't completely innocent the day you were born."

"Ahh, Luce, you know me so well. It's not my fault I was born with a hint of the devil in me. But you love me, devil and all."

"It seems I do."

When he'd applied the sunscreen stick to her face and nose, he leaned in to kiss her. "Now do your lips. I need them nice and soft later."

She hooked an arm around his neck to keep him from getting away.

He raised an eyebrow. "Yes?"

"I just want you to know . . ."

His arms encircled her waist. "What do you want me to know, babe?"

"That even when I'm dying of embarrassment, which is often when you're around, I love every minute we spend together."

His eyes went soft with love and his smile lit up his handsome face. "Does that mean I'm forgiven for the Boy Scouts?"

She stole a kiss since he was so close, and his lips were always so appealing. "Not even kinda." Lucy released him and headed for the canoe, smiling at the deep groan that followed her.

CHAPTER 3

———◆———

Lucy would never admit it, out of fear of having to go camping again, perhaps frequently, but the rest of their day was extremely enjoyable. When she and Colton caught up with Will and Cameron, they'd already found a place to camp and had set up their tent.

While Will helped Colton unload the canoe and pitch their tent, Lucy and Cameron enjoyed glasses of wine and watched the men work.

"I feel sort of decadent letting them do all the work," Cameron said.

"I don't," Lucy replied. "This was their big idea. We're just the guests."

"True." Cameron glanced over to where the brothers were arguing about the best nozzle to use on the battery-powered air pump they'd brought to inflate the mattresses. "Boys, don't fight. You're ruining our cocktail hour."

"Well, we can't have that, now can we?" Will asked with a droll smile for his girlfriend.

"They're like a couple of little kids sometimes," Lucy said.

"*All* the time. So where did you guys disappear to earlier?"

"Speaking of little kids," Lucy said, feeling her face heat with embarrassment all over again.

"Oh do tell! It must be good if your face lights up like that."

"It's good all right." She relayed the story of their outdoor sexcapade and how they'd almost been caught by a Boy Scout troop.

Cameron nearly peed her pants laughing, especially at the part about Lucy's underwear hanging from a bush. "Oh my God, stop it," Cameron said, panting and wiping tears. "Panties on a bush. Isn't that perfect?"

"It was positively magical."

"Will, you've got to hear this!"

"Cameron! Don't tell him!"

"I have to. We tell each other everything."

"Not this."

"Oh yes, especially this."

The guys joined them, and Cameron regaled Will with the tale of the riverbank and the Boy Scouts. By the time she was finished, Will was bent in half with laughter. "That's so awesome. *Why aren't they camping in a tent?*" He lost it laughing again.

"My favorite part is the panties in the bush," Cameron said with a wink for Lucy.

"We're glad to be able to entertain you two," Colton said as he refilled Lucy's wineglass. "Drink, honey."

"He's trying to butter me up so he can get lucky again later. He's shameless that way."

Cameron wiped the tears from her eyes. "Thanks for the best laugh I've had in ages."

"Happy to be of service," Colton said, filling her glass, too.

"Now isn't this fun, ladies?" Will asked.

"It doesn't totally suck," Lucy said.

Will raised his beer bottle in a toast to Colton. "Victory!"

"It's a little early to declare victory," Lucy said. "Anything could still happen."

"We'll take the points where we can get them," Colton said, squatting beside her chair for a kiss.

The brothers cooked burgers over the open fire and produced a salad one of them had made before they left home.

"They're pulling out all the stops," Cameron said to Lucy. "This might be the best burger I've ever had."

"It is good," Lucy said.

"And the salad," Will said. "Nice touch, right?"

"Very nice, honey," Cameron said with a pat on his head.

"We know what you girls like," Colton said. "Wait till you see what's for dessert."

"Mmm," Cameron said. "There's dessert?"

"Duh," Will said. "You can't camp without s'mores."

"S'mores." Lucy moaned with pleasure. "My favorite."

"Don't moan like that," Colton said. "It gives me ideas."

She rolled her eyes at him. "Everything gives you ideas."

Cameron laughed. "His brother suffers from the same ailment!"

Will puffed out his chest. "It's in the genes, ladies."

"He means j-e-a-n-s," Cam said to laughter from the others.

By the time they began to toast the marshmallows for the s'mores, the sun had set and darkness had rapidly descended. By darkness, Lucy meant darkness like she'd never seen in her life, except perhaps on Colton's mountain. But it was different knowing they'd be sleeping outside with only a thin canvas tent between them and anything that might want to get to them. The thought made her shiver.

"Are you cold, honey?" Colton asked, tuned in to her as always.

"No."

"Then why the shiver?"

"What if there's a bear or bobcat that wants to eat us while we're sleeping?"

In the glow of the fire, she could see him trying to hold back a laugh. "They won't bother us."

"How do you know that?"

"Because, for the most part they're more afraid of us than we are of them."

"Right . . . A big grizzly is really afraid of us."

"It's pretty safe," Will assured her, "or we never would've brought you here."

"That's right." Colton put his arm around Lucy and kissed her temple. "You girls are far too precious to us to ever risk you to bears or bobcats. Don't be scared, okay?"

Surrounded by his muscular body and warmed by his assurances, Lucy relaxed against him, still trying to be a good sport for his sake even if the thought of wildlife visiting in the night scared the hell out of her.

With the darkness came mosquitoes in swarms. Colton produced the can of bug spray that they all took turns applying yet again.

On the other side of the fire, Cameron sat on Will's lap, whispering and kissing.

"Let's take a walk," Colton said.

"A walk? Where?"

"Not far. I want to show you something."

"Is that a pickup line?"

"I'd be suspicious, Lucy," Will said.

"I *am* suspicious."

"Thanks for the vote of confidence," Colton said, chuckling. "But it's not a line, and I really do want to show you something."

She had no desire to leave the relative safety of the campsite, but she didn't want him to think she didn't trust him. So she took his outstretched hand and let him help her up.

"We're going to hit the hay," Will said. "We'll see you guys in the morning."

"Sleep tight," Colton said to his brother.

"If we're not back by morning, send help," Lucy said.

Cam laughed at her distress. "We will."

With a flashlight in hand, Colton led her to a well-worn path that led into a densely forested area.

"You're sure this is safe?" Lucy asked.

"Positive." He squeezed her hand in reassurance. "It's not far. Just up a short hill."

His idea of a "short" hill was her idea of a mini-mountain, and by the time they emerged from the trees at the top, she was winded and sweaty. Then he turned off the flashlight, and she gasped at the astonishing view of the stars that seemed close enough to touch. "Oh, wow," she said with a sigh.

"I wanted you to see that, and it's so much better up here."

"It's amazing. I've never seen anything like it."

Colton stood behind her, his arms looped around her and his lips nuzzling her neck. Against her ear, he hummed the chorus to "Lucy In The Sky With Diamonds."

Thrilled to be sharing such a moment with him, she smiled and took hold of his hands.

"Any time I hear that song from now on I'll think of the first time I took you camping."

"So will I. Thank you for bringing me here, for showing me that new things aren't always bad things."

"*Now* I'm forgiven for earlier. All it took was a few million stars."

"Not forgiven yet."

His laughter made his body shake behind her. "Does this mean you might let me take you camping again?"

"Don't press your luck. All I'll say is maybe. I have to admit you and Will did a great job anticipating our every need, right down to the wine, the bug spray, the sunscreen and the salad."

"Don't forget the toilet paper."

"Don't you always bring that?"

"Nah, we're *men*. That's for sissies."

"I'm not even going to ask . . ."

"It's better if you don't." He rubbed his hard cock back and forth over her bottom.

She pushed back against him, making him groan. "Ahh, there he is. I was wondering where he'd gotten off to the last few hours."

"He's been there all along, sad and lonely, hoping you might notice him."

"Poor baby. He's so neglected."

"I'm glad you feel for his plight."

"What do you say we make it an early night? I heard that air mattress you brought is ultra deluxe."

"Only the best for my girl."

She took one more look at the incredible sight above, committing it to memory. "Lead the way."

He helped her down the steep incline, keeping her from tumbling a couple of times as they worked their way back to the path that led to the campsite.

"How long do you think it'll be before I can walk down a steep Vermont hill without your assistance?"

"A few more months. It takes a while to get acclimated to mountain life. You shouldn't be expected to figure it all out overnight. You're doing great so far."

"Am I? Really? I sort of feel like I must be a drag because you're so good at it."

He stopped walking and turned to her. "You could never be a drag to me, Luce. I get us around in the mountains. You get us around in the city. It all comes out in the wash."

"Yes, I suppose it does."

"I love that you've never done any of this before. I love that I get to share these experiences with you and introduce you to things I enjoy doing. And I love you—no matter what we're doing."

"I love you, too." She reached up to place both her hands on his face and tugged him close enough to kiss. "In fact, I might be prepared to show you just how much I love you."

"Tent. Now." He moved swiftly through the trees until they emerged into the campsite where Will and Cameron's tent was aglow from the lantern they'd lit inside.

"Oh shit," Colton whispered as their silhouettes came into focus, showing exactly what was going on inside the tent. "Someone please remove my corneas."

Cameron was bent over Will, making all his camping fantasies come true.

"Turn off the light, Romeo," Colton called to them. "Your tent is see-through."

Cameron let out a scream. "Will! Oh my God! They can see us!"

"How's this my fault? I didn't know it was see-through. I've never had sex in this tent before."

Lucy was crippled with laughter as Will begged Cameron to continue what she'd been doing before they were so rudely interrupted.

Colton nudged her toward their tent. "I believe certain promises were made," Colton reminded her as he unzipped the mosquito screen.

"I need to pee and brush my teeth."

"I can assist with both those things."

After they'd attended to business, Colton was more than happy to help her out of her clothes and into the sleeping bags he'd zipped together earlier to make one big bed for them.

The soft flannel felt incredible against her bare skin but not as good as he felt when he joined her.

"Shut the light off. I've been on display enough today."

"Yes, ma'am." He flipped the switch on the lantern and plunged them into darkness.

"Wow, that's dark."

"Uh-huh." He nuzzled her neck. "No one will see a thing." With his lips and tongue and teeth, he set her on fire.

Something about the cocoon of the tent, the sleeping bag, the pervasive darkness and the nearness of the man she loved had all her inhibitions melting away as she gave herself to him with the kind of abandon she'd rarely experienced.

"Jesus, Lucy," he whispered at one point. "I need to take you camping more often."

She laughed and threw her arms over her head, giving him free rein to take whatever he wanted. Her obvious capitulation seemed to make him a little crazy, and they went at it like they hadn't had sex in a year . . . Until a loud pop followed by a hiss stopped them cold.

"What the hell was that?" she asked as he froze above her.

Colton lost it laughing as the air mattress below them rapidly deflated. "You broke the bed, babe."

"*I* broke the bed?"

"Yep, it's all your fault. You went all wilderness vixen on me. And besides, I was told I had to provide the hottest sex of your life to get you to go camping again. I was just doing as directed."

Laughing at the term *wilderness vixen*, she said, "I thought this air mattress was super ultra deluxe?"

"It is, but it's no match for Lucy when she lets loose."

She smiled and reached for him, kissing him with abandon. "If you finish me off in spectacular style, I might forgive you for *all* of this."

He pushed into her, apparently up for the challenge. "Ohhh, really? You're on."

"So, wilderness vixen?"

"You like that, huh?" he asked, sounding more breathless by the second.

"I love it."

"I love you, my wilderness vixen."

She put her arms around him and held on tight as he finished her off in very spectacular style. "I love you, too."

"Told you tent sex was the hottest sex you'd ever have in your life."

She squeezed his lips shut. "Stop talking before you ruin it."

He nibbled his way free of her fingers. "Yes, dear."

Lucy held him close, happy and in love with him no matter where they were, even in a tent in the middle of nowhere, Vermont.

With special thanks to Holly and Erica, last names omitted to protect the saucy, for sharing some of their favorite camping stories, and to all the readers who made me laugh so hard with their camping (mis)adventures. This is why I'm with Lucy—give me a resort and spa ANY day! And thanks to Julie, who came up with the PERFECT name for this story over a fun dinner in San Francisco.

Turn the page for a preview of the
next book in the Green Mountain series

AND I LOVE HER

Coming March 2015 from Berkley Books

Business opportunities are like buses,
there's always another one coming.

—Richard Branson

W hen her sister and brother-in-law said they wanted to talk to her after closing, Megan Kane assumed they were going to tell her they were finally expecting the niece or nephew she'd wanted for as long as they'd been married. But the words that came from Brett and Nina in stuttering, halting sentences had nothing to do with babies.

"Moving overseas."

"Selling the diner."

"So sorry to do this to you."

"It was an amazing opportunity."

"We couldn't say no."

"You can come with us." Nina seemed crushed to be delivering this news to her "baby" sister, who was almost twenty-eight and hardly a baby anymore. "I'd love that. We could run around and explore together while Brett is at work. It would be so fun."

Megan shook off the shock and found her voice. "No. You've been taking care of me since you were twenty-two, Neen. It's time to go live your life. I'll be fine."

"We really do mean it when we say you should come with us," Brett said. He was always so kind to her, never once in all these years acting as if her tight bond with his wife was a problem for him.

"I can't do that. I can't crash your party. I've been around your necks long enough as it is."

"You're hardly around our necks, Megan," Nina said. "We could have so much fun! Would you think about it before you automatically say no? Please?"

"Fine." Megan said what her sister needed to hear. "I'll think about it."

"Great!" Nina said, beaming with pleasure at the small victory.

"If you decide to stay here, we'll help you find another job," Brett said. "Maybe the new owners of the diner would want to keep you on. They'd be crazy not to."

He'd been a terrific brother-in-law to her since he married her sister nine years ago. A teacher at a nearby boy's prep school, he'd apparently applied for overseas positions in the past but they'd never materialized until now.

Work at Nina's Diner without Nina? Unthinkable. "I'll figure something out. You guys don't need to worry about me."

"Of course we'll worry about you, Meg." Nina reached for her sister's hand across the table. "I don't know how *not* to worry about you."

"It's probably time I got a life of my own." Megan tried to stay calm even as she panicked on the inside. Not see Nina every day? Unbearable. "Mom and Dad would be horrified if they knew I was still living in the garage apartment."

"They'd be proud of you."

"No, they'd be proud of *you*, but you deserve it. You've created such a wonderful business here, and now you have this fantastic opportunity to travel. I'd never hold you guys back from doing what you want."

Brett's relief was so visible he practically sagged under the weight of it. Obviously, they'd worried about telling her their news. "You really can come with us if you want to, Megan," he said. "It would be great to have you in France."

"I'd love to come visit while you're there, but this is home." In reality, *Nina* was home to her, not Butler or the house where they'd once lived with their parents, but Megan kept those thoughts to herself.

"You said you'd think about it!" Nina said.

"Neen, I can't just go traipsing off to France, as fun as that sounds. I need to figure out my life and what I'm going to do with it. I can't do that in France. I don't want either of you to worry about me. I swear I'll be fine."

"Are you sure?" Nina asked tearfully. "You'd tell me if you didn't mean that, wouldn't you?"

"I'm very sure." Megan kept her emotions out of it—for now anyway. "This could turn out to be a good thing for me. It'll give me the kick in the butt I've needed to move on." Megan had been marching in place for more than ten years, since the snowy night they lost their parents in a car crash during her senior year of high school.

Nina had been her rock ever since, acting as mother, father and big sister all rolled into one. The sisters had held on to each other for all these years, and the thought of everyday life without Nina was unfathomable to Megan.

"If you agree, we're going to rent the house," Brett said, "but the garage apartment is all yours for as long as you want or need it. We told the Realtor it wouldn't be part of the rental."

"Of course I agree. No sense the house sitting vacant when you could be making some money." Her brother-in-law's sweetness nearly broke her emotional dam, but she refused to cry in front of them. Since there were going to be tears—and lots of them—she had to get out of there immediately. No way would she make them feel bad about something they were so excited about. Knowing she was on borrowed time where the tears were concerned, Megan gathered up her belongings and stood. "I'll see you guys in the morning."

"Let me drive you home," Nina said.

"That's okay. I could use the fresh air after being inside all day."

"You're sure you're all right?" Nina asked.

Megan bent to kiss her sister's cheek. "I'm fine, and I'm thrilled for both of you."

Nina held her tight for a minute. "Love you, Meggie."

Megan couldn't remember the last time Nina had called her by her childhood nickname. "Love you, too."

Feeling as if she'd been set adrift, untethered from the one sure thing in her life, Megan stepped out of the diner, taking a moment to breathe in the fresh, clean early-autumn air. The tears she'd managed to contain in front of Nina and Brett broke loose in sobs that had her looking for a place to hide until the storm passed.

She crossed the street and ducked behind the Green Mountain Country Store, planning to hide out until Brett and Nina left for home.

The last thing she wanted was for them to see her crying, and nothing short of a miracle would help her keep it together tonight.

After another twelve-hour marathon in front of the computer, Hunter Abbott stood and stretched out the kinks in his shoulders and back. As the chief financial officer for the Green Mountain Country Store and other Abbott family businesses, Hunter worked pretty much all the time. If it weren't for the pressing need for food that his body demanded every few hours, he'd probably work around the clock.

It wasn't like he had anything better to do. And wasn't that a sad, pathetic fact of his life?

His stomach let out an unholy growl that had him checking the time on his computer. Nine ten. Great, the diner was closed, which left pizza as his only option in town at this hour. He dialed the number to Kingdom Pizza from memory and ordered a small veggie and a salad. If he was resorting to eating junk, at least it was somewhat healthy. Before his twin sister, Hannah, had remarried over the summer, Hunter might've headed for her house to bum some dinner and conversation. But with Nolan now living with Hannah and the two of them in starry-eyed newly wedded bliss, Hunter steered clear.

He turned off his computer and glanced at the stack of files still awaiting his attention. Bring them home or leave them for tomorrow? After a brief internal debate, he shut off the light and left them. His tank was running on empty, and tomorrow would bring more of the same.

In the outer office, he was surprised to find the light still on in his sister Ella's office. He went over to knock on her door. "You're working late."

"As are you."

"Except I always do. What's your excuse?"

"Getting some new products entered into the system, and dealing with a pile of paperwork that never seems to get smaller no matter what I do."

"I hear you there. So much for being self-employed, huh?"

She smiled at him, but he noted a hint of sadness in her eyes that caught him by surprise. Ella was one of the most joyful people he'd ever known—always happy and upbeat.

"Everything okay?"

"Sure. Why do you ask?"

"You just seemed . . . I don't know . . . sad or something for a second there."

"I'm fine. No need to worry."

"Okay then." Hunter took a step back, planning to leave, but there it was again—the sadness he'd seen before. "You know if there's anything wrong, you can come to me, right? We may see each other a thousand times a day, but I'm right over there if you need me. No matter what it is."

"Thank you, Hunter. That's very sweet of you. I know you want to take care of everything for all of us, but some things . . . Well, some things can't be managed. They are what they are."

More confused than ever, Hunter wasn't sure whether he should stay and try to force the issue or give her some space to deal with whatever was bothering her. "I'm here, El. I'm right here. Don't suffer in silence."

Her smile softened her face. "I'll see you tomorrow."

"Do you want me to wait for you so you're not here alone?"

"No. I've got another hour or so, and I can lock up."

"Give me a quick call to let me know you got home okay."

"Hunter . . ."

"What? You'll always be my little sister, so call me."

"I'm only four years younger than you."

"And I vividly remember the day you were born."

"Freak."

Hunter chuckled at the predictable comment. His family teased him every day about his photographic memory and ability to recall facts and figures from years ago that should've been impossible to remember. Sometimes he wished he could forget some of the crap that rattled around in his brain, but it was his lot in life to be a walking, talking data warehouse. "See you in the morning."

"Have a good night."

"Call me."

"Go!"

Hunter went down the stairs thinking about what Ella said about him wanting to take care of things for everyone. Perhaps it was also his lot in life as the oldest of the ten Abbott siblings, but he wanted the people he loved to be happy and their problems to be few, even if that meant taking on more than his share of the load.

Hannah had been after him recently to work less and play more. If only he could think of something he'd rather do than work.

Totally pathetic. He knew it, but damn if he could figure out how to snap out of the rut he'd fallen into. When had he become an all-work-no-play stick-in-the-mud? If he were being honest with himself, he'd been in the rut for a long time, probably since he graduated from college and joined the family business full time. College had been the last time he'd been truly free of responsibility and obligation.

Thinking about the blissful college days had him remembering his late brother-in-law Caleb, Hannah's first husband, who'd died in Iraq seven years ago. If he came back to life and saw how ridiculously out of balance Hunter's life had become, he'd raise holy hell.

Raising holy hell was on Hunter's mind as he stepped into the cool darkness and waited for the motion-sensitive light to come on. Once it did, he turned to lock the door behind him. Ella would see to setting the alarm system. Leaving her alone at the store made him anxious, but he would check on her if she didn't remember to call him.

A sound to his left had him stopping to listen. Was that sniffling? "Who's there?"

"It's me, Megan. I'm sorry to scare you."

That voice . . . It cut through him like a knife slicing butter. Every nerve ending in his body stood up to take note of her nearness, which happened every damned time he came into any kind of contact with her. "Megan," he said in a voice that was barely a whisper. "What're you doing here in the dark?"

"Hiding out."

"Why? Are you hurt? What's wrong?" True to form, he wanted to make things right for her, no matter what it took. His heart beat quickly, as if he'd been running for miles, and his hands were suddenly sweaty and clammy. He'd never understand why this particular woman provoked such a strong reaction in him every time he laid eyes on her—or in this case, heard tears in her voice as she spoke in the dark.

"Nothing's wrong. I just needed a minute. Sorry to trespass on your property. I'll get out of your way."

"Wait. Don't go." The words came out sounding far more desperate than he'd intended. "At least let me drive you home."

"That's all right. I can walk."

"I wouldn't mind at all."

She stepped into the light, and the sight of her tear-ravaged face broke his heart. What could possibly be so wrong?

"It's out of your way."

"I've got nowhere to be." He watched her expressive face as she pondered his offer. Her lips pursed, which brought her cheekbones into sharper relief against the pale skin on her face. Exquisite was the word that came to mind whenever he looked at her, which was as often as he could. Knowing that until recently she'd been in major crush with his brother Will had no bearing whatsoever on how he felt about her. He looked at her, and he wanted. It was that simple.

Except, she barely knew he was alive, which was a problem.

"If you're sure you don't mind," she said after an impossibly long pause.

"I really don't."

"Thank you."

She walked with him to his silver Lincoln Navigator and stood by his side as he held the passenger door and waited for her to get settled.

As he got into the driver's side, his growling stomach reminded him of the takeout order. "Have you had dinner?" The words were out before he could take the time to overanalyze the situation.

"Not yet."

"I have a pizza and salad on order. I'd be happy to share."

"I don't know if I could eat."

"Come along and keep me company?"

"Um, sure. Okay." She reached into her purse, withdrew a tissue and wiped her eyes.

"Are you going to tell me why you were crying?"

"Do I have to?"

"Of course not." He was surprised that she would think he'd try to force it out of her. "But I'm told I'm a good listener."

She had no reply to that, so he turned the key to start the engine, lowering the windows a bit to get some air.

"I probably stink from working all day," she said.

"No, you don't." As he drove, he thought of a thousand

things he'd like to say to her, but none were the sort of things a guy blurted out when he finally had a moment alone with the woman he desired.

How exactly did you tell a woman who barely knew you were alive that you thought about her constantly? That seeing her upset killed you. That wanting her kept you awake at night. How did you tell her it didn't matter if she had once been obsessed with your brother? That there was nothing you wouldn't do to see her smile, to see her pale blue eyes light up with joy?

How could he say any of that and not sound like a total creep?

He couldn't, so he kept his mouth shut and hoped he wouldn't do something embarrassing like hyperventilate from the overwhelming effort it took not to say all of it.

FROM *NEW YORK TIMES* BESTSELLING AUTHOR

Marie Force

I WANT TO HOLD
YOUR HAND

A Green Mountain Romance

Hannah is heartbroken after losing her husband in Iraq,
but the attentions of a lifelong friend make her believe
in love again...

PRAISE FOR MARIE FORCE

"Marie Force makes you believe in the power
of true love and happily ever after."
—Carly Phillips, *New York Times* bestselling author

"Genuine and passionate."
—*Publishers Weekly*

marieforce.com
facebook.com/marieforceauthor
penguin.com

M1497T0514